THE
LAST
DIPLOMAT

Don Marrs

Copyright 2012 by Don F. Marrs

ISBN: 978-0-9883546-0-9

Cover art by Kyler Martz

Also by Don Marrs:

The Last Astronaut

This book is dedicated to Rudd Fleming.

ONE

It was her first spring in Idaho and Katie could hardly believe how green everything had suddenly become. When she arrived last September it had been dry and brown and it had remained like that all winter. But the spring rains and warm days of April had transformed it; it was beautiful now. She stood by an open window in the South Kuna High School teachers' lounge looking out across new-mown ball fields to the mountains beyond. A little snow still dressed the highest peaks, vivid white against an azure sky. In the middle distance a flock of gulls trailed a farm tractor plowing serpentine furrows across a muddy hillside. The air was sweet with the smell of fresh-turned earth.

Behind her on the lunch table stood a stack of ungraded test papers. She had intended to work on them during her mid-morning free period but gave up the task as hopeless. Who could grade papers on a day like this? For the last ten minutes she had done absolutely nothing.

A student walked past the window and waved to her. She waved back and felt a sudden stab of guilt. His paper was in the neglected stack on the table.

What would Phillips say, she wondered. If he knew she was playing hooky he'd have her on the carpet for sure.

Reluctantly she pushed herself from the window, took a seat at the table and picked up the first test paper.

She had done well in her first year of teaching and she knew that Phillips agreed, but no job was secure these days. The year 2031 had been terrible for the country, for the whole world.

The five-year-old global depression was grinding on and the government seemed powerless to affect it. Sixty million Americans were unemployed; twenty million were homeless. Their sad, tired faces haunted the daily television news. Where would it all end? No one knew.

Katie was one of the lucky ones; she had been offered a position just two months after graduation. She earned it—dean's list, summa cum laude—so she didn't feel guilty about her good fortune. But she did feel nervous about it; only a fool wouldn't. Her year in Kuna had been a gift. Idaho, like the rest of the agricultural heartland, was an island of calm compared to the lawless chaos of the big cities. The enraged crazies who stole and rioted and burned down neighborhoods there almost never troubled Idaho. Was it because they respected the fact that food must be grown? Or because no one in the farm belt had any money, only livestock and crops and machinery? Or was it simply because the crazies had no gasoline and couldn't travel to the countryside? Whatever the reason, Katie was grateful. She felt she had the best job she could possibly have and the best life available to her anywhere in this dysfunctional world.

She remembered her first meeting with Phillips. Her practice teaching days in Seattle had left her anxious about the prospect of a real teaching position. Was she tough enough? Phillips assured her that things were different in Kuna; there was no need for weapons searches at the main gate or police patrols in the hallways. It all seemed too good to be true.

But it was true. Her first day she realized she didn't need to fear these kids. They were brighter than she expected and they really wanted to learn. The anger the kids displayed in Seattle was almost totally absent here. It was strange, the entire Boise metro area seemed frozen in time, as though the twenty-first century with all its ugliness and violence and corruption had been denied admission here.

"Penny?"

She awoke from her reverie with a start. Her eyes focused on the test paper in her hand and she realized she hadn't read a word of it. She looked up and found Kevin Keegan standing a few feet away, pouring himself a cup of coffee. Keegan was a science teacher and the football coach. He was very good looking, with shaggy blonde hair, piercing blue eyes and an athletic body. She liked him well enough but had no interest in him romantically, something she had tried repeatedly to communicate to him. But no matter how many times she rebuffed him he persisted.

"Excuse me?" she asked.

He settled into the chair next to hers. "A penny for your thoughts. It's an old expression but I thought you might have heard it."

She shrugged. "Sorry, no." She was not in the mood for small talk.

"It means . . ."

"I can guess what it means."

"Well then?" He flashed an engaging smile.

He was attractive, she had to admit. On another day, in another life, maybe. But not here and not now.

"Waste of money," she said. "Sorry, Kevin, but my mind's a blank, a prefect vacuum. There's nothing to tell." She glanced at the clock on the wall. "Anyway, I have a class."

He watched her as she gathered up her papers and started for the door. Then he called after her, "You realize that's a scientific impossibility, don't you!"

She turned. "What is?"

"A perfect vacuum. There's no such thing." He tapped his forehead, and pointed at her. "There has to be something in there."

She laughed. "Don't bet on it, Kevin."

As she made her way through the crowded hallway toward her classroom her mind drifted back to her thoughts of a few moments earlier. Had she done well enough, she wondered. Would Phillips ask her back? She certainly hoped so. For some, Idaho's uniqueness was a problem; they saw it as completely unreal, a rural backwater, and felt cut off from the real world here. She saw the opposite. For her, Idaho's innocence seemed more real than the "real" world; it was the way the world should be. She desperately wanted to be asked back.

When she reached her classroom the students were

7

filtering in; some were in their seats, others stood around in small groups talking. She looked past them. Beyond the windows she saw ball fields and trees and small scrubbed houses, like a Norman Rockwell painting. Unseen beyond the houses, she knew, a vast expanse of barren sagebrush desert stretched away to the east. She loved that too. She loved all of it, the people and the modest houses and the miles of sagebrush that insulated Kuna from places like Seattle.

The bell rang. Katie waited while scattered conversations died down and the stragglers found seats. She smiled as she looked at the faces arrayed before her. She especially loved these kids.

"All right," she began. "Who remembers where we were yesterday?"

Hands were raised. She picked one.

"We were at the turn of the century, talking about the factors that led to the depression."

"Very good, Todd."

"They weren't all economic," the boy continued.

"That's true," Katie said. "But I want to stop before we get into that. I want to do the same thing now that we did a few months ago when we finished our study of the nineteenth century. Do you remember the question we asked then?" Again, hands were raised. "Jessica?"

"We asked what was the single most important development of the century," said Jessica.

"Exactly. We asked what development most clearly characterized and defined the century. I want to consider that question now for the twentieth century. We want a lot of discussion on this, so while you think about it let's move into round-table format."

It took less than a minute for the students to rearrange the room. When they were finished the desks formed a circle, beginning near one end of Katie's desk and ending near the other.

"All right," she said. "Who wants to start?"

Someone said, "Technology."

"The moon landing," offered another.

"The atomic bomb," said a third.

Katie raised a hand for quiet. "Order," she said smiling. One at a time, people. Let's do this right. Now, Melissa, I think you were first."

Melissa said, "technology." Immediately, three other hands were raised.

Katie waved them off. "Why do you think technology was most important, Melissa?"

"Because, think about it; the century started with people riding around on horses. There was no radio, no airplanes, no real cars, no television, no computers, no internet. In fact, practically everything we use today was invented during the twentieth century. That's what the century was all about."

"Miss Hogan!"

"Yes, Jeremy." Katie was pleased to see Jeremy Abel's hand raised. He was painfully shy and rarely contributed to class discussions.

"It can't be technology," Jeremy said. "Technology was the answer for the nineteenth century; it can't be the same thing twice."

"Can't it? Why not?"

Jeremy looked confused. "So Melissa is right? Technology is the answer?"

Katie felt sudden sympathy for him; he was so easily bruised. "No," she said. "I'm not saying Melissa is right. That's not for me to say. What's important is what you think. History isn't absolute, Jeremy, it isn't just a list of dates. It's about processes. We study the past so we can understand the processes that created our present world. That helps us plan for the future. You understand?"

Jeremy nodded and looked absently out the window. Katie could see him withdrawing back into himself and knew she had handled him badly this time. *I have so much to learn. Will I ever become a good teacher?* She wanted to say something to him, something that would bring him back. But it would have to wait. She had a responsibility to the others as well.

She looked around the room. "All right then, who's next?

9

Ryan?"

Ryan was Jeremy's emotional opposite. He spoke frequently and brimmed with confidence. "As I understand it," Ryan said, "what we're trying to figure out is the thing that had the greatest impact on mankind during the twentieth century, the thing that, if you took it away, nothing would be the same. Is that right?"

Katie said, "I guess you could put it that way."

"Well if that's true then I think we can eliminate a lot of things. For instance, in 1944 Hitler was defining the century. But he was eliminated so he's just a footnote now."

Several students laughed.

Katie said, "I think Hitler rates more than a footnote, don't you, Ryan?"

Ryan rolled his eyes. "Well, okay, but you know what I mean. You could say the same thing about the atomic bomb. In the '50s or '60s the bomb might have been our answer. But it's not our answer now. When the Soviet Union collapsed we stopped worrying about the bomb."

Katie nodded her agreement. "All right. So what do you think is the answer now?"

Ryan replied, "I think it was television. Or maybe mass communications in general. Television, radio, telephones, computers, the internet—all those things shrank the world in the twentieth century. So now we all know what's going on everywhere the minute it happens."

"Good!" Katie said. "Ryan nominates the creation of the global village. Any other candidates? What about you, Ashley?" Ashley was one of Katie's brightest students. She rarely volunteered but when drawn out almost always had something thoughtful to add.

"I think we've been looking in the wrong direction," Ashley began. "We've been talking about things; I think ideas are much more important. I think the event that defined the twentieth century was the rise and fall of communism. That's the century's legacy to us—communism lost, democracy won."

"Objection! Objection!" On the far side of the circle an

overweight boy in filthy blue jeans and uncombed hair sat with his hand upraised. When all eyes had settled on him he announced, "The shadow minister demands equal time."

Ashley glared at him. Katie said, "I've told you before, Nathan, this is not a parliamentary democracy, it's a dictatorship. You will speak when I recognize you, not before." There was scattered laughter. "Go on, Ashley. You were saying . . ."

Ashley smiled triumphantly at Nathan and said, "I was just going to say that the defeat of communism set the whole world free, and that is clearly the most important thing that happened in the twentieth century."

Katie thanked her and nodded to Nathan. "All right, Nate."

Nathan sat up in his chair and addressed Ashley directly. "First, I agree on one point—European communism did collapse. But in case you hadn't noticed, 30 percent of the world's population is still Communist, in Asia! And as for democracy winning . . ."

"You're talking about China?" Ashley interrupted. "China isn't Communist. It's been capitalist for over thirty years. Or hadn't *you* noticed?"

"It has restructured its markets, but its core ideology is unchanged. Every member of the central committee is still a Communist. Surely you must have noticed that."

"Not true," Ashley countered. "The reformers are winning. Within the next decade . . ."

It was Nathan's turn to interrupt. "As for democracy winning, democracies have collapsed too. All over the globe they've gone down just as hard as the Soviets did. We're in the middle of a global depression. Thirty percent global unemployment, currency dislocations, market chaos. And no one sees an end yet. You may call that winning, but I . . ."

"Enough!" Katie stood and walked to the center of the circle. "We're getting way off the subject, people. Let's stick to the twentieth century, shall we. This is a history class; we're not here to discuss current events."

"We *are* discussing the twentieth century," Nathan objected.

11

"No you aren't! The depression didn't start until 2026."

"But the roots of the depression were already sown before the turn of the century. Are we supposed to ignore all that? That's called sophistry I think. Isn't it?"

Katie eyed him impatiently. "It's called doing what I tell you, Nathan. Now get back to the subject, or . . ."

She stopped in mid sentence, startled. What was she seeing? Outside the windows the daylight had grown suddenly brighter.

The students all turned to look. The light quickly flared to incredible intensity, then just as quickly faded and returned to normal. The entire incident had taken perhaps four or five seconds.

A number of kids left their desks and moved to the windows, looking around in all directions, trying to find some clue to what they had just seen.

"What the hell was that?" someone asked.

"It was like lightning."

"Except that it's broad daylight and there's no clouds."

"Yeah! And it lasted longer than lightning."

"Hey look! The lights are out."

Katie looked at the ceiling and saw that the lights were indeed out. She walked to the door and tried the switch. Nothing. She opened the door and looked into the corridor. It was dark. And suddenly a nameless dread washed over her. She had read a story once in which these same things happened. But it couldn't be that, could it? No, there had to be another explanation. Still, could she afford to ignore the possibility?

Jeremy Abel was standing nearby, apart from the others. She went to him and asked quietly, "Jeremy, how far is it to the airfield?"

"You mean Gowen?"

"No. Not Gowen. The air force base."

"Mountain Home?" Jeremy paused a moment to think. "Thirty or forty miles give or take. Right out that way." He pointed out the windows toward the south.

Katie began doing a calculation in her head. Sound traveled

a mile in about five seconds she thought. So thirty miles would take a hundred and fifty seconds—two and a half minutes. She guessed it had been twenty or thirty seconds since they saw the flash.

She walked quickly to the center of the room. "People! I need your attention please." The students turned and faced her. "I want everyone to move into the corridor. Leave your books and don't anybody run, but don't waste time either. Do it now people. Let's move!"

It took less than a minute for all of them to clear the classroom; Katie was the last to leave. She closed the door behind her and strained to see as her eyes adjusted to the dim light in the corridor.

Her students clustered nearby. Down the hall, where light spilled weakly out from the small windows in classroom doors, she could see that the corridor was empty. No other teacher was taking this precaution. She felt suddenly foolish and wondered if she should take everyone back inside and resume the class. But she decided against doing that. They would know soon enough—a minute more, a minute and a half at most and they would know.

A student asked, "What's going on, Miss Hogan? Why are we out here?" She looked toward the voice and found Nathan. Her eyes had now adjusted to the light and she could see him clearly. He looked frightened.

"I'm not sure," she said. "I just thought discretion was the better part of valor in this case. But I seem to be the only one who thinks so."

"The only one who thinks what? What are we hiding from?"

Katie had a sudden vision of Nathan at home this evening, trying to explain this incident to his parents. No matter what he told them she was going to look foolish. She wondered if she should tell Nathan what she was thinking so he could explain it to his parents. No, she decided. No one would understand; you had to be here. So maybe she should just give it up. After all, it had already been over two minutes and . . .

Before she could complete her thought the building was

13

struck by a deafening concussion. The walls shuddered and seemed to bend and wave as though they were made of rubber. From every direction she heard the sound of glass shattering. A light fixture dropped from the ceiling a few yards down the hall and exploded as it struck the floor. Several students screamed. Ceiling tiles dropped, one narrowly missing her. There were more screams, several groans of pain and shouts of alarm from nearby classrooms. Then there was a sound of incredible power, like a steam locomotive being driven right through the school. The building shook and creaked for what seemed like minutes but was probably only seconds. Then it was over.

Katie steadied herself against a wall and looked around. It seemed darker than it had before and she didn't understand why until the door to the nearest classroom flew open, spilling light out into the corridor. The air was thick with dust! A student stumbled out through the door, followed by two more. Katie moved toward them. "Is everyone all right?" she called.

In the doorway a girl turned and faced her. Her expression was blank and blood flowed from a cut on her forehead, coloring the side of her face and staining her shirt. She said, "Miss Hogan. What was it, Miss Hogan?"

In the classroom beyond, Katie could see that all the windows were blown in. Broken glass was everywhere and nearly all the desks near the windows were overturned. Several students were lying or sitting on the floor. Others were standing. Everyone looked dazed, except for a small group of four or five who had gathered around their teacher, John Caper. Caper was barking orders to them, directing their efforts to assist the injured.

Katie looked at the girl immediately in front of her. "You need the nurse," she said, examining the cut on the girl's forehead. Then she called, "Nathan!"

"Right here, Miss Hogan." Nathan had been standing just behind her. He too was looking into Caper's classroom.

"We have to get organized here, Nate. Round up some of your friends and find Nurse Stewart. She's going to be very busy and I'm sure she can use all the help we can give her. See if she can give you some supplies to bring back here. We need bandages,

14

antiseptic—she'll know."

"Yes ma'am," Nathan said and hurried off.

Down the corridor all the doors stood open now and the hall was growing crowded. A constant hum of sobs and weeping and anxious conversation filled the air. Katie wondered what she should do next. She decided to offer her assistance to John Caper.

Glass crunched underfoot as she entered Caper's classroom. Caper was tearing a strip of cloth from his shirt. As she approached he wrapped it around a boy's arm. The remains of the shirt lay beside him; he was naked from the waist up. She watched for a moment. When he was finished she said, "I sent some students for medical supplies. They should be back soon."

Caper looked up. "Good. Are you okay, Katie?" There was a deep gash across his right cheek, still bleeding. He patted it dry with another piece of his shirt but the blood returned immediately.

"Not a scratch." She felt embarrassed saying it. She was the only one in the room who appeared to have sustained no injury.

"Have you seen it?" he asked.

"Seen what?"

He was moving to the next victim, a girl with blood flowing from a cut on her arm. He tore another strip from the shirt and began dabbing at the wound. Without looking up he said, "Seen that?" and tilted his head toward the window.

She looked in the direction he had indicated. Outside, the schoolyard was littered with downed tree branches. At the edge of the school property was a line of small poplars; all were sheared off near their bases and now lay on the ground in a perfect row, like arrows pointing directly at the school. In the far distance, beyond the poplars, was a tall boiling column of smoke.

Twenty minutes later order had been established. They were coping amazingly well, Katie thought. Nurse Stewart had converted the teacher's lounge into a makeshift infirmary and only ten or twelve students now remained in the hall outside awaiting treatment. The rest of the student body had been assembled in the gym where a team of teachers was arranging for their transport home. Busses were unavailable—no one had been able to contact

15

their drivers—so teachers and students who drove to school, and whose cars were working were being pressed into service. Serious injuries had been sustained only in the wing that faced southeast, so the disaster, at least at the school, had not been nearly as bad as first feared. They had little information about what was happening beyond the campus.

"How did you know, Katie?" The question came from John Caper. He and Katie and a teacher named Karen Sullivan were standing in the hall outside the gym. None had a car on campus, so for the moment their presence was not required.

"I didn't know," Katie said. "I guessed. But even while I was moving the kids into the hall I was sure I must be wrong. It just seemed too fantastic."

Caper said, "Well, it was a damn good guess. And damn lucky for your kids."

"It certainly was," Karen agreed. "If only I had known what you did." Her words trailed off and tears welled up in her eyes. She put a hand to her face in embarrassment. She was a sixty-year-old widow who had always struck Katie as brittle and opinionated. Now she seemed merely fragile. Katie put a hand on her shoulder in sympathy.

"There's a girl in my class," Karen said, dabbing at her eyes. "I think you know her—Allison May? Such a pretty little thing, and she was cut so badly. I think she may lose an eye."

Katie shuddered. She did know Allison May.

"If only I'd known."

"You couldn't have known," Katie reassured her.

"You knew."

"No I didn't. Nobody knew."

Neither of them spoke for a moment. Then Karen said, "I wonder if we'll ever be told the truth? After all these years you'd think the system would be failsafe. How could this have happened?"

"No system is failsafe," Katie said irritably. "Murphy always wins; accidents always happen eventually."

"That's true," Caper agreed. "But it has nothing to do with what happened here. This was no accident."

16

"It has to be," Karen objected. She seemed to have regained her composure. "There was no warning, John. If it had been anything but an accident there would have been sirens or something."

"Well, that would be true if it was a missile attack. We probably would have had some warning then. But this was something else."

"What else?" Karen asked.

Caper shrugged. "I'm not sure."

"Then how can you be so certain it wasn't an accident?"

"I'm certain because of that cloud we've been watching, wondering where the wind was going to take it. The cloud isn't over the air base. It's over Boise."

Karen looked stunned.

Katie said, "But that means . . ." she stopped, unable to say what she was thinking.

"It means we've been attacked," Caper said.

Katie found her voice. "By whom? And why? Why would anyone attack a small town in the middle of nowhere?"

Again, Caper shrugged. "I can't even guess."

Karen asked, "Are the phones working? I need to talk to my daughter."

"We can't call," Katie said with authority. "The phones are going to be down for a long time."

"Why?"

"Something called EMP. Nuclear explosions destroy electrical equipment. That's why the power is out."

"So that's how you guessed it," Caper said.

"That's right."

"But how did you know? I've never heard of EMP."

"I read it somewhere. I don't remember where."

Caper eyed her with sudden respect. "So what should still be working?"

"I'm not sure. Satellite radios maybe. Car radios."

"Good. Let's find one. Round up a few of the kids and . . ."

As if on cue the school principal rounded a nearby corner. Caper started to say something to him but stopped. Phillips face

17

was ashen; he looked like a man who had just heard his own death sentence.

"I found a radio," he said, fighting back tears. "This wasn't an accident. There have been others: Washington, Chicago, San Francisco—"

Katie blurted, "Oh God!"

Karen reached toward the wall for support, missed and fell against it. Katie tried to catch her but succeeded only in easing her descent to a sitting position on the floor.

Phillips continued, "They aren't sure how many yet but it's at least five." He looked at Caper, his eyes pleading. "It's too horrible to contemplate. This can't be happening, can it?"

"Who is attacking us?" Caper demanded.

"They didn't say. I don't think they know. I don't think anybody knows."

"The military damn well knows," Caper spat. "If the media don't know yet it's because the military haven't told them. Secretive bastards!"

Phillips shook his head. "They may know. I couldn't say."

"I'm leaving," said Caper. "We all need to go home and find our families."

"But where should we go then?" Karen asked no one in particular. She had not lost consciousness and was watching everything from her seat on the floor. "Where is it safe?"

"That depends," Caper answered her.

"Depends on what?"

"On which way the wind blows." He wheeled and marched off toward the exit.

Karen held a hand up to Katie, who took it and helped her to her feet. Then she asked, "Where are you going?"

Katie thought for a moment. "To find my parents."

"In Seattle? You can't go . . ."

"No! They moved six months ago. They're in Salem, Oregon now. How about you? Where will you go?"

"I don't know." Karen sounded numb, bewildered.

"You must have family somewhere. Brothers? Sisters?"

Karen's eyes clouded. "In San Francisco," she sobbed.

18

Katie embraced her and looked at Phillips. "Can we leave?"

Phillips nodded. "Go," he said solemnly. "Of course, go."

The two women started down the hall and Phillips called after them, "God be with you. God be with you both."

TWO

"How much further?" Captain Sandiman asked.

His driver replied, "About twenty miles."

"Good. Almost home."

The driver said, "If you'll pardon the observation, Sir, I'm afraid the worst is still ahead of us. In a few miles there's a stretch that's been very bad."

"That so?" The captain pulled himself erect. Convoy duty was new to him, but his driver was an old hand. "How many times have you made this run, Corporal?"

"This makes thirty-one. I think it's some kind of record."

"Well, let's hope your luck holds again this time."

They were rounding a curve. Sandiman took the opportunity to look back along the line of trucks trailing the Humvee. They were all tucked in tight, just as they should be. It had stopped raining and the sky had lightened from dark grey to pewter. It looked like they might have good weather by noon.

"I'm afraid I can't claim real luck," the corporal said. "I've been on four convoys that were hit. We were just never stopped."

"That qualifies in my book," Sandiman said. "Nobody's perfect."

They rode for a while in silence and the captain looked out at the rolling countryside of central Virginia. It amazed him how absolutely normal everything seemed here despite all that had happened. Fifty million Americans were dead and thousands more were dying of radiation sickness every day. Still others were falling victim to the gangs roaming the hills. An unknown number were starving and millions more would undoubtedly be lost this winter. Yet here there was no sign, no visible evidence of any of it. Except for the absence of traffic on this road, this could be a day in mid-

July of any recent year, before anything happened; before his wife and his two daughters . . . No! He didn't want to think about that, not today.

He turned to the corporal and said, "It's a hell of a mess, isn't it?"

"What is, Sir?"

"Everything. All of it. The fact that we have to band together like a herd of wildebeest for protection against the jackels that might be lurking over the next hill. It isn't natural. Americans shouldn't be preying on other Americans."

The corporal nodded. "You got that right. But I don't guess there's anything more unnatural than nuclear war, is there, Sir."

Sandiman said, "Corporal!"

"Yes, Sir."

"Please stop calling me sir. My name is Paul. I'm National Guard. Two months ago I was a civilian and I still feel like a civilian. Understood?"

The corporal nodded but did not answer. He was studying the woods flanking the road, looking first to one side, then to the other.

"Is this the area?" Sandiman asked.

"Coming up very soon now. There's a bridge just over this next rise that always worries me. They've never hit us there but it would be a good spot for it."

Sandiman dropped a hand to his side and rested his palm on the butt of his service automatic. The feel of the weapon was reassuring, but the muscles in his legs still tensed as the convoy crested the hill and started down toward the bridge. The trees were closer to the road here, arching out over the pavement so only a narrow band of leaden sky showed between them. It was dark under the woodland canopy; there were a thousand shadowy places where a man could hide. The corporal was right—this spot was bad.

Sandiman thought he saw a glint of light reflect off something metallic. His head snapped around and he fixed his gaze on the spot. But he realized immediately that it had been imagination, his eyes playing tricks. On this overcast morning

21

there was no sun so there could be no reflection.

They moved onto the bridge. He braced himself for the possible explosion, half expecting the pavement to erupt beneath him and hoping the corporal couldn't see his fear. Then they were across and moving up the next rise. The tension drained out of him.

"I'm going to ask for you next trip," he said to the corporal. Your luck seems to be holding."

"Might not be a good idea, Sir," the corporal grinned. Sandiman frowned in mock anger.

"Sorry. I mean 'Paul'. You know as well as I do, the odds are stacked against me now. There's thousands of people out here beyond the perimeters. They're all armed and they all have to eat and they all hate us. One convoy in ten doesn't make it. I can't stay lucky forever."

"It won't go on forever," Sandiman assured him. But his tone was merely hopeful, not really confident. "They'll come in eventually. Sooner or later they'll realize we all have to work together on this.

The corporal regarded him doubtfully. "You really believe that?"

Sandiman didn't answer; he was studying a grove of trees approaching on the right.

The convoy rolled on toward Richmond—twenty truckloads of food and fuel and medical supplies. It would be the only convoy today for the five hundred thousand housed there, jammed into the city and camped along the river.

They were barely keeping them alive, Sandiman knew. Something had to change soon or all hell was going to break loose. The ones inside the perimeter would try to break out or the ones outside would try to break in. Either way, the military would be caught in between. How had it come to this? How had an entire nation dissolved in just two months? Now, except for the army and the martial law, it was every man for himself, worse than a civil war. Out in the countryside there was anarchy.

They were approaching the last checkpoint, an outpost that

provided support for the convoys and served as headquarters for patrol operations in this sector. A decade ago in Central America it would have been called a firebase and the patrols would have been called search and destroy. They weren't called by those names here, but it was the same. Squads went out from this base to locate and engage the lawless bands in the nearby countryside. American soldiers went into the hills of Virginia to make war on American civilians. Sandiman shuddered when he thought about it.

"Something's going on!" The corporal slowed the Humvee and the convoy slowed behind them. Sandiman saw it too; there was more activity than usual at the base. Trucks were moving in and out and more trucks were lining up near the center of the compound. For some reason an enormous convoy was being formed. They rolled to a stop at the barricade and waited.

A private hurried over to them and saluted. "We need your trucks, Sir."

Soldiers were running in every direction. Work details were breaking down the tents. They appeared to be packing up the entire camp.

"What's going on?" Sandiman asked, looking past the soldier to the confusion beyond.

"Your trucks," the soldier insisted. "We have to have them, Sir. It's orders."

Sandiman looked at him and growled, "Well you can't have them. They're loaded with supplies for Richmond. Now what the hell is going on here?"

"We've been invaded," the private snapped. "Sir."

"Invaded? You mean Richmond? You mean the crazies in the hills?"

"No sir, not Richmond. Along the coast. Amphibious landing forces, thousands of troops. Now, I say again, we need these trucks."

Sandiman was out of the vehicle in an instant, standing stiffly in front of the private. For the first time in his life he was acutely conscious of being military, really military, and of being faced with a great and necessary duty.

"Now let me get this straight, Private." His words sounded

23

strange to him; the calm voice bristled with authority. "Who is coming in along what coast."

The soldier stood his ground, looking just as military as Sandiman felt. "The Chinese," he answered.

"The Chinese!" Sandiman felt an irrational impulse to laugh. That was ridiculous, absurd. "Where?" he asked, amazed that his voice still sounded calm. Somewhere inside him the officer, Captain Sandiman, had taken control.

"Someplace in New Jersey, south of Atlantic City. That's why we need the trucks. You can dump your loads right over . . ."

Sandiman looked past the private. A major was striding toward them from the compound. He stopped beside the private, returned Sandiman's salute and said sternly, "Have your men dismount, Captain, and start unloading these trucks. We move in twenty minutes."

"I can't do that," Sandiman objected. "This is the only convoy scheduled into Richmond today. Those people have to eat."

The major cocked his head to one side and glared back. "Those people will have to eat tomorrow, Captain. Because if we don't get these trucks, this time next week there won't be any city of Richmond, or any Goddamn state of Virginia. Do I make myself clear?"

Startled by the major's outburst, Sandiman said weakly, "Very clear, Sir."

"I'll need everything, trucks and APCs. You can keep one truck to get your men back to Richmond. That's all I can spare. Now move!" He stomped off without returning Sandiman's salute.

Sandiman walked back along the line of trucks giving the necessary orders; then he returned to the Humvee. He was shaking as he climbed in beside the corporal, half from anger at the major, who seemed to care nothing for the people in Richmond, and half from the realization, slowly creeping over him, of what was beginning. How could the Chinese have mounted an offensive so quickly? Landed troops on the beaches of New Jersey in only two months? It simply wasn't possible.

The private raised the gate and they lurched into motion, leading the convoy into the compound.

24

If it was true, what defense could they offer? Where would they find the manpower to repel an invasion? Regardless of what the major had said they could not simply abandon the refugees. And it was taking all their resources just to keep the camps supplied and the countryside patrolled against the rabble. Maybe the invasion would change that. Maybe the rebels outside the perimeters would join with the military to fight the common enemy. Or maybe not. There was so much distrust of the military; the rebels might refuse. Or they might not believe what the army told them until it was too late. There was simply no precedent for the disillusionment that swept the country in the last nine weeks.

Inside the compound the troops dismounted and began unloading the trucks. Sandiman rounded up some soldiers from the compound to help, then rejoined the corporal. He wasn't needed here and he wanted to get back to Richmond. At the far end of the camp they checked out through the east barricade and headed into open country. It was eleven miles to the Richmond perimeter. They were alone and unprotected but he knew there was little danger. The gangs wouldn't bother a single Humvee carrying no supplies. He returned to his thoughts.

Thousands of Chinese, the private had said. How many thousands? Ten? Fifty? A hundred? He wondered if it was happening only here or if this invasion was part of some grand global conceit, some ancient dream of world domination. Conditions had never been so perfect.

There had been a total of nine nuclear targets struck, six in the United States. Of these, only one—Washington, D.C.—suffered multiple strikes, four small (one or two kiloton) bombs. The other major targets—San Francisco, Chicago, London and Brussels— were struck by single, large devices, smuggled in aboard cargo ships and trucks and detonated in place.

No one was certain who was responsible, but the most plausible speculation focused on the third world. It had long been suspected that a number of third-world nations were in possession of nuclear weapons, obtained decades earlier after the Soviet Union disintegrated, or purchased on the black market or manufactured in country. Now those governments had motive.

25

The global depression of the last five years had so decimated the global economy that developed nations were forced to abandon their foreign aid programs, enraging many third-world leaders. According to the theory, some of those leaders might have become sufficiently angry or desperate to do the unthinkable, perhaps in partnership with Muslim terrorists.

Two facts supported this thesis. First, at the time of the "war" there was no active crisis playing out among the major global powers that might have motivated nuclear aggression. Second, no missiles had been used against the targets struck in Europe, the United States or Japan. All these strikes had been ground bursts, the weapons apparently smuggled to their targets. The entire war therefore bore the unmistakable stamp of the third world. Terrorists and guerrilla fighters employed these tactics; professional standing armies did not.

The holocaust in the Middle East was a different matter. Missiles were used there, but the warheads were not nuclear and they were not deployed until hours after the initial bombings. Analysts concluded that the fighting in the Middle East had been an unplanned reaction to the larger conflict, a separate and distinct war of opportunity. In consideration of these facts it was generally agreed that the Mideast missile war did not controvert the "Third World Thesis."

But this new development could controvert the thesis, Sandiman thought. Chinese troops were landing on the North American mainland just nine weeks after the bombings. That certainly suggested that China, not some deranged third world dictator, may have masterminded the war.

The lone strike sustained by the Chinese had been delivered by missile from Kazakhstan. Was that aggression the product of ancient hostilities? Or was it retaliation? Did the Kazakhstanis know something about China's role in the war that no one else knew? If they did the world might now be facing monolithic evil on a scale even Hitler never dreamed of, a scale that . . .

"Trouble, Sir!"

Sandiman blinked. They were cresting a hill and just ahead

26

of them, perhaps a hundred yards distant, a tree lay across the road. He reached for his pistol. As he did he saw something move close beside them, at the limit of his peripheral vision. He turned, but they were already past whatever it had been. Then he heard the splintering of wood, a loud rustling of leaves, a crash.

"We're boxed," the corporal announced, looking in the rear view mirror.

Sandiman swung his head around. A second tree now blocked the road behind them. He shouted, "Get off the road!"

"Where?"

Sandiman pointed. "There!"

"No good. The bank's too steep!"

"Try it anyway. You have to try."

The corporal slowed and started turning.

They both heard shots. Bullets splattered across the windshield. The corporal jerked sideways and pitched out onto the highway. The Humvee spun on the rain-soaked pavement, slid backwards and slammed into the embankment. Sandiman was thrown clear.

He was dimly aware of voices shouting and the sound of running footsteps. He opened his eyes. He was lying on his back and there was a man looking down at him. The man had shoulder-length hair and a ragged beard. He leaned down close and pulled the automatic from Sandiman's holster. His breath smelled foul.

"Are you going to kill me?" Sandiman asked dully.

"Should I?" The man flashed a grotesque grin and took a step back. "Let's see." He reached into his pocket with his left hand, withdrew a quarter and held it between his thumb and forefinger. "Heads I snuff you, tails I don't." He tossed the coin and watched it bounce in the gravel at his feet. Then he bent down and peered at it. "Your lucky day," he announced. "It's tails."

Sandiman's head was slowly clearing. He balled his hands into fists and flexed them, trying to determine if he was in any condition to fight. He wasn't; the pain that shot up his right arm told him it was probably broken. "Is that all this is to you?" he asked disgustedly. "Some kind of fucking game?"

The man waved the pistol menacingly. "Don't press your

luck," he warned.

A few yards away, two men had been working to get the Humvee back on the road. The engine roared now and the vehicle lurched up onto the pavement. Sandiman's captor started walking toward it.

With his left arm Sandiman pushed himself to a sitting position and shouted, "How's my driver?"

The man paused. "'Fraid he bought it," he said, flashing that ugly grin again. "Got a big hole in his gut."

A wave of revulsion swept over Sandiman; he felt sudden rage. He wanted to wipe the grin off the man's face, wanted to blow a hole in *his* gut, wanted to lash out and—but there was nothing he could do. There were three of them and there was no point in getting himself killed. So instead he lay back on the embankment and closed his eyes.

He listened as the attackers moved away. He heard the sound of a chainsaw cutting through one of the fallen trees. Then the Humvee accelerated away. He heard the drone of its engine fading into the distance. A minute later he sat up.

The corporal's body lay face down on the far side of the road. The sun was just breaking through the clouds.

THREE

They were moving him again. As always there had been no warning, they simply summoned him and ordered him to collect his things. "You have five minutes, Mr. Craighill," the lieutenant said. "A car is waiting."

Such treatment would have angered him once; he would have demanded to know where they were taking him and why. But that time was long past. They never answered his questions and he finally abandoned his ritual resistance. Now he simply obeyed.

He did not consider this to be surrender, rather a recognition of reality and a means of conserving his strength. Life in the labor camps was hard enough; there was no point in making it harder. Defiance enraged the Chinese and accomplished nothing.

Still, submission had not come easily to David Craighill; he was accustomed to being treated with respect. Before the war he had risen high in his profession—a nightly TV news anchor in Los Angeles, he had enjoyed membership on a televised weekly public affairs panel, speaking engagements, VIP privilege. He had been a father figure to generations of southern Californians, recognized and respected by millions. His new status under the Chinese occupation had been difficult for him to accept and in the early days he rebelled. His celebrity caused his fellow prisoners to look to him for leadership and he had not disappointed them. He argued in favor of tacit cooperation with their captors, then organized an escape attempt. For six months his team worked tirelessly, planning and preparing. But their plans were discovered and two members of the team were executed.

Craighill grew cautious then, electing to wait out the changes that must inevitably come. They had time, he told himself. Time passed, a month, six months, a year. Conditions in the camps did not change. He was both frustrated and encouraged by this. The Chinese seemed to have no plan and their conduct of the occupation had grown stagnant. They were accomplishing nothing and eventually they would grow weary of failure, he was certain of it. When they did, he and the other prisoners would be ready. They would need all their strength when the opportunity presented itself. He explained this to the others over and over and kept reminding himself as well, trying to keep his spirits up. Someday there would be an opportunity and they would all need to be ready.

But now they were moving him again and he would have to start over in a new camp with a new group of inmates.

He leaned back in the car seat and tried to force his body to relax, tried to invite sleep. It was dark now; they had been on the road for several hours and it had been dark for most of that time. Still, sleep would not come. It was always like this when they moved him. Why did it still excite him? He should have learned to accept it as routine by now. But of course he knew the reason— moving represented change and change was the thing he longed for most, the thing his mind lusted after. Anything was better than the monotony of life in the camps.

He closed his eyes. Somehow he must sleep. He tried to think of something calm, tranquil. He saw water, a cloudless sky, a tree-lined lake shore. There was a cabin in the trees with a grassy lawn leading down to the water. A young boy moved toward him, riding a bicycle unsteadily, a mixture of fear and laughter on his face. It was his son, Michael. The bicycle turned, moved away, disappeared around a corner of the cabin. He followed, turned the corner and found a woman kneeling by the edge of a flower bed beside the front porch. Her back was to him as he approached; she was wearing a two-piece swimsuit and he could see the muscles in her shoulders rippling under smooth, tanned skin as she prodded the earth with a trowel. He stopped as he reached the steps beside her and she turned toward him, holding a hand up to shade her eyes from the afternoon sun. A stray wisp of hair fell across her face and she brushed it aside carelessly, still looking at him, squinting now, smiling. "Hi, Pug," she said.

He remembered it all so well. He had known at that moment that this image of her would remain frozen in his memory forever, like a snapshot in a photo album. It was still there, thirty-five years later.

He tried to discard it. He wanted peace, a few hours of serenity, not this pain. But it was beyond his control, had taken possession of him. *Annie! Oh, Annie, where are you? Are you still alive somewhere?*

Other memories drifted back to him. A ski trip to Zermatt—the one time she had accompanied him to Europe. They stayed near the base of the magnificent Matterhorn in a four-hundred-year-old chalet and rode around in horse-drawn sleighs, shivering against the chill of the incredibly clean alpine air. They had been so happy there. On a vacation in Hawaii he heard his daughter's laughter, saw his father's face, smelled the sweet fragrance of Ann's perfume. In a hospital room he saw the look in her eyes the day Michael was born.

He slept. The car moved on through the night and David Craighill moved on through sixty years of accumulated memory.

He was still sleeping when the car rolled to a stop at a security gate. It was late and he had passed through many such gates before so he did not awaken as his escorts and the camp guards discussed credentials and clearances. The gates were raised and the car moved through into the compound. It drove along a road encircling the perimeter of the camp. On the left were rows of blocky, solid-looking barracks; on the right, a high chain-link fence topped with coiled razor wire paralleled the road. At fifty-yard intervals along this fence tall platforms were placed. Sentries stood on each platform, armed with machine guns. The entire perimeter was floodlighted.

The soldier sitting in the car's right seat whistled softly as he took it all in. "What's this one done?" he asked. "I've never seen security like this."

The driver shrugged. "I only transport them. No one tells me anything."

31

They turned left onto a road that passed between two rows of barracks. Twenty yards ahead two camp guards stood by the entrance to the second building. The car pulled up beside them and stopped.

One of the guards leaned over and addressed the driver, "Any trouble?"

The driver glanced at Craighill. "He's been asleep. Hasn't said a word."

The guard nodded, moved to the rear car door and opened it. Craighill blinked and sat up groggily. The guard took his arm and helped him from the car. Then he closed the door and motioned to the driver. The car pulled away.

Craighill shuffled slowly the few feet to the steps leading up to the barracks' entrance, pausing to rub his eyes. He yawned. The guard said, "Come on, Mr. Craighill." The newsman started up the steps, then abruptly stopped. The guard tightened his grip on Craighill's arm and pulled him toward the door. Craighill resisted. Something had caught his attention. Something was different, but what? He took several hesitant steps, trying to shake himself awake.

They were solid! Of course, that was it. The steps were solid. How long had it been since he had seen steps made of anything but wood? Those stinking temporary barracks.

"Where am I?" he demanded.

They were almost to the door. Clumsily he tried to pull his arm free. But the guard only gripped tighter, drew him along more insistently. The second guard took hold of his other arm, together they were almost carrying him.

"What is this place?" Craighill shouted.

Then they were inside. His head was clearing now. He had seen . . . what? Stucco? The building was made of stucco. And there had been something in the distance. Fences? Floodlights?

"You'll find out soon enough," the guard said. His voice was soothing but his grip on Craighill's arm did not relax.

They led him down a corridor. Everything was stark white: walls, floors, even the doors they passed. *A plaster building with concrete steps; a permanent structure*—he ran through the

32

possibilities in his mind—*a prison compound of some kind, but inside it looks like a hospital.*

Halfway down the hallway was an open door. They led him through it into a small room. Again, everything was white, even the furniture. There was a single bed with clean white sheets, a desk, a chair, an empty bookcase, a toilet.

It is. It must be! They've brought me to a hospital.

They were undressing him. He felt suddenly anxious, frightened. But why was he frightened? This was what he wanted, wasn't it—change! It was finally changing.

When the guards finished they sat him on the bed dressed only in his underwear. The first guard said, "Try to get some sleep now. Will you need a sedative?"

"No," he replied. "I'll be fine."

The door closed. He heard the click of an electronic lock, then silence. Moments later the lights went out.

He was still not fully awake and only half sure he hadn't dreamed it all. But he was here wasn't he, sitting on a good firm bed? He ran his hand across the sheet for reassurance. The tiny room seemed to press in around him. *What kind of place,* he wondered. *A Chinese Auschwitz? Possibly. But then why the private room?*

Other questions suggested themselves. But he had no information, no basis on which to even guess at answers. That was always the way in Sino-America, there was never enough information. And nothing was more useless than a newsman without the facts.

He sat for a while, staring into nothing, thinking. The room was as dark as the mountains the car had driven through. For a moment, after the guards had left, light had washed in beneath the door, but before his eyes could adjust even that had been extinguished. Still he had noticed something; he struggled to remember. And finally it came to him. He bent down and ran his hand over the floor. It was carpeted. A carpeted prison cell?

"Damn," he said aloud. "Dammit to hell, what is going on here?"

He awoke to the sound of muffled voices and opened his eyes. For a moment he couldn't remember where he was, but it came back to him as he felt the clean, soft pillowcase against his cheek. The room was still dark, but not as dark as it had been; light was coming in from somewhere. He rolled over.

The door was open and there was a figure standing in the doorway, silhouetted against the brightness of the hallway beyond. The figure looked tall and athletic; Craighill didn't think it was one of the guards.

"Morning, Mr. Craighill. Did you sleep well?"

"Yes." He sat up squinting, trying to make out the man's face.

"It's late," the man said. "You've missed breakfast."

It was not a guard, the voice told him that. But if it was not a guard then where were the guards?

"I don't understand," he said. "You say they let me oversleep? What time is it?"

The man laughed. "No idea. The last time I knew it was late afternoon. But that was three or four days ago. Things are different here." He flipped a switch in the hallway. The room lights came on and Craighill saw the man clearly for the first time. He was perhaps thirty-five years old, a tall, muscular black man with a round, open face. Craighill was certain he had seen him before. The man walked into the room, drew the chair away from the desk, swung it around backward and sat down, straddling it with his arms resting on the chair back. There was an easy looseness to the way he moved and that too seemed familiar. The newsman was even surer now that he recognized him.

"I know you," Craighill said.

The man grinned and extended his hand. "Lonnie Murphy."

The pieces fell together. "Of course! Lonnie Murphy, the Kansas Tornado! I used to watch you at the Staples Center. I was there the night you scored sixth-eight points."

Murphy's grin became a crooked smile. "That was a long time ago."

34

"Not so long. What was it, eight years? Ten . . ." Craighill caught himself, suddenly embarrassed at the stupidity of what he'd just said. "Excuse me, Lonnie. For a moment I just forgot."

"I try not to think about that stuff."

"I understand."

"Counterproductive, as they say."

Craighill swung himself half out of bed and sat with his feet on the floor, looking around the room. "So what is this? A hospital or what?"

"A hospital?" Murphy's infectious grin returned. "Well I guess I can see why you might think that, but no, it's a prison all right. A very unusual prison, but a prison just the same. They have something special in mind here but we're not sure what. You'll understand better when you meet the others."

"The others?"

"We've all just arrived. I got here four days ago. There were only three of us then but every day since one or two more have come in. And that's just in this building. We don't know how many more there are in the other buildings."

Craighill began pulling on his clothes as Murphy talked. When the athlete paused, he asked, "So what do they have you doing?"

"That's one of the mysteries; we aren't doing anything. No work details. They've left us completely alone. They bring us food and a couple of times a day a guard walks through. Each night they lock us in our rooms. Aside from that—nothing."

"Strange," Craighill said. He finished tying his shoelaces and rose from the bed.

Murphy rose and pushed the chair back under the desk. "So. Let's go out and meet everyone, shall we?"

In the corridor Craighill's attention was immediately drawn to a card displayed in a bracket on the door opposite his. *Dr. Eugene Palitz* it read. On Craighill's own door was a similar card, bearing his name. There were brackets on each door along the corridor. In one direction all held cards; in the other, toward the building's outer door, the brackets were empty. Craighill looked at Murphy. "Is Palitz here?"

35

Murphy nodded. "It's a very unusual group. You'll see."

As they walked down the hallway Craighill read the names off to himself. There was Palitz, whose medical group had been instrumental in the development of the Altzheimer's drug therapy; a screenwriter named Roger Simone; Derek Kowalski, an NFL linebacker; Dr. James Summerland, a physicist who had once toured the country, campaigning for increased NASA funding; Murphy; a television actor named John Grant; and a consumer advocate named Paul Sandiman.

"I see what you mean," Craighill said as they passed the last door. "Quite a mixed bag."

Murphy shrugged. "Palitz and Summerland are a pair I suppose. Kowalski and I were professional athletes. Then there's Simone and John Grant; they were both in the entertainment business. But I don't know what to do with you and Sandiman. Any ideas?"

"Not off the top of my head. Sorry."

They had reached the end of the hallway and were standing at the entrance to a large room furnished with heavy upholstered sofas and chairs. On one side were three game tables; the opposite wall was lined with well-stocked bookshelves. The roof beams had been left exposed and ceiling fans hung from two of them. The overall impression was of an inexpensive men's club, modest but comfortable.

The men whose names David had just read were rising from positions around the room and moving toward the new arrival. Craighill recognized all but one. The stranger had to be Roger Simone; David had never met him.

Murphy waited until they were all gathered together and announced, "Gentlemen, welcome David Craighill, the newest member of our team."

FOUR

For the first time in nearly two years, Chen Loying was feeling satisfied. The fighting was over, the waiting was over and he had won.

He was seated at a small desk in a small, sparsely furnished office. Aside from the desk, the office contained a single chair, a file cabinet and a bookcase. The walls were bare of decoration. The average visitor would undoubtedly find the room dreary and assume that its occupant must be a person of little consequence. This did not matter to Chen. He had never cared for the trappings of status and everything he needed was here. In this place he held the world—the new world—in his hands. What he was about to do here would shape the destiny of millions.

He was eighty-eight years old. His muscles frequently ached without provocation, his stomach sometimes rejected even the mildest foods and his bowels often refused to function as they should. None of this mattered to Chen. He saw old age not as a curse, but as a gift. The years were stealing his physical abilities, but they were also providing him the time he needed to complete his work. And his work was all that mattered to him. It invigorated him. Not since Tienanmen Square had he experienced such excitement or such dedication to a task.

He could hardly believe this opportunity was finally at hand, and that the experiences of his lifetime had conspired so specifically to prepare him for the task now before him. Scholar, teacher, diplomat—the skills and experience gained in each of these disciplines would be required if he was to succeed. Strange, he thought, the random events that determined the course of a life. In his case the first of those events had occurred nearly a hundred years earlier, long before he was born.

Chen's father, Jie-do, had been just eleven years old in 1934. That year, Chiang Kai-shek's Kuomintang army completely encircled the Communist stronghold in southern Jiangxi province and began methodically starving the insurgents into submission. Jie-do's family lived in Jiangxi and Jie-do's father was a Communist.

The blockade imposed great hardship on the Reds; there was very little food. And the Kuomiutang was steadily drawing the perimeter in, pulling the noose ever tighter around the Reds. Then, one day in October, Jie-do's father called the family together to tell them what their leaders had decided.

"We are going to break out," the father said, with such calm assurance that Jie-do could not possibly have understood the difficulty of such a thing. "We are going to the west, to Sichuan," the father told them.

Two days later they set out at dusk and walked all night toward the south to join the thousands gathering near Yudu. Three days after that, the epic "Long March" began. A hundred thousand soldiers and peasant partisans trekked south and west toward Hunan province on the first leg of their incredible journey.

During the months that followed, the Red Army fought constant battles with Kuomintang troops who were dug in along their route. Jie-do saw little of this fighting, but he could hear it. The thudding of artillery and the clatter of small-arms fire was constant as the rear guard made its way along roads that the advancing army had captured for their passage. There were dead and wounded all along these roads, and many times Jie-do and his family were forced to take cover from low flying Kuomintang aircraft that constantly bombed and strafed the column.

Most of the time they moved by night. By day, Jie-do and his father and the Young Vanguards held meetings with local peasants, and these meetings served to crystallize the boy's understanding of their cause. "We must succeed," they told the peasants. "We are the hope of the people." And the people flocked to them. They gave food to the Reds and by the thousands joined their ranks to fight against the oppression of the landlords and the tax collectors.

In May Jie-do joined the Vanguard, having finally received permission from his father. Just turned twelve, he marched with the Red Army and carried a rifle. He missed the initial engagement of the army's crossing of the great Tatu river because he was in the second line of march. When he arrived, the river town of An Jen Chang had already been taken and the boats were furiously working against the rising waters of the Tatu Ho, transferring men and supplies to the far shore. The river was swelling rapidly, and each crossing was more difficult than the last. It was clear that another route would have to be found, and there was only one alternative—two hundred and fifty kilometers to the west was a bridge, the Liu Ding Jiao.

At last the twelve-year-old revolutionary saw his chance to make a real contribution. He was young, but strong for his age. And he was determined. He pleaded with his commander to let him go with the hand-picked soldiers being sent to race the Kuomintang troops on the far side of the river, west along the Tatu Ho to the Liu Ding Jiao.

"It is not a task to be left to a boy," his commander said at first. "Especially not to one so new to the army."

'But it is because I am new that I should be allowed to go," Jie-do argued. "It is my first opportunity to fight for the revolution. I will give my last breath."

Finally, when the boy's father argued in his behalf, the commander relented.

For three days and nights the two armies pursued their routes along opposite banks of the river, through some of the roughest terrain in China. The trail took them from the knee-deep mud of the river lowlands to the tops of sheer canyon walls, where the Tatu wound its way thousands of feet below, swift and narrow as the blade of a knife. Except for brief rest intervals there was no stopping along the way; for three days they did not sleep. They pressed on and gradually drew away from the enemy soldiers on the far shore.

The bridge was constructed of heavy chains supporting thick wooden planks which formed the roadbed. When they

39

reached it, they found the planks on their side missing. Halfway across the gorge the roadway ended and from this point to the great abutments where the structure was anchored on the near side of the river the chains hung naked. On the far side, a regiment of troops stood guard, with a machine gun at the bridgehead to discourage any attempt at frantic heroism.

But nothing could deter the Reds now. Despite the enormous risks, soldiers weary from three days of constant marching without sleep swung out onto the chains and started toward the far shore while their comrades laid down a fusillade of covering fire. Many died in the attempt, but miraculously a few made their way to the security of the planking at the center of the span. One, then another, then ten and twenty climbed onto the roadbed and began throwing grenades at the enemy. The Kuomintang soldiers broke and ran. The Liu Ding Jiao, the bridge built by Liu, had been taken.

Jie-do had not been among those who climbed onto the chains in this incredible display of individual courage; he had been one of the hundreds on the south shore laying down covering fire. But in the minds of his fellow revolutionaries there was little difference. He had done his part, he had made the march and he had been there at the end. Of all the Reds in China, for all time there would only be a few hundred who could say they had been at the Liu Ding Jiao. Jie-do was one and for the rest of his life this fact would open doors, leading to a distinguished career in the Red Army and recognition as a true hero of the revolution.

Later, it would open doors for his son as well.

Chen Jie-do had big plans for his son. A second generation soldier, Chen Loying would rise quickly through the ranks and take his place among the leaders of the new China. He would benefit from advantages his father had not had—education, a culture that was emerging from darkness into light, friends in the highest places. The father foresaw a future virtually without limits for the boy.

But it was not to be. Chen Loying had no interest in the military. He did not want to disappoint his father but he knew

40

pursuing a career that did not ignite his passions would guarantee failure.

"I do not belong in the army," he told his father. "Please, try to understand."

After much discussion his father agreed that the boy must do what was right for him.

Given his father's permission, young Chen's passion for history determined the path he would pursue—a life of scholarship: forty years as a professor of Western Studies at Yenan University, assignment to a number of government panels and think-tanks studying China's relationship with the West and, late in life, selection to a post on the Chinese delegation to the United Nations. Then, just when he thought his career was at an end, a final appointment.

The Central Committee of the Chinese Communist Party named him to chair a secret task force, operating under the strictest possible security. Chen's team was ordered to establish policies and develop procedures for administering the postwar pacification and reconstruction of the North American continent. It was absurd, the aging historian thought, a futile exercise. The western democracies were weak and growing steadily weaker, but there would be no war! Not even China was ready to challenge the United States militarily, and the whole world knew it. Regardless, the task force worked diligently, and its plans were approved in due course.

Four years later Chen was enjoying a comfortable retirement when the world exploded, and the Chinese moved to restore order. When the occupation of North America was complete the implementation of his task force's recommendations should have been automatic. But there were unforeseen difficulties.

Following the nuclear bombings, anti-American sentiment in China rose to unexpected levels. There was evidence that the bombs were of Russian, not American manufacture, but the terrorists who deployed them had been motivated by the global depression, and most in China held the Americans responsible for the depression. Greed had driven the global economy into chaos, the anti-Americans asserted; many nations had played a part, but they were following the example set by the Americans.

A groundswell of public outrage erupted. There were demonstrations in the streets of every major Chinese city. The people demanded retribution. "The Red Army must sweep the North American continent clean of all capitalist devils," they shouted. "Like a scythe felling wheat!"

Their rural imagery was borrowed from a China that no longer existed, but the passion it expressed was real and malevolent.

Cooler heads argued mightily against genocide, reminding the demonstrators that it was not the American masses, but the American leadership which had been responsible, and that the Chinese people had long been the friends of the American people.

The radicals countered with mathematics. They pointed out that among the world's remaining six billion souls there were barely two hundred million Americans; their presence was a threat, their absence would hardly be noticed.

At one point, even the Central Committee seemed to waver and Chen feared the worst.

In the end, however, the Party stood firm. As weeks became months, the riots grew less frequent and the rhetoric less inflammatory. Eventually the demonstrations and the demands ceased altogether.

Once the North American continent was secured, however, Chen discovered that anti-Americanism had not completely died with the decision to imprison rather than eradicate the American population. His attempts to initiate his carefully conceived program produced almost no results. Requests for manpower and equipment routinely met with excuses and delay. Progress was agonizingly slow. The North American reconstruction lagged far behind the other continents, and conditions in the North American camps were the worst in the entire world.

Conditions in the camps were not of direct concern to Chen or his organization; the camps were temporary quarters run by the army and Chen had no control over their administration. They did, however, form the environment within which his team was forced to work, and that environment was rendering their work virtually impossible. Denied Chinese crews to construct the facilities they needed, they were forced to rely on captive labor. Low morale among the captive population caused this labor to be slow and ineffective. Time was slipping away, time that Chen was convinced they could not afford to lose.

For over a year he pursued his needs through normal channels, until finally, convinced that he could wait no longer, he circumvented the military hierarchy and went directly to the continental administrator, Lin Chiao-tu. It was a violation and a risk; it could have led to Chen's dismissal.

Lin was angered by Chen's request for a meeting. It placed him in a position which could compromise him as well. But he agreed to hear his old professor's arguments because he remembered Chen fondly from his student days in Yenan, and because he respected Chen's many contributions to China and his established dedication to the Party.

Chen argued persuasively. "The situation in North America is unparalleled among the six continents," he told Lin. The population here will not be swayed by traditional propaganda; these people are accustomed to forming their own opinions. Slogans, regardless of how clever or correct they may be, will prove insufficient to encourage their cooperation. Have you not already found this so?"

Lin listened and asked what alternative Chen offered.

Chen answered with an outline of the program which had been approved by the Central Committee nearly five years earlier. The program was the product of careful planning, he explained, by men who were intimately familiar with the American population.

It was an impressive presentation, complete with voluminous documentation to justify his requests. He spread it all out on Lin's desk, explaining exactly what must be done and why.

Lin listened patiently to all that Chen said, then raised the obvious objection: "I understand your position, Professor. But this camp you propose to construct—while I can assure you that it will be built eventually, I don't see how I can justify its construction now. By your own admission, it is special; it is designed to

43

accommodate a special class of prisoner. Yet, as you well know, parity is the first priority.

This repetition of dogma was less than Chen had hoped for from Lin but not less than he had expected. There were political implications in his request that Lin could hardly ignore. Despite his high office, Lin was not free to operate autonomously; the Party would not permit any man to disregard the established order. Chen knew, therefore, that his only chance lay in making his request appear to fall within the guidelines of the First Directive: *Parity is the first priority.* He had anticipated Lin's objection and was prepared for it.

"Parity," Chen said, "is a relative thing. We agree, for example, that it is necessary to provide sufficient food for each inhabitant of the six continents, and this is clearly a proper goal of the new order. But you will admit that we do not mean by this that every individual, whether infant, adult man or adult woman, should receive exactly the same ration. Instead we mean that each must be provided a ration sufficient to his needs. An adult man may be given five times what an infant receives and that may constitute parity. Is this not true? It is the same with my request, Comrade Lin. The needs of these Americans are unique. We cannot provide for them as we provide for the populations of Africa or India or South America and call it parity."

Their discussion continued for a half hour. When the interview was concluded, Lin politely refused to grant Chen's request. But he did not dismiss it altogether. Instead, he promised "to consider the matter over the next few days." To assist him in his deliberations, Chen left with him all the documentation he had used in making his presentation. Then he returned to his duties and awaited Lin's decision.

Of course, even in this last desperate attempt to obtain what he needed, Chen had not explained to Lin all his reasons for pursuing his program with such determination. For many years now a heresy had been growing in Chen's mind and it was this, far more than any belief in justice or the true nature of parity, that motivated him.

For nine years during the mid-1990s and early 2000s,

44

Chen had been attached to the Chinese delegation to the United Nations. He had used that time to conduct a careful study of the American people: their history, their ideology, their weaknesses, their strengths. The American economy had been in turmoil for many of those years, but by any normal measure was still enormously successful. Chen wanted to know why.

He was aware that America was incredibly rich in natural resources, but it was not possible to dismiss the American phenomenon as a mere accident of geography. Other nations were also rich in resources but had not begun to claim proportionate achievement. There had to be other reasons and Chen was determined to understand them.

Whenever possible he sought out Americans and spoke with them. He experienced first-hand their curious confusion regarding political priorities, their pride in and simultaneous apathy toward their institutions, their alternately profound dedication to social causes and hopeless lack of coherent social consciousness. He observed that with few exceptions they seemed unconcerned with the concepts of family or community or national identity; instead they were inner-directed, selfish and acquisitive. At the same time they could be extremely generous. Yet curiously, their generosity was almost always directed toward strangers; they gladly donated food to the famine-stricken populations of Africa, but turned their backs on the poor and disadvantaged in their own midst. It was all extremely confusing.

In the end Chen concluded that, from a Chinese perspective, they were hardly a society at all, but rather a random collection of subcultures which found themselves accidentally occupying the same space. They had almost no common tradition and little real regard for one another. Yet they prospered.

It made absolutely no sense. If they were not really a society, and if the answer to their remarkable success could not therefore be found in any collective mechanism, what was its source? For all his study Chen was unable to answer this question. On the day of his departure from New York he still had not penetrated the mystery to his satisfaction.

And the mystery gave birth to his heresy. For although he

admitted that American society, through its excess of misdirected freedoms, had spawned more insidious social inequities than any other on the face of the globe and was now clearly in the process of self destruction, he was still unable to dismiss its earlier successes. Its successes must be explained and understood.

Those successes were not the product of democracy—he was certain of that much. The American people had long ago surrendered their democratic institutions to the politicians and the corporations. They ignored their democracy; most didn't even bother to vote! That left only a single plausible candidate—their success must somehow be the product of capitalism. Not the capitalism practiced for the last four decades in China, where a massive government bureaucracy oversaw and controlled every aspect of the nation's economic life, but rather a wild, chaotic and almost completely uncontrolled free-for-all, a rigged game which promised riches for all but rewarded only a very few. Was this what motivated their success? Did the remote possibility of huge wealth provide them more motivation than the Chinese model, which promised a good and stable economic life, but no realistic possibility of wealth?

The mere suggestion of this idea was repulsive to Chen. To accept it he must reject many of the ideals to which he had dedicated his life. And yet the conclusion seemed unavoidable. Was it possible that a man would work harder on his own behalf than he would for his family, his village, his nation? As Chen pondered this question during the last years of his time at the UN and studied the results of China's decade-long experiment with capitalism, an idea began to form in his mind. And the idea became the foundation of his heresy.

Chen had always believed that personal incentives could not foster greater effort among the Chinese; they could only foster selfishness and greed. Now, however, he saw that the new Chinese capitalism was succeeding. It was a shock to him. He wondered if there might be another aspect to the relationship between effort and reward that he had previously overlooked. In China, hard work was expected and workers who put forth great effort were rewarded with recognition. But the work and its reward were

46

almost always contained within a strictly defined context. And the most strictly defined work was almost always most greatly rewarded because it was most easily recognized and quantified. Innovative thinking was rarely rewarded and was, in fact, often discouraged. Thinking outside the box was considered dangerous—new ideas led to unpredictable outcomes.

Was this the key? Was the capitalist West more successful because its system of rewards encouraged workers to be clever and ingenious rather than to simply work hard?

The more Chen considered this idea the more he came to believe it was true. For a Chinese there was satisfaction and recognition in work, any work. But for a capitalist, rewards were based on results, so there was incentive to learn how to produce more, even if that meant that less work was required. Armed with this realization, Chen began to view capitalism not as a monolithic evil, but as a simple tool which could encourage progress. This was his heresy.

He discussed it cautiously with close associates after leaving the UN and discovered to his surprise that many of them shared his view. A year later, even some members of the Central Committee began talking quietly about expanding the experiment with free market structures. A decade later, however, with China rapidly emerging as a new global superpower and the western economies struggling, the Central Committee began slowly reasserting its control over the Chinese economy. The capitalist world was about to drown in a sea of red ink; the Central Committee was determined that China would not share in the West's collapse. To the contrary, China must survive and emerge intact, ready to dominate the globe.

To this end the Central Committee began designing contingency plans. Capitalism would not go quietly, it feared. There would be mass riots, class warfare, possibly some form of global conflagration. When it was over, China must be prepared to wrest order from the chaos.

It was at this time that Chen was ordered to prepare his plan for the North American reconstruction.

The end came later than most expected, and no one

47

anticipated its final form. But it did come. The invasions were mounted then, and the six continents were occupied. Chen began his work six months to the day after the troops landed on the North American beaches.

He did not mourn the passing of the America he had known so well. That America had been corrupt, even he could not deny that. But he was still convinced that the corruption was not fundamental and that the idea of capitalism had not been the source of the corruption. Others believed it had, but Chen's heresy remained intact. He was convinced that capitalism should not be discarded, that it represented a tool which could be extremely useful to the new order. And he was determined to demonstrate that fact here in North America.

Of course he had not been able to explain the depth of his feeling on this to Lin or to anyone else, but it was this belief that prompted his visit to the continental administrator's office. Elements of capitalism had been carefully woven into the program he presented to Lin, but he advanced them with great care, explaining that they were to be offered as concessions to the Americans, as bait to trap their quarry. He did not tell Lin that he himself believed in their power.

Lin kept him waiting for two weeks before delivering his approval. Ten days later Chinese crews and material arrived on site and construction of Chen's special camp began in earnest. The work progressed quickly. By mid-September the facility was complete. A week later the staff was in residence and the selection of the first group of Americans had begun. On September 29th three prisoners were moved into barracks four. Others were now following in rapid succession.

Soon the real work would begin, work which would lead, hopefully, to the enlistment of American cooperation in the creation of a new and infinitely superior society.

Chen smiled as he considered what was about to begin. The world made whole. An end to war and human suffering. An opportunity to solve global problems on a global basis. Not even Mao could have imagined such a thing.

FIVE

Sunday, October 3, 2032

Today is the first day of my incarceration in a very unusual prison. My jailers have provided both time and writing tools so I have decided to maintain a journal. I am David Craighill, formerly of Los Angeles, California. I have been a prisoner of the Chinese North American Military Command since July 30, 2031. Until yesterday, I had been confined in three separate farm labor camps, all physically and functionally similar. Last night I was brought here.

This place is completely unlike the other prisons. It is a maximum security facility. My barracks is built of stucco with a concrete floor. There are no windows. The prison compound is surrounded by a high wire fence with guard towers. The perimeter is floodlighted at night.

There are seven other inmates housed in my building with more arriving each day. None of us has any idea why we have been brought here. The Chinese have explained nothing and are, in fact, ignoring us. They have assigned us no work details. It is all very puzzling.

My fellow prisoners are an interesting group. In order of their arrival here they are: Paul Sandiman. Age 42. Paul was a consumer advocate before the war. Wrote a best seller on consumer fraud. A born activist, he interviews every new arrival, collecting intelligence. Talks about planning an escape, but no one else seems interested.

John Grant. Age 39, film actor—

Bell just rang. Lights out in one minute. I'll block out more time for this tomorrow.

SIX

Two more prisoners arrived Sunday night. They were Michael Wiedemier, a NASA astronaut, and Alex Hammil, a columnist with the Sacramento Bee. Craighill did not know Wiedemier but he knew Hammil well enough to be pleased when he saw the card on Hammil's door Thursday morning.

As usual, Murphy did the breakfast introductions. Hammil recognized Craighill immediately. The two shook hands and stood for a moment groping for something to say. Finally, Hammil muttered, "It's been a hell of an ordeal, hasn't it?"

David nodded his agreement. He wanted to say, "Alex, you look terrific," or, "Alex, you haven't changed a bit." But neither was true. Hammil had aged twenty years. He looked as though he had, in fact, been through a hell of an ordeal.

One by one the others welcomed the newcomers, all except Palitz and Summerland, who were off by themselves in a far corner of the room.

John Grant clapped Hammil on the shoulder and asked if he wanted a drink. Noting Hammil's obvious surprise, he said expansively, "No shit! We have all the comforts here and today is your day. Yours too, Wiedemier. Now, what'll you both have?" He swung open the doors of the bar cabinet and waved a hand theatrically at the bottles arrayed on the shelves within.

Hammil glanced doubtfully at Craighill and shook his head in disbelief. "I never drink this early in the day," he said. "But it's been two years. . . . What the hell, I'll have a gin, neat."

"Good man," said Grant.

Craighill explained the new arrival tradition to Hammil and led him to his place at the head of the table. Wiedemier sat at the far end. Kowalski brought their food, and Hammil began reciting his experience in the camps.

It was more gruesome than most. Hammil had been in a camp where the workers staged a slowdown. There had been retaliation—beatings and an execution. Later, in another camp, there had been an escape attempt. Five men actually got away, only to be recaptured the next day. They were lined up against a wall and shot.

"The next six months were absolute hell," Hammil said, the pain of the recollection written on his face. "The guards beat us indiscriminately. They raped two women, cut our food rations, forced us to work long hours; they even withheld heat from our barracks. The worst of it was they actually seemed to enjoy it, the bastards. I never saw such cruelty."

The table fell silent for several seconds, then Kowalski said, "I imagine they really did enjoy it. Under those circumstances cruelty is natural. I was a psych major in college and I saw a study once that would amaze you. Some university students created . . ." He paused, recognizing surprise on the faces around the table. "What? You think because I was a jock I studied basket weaving? I carried a 3.2 average! I graduated!"

Sandiman reassured him: "No one doubts that, Derek. Go on."

"A group of students created a mock prison," Kowalski continued. "Some played the part of prisoners, some were guards. I don't recall the scheduled timeframe, but the university had to terminate the study early. Because it worked too well. The student prisoners started acting like real prisoners. They became devious and petty. They created a degenerate subculture. It was the same with the student guards; they became mean. There were instances of real cruelty."

"The point is, we all accept roles in life. We live up to the expectations our culture places on us. We become our roles. None of this is unique to the Chinese. There was plenty of cruelty before the Chinese came. That last year before the bombs was terrible. I saw things that turned my stomach."

"He's right about that," Grant said. "I lived in Malibu and I can tell you, Malibu was a war zone that entire last year. I don't know how many houses were torched or how many people were killed, but the gangs that came out from L.A. were vicious. My neighbors armed themselves, bought guard dogs, hired private security; none of it helped. An entire family two doors up the canyon from me was massacred."

Weidemier nodded. "It was bad everywhere. My brother in Baltimore was killed by a black kid. He was only eleven years old."

"You had an eleven year old brother killed?"

"My brother wasn't eleven, the black kid was." Weidemier glanced nervously at Murphy. "No offense, Mr. Murphy."

Murphy shrugged. "None taken. You're not talking about

51

my people, Alex. I lived in Bel Air. My house was shot up three times."

Sandiman asked, "The eleven year old kid—they caught him?"

Weidemier shook his head. "Hell no, they didn't catch him. They never caught any of them, did they? We're talking about an army of terrorists, pouring out of the center cities into the suburbs. It was a civil war; the police were helpless."

"So how did you find out the kid was only eleven?"

Weidemier's eyes were tearing and his jaw was beginning to quiver. He said, "Some reporter told my sister-in-law. He said the kid had been bragging to other kids about it."

Simone looked at Kowalski. "So how does psychology account for that, Derek? What cultural role were these people acting out?"

The halfback settled in his chair and thought for a moment. "Victim, I suppose. The problem was the culture assigned them no role; it neglected and abandoned them. They took it for a long time, then they snapped. They felt like wild animals, wounded and backed into a corner."

Simone groaned. "Oh, spare me! Good God, Derek, I thought that kind of bullshit thinking disappeared twenty years ago. We bankrupted the country trying to prop up the huddled masses. You can't believe . . ."

"I suppose you prefer the bullshit thinking of ten years ago. Or five. Look around you, Roger. This is what your bullshit bought us."

"Stop!" Sandiman called out suddenly. "Time out! This is old business. I thought we all had our fill of this argument a long time ago. In any event, it's moot now; it serves no purpose."

"It's cathartic," Simone insisted.

"It's a waste of time. We have better things to do."

Kowalski laughed derisively. "Such as?"

"Well, I'd like to talk to the new arrivals, if it's all right with you."

Simone delivered a mock salute. "I almost forgot, you're the CIA operative in this camp, aren't you?"

Sandiman returned a crooked smile. "It's a dirty job, but somebody has to do it."

Simone pushed himself to his feet. "Suit yourself, but I don't have to watch. Derek, I wasn't finished. Were you?"

"Just getting started," Kowalski replied. They headed off to

52

continue their argument.

Craighill looked at Sandiman. "Talk to Weidemier first, okay? Alex and I have some catching up to do." Sandiman nodded.

Grant pushed himself away from the table and announced, "The drinking lamp is lighted, boys. Fill 'em if you got 'em."

There were no takers. This morning he had the bar to himself.

Tuesday, Oct. 5

There has been a change here, although we don't understand what it may signify. In the past, our guards contented themselves with delivering our meals and walking through the barracks occasionally on brief inspection tours. This afternoon two of them stayed with us for nearly half an hour. They made no attempt to speak to us (although we're convinced they understand at least some English) but they did smile whenever one of us looked in their direction and seemed generally more curious than hostile. They left without speaking even to each other, but we are nevertheless hoping that it may signal the beginning of a dialog.

I should mention that these guards were unarmed. None of the guards who have come into this building since my arrival has been armed. Still, we've given no serious consideration to capturing any of them to hold as hostage. We have no doubt that just beyond the outer doors other guards are stationed, and they certainly are armed. Nor do we doubt that the ones who come into the building would be ready to die if necessary, and their comrades on the outside understand this and would expect nothing less. They are an intensely dedicated people, these Chinese. Despite all of this, however, I must admit that the absence of weapons inside this barracks has had a calming effect on all of us.

Two new arrivals today:

Kevin Sutton. Age 35, our second actor. Has done it all: theater, film, television, commercials. Six foot two, blonde hair, blue eyes. The rugged, outdoor type.

Ken Fogarty. Age 55, editor of 'Whistleblower' magazine. Fogarty stepped on a lot of toes during his maverick career, but his wealth made him immune to the forces which were often marshaled against him.

Wednesday morning two guards entered the barracks shortly after breakfast, their arms loaded with boxes, and made their way directly to one of the game tables in the great hall. One emptied the contents of a box onto the table while the other (in perfect English) directed the prisoners to gather around him. He said they were going to teach them a game.

The prisoners complied enthusiastically, all displaying real interest, not in what the guard was saying, but in the way he said it, his mannerisms and inflections. It was an opportunity for them to gauge his attitude toward them.

He introduced himself as Ho-ting, and as he began his instructions it became obvious that he was enjoying himself. Much of his enjoyment seemed to derive from his enthusiasm for the game itself, and the Americans found this puzzling. The game seemed to be little more than a modified form of the board game 'checkers.' Ho-ting gave every indication of being quick-witted and intelligent, and they were baffled by his apparent fascination with such childish entertainment. Baffled, that is, until he explained the final step in preparation for a contest.

The game was played on a board approximately twenty-four inches on a side with its face marked off into a grid of squares. The board was black, the grid boundaries a vivid crimson. The grid was twenty squares by twenty squares or four hundred squares in all. The player's pieces, thin metal discs with small pegs in their centers which allowed them to be picked up and moved, were arranged in the first three rows at each end of the board, one disc in each square, sixty discs for each player.

The game proceeded with the players alternating moves. In the course of one move it was possible to move a disc a considerable distance by jumping over adjacent discs to the next available vacant grid square. It was thus possible, Ho-ting explained, to break off a force of ten or fifteen discs and move them across the board as a squad, keeping them always together by always moving the rearmost disc to the next open square at the head of the squad.

As the play proceeded, squads and larger armies would engage in battles, coming face to face with each other. In this situation, stalemates would occur unless one player's squad was numerically superior to his opponent's. One disc standing in the path of an enemy disc was sufficient to block the progress of the enemy. However, if a player stacked a second disc on top of his first, then with his next move he might bridge the opposing disc, taking a position in the vacant space beyond. He could do this with the second (stacked) disc or with any of the discs behind in the same squad. Similarly, three discs may be stacked to bridge two, four to bridge three, and so on.

Here, Wiedemier asked him why it would not be easier to go around, to simply flank the enemy squad. Ho-ting smiled and said, "You will see, Mr. Wiedemier. Very soon you will see."

The object of the game was to move one disc completely across the board into the last row, the opponent's first row. The first player to accomplish this was the winner.

When Ho-ting had finished, Sandiman asked, "Is that all there is to it?"

"That is all there is to the rules," Ho-ting said. "Now, who would like to play?"

No one stepped forward. Ho-ting stood with his arms folded across his chest, waiting. Craighill, who had no real interest in the game, was about to offer to play, fearing that Ho-ting might take refusal as an insult, when the guard leaned forward, placed his hands palm down on the table and said, "Gentlemen, believe me, I understand how you feel. There are more important matters on your minds than games. But I am afraid I must insist. It will be necessary for someone to play this game now. Later it will be necessary for everyone to play. Starting today, there is going to be something required of you every day. So! Mr. Sandiman, please take a seat . . . there." He indicated the chair opposite his.

When Sandiman had seated himself, Ho-ting resumed his smiling affability and continued as though no interruption had occurred.

"You are certain that you understand the rules?" he asked. Sandiman assured him that he understood.

"Good. You will have ten seconds for each move. After you have become more familiar with the play, this will be reduced to five. But for now, for a beginner, ten is difficult enough. I will begin by pressing this button on the side of the game board, after which you will have one minute to study the board. Understood?"

Sandiman frowned. "Study the board?"

Ho-ting pressed the button.

There was a mechanical click and a faint whirring sound, like a tiny electric motor engaging. Suddenly, some of the crimson grid boundaries rose up from the board surface to a height of about a half inch. These tiny "fences" were themselves crimson colored and formed a random geometric pattern against the black background of the board face.

At first Sandiman was aware of no particular order to the pattern. Then he realized that it was a maze.

"All movement of pieces must be within the lanes formed by these barriers," Ho-ting instructed. "At no time may the barriers be breached."

Sandiman studied the pattern of the maze. "But you have me at a disadvantage," he objected. "I can't learn this maze in one minute and play you a fair game. You've played it many times before."

"I have never played this maze before," Ho-ting assured him.

"But you said you had," Sandiman countered.

"No. I said I had played the game many times. But not this maze. Look, I will show you." Ho-ting pressed a second button on the side of the game board. The red panels withdrew. He again pressed the first button. The panels reappeared.

"I see," Sandiman said. They all pressed in for a closer look. Michael Weidemier, who was standing next to Craighill, nodded approvingly and said, "Interesting!"

The pattern had changed; it was not the same maze.

"I can't say that it never repeats," Ho-ting said. "But there are so many different mazes that it never seems to repeat. Each time it is different, you see?" He cycled the buttons several more times. Each new maze was different from the others. "So, are you ready now?"

Sandiman agreed that he was ready; Ho-ting cycled the buttons a final time. The two players studied the board, and Ho-ting made the first move, taking a disc from his first row and moving it forward four squares to the entrance to one of the avenues that led into the maze. Sandiman imitated the maneuver, also moving one of his first row pieces to a position in his fourth row.

The Americans found it impossible to assess the wisdom of these initial maneuvers. The introduction of the maze into what had originally been a very simple format rendered it extremely complicated. To begin with, apparently opposite moves were not necessarily opposite, as they would have been on most square-grid board games. A move by one player, which seemed to counter the second player's move at the far end of the board because it was directly opposite, might actually bear no relation to it because the two avenues entered might never touch once they made their way into the depths of the maze.

There were many tracks through the maze, some shorter than others. There were also a number of places where gaps appeared in the walls allowing passage from one track to another. A player was therefore required, while planning his own attack strategies, to simultaneously consider all the possible avenues his opponent's moves might lead into and set up adequate defenses. All this had to be accomplished in the space of ten seconds and, according to Ho-ting, once a player achieved a degree of proficiency this time limit would be reduced to five seconds.

Craighill was fascinated by the complexity of it all. It was, he decided, about as difficult as chess. The others seemed equally entranced. All of them watched intently as the two players developed their individual strategies.

The completion of that first game took well over an hour. Each player was making only three or four moves per minute on average (although Ho-ting sometimes moved in considerably less than the allotted ten seconds) and there were a great many moves which had to be made before any significant progress was evident. Still, none of them grew bored with it. And when the action reached the center of the grid and confrontations were entered between the opposing sides, enthusiastic heckling broke out all around.

Ho-ting emerged an easy victor. Sandiman seemed embarrassed by his poor showing and, when challenged to another game by John Grant, begged off, saying he'd prefer to watch someone else try. Ho-ting and the other guard pulled game boards from the other boxes and insisted that everyone but Sandiman take part in a second round. Sandiman could sit out if he preferred, there was an odd man anyway.

They all behaved like children for the rest of the day. Craighill played a game with Wiedemier, which he managed to lose in record time. Ho-ting and the second guard, whose name was Chun, wandered around the room, smiling as they had the day before and saying little. They left just before lunch and did not return.

That evening there was just one new arrival:

Peter Bell. Age 43, an attorney who made a career of representing underprivileged clients against oppressive (his characterization) governments and corporations. As liberal influence in Washington steadily eroded during the last three decades, liberal activists turned increasingly to the courts. Bell was their most vocal spokesman. He was the thirteenth arrival at the barracks.

Thursday, October 7th

We resumed the old routine today. Ho-ting and Chun did not return. Everyone is disappointed (We were told to expect required activities every day now.) and expecting something to happen soon.

The game remains a popular diversion. Weidemier organized a tournament this afternoon, which he won. Kowalski finished second and the final match was a real battle, judging by the shouting and loud applause that accompanied it.

I spent most of the day reading Mao Tse-tung. I feel the need to at least try to understand the Chinese mind, and this seemed as good a place to start as any.

Two newcomers today:

Billy Dupree. Age 26, musician. He seems pleasant, but I have no knowledge of his work. Grant tells me he was the leader of a popular rock band called "Crystal Sludge."

Nathan Moore. Age 59, board member of a half dozen major corporations. In the last years prior to the war, he was a frequent spokesman for American business, constantly being interviewed by TV, print and electronic media regarding the commercial crisis or controversy du jour. I interviewed him myself once, six years ago. An unpleasant, sour individual.

SEVEN

There was no breakfast Monday morning. The guards unlocked the rooms as usual, but when the prisoners began wandering into the great hall they found the tables empty.

What did it mean? Had they been awakened early? Had the cooks overslept? No, there was more to it than that, they decided. Last night there had been no new arrivals. Together, these two developments must signify a change. Something was about to happen.

It was a half hour before their suspicions were verified. They heard the outer door swing open and the sound of footsteps in the hallway. Ho-ting marched into the great hall alone. At the center of the room he paused, hands on hips, and looked around as though searching for something. All conversation stopped. For the first time he was armed; a pistol rested in a holster strapped to his belt. His expression was stiff and businesslike.

"Mr. Sandiman," he said, "over here please. Mr. Grant and Mr. Murphy, you will please come with me also."

The three whose names had been called rose and joined him. He motioned in the direction of the hallway and they started toward it. Sandiman began to say something, but Ho-ting raised a hand in a gesture for silence. The four of them proceeded to the hallway where Ho-ting turned, made a half bow, and said, "The rest of you will go about your normal routine." Then he turned and followed the others. The prisoners heard the outer door close, then silence.

For a moment everyone stared mutely after the four who had just left. Then murmured conversations broke out in every corner of the room.

Simone bolted to his feet. "What do you make of that?" he said to no one in particular.

"I expect it's the beginning of phase two," Craighill offered.

"Phase two?"

Wiedemier said, "What else? It's what we've been expecting."

59

"Well of course, but . . ." The screenwriter's voice trailed off and he sank back into his chair.

Craighill watched, feeling sorry for him. The seemingly endless waiting since their arrival had been hard on all of them but it seemed to have been hardest on Simone, perhaps because in his former life he had enjoyed such autonomy. He had worked for no one and no one had ever told him what to do before the war.

"I think I must be going crazy," Simone sighed. "I realize this had to happen, of course. But I hate it. I hate the fact that we're so helpless."

"Maybe when they bring Sandiman, Grant and Murphy back we'll get some answers," Craighill said hopefully.

Ho-ting returned fifteen minutes later and the procedure was repeated. This time Summerland, Kowalski and Simone were escorted from the building.

It was following in logical sequence, they noted—in order of their arrival at the camp. So the next to go would be Palitz, Craighill and Wiedemier. Tension hung in the air and Craighill was aware, much as he tried not to notice it, that his heart was beating a little faster than normal.

Ho-ting returned on schedule and the next trio was led to the doorway.

The first impression Craighill received when the outer door opened was of blinding light. And heat. He held up an arm to shield his eyes from the glare and squinted against the blazing sun.

They were in the desert; they had guessed right about that. Craighill thought the temperature must be near a hundred. And from the look of the shadows it was no later than 10:00 a.m. He began sweating almost immediately, but tried to put the heat out of his mind and concentrate on observing the camp as Ho-ting led them away from their building.

Compared to the other camps he had been in, this one was small. He counted only eight buildings. There was room to the south, beyond the last building he could see, for perhaps two more barracks, but no more. He knew there could be no more because he could see the top of the perimeter fencing as they walked down the road that ran between the rows of buildings. The fences were high enough to be seen above the roofs of distant buildings, and even where the buildings were so close that they obscured the fences he could still see the watchtowers. The entire complex was perhaps two hundred yards long by seventy-five wide. He counted a total of eight watchtowers.

The barracks themselves were much the way he had imagined them. But there was one detail he knew Sandiman hoped would be different. Just yesterday, Sandiman had suggested cutting through the ceilings of the private rooms as a possible route of escape. Once into the closed attic above the rooms, he thought they might cut through one of the end gables to get out of the building. By working slowly and carefully enough, he reasoned that they might construct a trap door, hinged at the top, which when closed would have remained undetectable. It would have been long and difficult work, but if the gables were faced in shingles or lap siding, he believed they could manage it. Now Craighill saw that they were faced not with siding, but with stucco, right to the soffits. There was no way to cut through that smooth material without leaving a visible scar, and it would be too heavy to work with anyway. The attic escape route was the only reasonable idea Sandiman had come up with and now it was clearly impossible.

There was another disappointment. Their barracks was located at the center of the camp; the nearest section of fence was at least twenty yards distant and beyond the fence lay desert, flat as a billiard table and completely barren. For at least a mile in all directions the vegetation had been bulldozed, leaving no cover.

They were approaching a large building, one of only two two-story structures in the camp. Ho-ting was at the head of the group, followed by Palitz, Craighill and Wiedemier. Three more guards trailed four or five paces back. It had taken only thirty or forty seconds to cover the distance between the two buildings, but in that short time Craighill had seen enough to conclude that there could be no escape from this place. His lips formed a perverse grin as he imagined how Sandiman must have reacted to all of this. Poor Paul! He had been so determined to escape; now all his hopes were dashed! He would be inconsolable. He must be sinking into the depths of a suicidal depression.

At that moment Paul Sandiman was feeling wonderful. He was vaguely aware that he had not always felt this good, but he couldn't remember why and anyway the whole subject of how he had previously felt no longer seemed important. The present moment consumed all his attention and the present moment was beautiful. Clearly, feeling good was the natural state of things.

He was sitting on a low cot and there was a man standing

in front of him. The man had a kind face. It was not like his father's face, he thought, but it was equally as pleasant as his father's face. He smiled at the man. Then he looked around the room.

It was a very pleasant room; small, but very pleasant. The cot on which he was sitting was the only furniture and the walls were painted white. There was a door, which was closed, but no windows. A long fluorescent fixture overhead provided beautiful, warm, soft light. He could feel the warmth of this light creeping into the pores of his skin. It was a good feeling.

The floor of the room was vinyl tile in a black and white checkerboard pattern, the kind of floor often seen in the basement recreation rooms of very old suburban homes. He liked the floor because it reminded him of places where people had a good time. He was looking at the floor when he noticed his feet dangling over the edge of the cot.

But they couldn't be his feet. They were so far away!

He traced a path with his eyes from the feet up the legs to the body. His body. So they must be his feet. But they were so far away! He heard himself laugh and felt suddenly dizzy. He swayed unsteadily and the man who stood in front of him stepped forward and helped him to lie back on the cot. That eased the dizziness some, but his head was still spinning.

The man leaned over him, so close their faces almost touched. Paul felt a hand brush lightly on his arm and heard the man say something that he didn't understand. Then the man backed away.

He turned his head to see where the man had gone but the room was empty. He was alone. He heard himself say "Daddy" in the voice of a small child, and started laughing again. The laughing felt very good and he laughed harder and harder until he had to stop to catch his breath. Then he lay still for a while, breathing deeply and looking at the soft, warm ceiling light.

As he looked at it, the light began to change. It was disassembling, refracting into all the varied colors of the rainbow. He blinked but the effect persisted. There was red and pink and orange, green and blue and deep purple; a million swirling colored splinters danced before him like the facets of a gem, like diamond dust. He closed his eyes and held them closed, then opened them slowly. The fragments were still there; the diamond dust still swirled.

He raised an arm toward the light and saw his hand sway

disconnectedly. Then it dropped back and struck him on the cheek. He heard himself laughing uncontrollably as the hand groped clumsily along the contours of his face and came to rest on the bridge of his nose. He rubbed one eye with the hand, then looked back at the light. There was no change. He rubbed the other eye and looked again. The colored splinters still spun and tumbled.

For a moment he thought he should be frightened. But he couldn't be frightened of this. It was too beautiful. And he felt too good to be frightened. He moved his hand and the sparkling particles of light flickered through the space around his hand like fireflies. He stretched his arm up toward the light again and waved at the fireflies. In response they rolled and churned like leaves caught in the wind.

So that was it, it wasn't the light, it was the air! He was actually seeing the air!

His body tingled with a thousand unfamiliar sensations. He tried to raise himself but fell back dizzily on the pillow. His head spun and the flickering shards tumbled, grew denser, enveloped him in a kaleidoscopic fog.

Then the man was there again, standing above him. And there was another with him. The second man was tugging at his feet. They were pulling him, lifting him from the cot. They stood him on the floor and as they did the dizziness increased. His legs felt useless, rubbery.

Then he lost consciousness.

EIGHT

Cold. It was bitter cold! Katie's mind struggled toward consciousness but something in her resisted, as though it was afraid of what she might learn if she engaged her senses. So at first she was aware of nothing but the cold.

She lay motionless, trying to order her thoughts. Where was she? Why did she feel this nameless terror? Cautiously, she opened her eyes.

She saw featureless white light. Immediately in front of her, along the left side of her field of vision, she saw something dark and very close. She heard a faint sound, like popcorn popping.

And there was pain. Her head throbbed.

She started to reach up to touch the source of the pain and saw the dark shape in front of her move. Her arm! It was her own arm! Some instinct suddenly commanded her to ignore the pain and lie still. Because movement would expose her to danger!

The popcorn popped again, much louder this time and different, sharper and higher pitched. A moment later she became aware of an acrid odor in the air, the smell of . . . cordite! And everything came back to her with a rush.

They had been on a routine harassment patrol, a simple mission where nothing should have gone wrong. The target had been a remote microwave tower, part of the Chinese communications network in these mountains. There had been four in the patrol and only two Chinese guards. The guards had been careless and her team had killed them easily. Then they placed the charges, set the timer and started down the mountain.

What happened next was simple bad luck. They heard the charges explode behind them and turned to watch the tower fall. Then, just as they started walking again, there was gunfire.

They had been careless themselves, that was clear now. Why hadn't it been clear to them at the time? Why hadn't they sought cover? Why had they risked traveling on the road?

Because of the snow, that was why; because there had been

a storm yesterday and they could move much more quickly on the road. And also because they had known that the guards wouldn't be relieved for two more days and there would be no Chinese within twenty miles of this mountain until then.

But they had been wrong. Either their intelligence was bad or the Chinese had changed the rotation schedule. Whichever it was, relief guards had appeared around a bend in front of them, no more than fifty yards away, at the very moment the tower blew. And the team had been caught on the road.

Jerry Haskell went down immediately, hit by the first shots the Chinese fired. From the way he fell she was certain he was killed instantly. The rest of them had dived off the road. She remembered that, it was the last thing she remembered.

Her head was clearing now, but she had no idea how long she'd been out or how bad their situation was. She knew only that at least one other member of the patrol was still firing, the one whose shots she had just heard off to her right. She rolled her head slowly in that direction.

It was Devin. Thank God! Devin was the only professional soldier among them. He was a Marine and a first-rate fighter; the rest of them were amateurs. As she watched, he rose up on one elbow and fired a quick burst, then ducked back down behind the tree he was using for cover. The response from the Chinese was immediate; bullets splattered all around his position.

Without moving, her cheek still pressed into the snow, she called to him. "Sergeant!"

"Hogan?" Devin looked over and grinned. "Welcome back. You picked a hell of a time to doze off."

"I was hit."

"I know. How bad is it?"

"I've got a hell of a headache."

"Can you move?"

"I'm sure I can, but I'm afraid to."

There was a sudden burst of fire from a spot several yards beyond Devin's position; she saw flashes from the rifle muzzle. So McKee was okay and there were still three of them. That made her feel better.

Again, the Chinese returned fire. She heard bullets pass over McKee's position. One splintered a tree ten yards behind him.

Devin glanced at McKee and back to Katie. She was still lying face down, afraid to move. "Okay," he said. "The first thing we have to do is get you to cover. There's a downed tree about ten feet to your left. When Jack and I start firing, I want you to roll over there. All right?"

"Ready when you are."

"Don't forget your rifle."

"In my left hand."

Devin looked at McKee, who nodded his understanding.

"On three. One—Two—Three!"

In unison, Devin and McKee opened up on the two Chinese, who were huddled behind their jeep. As Katie rolled to her left, she heard bullets carom off metal and glass shatter. There was an instant of silence before the Chinese responded.

Safe at last, she checked her wound. She had been struck two inches above her left ear. The bullet had removed a strip of scalp about a half inch wide and three inches long. Her hair was wet with blood, which was still flowing. But curiously there was no pain when she touched it. She was sure she felt bone.

"You okay?" Devin called across to her.

She waved back to him.

"Okay then. I figure we have ten or fifteen minutes before the choppers get here. We only get one chance at this so wish me luck."

She knew what he meant. Devin carried a single rifle grenade, which he now loaded. When he was ready, he signaled to her and McKee.

"On the count of three. One—Two—"

Katie and McKee both anticipated the count. By the time Devin said "three" they were already laying down a covering barrage on the jeep. Devin rose quickly on one knee, took careful aim and fired.

From the corner of her eye, Katie saw the grenade fly toward its target, saw it disappear into the shadows beneath the Chinese jeep and saw it explode.

Was it luck that placed it so precisely, or was Devin really that good? Whichever, it was a perfect shot. The grenade exploded directly under the jeep's rear axle and the vehicle cartwheeled into the air, spewing flaming gasoline from its ruptured fuel tank. In an instant, the jeep, the road and an area ten feet in every direction were ablaze. Black smoke billowed. A single Chinese soldier emerged from the inferno, his uniform afire. McKee shot him as he staggered forward, screaming and flailing his arms wildly. The soldier dropped to his knees and pitched forward into the snow. They saw no sign of the other Chinese.

66

Devin rose up on one knee and fired several long bursts into the smoke. Katie and McKee followed suit. Satisfied, they stood up.

"All right," Devin barked. "Let's move. Katie, you go east!" He pointed out the direction he wanted her to take. "Jack, you start to the south. I'm going north. You both know the drill; nobody goes near the base camp for at least two days. And be damned sure you've lost them before you come in. That's it. Good luck."

Neither McKee nor Katie said anything; they simply turned and started down the mountain. As Devin had said, they knew the drill so there was no reason to say anything. And there was no time. Each of them would have to travel over half a mile before they would clear the snow line. Until then a blind man could track them; the helicopters could follow them from the air. There was about a half hour of daylight left. Katie knew it was going to be the longest half hour of her life.

She had covered only two-thirds of the distance to the snow line when she heard the helicopters. She was in the trees by then and feeling a little more secure, but not much. This high up the forest was only thin scrub; it provided minimal cover but didn't block much of her view back up the mountain. She stopped for a moment and leaned against a tree, breathing heavily. There were two choppers hovering near the peak where the tower had stood. She watched as they moved down along the road toward the smoke, which was still rising from the burning jeep. She saw them land there.

She was embarrassed by her first reaction when she saw that there were only two helicopters. *They can't follow all three of us,* she thought. *Maybe I'll be the lucky one. Maybe they'll track Devin and McKee and miss me completely.*

It was natural enough, she guessed—after all, wasn't survival supposed to be the strongest human instinct? But she was still glad that no one would ever know what her thoughts had been at that moment.

She didn't wait to see whose tracks they followed. Instead she turned and rushed on down the slope. The brief rest had rejuvenated her and she made good time. Soon the trees grew larger and there were bare patches on the forest floor where overhanging branches had blocked the snowfall. She chose her route more carefully now, running in the bare spots wherever possible, trying not to leave tracks that could be seen from the air.

67

With about twenty minutes of daylight left she cleared the snow line. Five minutes later she came to an area of open, exposed rock. Except for a few scattered scrubs it was clear of trees for fifty yards off to her right and perhaps a hundred yards to her left. It was exactly what she needed; it could be the key to her escape. On the rocks she would leave no tracks at all. But could she risk fifty yards of exposure with no cover, a hundred yards if she chose to go to the left?

She stood at the edge of the trees for a moment, listening. She heard nothing—no helicopter sound, no clamor of troops. Since she had seen the choppers land up by the jeep site, she had neither seen nor heard anything that indicated she was being followed.

She decided it was worth the risk. More, she decided to take the long route, to the left. *They'll never expect me to go that way,* she told herself.

Out in the open, she moved more quickly than she had in the trees. But she still did not run. There were loose stones on the exposed rock face; in some places there were even patches of gravel. If she was careless it was possible to leave tracks even here. The situation reminded her of a classic movie she had seen on television once, *Butch Cassidy and the Sundance Kid.* In one scene, the two outlaws were being followed by Pinkerton men, the best trackers in the world. Butch and Sundance had done exactly what she was doing now, choosing a route across an open expanse of solid rock. And the Pinkerton men had tracked them right across the rock. She wondered if the Chinese had any super trackers with them who would leave her wondering, as Butch and Sundance had, "Who are those guys?"

She was about two-thirds of the way to her destination when she heard the helicopter. It sounded far off at first but could have been close, behind a nearby hill; she couldn't be sure. The way sounds echoed in these mountains she couldn't even be certain which direction it was coming from. The only certainty was that it was moving toward her; the sound was growing rapidly louder.

Discarding her previous concern about tracks she broke into a run.

The helicopter drew nearer. The whine of its engines was very loud now, just beyond the ridge to her left. It was going to burst over the trees at any second! And she was still fifty yards from the nearest cover. Why had she been so foolish? Why hadn't

68

she been satisfied to take the short route? Why . . .

Suddenly, she saw an opportunity, maybe her only opportunity. A few yards ahead there was a rock shelf with a small cave beneath, a narrow cleft just large enough for her to squeeze into. She rushed for it and dove headlong into the opening, pulling her rifle in behind her. Then she twisted around so she could see out, and held her breath.

The sound of the helicopter rose to a deafening roar. Dust and debris churned in the air and she realized that it must be directly over her and very low. A moment later it emerged into her field of vision, no more than thirty feet above her. It traveled across the rock face slowly for fifty yards, then rotated ninety degrees and settled to a landing.

So they had seen her and she was about to be captured. Impotent rage welled up in her and again she cursed her stupidity. How could she have allowed herself to be trapped like this? She had acted hastily, irrationally. She hadn't thought it through and now . . .

She knew what she had to do; everyone in the clan knew what they must do if they found themselves in this situation. She fought back tears as she unfastened the flap on her holster and withdrew the 9 mm Glock she carried. The Chinese were merciless; everyone had heard the stories. They tortured prisoners and if torture didn't succeed they used drugs. No one could resist the drugs and she knew far too much to allow herself to be taken alive. This was better; there would be no pain and the others would be safe.

She was amazed at how calmly she was approaching this final moment. There was no fear, only resignation and profound satisfaction at the prospect of denying the soldiers their prize.

She raised the pistol to her temple and held it there as she looked out at the helicopter. The pilot shut the engine down. Two soldiers climbed out and began looking around. But curiously, they did not look at her. Instead, they spread maps on the ground, bent over them and began pointing to nearby landmarks. Was it possible they had not seen her? Could their landing at this spot at this precise moment be purely coincidental? She lowered her pistol.

Five minutes passed. The second helicopter appeared and landed beside the first. Soldiers climbed out and joined the group by the first helicopter. It was now nearly full dark and she was having trouble seeing. In a few minutes she could consider escape;

she was only thirty yards from the tree line.

Ten more minutes passed. She could no longer see the soldiers and she was certain now that she could reach the trees without being seen. She was just about to climb from her hiding place to attempt it when she heard voices approaching her position.

Three soldiers had moved away from the helicopters and were walking toward her. They were carrying flashlights and, for an instant, one shone directly into her face. But the soldier who had aimed it at her had apparently not been looking at the time. At least he gave no indication that he had seen her. One of the three moved off to her right and she raised the Glock to her head again. But he returned several minutes later with an armload of wood and began building a fire. The trio of soldiers gathered around as it flared to life.

Several other fires appeared further off on the rock clearing. And Katie finally realized what was happening—the soldiers were making camp for the night. In the morning they would undoubtedly resume their search; for now she was a prisoner. Light from the fires did not penetrate her hiding place— the nearest one was off to her right and its glow cast a deep shadow across the mouth of the cave. But as long as it burned just twenty yards from where she sat, escape was impossible. It was maddening!

She tried to push herself further back into the tiny cave but it was too narrow; she was already wedged in as far as she could go. She waited, her rifle resting between her legs, her pistol cradled in her right hand.

Had the soldiers posted sentries for the night? She didn't know. If they had, she probably couldn't risk an escape attempt even when the fires burned down. But if they hadn't and she didn't make the attempt, she might be giving up her last chance to escape. Could she risk waiting, simply hoping they wouldn't see her in the morning?

It was three hours before she was sure the soldiers were asleep, another half hour before the fires burned down to glowing coals. She waited, listening and watching and considering her options. Her head ached and the sound of her pulse pounded in her ears. She had been wrong before; she had acted too quickly and it had almost cost her her life. This time she would be more careful. This time she would not move until she was certain.

NINE

Saturday, October 9

This entry will be brief because I remember very little of what happened yesterday. (I'm assuming it is now the morning of the 9th. If it is still the 8th, then it is the events of earlier today which I don't remember.)

We were taken outside in groups of three. I was in the third group. I assume that the remaining six followed in due course, so that all of us have now seen our prison compound.

As an intelligence-gathering expedition my moment in the sun wasn't very productive. To me, the camp seemed escape proof. I haven't had a chance to speak to any of the others yet but I doubt that any of them noticed any weakness I missed.

The camp consists of six or eight total buildings, all but two of these apparently being barracks identical to our own. We were taken into one of the non-barracks, a two-story building which gave the appearance of being a hospital. Once inside we (myself, Dr. Palitz and Michael Wiedemier) were separated and taken to small, individual rooms in the company of a pair of Chinese doctors(?). I was immediately instructed to roll up my sleeve and given an injection.

I was aware of a tingling sensation over my entire body, then a sudden unreasoning sense of well being. This was followed by bizarre hallucinations, disorientation, dizziness and finally loss of consciousness. I remember nothing more until waking in my room this morning.

At this moment my door remains locked and there is no light in the corridor. I am working by the light of my desk lamp. (What penalty will I incur for this offense, Ho-ting?) Of course, since there are no windows in this building it could be any time of day. It could be only a few hours since I was injected, but I doubt it. I feel as though I have slept for a week.

As to what all this signifies, I can't guess. Perhaps this camp is dedicated to medical experimentation. I'm anxious to talk to Palitz. He may know what kind of drug was used and that may tell us something about the Chinese purpose in administering it.

Apparently no more new arrivals. I believe we are still 15.

Saturday, October 9 (evening)

Palitz could not identify the drug. I suppose this fact in itself is somehow significant. He says (in his typically cautious and circuitous manner) that "there are symptomatic elements consistent with those associated with certain known drugs" but also that "certain of the symptoms fall outside the established norms for drug-induced hallucinations."

He seemed most puzzled by the consistency of our separate hallucinations. All of us apparently saw the same things and experienced the same symptoms.

During the 1960s, when the drug culture first became a popular topic, there was a great deal written about consciousness expanding or mind expanding drugs. I distinctly recall reading that it was then an article of faith among medical professionals that, although experimental use of these substances under controlled conditions promised certain benefits, indiscriminate use was potentially dangerous precisely because different personalities would react differently to them—there would be good trips and bad trips. Palitz confirms this and it is the absence of this symptom which seems to disturb him most. Fifteen different personalities simply cannot experience identical hallucinations. Yet that is apparently what happened.

Again, no new arrivals today. We are now quite certain that our internment here has entered a new phase.

Wednesday morning, for the first time, the guards remained in the barracks while the inmates ate breakfast. Their presence had the effect of discouraging normal mealtime conversation.

Immediately after breakfast, Ho-ting instructed them to pull the furniture in the great hall into a semicircle. Other guards then brought in a lectern, a blackboard and a large tripod easel. The prisoners were told to take seats and three Chinese they had never seen entered the room. One of these three was very old, and from the deferential attitude the guards displayed toward him it was immediately obvious that he was in command. Even without

72

this indication, however, they would have known. It was written in every line of his face, and in the alert and penetrating gaze he fixed upon them.

He walked to the lectern and stood for several moments, studying the prisoners before he spoke. His outstretched hands rested on the lectern; the left was missing a finger. When Craighill saw this hand, he recognized the old man. During his early years at NBC, the young reporter had frequently visited the UN. He had seen Chen Loying there twice, once addressing the General Assembly, a second time in a hallway in earnest conversation with several Americans. Chen had impressed Craighill then as one of the most reasonable and moderate members of the Chinese delegation.

He introduced himself now and began, "Gentlemen, we have been subjected these past two years to an agonizing ordeal. Our gravest fears have been realized; the world we knew has ceased to exist. But that is not important. No, it is not important at all. What is important now—and this is absolutely true—is how we administer the world we have inherited. Is there anyone here who disagrees with this?" He seemed to expect no response and he received none. He paused for only a moment before continuing. "Now, it may seem to you that what has happened has been harder for you than it has been for us. But I submit that we have suffered about equally. We—the Chinese people—lost fewer lives than you did during the chaos, that much I grant. But in the years since, we have been forced by circumstance to shoulder the enormous burden of reconstructing this ravaged globe without assistance. Despite what you may believe, it was not a task we welcomed, but one we undertook out of necessity.

"The errors of the past must never be repeated—we should all be able to agree on this at least. But putting aside this point of consensus, a vast gulf separates us. You have lost a war and are prisoners, we have won and occupy your lands. You believe in freedom for the individual, we believe in suppression of individual rights. Or so it must appear to you. But you are wrong in this.

"Despite its appearance, gentlemen, this is not a prison; it is a school. You have been brought here to learn. Whether or not you do is up to you. We cannot force understanding on you; we can only provide the opportunity. Those of you who choose to reject it will be returned to their previous duties. Those who choose to learn will be offered positions in the reconstruction."

He paused for several seconds, studying their reactions to

this. Then he continued. "I would not expect you to feel differently. I understand and respect your skepticism, which is entirely reasonable under the circumstances. But I caution you against prejudging us. We are seeking cooperation, not collaboration. We Chinese have accomplished all that we can alone. If we—our people and yours—are to progress further, it must be together."

The sincerity with which he delivered these lines impressed Craighill. The old man appeared to be making an honest appeal for their assistance. But was it legitimate? Chen had been careful to emphasize the distinction between cooperation and collaboration. When they knew the details, would they agree with his interpretation of these terms, or conclude that he was merely arguing semantics? And what part did the drugs play in all of this? As far back as the Korean War there had been rumors of elaborate Chinese plans to enlist the collaboration of American POWs by means of hypnotism and psychological torture. Drugs were thought to be part of those experiments. Could the drugs they were now using represent the final product of those Korean experiments? Clearly, the prisoners had no choice but to maintain a healthy skepticism.

Chen spoke for several minutes more, reciting his version of Chinese global accomplishments since the war and outlining what he felt to be the major problems now facing all of them. His tone was conciliatory and fraternal. He took great pains to include the Americans in his blueprint for a new society. He then introduced a second speaker.

The second speaker was a far less imposing personality than Chen and much younger. But he carried himself with the same air of calm assurance. As he proceeded, Ho-ting and the other guards (there were four guards in the room, all unarmed) listened with interest to him and nodded whenever he made a point that they considered particularly important. He was, the Americans realized, their first teacher. Before they had even begun to digest Chen's opening remarks, class was beginning.

The subject was Chinese history. In less than an hour this first instructor reviewed the long succession of Chinese dynasties, compressing four thousand years of social evolution into a fairy tale of war and oppression that even Craighill, who knew very little of the Asian past, recognized as pure propaganda. It was the Chinese Communist Party line—pre-Communist China was degenerate; the governments were corrupt, the peasants were exploited, the landlords prospered unconscionably at the expense

74

of the Chinese people.

If this was typical of what their school was to offer, Craighill thought, there would be no real option presented and no legitimate line drawn between cooperation and collaboration.

He glanced at Chen several times during this lecture, looking for some indication that the old man was aware that this history was a fraud, or for some sign of concern that his prisoners might not be sufficiently gullible to accept it. But there was none of this. Most of the time he seemed to be only half listening, apparently preoccupied with private thoughts.

The lecture had progressed to the year 1900 when the speaker broke off and announced an intermission. Pots of coffee and tea were brought in and the Americans were invited to relax for a few minutes before the class resumed. The prisoners collected refreshments and retired to one side of the room while the Chinese clustered in a little group around the speaker. Chen remained apart, standing off to one side. Craighill made his way over to him and addressed him by his hororary UN title of "Ambassador."

"You recognize me, Mr. Craighill?" He seemed genuinely surprised. "I am flattered."

"Yes, I recognize you. And I admit I'm puzzled."

"Oh? And what is it that puzzles you? Perhaps I can help." Chen motioned toward two nearby chairs and suggested that they make themselves comfortable.

"I'm puzzled by your presence here," the newsman said, when they had taken seats. "Are we being offered official diplomatic recognition?"

Chen smiled. "It is good to see that you haven't lost your sense of humor in these . . . difficult circumstances. Of course, the question of diplomatic recognition is moot since we are all now citizens of the same State. But I was not always a diplomat. For most of my life I have been a teacher. That is what brings me here. It is exactly as I said; this is a school and I am here to teach."

Craighill restrained an impulse to comment on the teaching of the first class and asked, "To teach what?"

Chen refused to answer. Instead he said, "Let me ask you this: When you read a book, do you read the last page first, before beginning? If you did I'm afraid you might summarily dismiss the writer's conclusions and decide never to begin."

Craighill assured him that he was not in the habit of reading books from the back forward.

75

"Then I ask you to show me the same consideration you would show a book. Much of what you will hear in the coming days will seem tedious. Some of it you will undoubtedly reject as incorrect. But you must hear all of it before I allow you to read the last page. You will be free then to make your own decision, I promise you."

"Is our cooperation so important?" Craighill asked. "It seems to me you could simply order us to do whatever you wish."

Again, the old man smiled. "We will give no orders. You will understand soon enough why it must be this way."

Craighill could get nothing more specific from him. Clearly, Chen was asking for permission to propagandize them. To what purpose? On one hand this brief conversation made Craighill even more suspicious than he had been before. On the other, he was compelled by Chen's sincere manner to grant him the benefit of the doubt.

The lectures continued through the day with several speakers alternating. They spoke about nothing but China and discussed the Long March and the Communist Revolution in great detail, concentrating on ideology and the benefits enjoyed by the peasantry since 1949. Craighill had recently been reading books from the prison library concerning this period and was better able to assess the accuracy of these presentations. (If he could trust the accuracy of the library texts. Many were ostensibly by occidental authors: Snow, Tuchman, Barnett, Lifton. But whether these copies remained unedited he had no way of knowing.) If the library texts were unedited, then he was forced to admit that the discussions of this period seemed more accurate than the discussions of Imperial China before the revolution. Some time was even devoted to a review of Party failures, including the terrible excesses of the Cultural Revolution, the repressions following the Tienanmen massacre in 1989 and the economic recession of the late teens. All in all, he was somewhat encouraged by the content of these talks. They appeared more realistic and less laced with propaganda than the morning's presentation.

Or were they merely more skillfully staged? Had their instructors purposely overstated the inaccuracies in the earlier lectures so the prisoners would be more likely to accept this new information?

Craighill was unable to discuss these questions with his fellow inmates. The guards remained with them through dinner, after which the prisoners were locked in their rooms.

Monday, October 11

More lectures today, this time reviewing the last thousand years in western Europe. It was an interesting if somewhat twisted summary of the complex history of that part of the world. Again emphasis was placed on the influence wielded by oppressive hierarchies—governments, churches, caste systems— and on the detrimental effects of this oppression on the masses.

Although the parallel was never specifically drawn, it was clearly implied that the cultures of Imperial China and Europe were, in social terms, virtually identical. Technologically, European accomplishment was shown to be superior, but the gap between aristocratic affluence and peasant poverty was portrayed as equally vast in both cultures. To our instructors, it seemed this was all that mattered.

The fact that socially and politically democratic systems began to evolve in Europe hundreds of years ago was ignored. Instead, when the speakers arrived at the chronological point where social reforms took place, the thrust of their expositions shifted abruptly from social institutions to evolving technologies and the "tyranny of wealth" they produced. The result was a virtual duplication of yesterday's lecture. European history was made to appear identical to Imperial Chinese history, an unbroken litany of war and oppression.

What they hope to accomplish with all of this remains a mystery. I don't deny that they have been presenting facts and, as a consequence, a kind of truth. But it is a half-truth at best. And there is not a man among us (with the possible exception of Billy Dupree) who is not sufficiently well read to recognize the obvious omissions and distortions.

Perhaps the answer is that they are so immersed in their dogma that this is the way they truly view all history. In any case, we are growing weary of it.

TEN

When the Chinese helicopters arrived at the microwave tower the assault force commander was enraged by what he found. The tower had been destroyed and four Chinese soldiers were dead. One bandit had been killed but three had escaped; their tracks were clearly visible, leading down the mountain in three different directions. And the commander's helicopters could follow only two of them.

The proper strategy was self-evident. He directed the helicopters to track the two who had headed north and south and drive them toward the east, toward the one who had headed in that direction. In this way he hoped to capture all three.

Jack McKee knew nothing of the commander's strategy. He knew only that one of the helicopters was following him. He had seen both choppers circle the microwave tower, then lost sight of them when they dropped down toward the spot where the jeep was burning. For the next ten minutes he rushed down the mountain, hoping to reach the snow line before they reappeared. He almost made it. He was into an area where the trees were larger and stood closer together when he heard the sound of a single helicopter approaching. He paused for a moment, looked back, and saw it descend into a small clearing about four hundred yards behind him. It settled to within a few feet of the ground and four Chinese soldiers leaped from it and dropped to the snow. McKee thanked God for the larger, denser stand of pines here where he stood. It was only these trees, he knew, that had forced the troops to jump off so far behind him. If he could stay ahead of the soldiers for another fifteen minutes he should be all right; it would be dark by then and he was sure he could lose them in the dark.

He veered off a little to his left as he continued down the mountain. He couldn't allow his route to become predictable. If he did that, the helicopter could intercept him; it could fly on ahead and set more soldiers down in front of him.

A few minutes later the wisdom of this tactic was confirmed. He heard the helicopter again, and when he looked back he saw it flying low above the treetops, directly above the spot where he had stopped to watch it drop the troops that were now tracking him. It flew on down the mountain following his original route. When he saw this he altered his course a little further to his left, toward the east. *And toward Katie,* he thought. *I can't go too far in this direction or I'll lead them right to her.*

He continued on this course for only four or five hundred yards. Then he swung back to the south and headed straight down the mountain for the next ten minutes. He was clear of the snow now and it was beginning to get dark; in another ten minutes he would have trouble seeing. But so would the soldiers. The darkness promised safety. He changed direction again and headed a little more to the south, moving as quickly as he could while he could still see.

It had been at least fifteen minutes since he had last seen the helicopter, but he could still hear it. The sound of its engine had never been very far away. As he listened now, it seemed to change direction and move toward him. He looked up, scanning the few patches of dark blue sky visible above the trees. He was sure the chopper was getting very close. He pressed himself against a tree, watching. And finally he saw it, a dark shape sweeping low above the trees a hundred yards up the mountain from his present position. He lost sight of it a moment later but he could still hear it, droning steadily off to the north. The sound quickly grew fainter and finally disappeared.

Had they given up? No. The helicopter had left because of the darkness. But there were still the soldiers. Was he outdistancing them or were they gaining on him? He looked back up the mountain along the route he had just traveled. He could see nothing. If they were there he should see their lights. Unless they *had* given up. But that would be too much to hope for; they wouldn't have surrendered so easily. No, they were there all right, still tracking him. And they would continue tracking him, trying to wear him down. They were probably not using lights because they didn't want him to know how close they were.

He took a deep breath to steady himself and headed down the mountain again.

He was moving slower now. It was almost full dark and it was getting really hard to see. In the next five minutes he covered less than a hundred yards. He looked back up the mountain repeatedly but saw no sign of the soldiers. That was encouraging because he knew that they could not be following him now without lights. Perhaps they had given up. Or perhaps they were content to wait out the darkness and resume their pursuit in the morning, assuming that he too would be forced to stop. If that was their hope they would be disappointed. Because he was not going to stop. His progress would be slow, but he would push on through the darkness. By morning he would be miles away.

He heard a sound and froze. He wasn't sure exactly what he had heard, but he had heard something. A dry twig snapping as someone stepped on it? He crouched low, listening.

He heard a faint metallic click. A rifle bolt sliding into place? Then there was a rustling noise, like footsteps on the pine needles. He held himself absolutely still, trying not to even breathe.

Jack McKee had been born with exceptional hearing, hearing so acute that when he had participated in experiments at Oregon State University once he had been called back for retesting. "The equipment must have been faulty," the tester had explained with some embarrassment. But the retest had produced the same result and he had been told that his hearing was the auditory equivalent of 20/05 vision, the most acute the testers had ever encountered. He had shrugged it off as unimportant then, a curiosity and mildly interesting, but of no real value. Now, he realized, it might have saved his life.

He was hearing sounds made by a small squad of Chinese soldiers, sounds that perhaps only one human in ten thousand could have heard at this range. He heard them moving around. He heard two whispering to each other in Chinese. He heard one drink water from a canteen. He couldn't be certain but he believed there were five of them.

They were about a hundred and fifty yards down the mountain from his position and directly on the route he had been following. He was sure they were not the soldiers who had been following him; there was no way that group could have flanked him and set up a position this far ahead. So the helicopter must have dropped these to intercept him.

They would be surprised in the morning, he thought. At first light they would discover his tracks and find that he had simply walked around them in the darkness. He wished he could see their faces in the morning.

Carefully choosing a route that circled five hundred yards south of the soldiers' position he made his way down into the canyon below. He took great care to be quiet and the journey took a long time. But he had time; he had all night. He was certain now that he was the only one moving.

At the bottom of the canyon he found a creek. Its rocky bed was perhaps ten yards wide but the creek itself was only a brook at this time of year. The dry stream bed on each side of the brook formed a natural highway through the wilderness. It was well past midnight when he reached it. The crescent moon had just risen and there in the open stream cut it provided enough light for him to move more quickly. Still following Devin's instructions he headed downstream to the south.

He moved confidently, grinning at the thought of the happy genetic accident that had made his escape possible and at the arrogance of the Chinese who thought they had trapped him so cleverly. He took great pleasure in the images that formed in his mind when he thought of the soldiers. He imagined the consternation on their faces when they discovered what he had done, and the fury their commander would display when he was told what had happened. He chuckled aloud as he pictured it all.

It was at that moment that he fell.

It was a clumsy misstep, caused by simple carelessness. He brought his right foot down on a rock in the stream bed. The rock rolled from beneath the foot, which then slid into the gap between two larger rocks and wedged. He was thrown off balance and stumbled sideways, falling heavily on his right shoulder. He heard a loud crack as his ankle joint shattered and felt excruciating pain. He bellowed, half in agony, half in rage at his own stupidity, then forced himself to lie still and quiet. Tears welled up in his eyes.

How bad was it? His shoulder hurt, but that pain was nothing compared to the fire in his ankle. His ankle felt as though a knife had been plunged through it and was being twisted back and forth.

With great effort he pulled himself to a sitting position and surveyed the injury. His foot was still wedged between the two rocks, the ankle bent at a grotesque angle. He leaned forward to see if he could pull it free and felt a stab of pain in his shoulder. Fearing that it too might be worse than he first thought, he examined it and decided it was badly bruised, but nothing more. Then he returned to the ankle. It took several minutes, and he was forced by the pain to stop several times, but he finally managed to pull it free. Then he tried to stand.

It was impossible. And if he couldn't stand he certainly couldn't walk. So his flight was over; he was going no further than this spot, or at least this area. He looked around, carefully assessing his options. He had to find cover, some hiding place where there would be a chance, however remote, that the Chinese would overlook him in the morning.

He had traveled only a few hundred yards since reaching the stream bed and this, he realized, was his single advantage. If he could find cover near enough, some place he could reach without having to climb the soft stream bank and leave tracks, they might pass right by him. Because they were sure to expect that he would follow the stream for a considerable distance before heading back into the trees. If he hadn't been hurt, that was exactly what he had planned to do.

He saw nothing nearby. But thirty yards upstream there was a spot that looked perfect, if he could reach it. There a large Douglas Fir had been undercut by the stream and had fallen into the stream bed. Its trunk lay on the dry rocks, pointing diagonally downstream. Its large uprooted stump was intact and underneath was a dark hollow, like a cave, created by the stump and the angle of the trunk against the bank. The hollow appeared to be just the right size.

He looked downstream once more to be certain that this tree was absolutely his best opportunity. Convinced that it was, he began making preparations for the thirty-yard journey.

He knew he could afford no oversights and no mistakes. Movement was going to be very difficult; in the next hour his ankle would undoubtedly swell and it would become impossible. He began collecting his gear. A compass had flown from his pack when he fell; it was ten feet away and he almost failed to see it. That made him doubly cautious. He crawled to the spot where his rifle had dropped and, using it as a crutch, struggled to a standing position. Then he studied the area around where he had fallen. He found his ball point pen (why had he even carried a pen on a demolition patrol?) but saw nothing else.

So he was ready to start. He turned in the direction of the fallen tree and hesitated. There was something else, something he'd forgotten. He tried to think what it could be but his mind wasn't functioning very well. He felt nauseous and he was shivering. He knew he must be pretty shocky by now, and he couldn't allow it to get him killed. What had he forgotten?

It was several moments before it came to him. Camouflage! It was two long painful steps to the edge of the water but he had to take them. Then he lowered himself back down onto the rocks. He sat for a while, wincing at the pain in his ankle, then reached down into the stream, gathered mud from the bottom and spread it on his face and neck and hands.

There were now five, maybe six hours left until sunrise. Had he thought of everything? Had he done everything that Devin would do? He wasn't sure. And he couldn't be sure. He had done everything he could think of; that would have to do. Painfully he pulled himself back to his feet and began the long slow trek to his hiding place.

He didn't know if he slept that night, didn't know whether the visions that filled his mind were dreams or simply random hallucinations brought on by the fever that left him shivering. He saw his parents and his sister, his grandparents and the people at the base camp. Devin was there, and Katie, and there were even several actors he used to watch on TV. Carol was there too, with their son Evan. At a backyard lawn party at their house in Lake Oswego, the President of the United States appeared, looking like a caricature of himself, hungrily devouring hamburgers and potato salad and gladhanding everyone in sight. They were all mixed up together, people he knew and people he didn't know, people who'd met each other and people who never could because some of them were dead now. It was all very strange.

Less than two miles away, Katie Hogan sat calculating her options. She had heard no sound from the Chinese for many hours. Were there sentries? Should she risk flight or stay put?

The cold finally forced her decision. Her fingers and toes were growing numb; if she waited any longer she feared she might not be able to walk, so she gathered her courage and pushed herself from the small crevice where she had been hiding.

Escape proved surprisingly easy. The sky was clear and the moon provided just enough light for her to make out the shapes of the soldiers sleeping nearby. In the distance she could see the helicopters and several more small groups of sleepers. But if any sentries had been posted, she didn't see them. She saw no one and heard nothing until she reached the edge of the clearing.

"Katie!"

The greeting was whispered, barely audible. Even so, she recognized the speaker.

"Ben?"

"Over here."

She picked her way carefully toward his voice. The faint

moonlight didn't penetrate into the trees—she could barely see her own hand—so she was nearly close enough to touch him before she could make out his silhouette.

"What are you doing here?" she whispered.

He placed a hand gently over her mouth and said, "Later. Follow me."

They didn't speak for nearly half an hour. In that time she guessed they might have covered a quarter mile; their progress was painfully slow in the darkness. Devin guided them laterally across the face of the slope for several hundred yards, then uphill, back toward the microwave tower. Just below the snow line he turned north. Several times he stopped and crouched down, studying the terrain they had just covered and listening. Finally, after one of these observations, he said angrily, "That was a dumb stunt, Katie. What in hell were you thinking?"

The sky was just beginning to lighten and she could make out his face now. He was trying to look stern, but managed only a kind of worried concern; she had seen the same expression on her father's face the day she broke her nose playing touch football with the neighborhood boys.

"I don't know what you're talking about," she objected. "What stunt?"

"I'm talking about crossing that clearing. You were damn lucky."

"You saw that?"

"The whole thing."

"You were supposed to be miles away. Why were you . . ."

He cut her off abruptly. "We have to keep moving. You lead for a while. That way."

She started off in the direction he had indicated and he fell in behind her.

"I was there because they cut me off," he explained. "One of the choppers followed my tracks and dropped soldiers behind me. Then it flew on and dropped more ahead of me. I had to circle back. I couldn't believe it when I saw you out there in the open."

Defensively she said, "But I almost made it. I would have if the helicopter hadn't shown up when it did."

"The helicopter had to come, Katie, that's the point. It was almost dark so the choppers had to land. The clearing was the only place where they could. Didn't that occur to you?"

She glanced over her shoulder at him, a look of sudden recognition on her face. "It will next time," she said.

He mumbled something she didn't understand, then said sharply, "Come on, move! We're wasting time."

They followed the snow line to the far side of the mountain, the west side, with Devin forcing a quick pace. When they came to a small creek they followed it downstream for several miles. Then they turned north again.

About an hour after sunrise they heard a single dull report, an explosion of some kind, far off to the south.

McKee's hallucinations ended abruptly. He had heard something, something not from his visions. He opened his eyes to bright sunlight.

He peered out through the brush he had placed at the entrance to his hiding place, out along the tapering trunk of his tree to the stream beyond. There was no one in sight, but he could hear voices speaking Chinese. He counted them: two—three—he thought there were at least five. The same five he had avoided last night? Probably. The other four, the ones who had been behind him last night, would be searching upstream.

He wondered what time it was. About an hour past sunrise, he guessed, from the length of the shadows on the nearby hills.

The soldiers were moving down the stream bed and, although he couldn't see them yet, he could tell that they were almost directly opposite his position, on the far side of the stump.

His ankle throbbed dully. He held his breath and waited.

One came into view, then another. At first he could see only their heads above the trunk of his tree, bobbing comically as though they had no bodies, like targets in a carnival shooting gallery. Then, as they moved further downstream, he saw them clearly. They were walking quickly, exactly as he hoped. The first was following the water's edge and looking intently at the ground; the second was on the far side of the stream examining the stream bank. There would undoubtedly be another on this side, examining this bank. He pressed himself further back into his hollow.

It was time to consider the possibility that they would not overlook him. He had faced that prospect last night in a moment of lucidity and decided on a plan. He remembered that plan now and checked his equipment. He was ready. Whatever happened, he was ready.

He heard a scuffle of footsteps, very near. There was a soldier no more than ten feet from where he sat, moving around

85

the far side of the stump. A helmet appeared above his tree trunk; the soldier moved along the far side of the trunk and his head and shoulders came into view, then his lower body. His attention was on the bank opposite where he was walking, only a few yards downstream from McKee's position. When he reached the lower end of the tree, he stepped over it and took a few steps toward the bank. Then he turned and looked directly at the hiding place.

In sudden terror, McKee realized his mistake.

My eyes! He will see the whites of my eyes!

He squeezed his eyes shut, counted ten very slowly, then opened them just a slit.

The soldier was still there. He was staring at McKee and smiling triumphantly. As McKee watched, the soldier raised his rifle to his shoulder, aimed it at his captive, and shouted something in Chinese.

There was the sound of many footsteps clattering over the rocks, and several shouted replies. McKee heard water splash as the soldier on the far side of the stream rushed toward him. Then they were all there, gathered around the opening, peering in. His count had been correct, there were five of them.

The soldier who had found him moved nearer, waving his rifle muzzle from side to side. Another climbed over the fallen tree and stepped close to the opening of the hiding place, brandishing an automatic pistol.

"Out!" the newcomer commanded. "Climb out!" He pulled the brush from the entrance to the hiding place.

So this one speaks English! He must be the leader. He is the one I want!

"I can't," McKee responded. "I can't move. Broken ankle."

The soldier moved nearer. He looked down at the crude splint McKee had lashed to his ankle the night before. "This ankle?" he asked with a leering smile. And he rapped the splint hard with the muzzle of his automatic.

"Yes!" McKee cried out. "God, yes, that ankle."

"Then we will have to pull you out. Your rifle, please."

McKee pushed his rifle toward the soldier, who took it and tossed it aside, then motioned for one of the others to help him.

That's right, come to me. Come to papa.

Together, the two soldiers squeezed into the narrow opening, grasped McKee's clothing, and began pulling him toward them. As they did, McKee's left hand, which had been hidden beneath his body, swung free. The English speaking soldier saw it and saw what it was holding. He looked at McKee, surprise and disbelief written on his face.

That's right! You got me, but I've got you too.

He could see that the soldier knew there was no time, no possible escape; the opening was too narrow and he was wedged in too tight. The lever on the hand grenade had already been released.

McKee grinned at him. "So long!" he said, and thrust his hand out, driving the grenade into the soldier's belly.

There was a brilliant, blinding flash. Neither man heard the explosion.

But four miles to the northwest, Devin heard it.

"What was that?" Katie asked.

It was a sound Devin had heard a thousand times before. He paused, waiting, listening for accompanying rifle shots, the sounds of battle. There were none. And that, he realized, almost surely meant that Jack McKee was dead.

"I don't know," he replied.

"Rifle shot?"

"Can't be sure. Anyway, it was a long way off." He quickly turned away from her and resumed walking.

She hurried to keep up. "What was it, Ben," she insisted. "You think it had something to do with McKee, don't you?"

He didn't look at her. "It could have been anything," he said gruffly. "Now come on, we have to keep moving."

By noon they had covered about fifteen miles. Katie's legs were aching, her head was throbbing and she was breathing hard. She wished Devin would stop and let them rest for a while, or at least slow down. They had heard one helicopter several hours earlier but it had been miles away to the south and they had never seen it. Since then there had been nothing. Surely they must be out of danger now.

But Devin pressed on for another hour. He marched them north and east until finally, by a small spring high up at the base of a rocky escarpment, he swung his pack to the ground and leaned back against a large boulder.

"You're okay, Katie," he said. "You're doing real well."

She propped her rifle against a tree and sat down heavily without removing her pack. "Have we lost them?"

"Don't know. I'm going up to have a look." He pointed up, indicating the escarpment looming above them. "In the meantime, you get some sleep. You didn't sleep last night, did you?"

She shook her head wearily.

"And clean that wound." He walked over to her and knelt down, examining the scab above her left ear. Dried blood matted the hair around the wound and stained the front of her jacket. "How does it feel?"

"It feels like I've been shot. How should it feel?"

"It'll be fine if you take care of it. There's bandages and a first aid kit in my pack." He stood up and smiled down at her. "We're going to be okay, Katie."

For an instant her fatigue and the tension of the last eighteen hours seemed to overwhelm her and she thought she was going to cry. But she fought it off. "I believe you," she said bravely. Then she remembered the incident early this morning, the explosion they had heard, and she added, "And McKee? Is he going to be okay too?"

"Yeah, McKee's going to be fine. Day after tomorrow he'll be at the base camp waiting for us."

He climbed to the top of the escarpment. The majestic panorama of the Oregon Cascades spread before him with Mt. Hood dominating the northern sky. He could see for fifty miles in every direction. He waited there for an hour, watching and listening. He saw no helicopters and no evidence of troops. He heard nothing but the rustle of the pines in the October breeze.

When he climbed down he found Katie exactly where he'd left her, sleeping soundly.

ELEVEN

Despite its limited scope, the nuclear terrorism which preceded the Chinese invasion had rendered large areas of the North American continent uninhabitable. This desolation was the legacy of dirty bombs, ground bursts which injected thousands of tons of intensely radioactive material into the atmosphere.

Winds carried debris from Chicago across the upper Midwest and southern Canada and on into New England. The city of Chicago was now a dead zone, and a hundred thousand square miles of densely populated country to the east and north was a radioactive wasteland.

The city of San Francisco had been struck by a very large bomb, apparently smuggled into the bay on a cargo ship and detonated in place. The devastation in San Francisco was the worst in the world, but favorable winds carried most fallout south and west, away from inland areas of California. The cloud from Boise drifted north and east, across the sparsely populated upper tier states and southern Canada. Fallout from the Washington, D.C. bombs moved east, blanketing Delaware, Maryland's eastern shore and northeastern Virginia before storms carried most of it into the western Atlantic.

It seemed impossible that just five relatively small nuclear bombs (and one large device) had so completely destroyed the American economy. But what seemed more impossible was that the world's military arsenals had contained tens of thousands of much larger, much more destructive devices, but none were deployed.

We had been lucky; our madness, when it finally descended upon us, had been limited by circumstances beyond the terrorists' control, and the damage had been moderate.

Still, in the wake of the disaster, the nation had descended into chaos. The military's attempts to restore order met with open, often armed, resistance. Food was in critically short supply and hunger turned men against men, the people against their government and everyone against the army. Many starved to

89

death. When the Chinese invasion came two months later, some actually welcomed it. The war lasted just ten weeks. Once they assumed control, the Chinese designated Houston the new Continental Capital.

Chen Loying arrived in Houston on the morning of October 12th. As he boarded the van that would take him from the air terminal into the city his face was fixed in an expression of deep concern. His presence here on this occasion was not related to the city's status as Continental Capital; he was on a personal errand.

He had been sent by his camp physician to undergo testing. The doctor had been evasive about specifics, but although Chen was not now experiencing any pain or discomfort, he had no doubt that he must be a very sick man. The prospect troubled him greatly.

He could not recall having been truly sick a single day in his life. But it was not merely the novelty of illness that concerned him. At his advanced age any illness was cause for worry. Even minor maladies could prove dangerous to an octogenarian, and Chen feared that this illness, whatever it was, was not minor. The camp doctor had not insisted that he travel all the way to Houston to consult a specialist about simple fatigue. No, there were ominous implications in his symptoms, implications which might prompt even a younger man to experience the anxiety he was now feeling.

He was not afraid of death, having long since come to terms with that inevitability. But he was afraid of work left undone. Ten years earlier he would have accepted the prospect of death with equanimity, because at that time he had felt that he was at the end of a long and distinguished career. But now he was involved in work that was much more important than any he had attempted before, work that was just beginning. His body must not fail him now. The work must be completed.

In his preoccupation, he did not think of his old friend and former student, Lin Chiao-tu, the man who, four months earlier, had made the decision which had permitted Chen's work to proceed.

But his old friend was thinking of him.

Lin Chiao-tu, Vice Chairman of the Communist Party and Administrator of the North American Continent, learned of Chen's visit to Houston only an hour before Chen's arrival. He had not seen his old teacher since the meeting four months earlier when Chen had presented his proposal for the special camp. There could be only one reason why the old man was coming to the Capital now, the Vice Chairman reasoned. He was coming to express his appreciation for the approval of his project and to report his progress.

Angrily, Lin keyed his intercom and called for his secretary.

"Why was I not told of Comrade Chen's visit?" he bellowed when the door swung open.

The secretary, a slender, bookish young man with wire rimmed glasses, stepped into the office and stared back uncomprehendingly. "Comrade Chen?" The news had clearly taken him by surprise.

The Vice Chairman held out a sheet of paper listing VIP arrivals and departures from Houston on that day's flights. Rising from his chair he shook the paper at the secretary and said sternly, "Comrade Chen Loying is on this list. I should have been told days ago. He has undoubtedly requested a meeting with me. See that it is arranged."

The secretary took the paper, bowed and hurried from the office.

When he had gone, Lin settled back into his chair and sat with his hands folded across his ample stomach. His dark expression brightened slowly as he considered the fortunate coincidence of Chen's visit.

Of late the North American occupation had not been going well. There had been no riots like those currently raging in southern Europe, but the population here was not responding to indoctrination as Lin had expected. That reflected badly on his administration and ultimately on him personally.

Several times during the past week this situation had prompted him to recall his meeting with Chen and to consider the possibility that Chen's assessment may have been correct; perhaps these Americans did require special handling. If that were true, Chen's camp might prove more important than Lin had supposed when he had first given it his approval. It might even provide the solution to Lin's current problems. Each time this thought had occurred to him, however, the press of business had diverted his attention and he had failed to pursue it. Chen's appearance in Houston now reminded him once more. And this time he would not be diverted.

He opened the bottom drawer of his large desk, withdrew a

bound folder, and set it down in front of him. It was the presentation material Chen had left with him on the occasion of their last meeting. He had not looked at it since that day.

Lin tried to recall exactly what his old professor had said. Chen had requested construction of a special camp and the request had been granted. But there had been more, the Vice Chairman couldn't remember the details.

In the year since he had become Administrator of the North American Continent, Lin had rendered thousands of decisions. This one had seemed unimportant at the time. He did recall being surprised when the Central Committee approved Chen's request without question, and he remembered also that their reply had included the statement, "Comrade Chen is to be given every cooperation." But he had assumed they were merely humoring an aging hero. So he had complied with their instructions and promptly forgotten the matter. He had given Chen's project little real attention.

Had that been a mistake? He wasn't sure. But before today's meeting he wanted to know every detail of what his former professor was proposing.

He opened the file and began to read.

When Chen arrived at his hotel shortly after noon, he received an unanticipated and unwelcome summons. A message delivered to him by the desk clerk informed him that he was expected at Lin Chiao-tu's office at 2:30 that afternoon.

Chen had no desire to see Lin on this trip. But an invitation from the continental administrator could not be ignored, even if it conflicted with previous engagements. His medical examination, also scheduled for 2:30, would therefore have to be rescheduled.

He was shown to his rooms and spent the next half hour on the phone, making new arrangements with the doctor and with the transport authorities for his return trip. Then he visited the hotel dining room for a light lunch and took a car to the continental administration building. He arrived at Lin's office feeling slightly sick to his stomach and irritable. He was in the Vice Chairman's debt—he granted Lin that much—but he did not appreciate being ordered about like a camp prisoner.

He was shown to the Vice Chairman's private office immediately. Lin greeted him warmly and suggested that they sit in two large upholstered chairs by the window. The gesture puzzled Chen; such informality was unexpected. Four months earlier, Lin had remained at his desk with Chen sitting opposite. That meeting had been an interview, almost an interrogation, apparently this one was to be different, a discussion between relative equals.

"I'm pleased that you've come," the Vice Chairman said, once the preliminary pleasantries had been observed. "And I am anxious for news of your progress."

Chen, who had received no communication from the Vice Chairman since their last meeting, was encouraged by this expression of interest.

"It is proceeding on schedule," he said. "The first group is processing now."

"Then you are confident, I take it, that your program is succeeding? Your subjects are responding as you had expected?"

"It is too early to render such judgments," Chen replied. "Thus far they are behaving as we had hoped, but we won't be able to fully assess their response until they have been . . ." He paused, searching for the right word. "Until they have been challenged."

The Vice Chairman nodded, but his expression told Chen that he hadn't fully understood.

"What we are attempting has never been done before," Chen explained. "The success of our program requires the voluntary participation of these prisoners. Without that participation our task would become far more difficult, perhaps impossible. So we are proceeding cautiously with this first group and drawing them in slowly. We are allowing them to observe us and to learn from us while at the same time we are studying their reactions. We are actually learning more from them than they are learning from us. Based on what we are learning, we will decide exactly when we can invite their participation."

"I see," Lin said. "And how soon will that be?"

"We aren't certain. In two weeks perhaps, if all goes well."

The Vice Chairman leaned back and clasped his hands over his stomach. "Two weeks," he said thoughtfully. "Very good. Let us assume, Comrade, that your prisoners respond favorably and agree to work with us. How quickly can you have them ready to assume their posts?"

The question surprised Chen. He had come here fully expecting Lin to challenge him once again. But this question, and Lin's unusually cordial manner toward him, seemed to imply that the Vice Chairman had already decided to support his program. Was it possible that some member of the Central Committee had interceded in Chen's behalf?

"In that case," Chen replied, "the Americans could be ready in perhaps a month. But first there would be a great many details to be arranged. For example, many of the posts you speak of do not now exist; they would have to be created. Once the prisoners agreed to participate, I planned to approach you about this problem, but I saw no reason to trouble you with it before then."

Lin waved a hand in a gesture of dismissal. "Your consideration is appreciated, Professor, but waiting would only cause unnecessary delay which I cannot afford. I'm sure you understand what I mean."

Chen understood exactly what he meant. The problems Lin faced in North America were well known. For some time Chen had been counting on the Vice Chairman's difficulties to strengthen his own position when it came time to argue for final adoption of his program. Mentioning this now could only embarrass his host, however, so he merely nodded and said nothing.

"It appears that you were right," Lin continued. "Your predictions have proved accurate. The camps here are inefficient; the Americans refuse to accept our guidance. We are experiencing some of the same problems in Europe. And there is also the problem of the bandits. They are everywhere: in the swamps, in the mountains, on the fringes of the dead zones. And they are growing bolder. Last week, only fifty miles from here, they destroyed an oil storage depot. The fires could be seen from fifty different rural camps and the prisoners in the camps cheered when they saw them.

"So you see, we can waste no more time. For this reason, I have decided to grant you the opportunity you seek. Today, I wish to begin making preparations to put your program into operation."

Incredible! The Vice Chairman was offering his full support. This would accelerate the program considerably; it would save months. Chen nodded, but did not allow himself to smile. A smile could be misinterpreted. He still did not know whether Lin had arrived at this decision independently or if Chen's friends on the Central Committee had encouraged it.

"What do you need from me?" Chen asked.

"Your counsel and your guidance. I have cleared my afternoon calendar, Professor. I want you to tell me exactly what needs to be done and why and when it must be ready."

They worked through the afternoon. The Vice Chairman used the presentation file as his basic text and filled the margins with his notes. Several times the two men argued, but they always resolved the disputes. And when they had finally finished and Chen returned to his hotel, he felt that a great burden had been lifted from his shoulders. The future of the project was now secure, and the prospect of his scheduled medical examination no longer frightened him.

The next afternoon, as he boarded his flight home, his sense of satisfaction was complete. A year, the doctor had said, eighteen months if he was lucky. It was enough time. He would live to see the new world born.

TWELVE

Wednesday, October 13

I was drugged again this morning. I assume the others were as well but that is only supposition since we were not taken out in groups this time, but individually, directly from our rooms. The hallway is now dark and again I have no idea what time it is.

In the absence of organized activity I have been reading through a volume taken from the library in the great hall, a Chinese version of Who's Who. In particular, I have been studying the biography of our commandant, Chen Loying.

He is an interesting man. His father joined the Red Army on the Long March, where he distinguished himself (at the age of 12!) in a famous battle. Later, he rose to the rank of general.

Chen chose a very different path, the life of a scholar and diplomat.

One detail of his life disturbs me. Aside from a brief trip to Russia in 1974, Chen was apparently never out of China until his assignment to the UN, at which time he was in his mid-fifties. This may explain the dogmatism displayed by our instructors. Chen is clearly in command here and, in all probability, is responsible for establishing policy. A man who spent the first fifty-four years of his life insulated within China could hardly be expected to have gained a realistic view of world history.

I am now fairly convinced that it is Chen's view of history we are being taught. Of what value is this observation? Perhaps none. But if true, it may provide us with a slightly better perspective, and a better means of evaluating whatever proposal they are planning to make to us when our "education" is complete.

Thursday, October 14

As I suspected, we were all drugged yesterday. We

compared notes on the experience over breakfast and one more element has now been added to our common recollections.

We remember being taken to a small room where we were placed in a comfortable chair and attached to a machine. A kind of helmet was placed on our heads and wires were fixed to our wrists and ankles. We were then asked a series of questions. None of us can recall the questions we were asked but we did not find the experience unpleasant or in any way threatening. We were not interrogated. It seems instead that we were invited to engage in casual conversations. Was this some form of lie detector testing? We don't know.

During this breakfast conversation we realized that three of our number were missing. Murphy, Hammil and Moore have disappeared. We asked Ho-ting why these individuals had been detained but he could not (or would not) tell us.

Immediately after breakfast the lectures resumed, with Chen in attendance for the first time in three days. The instructors made no reference to the absentees, and when Simone tried to raise the question during one of the breaks, Chen dismissed him without explanation. "You are asking me to read the last page," he said. "Mr. Craighill knows what I mean."

Simone misinterpreted the comment and demanded to know what information I was withholding from the rest of the group. I was able to satisfy him that I had not become a collaborator but we still do not know what has become of Murphy, Hammil and Moore. As I interpret Chen's comment, I believe we can assume that they have been removed permanently, another supposition.

For the twelve of us who remain, the lectures continue as before. Today the last decade of world history was reviewed with great emphasis on the economic crisis of the years just prior to the war. For the first time the discussion included many references to the United States, it being virtually impossible to discuss those years without some mention of our part in (as our teacher put it) "precipitating the crisis."

The last few hours were taken up in a brief discussion of third world nations, their emergence from colonial protectorates to independent status, their brief and sometimes brilliant assertion of their right to recognition, and their subsequent decline into obscurity as the major powers turned their attentions inward, on their own debilitation.

I have little quarrel with the presentations made today. I

97

have noted the consistent pattern of these discussions before—when our teachers discuss the distant past, their interpretation of events often seems muddy and twisted, but as the lectures approach contemporary times they become increasingly accurate. Is this by design—do they misrepresent the distant past because they believe we can be fooled? Or do they simply misunderstand it themselves? I have no way of knowing, but I suspect the latter. Because the former seems to make no sense. What possible advantage could they gain by knowingly misrepresenting the distant past? This is another supposition and a harsh one, but it agrees with my former comments regarding Chen's background. If true, it means, in effect, that the entire world is now under the control of men who do not understand its past. What hope can there be then for its future?

Friday, October 15

Chen's warning to me is proving prophetic; the lectures are becoming tedious. Everyone is feeling it.

Kowalski fell asleep in class today and for this indiscretion was rapped soundly on the head by Ho-ting, who has begun carrying a long rod for this purpose as he paces the room. I thought I saw Chen smile at the yelp Kowalski let out but I couldn't be certain; the commandant's impassive features seem permanently fixed in the same enigmatic expression.

The first of our classes recalled to me my days long ago at NYU. (How did I survive the boredom then?) But I am now reminded more of elementary school. I almost nodded off myself a few minutes after Kowalski was whacked, and the delight I felt when I caught myself in time to avoid punishment could only be described as childish. It was as though I had returned to the third grade and narrowly avoided being nabbed passing contraband comic books to a classmate.

I am not alone in this reaction. I wonder if our instructors realize how bored their students have become. Where is this leading? And what do they believe they are accomplishing?

Today's subject was, for lack of a better term, comparative economic systems. Our instructors' Communist sympathies were clearly in evidence again. They stressed the advantages of the collective approach and the failure of capitalism to provide equitably for all its citizens. Many doubtful statistics were cited. But I must admit that when they focused on the West, most particularly the United States, I found myself agreeing with some of what they said. Is this a reasonable reaction? Have they made valid points, or is my mind somehow clouded by their drugs? I can only guess at an answer. I'll ask Palitz about it at breakfast.

Still no word about Murphy, Hammil or Moore. So we were apparently correct; they have been removed permanently.

THIRTEEN

In the heart of the Oregon Cascades, a hundred miles southeast of Portland, is a wild and eerie landscape known as the McKenzie lava fields. It is a place of unearthly beauty and utter desolation, a vast sea of brown, basaltic boulders strewn across sixty-five square miles of mountainous terrain. No vehicle can operate on these ragged lava flows; even pack animals have difficulty. It was here that two separate groups of war survivors had established their base camps, one near the northern boundary of the lava, the other ten miles to the south.

It was late afternoon when Ben Devin and Katie Hogan reached the northern rim of the lava field. In the three days since the battle at the microwave tower they had circled well north of the direct route to the camp, all the way to the Santiam River. They had followed the river for miles and hiked along several small creek courses as well. They had backtracked three times, until they were certain they could not have been followed. Now, finally, they were almost home.

They paused briefly when they came to Route 20, watching and listening before crossing the two-lane blacktop. Devin went first. When he reached the safety of the trees on the far side, Katie followed. Once onto the lava field, they traveled a route they knew well, a trail that kept to the low places and provided cover. It was raining and heavy grey-black clouds scudded low overhead so they didn't really need cover—there could be no aircraft. But they followed the familiar route anyway, out of habit and because it was procedure and because there was no reason to take unnecessary risks. They were determined that their carelessness at the microwave tower would not be repeated.

Four hundred yards from the road they approached the first sentry post. It was on the east side of their route, on a low ridge that commanded a broad view of the terrain to the north and west. They looked up at the position as they drew near, waiting to be recognized.

"'Lo Devin," the sentry said finally. "Hi, Katie." He was

perhaps ten feet above them, inside a small pillbox-like structure built of plywood with lava rock heaped on top, making it virtually invisible unless you knew exactly where to look. He stepped out so they could see him clearly and flashed a broad, welcoming smile.

Katie waved. "Hi, Zack."

Zack Zachary was a throwback, a twenty-first century mountain man. His six-foot-two-inch frame carried only a hundred and sixty pounds but it was all wiry muscle. Before the war he had been a bush pilot in Alaska and a fishing and hunting guide in Montana. He was a crack rifle shot so Anderson put him out on the sentry posts as often as Zack could stand the boredom. He was thirty years old but despite a full beard looked nineteen. Katie had rarely seen him without a smile on his face.

"Anything going on?" Devin called up to him.

Zachary squatted down to be closer to their level. "Matter of fact it's been pretty busy; trail's been like a freeway this afternoon. Cox's crew came through an hour and a half ago with a load of stuff from Sisters. And about a half hour ago, there was a stranger."

"Stranger?" Devin looked suddenly interested. "Where from?"

"Said he was from somewhere in northern California; Redding, I think. I've never been to California so I'd never heard of it. You know a town called Redding?"

Devin didn't answer right away; he was thinking. In the first year after the war there had been quite a few strangers; a lot of people were still moving around. But by last winter just about everybody had settled somewhere and no one had moved much since. Lately there had been rumors about turncoats, Americans who had thrown in with the Chinese figuring the resistance was finished. So all strangers were suspect now.

"There's a town called Redding," Devin said absently. "But it's a long way from here, three hundred miles at least. This fellow claimed he'd walked all that way?"

"That far and more, all the way to Washington. Said he was on his way back to California now."

"Did he tell you why he was doing all this traveling?"

"No. He said he had to talk to Anderson about something."

"Anderson? He knew Anderson by name?"

Devin's tone was growing insistent and Zachary was beginning to look as though the questions were making him nervous. He answered cautiously, "No, Ben, not by name. He just

101

wanted to see the leader of our group."

"And you let him through?"

"What else could I do?"

"You told him where the camp is located?"

"Ben, I'm sure this guy was okay."

Devin shook his head angrily.

"What was I supposed to do? Shoot him? I couldn't leave my post."

"You should have kept him here. You should have made him wait and taken him in with you when you were relieved." Devin motioned to Katie and said, "Let's go." Then he paused and looked back at Zachary. "Was he armed?"

"Was when he got here. Not when he left."

"You took his weapons? He gave you his weapons?"

"He didn't have much choice." Zack glanced at Katie and grinned. "I strip searched him. Made him take off his clothes and stand right where Katie is standing now while I went through his stuff. He had a pistol, a .357 Colt. That was the only weapon, except for a knife. The rest was just food, a sleeping bag, a tent, the usual gear."

Katie burst out laughing. "You strip searched him? Made him stand here buck naked in the rain?"

"Sure did. He took it pretty well too. Said he understood why I had to be careful." Zachary looked at Ben, trying not to laugh. "I told him I'd bring the pistol in with me this evening. You want it?" He reached behind him, retrieved the Colt and offered it to Devin.

Ben waved it off. "What'd he look like? How was he dressed?"

Zack jammed the Colt into his belt. "Medium height, maybe five-ten. Slender, almost skinny. Mid thirties, I'd say. You'll see him when you get to camp. Can't miss him; he's black."

Devin listened to this, then said evenly, "I want to know what he was wearing, Zack. If he's not in camp when we get there, we're gonna have to look for him."

Zachary stared back at Devin, looking angry at first, then embarrassed. "I didn't screw up, Ben," he said. "This guy is with a group just like ours in California. He's one of us."

Devin didn't say anything.

Zachary sighed wearily. "Okay. Maybe I should have kept him here. But it was raining and I wasn't due to be relieved for four hours, so . . ." The rain was pelting down, matting Zachary's hair and depositing little droplets of water on his beard. He looked at Katie, then back to Devin. "He was wearing a poncho just like yours. Camouflage color with a hood."

Devin nodded. Then he turned and started off in the direction of the camp. Katie smiled sympathetically at Zachary and started after Devin.

The sentry called out, "He was okay, Ben, I swear. He'll be in camp when you get there. You'll see."

Including children there were thirty-one people living in the north McKenzie camp and most of them were gathered in the main room of Tom Anderson's shelter. The Anderson house was the largest structure in the camp and on occasions such as this it served as the town hall. It consisted of a single room approximately twenty feet square with a low ceiling constructed of log beams and plywood. Heavy vinyl sheeting had been stretched over the planks, covered with fine lava sand, and overlaid with basalt rubble. A Coleman lantern, hanging from one of the ceiling beams, provided the only light. The furnishings were crude but surprisingly comfortable—benches, chairs and tables carved out of logs. A large hooked rug, appropriated from a farmhouse near Sisters, covered the floor in the center of the room.

For this meeting the group had drawn the furniture into a semicircle at the center of which Tom Anderson and the stranger who had just walked in across the lava fields were seated in two large upholstered chairs. Aside from the rug, these chairs were the only examples of pre-war luxury in the entire camp.

"So you won't tell us your last name," Anderson was saying. "Mind if I ask why?" He had been studying the stranger ever since his arrival in camp a half-hour earlier, trying to decide exactly what it was about him that he didn't like. There was something, but Anderson couldn't put his finger on it.

"Because John is enough," the stranger replied. "It's better if we don't know too much about one another. You've told me your name, Tom, but I don't want to know the full names of anyone else here. The less each of us knows, the less risk."

"I see." Anderson glanced around the room. Several in his group nodded approvingly. "Well, I suppose that makes sense. In any event, we're pleased to see you. It's been two, maybe three months since anyone new passed this way."

"And I'm glad I finally found you," John said. "We've

103

known for some time that there was a group in this area, but you're damn well hidden. I had a hell of a time locating this camp."

Anderson displayed a satisfied smile. He was a heavy-set, blocky man, physically the exact opposite of the slender intruder he was entertaining. Before the war, he owned a small trucking company in nearby Redmond. He was a dedicated survivalist and on weekends used his trucks to haul weapons and food and supplies into these mountains where he and several of his friends built and stocked four separate shelters. "There's going to be a civil war soon," he warned his wife. "When the shit hits the fan, we're going to be ready." His shelters had sustained the group through the first hard winter, and in the year and a half since, his knowledge and leadership had contributed greatly to their continued survival. All of this had earned him their unqualified loyalty and recognition as undisputed leader of the north McKenzie clan.

"We took great care in selecting the site," Anderson acknowledged. "And in camouflaging the structures. It's completely invisible from the air. In any case, no one would think to look for us here, out in the open."

John smiled and said simply, "I did."

Anderson's self-satisfied smile evaporated and he regarded the stranger with renewed suspicion. Muttered exclamations of surprise circulated through the room.

"But you just admitted . . ."

"That I had difficulty locating you? That's true. But I don't have spy satellites." John surveyed the faces arrayed before him. Then he looked back at Anderson. "Do you really believe the Chinese don't know where you are?"

"I believe exactly that," Anderson replied sharply. "If they knew, they'd be all over us. In force!" Several members of the group voiced agreement with this.

John shook his head. "I doubt that. They're stretched too thin. They've occupied the entire world, you know, and despite the fact that China is the most populous nation on earth . . ." He stopped abruptly, recognizing consternation on his host's face. When he looked around at the others he met similar, uncomprehending stares. "My God, you didn't know? What did you think? That they were only here?"

David Cox, the clansman sitting closest to John, asserted confidently, "They are only here. And maybe in Europe. We've heard rumors about world conquest but that just isn't possible."

Anderson demanded, "Exactly what are you claiming? And where the hell do you get your information?"

For the first time, John seemed uncertain of his ground. "Look," he said cautiously, "I think I'd better start at the beginning and bring you up to date. Okay?"

"I'm listening," Anderson said cooly.

"I represent a group headquartered in the mountains east of Redding, not far from Lassen peak. We've been in that area since the beginning, at least some of us have. We were only ten at first but by the time the war officially ended and the first winter set in there were sixteen more. By the next summer, there were fifty of us and we made contact with five other groups within a seventy-five mile radius. We spent that summer consolidating— collecting food and arms, setting up and stocking reserve camps and establishing a communications network."

"It was similar here," Cox offered. "Except that there weren't five other groups nearby. We only know of one other, south of here."

"Oh, there are a few more," John said, turning to face Cox. "Two groups near Mt. Hood, four down around Crater Lake. And that's only the ones we've made contact with. I don't know how many more there may be that we haven't found yet. But let me get back to what I was saying." He turned to Anderson. "We spent this last summer infiltrating the camps and setting up communications with the prison populations. That's where we get most of our information."

"Infiltrating the camps?" Anderson's eyes narrowed. "Chinese camp security is airtight. They patrol the perimeters constantly. So how in hell did you *infiltrate* the camps?"

John had recovered his confidence now and this was exactly the question he had expected. He said, "Security is tight in the camps near here. But in California it's much more relaxed. That's what I came here to talk to you about. It was actually easy for us to contact the field workers in our area. Sometimes we talk with them directly, sometimes we exchange notes at predetermined drops. Either way, we've been able to learn what's going on in the camps and they've learned that we're out here." He paused to emphasize his next point. "This communication is absolutely critical. Without the support of the camp populations, we're spitting into the wind. We can't win."

Anderson's expression darkened at this statement. What John said might be true—the California camp populations might be accessible. But the prisoners in the Willamette Valley camps were not. So loose talk about 'spitting into the wind' served no purpose and was certain to undermine his group's morale. That couldn't be tolerated.

"The situation is different here," he said gruffly. "Communication isn't possible. We know. We've tried."

John said, "It isn't possible now. But we think it could be."

Anderson stiffened. So that was it! This arrogant black bastard wanted to take over! The grand Pooh Bah from California was going to show the ignorant Oregon yokels how to whup the yellow menace. Like hell! Well, there was one sure way to deal with egomaniacs. If you gave them enough rope, they always hung themselves eventually.

"You really think it's possible?" Anderson asked, trying to appear interested. "I'd like to know how. What do you know that we don't?"

"We know a lot. To begin with, as I mentioned before, we know that the Chinese have occupied virtually the entire world. Asia, Africa, Europe, South America. We have no information about Australia but that doesn't really matter; there were only thirty million people in Australia before the war anyway.

"This tells us several things. First, it tells us that the Chinese have taken on an incredible task, more than they can handle. Second, it tells us that we're alone, that there's nobody anywhere who can offer us any help. Together, those two pieces of information have dictated our strategy."

A stunned silence had settled over the room as John spoke. The only sounds were the faint hissing of the Coleman lantern and the patter of rain on the roof of Anderson's house.

"I want to talk to you about that strategy," John continued. "We need to . . ."

Cox interrupted him. "Are you certain about this?"

"Absolutely. We have many sources: guards who talk to prisoners, prisoners who've moved around and heard things in other camps. One prisoner in particular was a dock worker in Galveston before the war and stayed there for about a year and a half after the Chinese takeover. He saw ships from all over the world, ships from thirty different pre-war countries. Their crews were from all over—Europeans, Africans, Asians—but every ship had Chinese military aboard. There are also radio reports; the Chinese broadcast music and a little news to the camps. You've probably picked up some of it."

106

Cox nodded. "We get a little. The mountains block most of it."

"Then you know that most of the news is propaganda. But there's some good information in it, things we can check against other sources. When we put all our information together there's no room for doubt."

Again, the room fell silent. Someone in the gathering said softly, "Jesus, if this is true, it's over. There's no point in staying here."

From around the room came muttered exclamations of alarm, a few at first, then more. In seconds the entire clan was reacting to the distressing news.

Anderson acted quickly to silence them. "That's enough!" he shouted. "We have no proof of these claims. And even if they were true, it wouldn't change anything."

John said to everyone, "Tom's right about that. What I've told you is true, but it actually works to our advantage. It would be much worse if the Chinese were only here, don't you see that? Taking possession of territory is one thing; holding it is another. The Chinese have taken so much that they're vulnerable. If we can exploit that vulnerability, the very scale of their success will be the cause of their ultimate failure."

He recaptured his audience with this. Several clan members voiced agreement. From the back of the room there was scuffling movement as log benches and chairs were drawn closer. John sat patiently, waiting for the commotion to die down.

Cox said, "Go on. Exactly how can we exploit it?"

Anderson shifted uneasily in his chair. He wondered if he had been wrong to invite the Californian to continue. Should he have challenged him earlier? A moment ago John had stumbled badly, but like a cat, had landed on his feet. He knew his subject and he was more authoritative, more persuasive than Anderson had expected. It was beginning to look like he might not hang himself after all. Still, there was no turning back now. All Anderson could do was pay out more rope and pray. "Go on," he said, echoing Cox. "If you have something to propose, propose it."

"In a moment," John said. "First, I have to ask you a question. How much do you know about guerrilla warfare?"

Anderson could hardly believe his ears. The intruder was actually questioning his authority! *My authority*, he thought in amazement. *My qualifications to lead this group!*
The visitor had finally made a real mistake.

"Guerrilla warfare?" Anderson smiled. "I'd have to say we're pretty good at it. If you could ask them, I'm sure the Chinese would agree. We've been giving them a very bad time."

The entire clan responded to this. "Damn right!" someone called out. The rest voiced loud agreement. Several fists were raised into the air.

"We're well armed," Anderson continued. "And we've used our weapons to good advantage. We've disrupted their communications, blown bridges and ambushed truck convoys. And we've done it all without a single casualty."

John paused before responding to this, as though he was carefully considering his next statement. Finally he said, "That's good, especially the lack of casualties. I'm impressed." But his tone clearly indicated that he was not impressed. "So what comes next? Where do you go from here?"

Anderson flashed a sarcastic smile. "I don't guess we should discuss specific targets. You said yourself, the less each of us knows, the less risk."

There was scattered laughter in response to this.

"Agreed," John said. "But I'm not asking about targets. I'm asking about your objectives. Exactly what are you trying to accomplish?"

Anderson hesitated. He sensed vaguely that John was trying to maneuver him into some kind of corner, but he couldn't identify the trap. The answer to his antagonist's question was self-evident.

"Our objective," he said evenly, "is disruption. Our strategy is terrorism. We intend to make life so uncomfortable for the Chinese that they'll pack their bags and go home."

John shook his head. "I wish it were that simple. Unfortunately it isn't. Let me ask you this, have you or anyone else here studied guerrilla warfare?"

Anderson said nothing, but his mute scowl spoke for him.

John continued, "It's a relatively recent development, a twentieth century invention. There've been cases where it succeeded and other cases where it failed. Given the proper conditions and waged properly, success is virtually certain; the government is powerless to resist it. But given the wrong conditions or waged improperly, failure is equally inevitable. The conditions here are not good. It's possible for you to win, but only if you conduct our operations flawlessly. You can't afford mistakes, Tom. And I'm afraid the strategy you've been employing is counterproductive."

John's eyes had been fixed on Anderson as he said this and the clan leader now glared back at him. He sensed that his followers were watching him, anxiously anticipating his rebuttal. But he felt powerless to respond. He had no idea what the stranger was talking about. John spoke of guerrilla warfare as though it was a subject that could be studied, like math or chemistry. That was crazy! By definition, guerrilla warfare was unstructured hit-and-run fighting, fighting without rules. It couldn't be studied. Guerrillas did what they could with the materials at hand. They sought to disrupt, to irritate, to terrorize by any means available. In short, they did exactly what the north McKenzie clan had been doing. This black bastard was purposely trying to confuse them. Why? Was it possible that John was working for the Chinese?

"That's bullshit," Anderson spat. "It's bullshit, and it makes no goddamn sense."

The clan reacted immediately, supporting their leader with shouted expressions of indignation.

At that moment the door to the shelter opened and two figures stepped through into the interior. The clan member nearest the door jumped to his feet and greeted the new arrivals warmly, then announced to the rest, "Hey everyone, Ben and Katie are back."

As the commotion died down and the newcomers acknowledged greetings from the members of the group, Anderson rose. "Ben!" he shouted. "Ben, come over here. I want you in on this."

Devin waved, pulled his poncho over his head and threw it on the pile by the door. A moment later he was standing next to Anderson. Katie remained at the back of the room, taking a seat next to Susan Agee, who began filling her in on the events of the last few minutes.

"How'd it go?" Anderson asked. "You're a day late. We were getting worried."

"I'll tell you about it later," Devin replied distractedly. He was looking at John, who was standing next to Anderson.

Anderson introduced them, taking care not to reveal Devin's last name. He was now convinced that, where John was concerned, such precautions might be well justified.

Devin had heard the commotion as he entered and he recognized the anger still clouding Anderson's expression. "What's going on?" he asked. "What have I missed?"

109

"Let's sit," Anderson said. When they had taken seats with Devin squeezing in next to Cox, he began: "John here claims to be an expert on guerrilla warfare. He says he's studied it."

Devin nodded. "I see. Well, that's good. We can use all the help we can get."

Surprise flickered in Anderson's eyes. He hadn't expected this reaction, hadn't expected Devin to accept the idea that guerrilla warfare could be studied. But he recovered himself quickly.

"You're our military expert," he went on. "So I think you should be the one to discuss this. John claims our tactics are counterproductive."

Devin looked at John and said, "Oh?"

"You've missed the background," John said. "Let me tell you what my group has learned." He quickly reviewed everything they had discussed before Devin's arrival. Anderson voiced disbelief or disapproval at several points.

Devin listened attentively. When John had finished, he said, "That's all pretty fantastic."

"Maybe. But it's true."

"You haven't offered us a shred of proof," Anderson said icily. He turned to Devin. "No proof, Ben. None."

Devin said, "I agree, Tom. But there's no harm in hearing him out." His eyes had been on John even as he spoke to Anderson and he now addressed the stranger. "You say our tactics are counterproductive. I'd like to know what you mean by that."

John leaned forward, resting his elbows on his knees. "I mean that your tactics are making it impossible for you to win. You've had some success, Ben, I understand that. But your success has been invisible to the people who matter, the prisoners in the camps. So it's gained you nothing. At the same time it's cost you a great deal."

"I told you," Anderson said angrily, "We haven't lost a single man."

Devin winced but said nothing. There was no point in bringing up the news about Haskell and McKee just now.

"I'm not talking about casualties," John said, glancing briefly at Anderson. "I'm talking about strategy. I asked a question earlier, but you weren't here, Ben. So I'll ask you now. How much do you know about guerrilla warfare?"

"I did a lot of training," Devin said. "Marine Corps. For the last two decades every little war that broke out was a guerrilla

110

war."

"Then you understand the problems. And the strategy."

"I guess everyone understands. In a guerrilla war you can't tell your friends from the enemy until someone starts shooting. You walk into a village or onto a city street and if there are twenty people in view you know that ten of them are guerrillas, but you don't know which ten. The others are sympathizers or they're so scared they won't talk to you. So the primary tactic you employ is patience. You just have to work it through slowly, gain their confidence. You have to get the good guys to realize that they have to stand up and fight."

John frowned thoughtfully. "That's all true," he said. "But I was really asking what it looks like from the other side, the side we're on now. Did you study the strategy guerrillas employ?"

"They hit and run," Devin replied. "They're terrorists."

"Those are tactics," John said, looking momentarily frustrated. "I want to talk about strategy."

Devin shrugged. "I was a non-com, a tactician. For strategy you need an officer."

Anderson laughed. Devin was making John look foolish, he thought.

But the black man was unperturbed. "You're an officer here, Ben."

"I guess that's true," Devin agreed.

John moved slightly closer to Devin. "Let me put this another way. Have you ever read Mao Tse-tung? Or Che Guevara?"

For an instant, Devin didn't react. Then his eyes narrowed and the muscles in his neck tightened.

"They're Communists," Anderson blurted. "Aren't they?"

"They were," John replied. "They both died fifty or sixty years ago."

"You're admitting that you're a Communist?"

John laughed, "Of course not! I'm telling you that since I'm now a guerrilla I wanted to know something about guerrilla warfare. I studied their strategy, not their politics." He addressed Devin: "Mao practically invented guerrilla warfare, Ben. And Che turned it into a science. He wrote a book on tactics and strategy. When I read that book, I understood why guerrillas succeed. In Southeast Asia and the Middle East and Central America they did exactly what Che told them to do, and it worked! It wasn't the situation that beat the central governments. It wasn't the rain or the mud or the heat or the ignorance of the peasants. It was the

111

guerrillas. They controlled the war. They employed the right strategy at the right time and the government never had a chance of winning."

Anderson looked at Devin. The anger was flickering in his eyes again. "He's a Communist, Ben, sure as hell," he growled. But Devin paid little attention. His brows were knit in a thoughtful expression and he was looking at John.

"At the very least he's a sympathizer," Anderson added. "He's probably working with the Chinese."

Devin nodded. "Maybe. But I'd still like to hear what he has to say." His gaze remained fixed on John. "You're claiming that the American leadership in Southeast Asia and Central America were fools. You can't really believe that all they needed to do was read a few books and we could have won the war?"

"No, I don't believe that. In fact, I'm quite certain that many of them did read Guevara's book. Or books like it. But it didn't matter—that's the point! When the right conditions exist, the right guerrilla strategy virtually guarantees success. The truth is, nothing we could have done would have changed the outcome."

Devin shook his head. "Now you're talking nonsense. For every strategy there's a counter strategy. There must have been something we could have done."

"There really wasn't, Ben. You see, guerrilla wars are successful only when certain conditions exist. There are four basic requirements:

"To begin with there has to be political instability. It doesn't matter whether the government is dominated by a single dictator or a corrupt bureaucracy; if the people believe it's abusing them, it's vulnerable.

"Next, there has to be an underclass, a group the government is abusing, which is large enough that by sheer weight of numbers it is potentially dangerous to the government.

"Third, there have to be rural areas where guerrillas can scatter and decentralize their operations. Urban bases won't work because in cities the government can mobilize its forces quickly in large numbers. But by operating in rural areas, guerrillas force the government to spread its army so thin that individual units are isolated and vulnerable.

"Finally, there has to be a rebel organization capable of doing two things: It has to outline goals the people can understand and it has to provide leadership to work toward those goals.

"It works like this: Once the rebels have set up rural bases the government has two choices. It can garrison the countryside and fight, but that will anger the peasants and make the government look even more oppressive than it did before. It won't work anyway because the countryside is so spread out that individual garrisons will be small and isolated. The guerrillas can attack them and win propaganda victories. So the only alternative open to the government is to abandon the countryside and garrison the larger towns. But if it does that, it surrenders large areas of countryside to the guerrillas, enlarging their area of influence and providing them with new sources of manpower and supplies. So again, the guerrillas win.

"You see? Either way, the government loses. That's what we were up against, Ben. You said the guerrillas wouldn't stand and fight. No guerrilla will. Because he isn't fighting for territory; he's fighting for the hearts and minds of the uncommitted population. Propaganda is more valuable to him than anything else. Because when the people become convinced that the rebels have a real chance of winning, they will join in the fighting themselves and the full scale revolt will begin."

John paused, apparently expecting questions. But neither Devin nor Anderson said anything, so he continued. "Now, consider how this relates to your situation here in Oregon.

"You're facing an oppressive government—nothing could be more oppressive than an occupying army. You also have a large underclass, a huge underclass, in fact. There are nearly two hundred million prisoners in the North American camps and only ten or fifteen million Chinese in all of North America. Those numbers clearly spell danger for the Chinese. If all the prisoners decided to revolt at once I doubt the Chinese would be able to resist them. Unfortunately, however, you can't satisfy the third and fourth conditions. There's lots of countryside, but it isn't the right kind. It isn't farmland with scattered villages and a rural population you can mix into. Instead, you are isolated in this wilderness, completely cut off from the populations in the camps. You've allowed yourselves to be locked out. The Chinese have chosen to leave you alone, in effect surrendering vast territories to your control, but you've won absolutely nothing as a result because you aren't in contact with the camp populations.

"Don't you see? Your military successes have netted you nothing in terms of propaganda. The camp populations don't even know you're here. That's a disaster! Because at this stage the only thing that matters is the camp populations. You can't fight the

Chinese by yourselves. Your only goal now should be to convince the prisoners in the camps to join you. You have to provide them with leadership. You have to design a revolution they can believe in and you have to make sure they know about it. Every action you take should contribute toward the goal of recruiting the camp populations.

"You haven't done that. In fact, the actions you've taken thus far have had the opposite effect. By harassing the Chinese, you've alerted them to your presence and caused them to tighten security in the Oregon camps. You've forced them to isolate you and thereby rendered yourselves useless as guerrillas."

Anderson brought his hand down hard on the arm of his chair. "Damn it," he bellowed. "I don't have to listen to this!" He glared angrily at John. "Who the hell do you think you are?"

John returned a look of such frigid intensity that after only a few seconds Anderson looked away.

"I know who I am," John said, "but you puzzle me." He looked quickly around the room. "You all puzzle me. We aren't playing a game here. No one is awarding us points for good intentions or honest effort. There are no rules and no referee and if we lose we get no second chance. We have to do this right the first time. I know what will work and I'm ready to help if you'll let me. But some of you seem to be saying, 'Go away! Don't confuse us with the facts.'"

Anderson rose from his chair and snarled, "Why you arrogant . . ."

But Devin grabbed his arm. "Tom! Calm down."

Reluctantly, Anderson sat down. Devin said to John, "Look, I don't know how this act of yours played in the other camps you say you visited, but it's not winning you any friends here."

"You're siding with him?" John made no attempt to hide his disappointment. "I misjudged you, Ben. I took you for a reasonable man."

"I believe I am; I believe we all are. But don't ask us to choose sides. You'll lose! We've been through a lot together and you're an outsider."

"We're on the same side," John sighed, "There's a lot more at stake here than simple loyalty. Don't you understand that?"

Abruptly, Cox shouted, "I don't believe this!" They all turned and looked at him. "Ben's right, John is an outsider. And I agree with you too, Tom, he may be arrogant as well. But what he was saying made sense and I'd like to hear the rest of it. So let's cut the crap and let him finish."

Self conscious laughter rippled through the room.

John eyed Cox with a mixture of surprise and gratitude. Anderson's face reddened but he said nothing. Devin smiled and nodded toward Cox. "All right, Dave, you have the floor."

Cox paused for only a moment, collecting his thoughts, then said, "John, a minute ago you said that you know what will work. I'd like to hear about that. Exactly what do you think we should be doing?"

John nodded to Cox. Then to the entire group he said, "That's obvious. You should be doing nothing. You should be conducting no raids. You should be trying to convince the Chinese that you've given up and are no longer a threat to them. Then, when they relax security in the camps, you can establish contact and begin laying the groundwork for the revolt."

"Is that why the camps in California are open?" Cox asked. "Simply because at first, you conducted no raids?"

"Exactly."

"But, then—I don't understand. You said that the California camps are still open. When you did begin fighting in California, why didn't the Chinese react? Why didn't they secure the camps?"

John looked puzzled. "But there's been no fighting in California. Not yet."

"None?" Anderson demanded. "Not even now?"

"I explained that," John said. "Last year the camps were still secure; the Chinese were still being cautious. This summer they relaxed their security and we were able to establish contact. Next spring we intend to move. For now, we're doing nothing to alarm them. Fighting now would serve no purpose. And it would cost us the element of surprise."

Anderson glared at Devin. "Did you hear him, Ben? They've done no fighting. He's up here lecturing us on guerrilla warfare, claiming to be an expert, and no one in his group has fired a shot!"

John too was looking at Devin. "Ben," he said, "Fighting is easy. Like you, we're anxious to fight. It's been hard doing nothing. But while you've fought many times and accomplished nothing, we've exercised restraint and accomplished a great deal. It's obvious which strategy is working."

Devin's gaze traveled from John, whose face was set in an expression of firm determination, to Anderson, in whose eyes anger smoldered, to Cox, who could only shrug helplessly.

"Nothing is obvious," Devin said finally. "This is going to take some time. We all need to think."

"I can't stay long," John cautioned. "I have work in California."

"You'll stay the night at least," Devin said. It was an order.

John nodded. "I have no choice, so of course I accept."

"You can bunk with me. We both need to get cleaned up. Then we'll come back here, get something to eat and discuss this some more." He turned to Anderson. "That all right with you, Tom?"

"Fine," Anderson said. He rose and announced that the meeting was over. The clan members began filing out.

A minute later only Anderson, his wife, Sarah, and Cox remained.

"How many for dinner?" Sarah asked.

Anderson thought for a moment. "Five," he replied. "You, me, Dave, Ben and our . . . our guest." He lowered himself into his chair with a weary sigh.

Cox started toward the door and Anderson called after him, "You know what I think, Dave?"

Cox turned. "I think you made that pretty clear."

"I think that son-of-a-bitch is working for the Chinese."

"Could be. But that's a hard thing to prove. So what do you plan to do about it?"

"I don't know. That's what worries me. Do you realize how dangerous this situation is? John is trouble; I can feel it in my gut. But there might not be a damn thing I can do about it."

FOURTEEN

Chen Loying strode into the great hall shortly after the prisoners had finished breakfast. He was flanked by Ho-ting and a second guard. The rest of his usual entourage—the instructors who had been delivering prepared lectures for the past two weeks—were conspicuously absent. This fact immediately caught the attention of his students, who were seated in their customary places, anticipating another day of tedious instruction.

"Well!" Roger Simone said, leaning toward Sandiman. "What's this?"

From behind them Wiedemier offered, "Looks like school is over and phase four is beginning. Or is it phase five? I've lost track."

Chen walked to the lectern, faced his audience and said, "You will be pleased to learn that Mr. Wiedemier is correct, your classes are complete.

Kowalski and Grant greeted this announcement with derisive applause. Ho-ting glared at them, but Chen accepted the sarcasm with apparent good humor. He waited patiently for them to finish, then said, "Your candor is appreciated, Gentlemen. I trust it will continue. If we are to accomplish anything together it is imperative that we be honest with one another. With that in mind I would like to ask you—any of you who care to answer— exactly what you feel you have gained from your lessons here."

There was an awkward silence, before Sandiman tentatively asked, "Do you really want the truth? Our honest opinions?"

"I want exactly that," Chen replied.

Sandiman shrugged. "Well, I can only speak for myself of course, but I don't believe I gained anything. I'm sorry, but to me the lectures seemed boring and pointless."

Chen nodded. "Thank you, Mr. Sandiman." He seemed curiously pleased with Sandiman's response. "Anyone else?"

"I agree with Sandiman," said Grant.

"I believe we all do," Wiedemier added. "If it was your

intention to convert us to your view of the world, I'm afraid you've failed."

Again Chen nodded. Again he gave no indication of disappointment or disapproval.

Craighill was next to speak. "We're frankly puzzled, Chen. At least I am. You've forced us to endure two weeks of blatant propaganda. Why? What did you hope to accomplish?"

Chen stepped from behind the lectern and stood beside it. "Would you feel differently, Mr. Craighill, if I told you that these lessons are not considered propaganda in China. Would it surprise you to know that these same lectures have been routinely presented to school children for the past half century there and that in China they are accepted as accurate representations of truth?

Craighill said, "No, that would not surprise me. Even if it did, it wouldn't answer my question. I still want to know why, with your knowledge of the world outside China, you chose to present these lessons to our group? This is not China, and we are not school children.

Again, Chen smiled. "I lived for many years in your country, David; I believe I know you. And one thing I know about you is that you know almost nothing about us. That was the primary reason for this school—we wanted you to understand our point of view.

"You've asked me a question; permit me to ask one of you. You have called our instruction propaganda. Please tell me exactly what you mean by that. Do you dispute the facts my instructors presented?"

Craighill said, "I admit that many of the facts they presented were accurate. But they omitted facts we consider important and emphasized points we consider trivial. The result was a distortion of the truth. As you well know, propaganda is seldom based on outright lies; it is usually more subtle, a slightly skewed presentation of truth and half-truth."

"I see. Then it is not our facts you dispute but our interpretation of those facts."

Now it was Craighill who smiled. "No, I won't let you off that easily. I'm not talking about simple interpretation; I'm talking about purposeful distortion. I can cite many examples, significant events which your lecturers mentioned only in passing or ignored completely, minor events which they . . ."

"Significant in whose opinion," Chen said abruptly. "Minor

according to what test?"

Craighill hesitated before answering, wondering if he had detected sudden irritation or even anger in the Commandant's tone. But there was no hint of either in his present expression. A small smile was playing around the corners of Chen's mouth. He seemed to be enjoying the discussion.

"According to the test of history," Craighill replied, you know exactly what I mean. The events to which I refer are well documented."

"In the literature of the West?"

"In the literature of the West, and of the East as well, I'm quite certain."

"Are you indeed?" Chen pursed his lips thoughtfully. I'm confused, David. A moment ago you said it would not surprise you to learn that these lessons are accepted in China. Now you say you are certain that the truth—your western truth—is understood in China and that these lessons have been purposely distorted. Which do you really believe? It can't be both." .

Craighill considered this and said, "But I do believe both. I believe that the establishment in China has access to the facts but presents a distorted view of those facts to the Chinese people. I believe that you propagandize your own people—in the schools, in the villages, in your national media. This too is well documented; you can't deny that it happens."

"On the contrary, I can and do deny it. You see, there is a fallacy in your argument, David. You assume the existence of an absolute, universal truth. Americans have always claimed a unique knowledge of that truth and accused all who viewed the world differently of deceit and distortion. Your western allies, the Europeans, were not so presumptuous; they understood, as we Chinese do, that there are many possible interpretations of truth and many equally valid conclusions which can be drawn from the same set of facts."

Chen stepped back behind the lectern and leaned forward, resting his elbows upon it. "Gentlemen, no universal truth existed before the war. We have presented these lessons to demonstrate that fact and to acquaint you with the traditional Chinese version of truth, our view of the pre-war world. From your perspective that truth may seem distorted, even corrupt. But you must understand that from our perspective your truth appears equally distorted, equally corrupt.

"For generations these differences have divided us and

119

caused us to view each other with distrust and suspicion. We must now put all that aside." He addressed Craighill directly. "Let me ask you this, David. When you apply the test of history to your American truth, what does it reveal?"

Craighill seemed uncertain. "I'm not sure what you mean."

"It's a straightforward question. Our separate truths are expressed in separate philosophies and those philosophies have produced very different social systems. Did your American system succeed or fail?"

Craighill said, "There's no simple answer to that question. It succeeded in some ways and failed in others."

"Agreed. But on balance?"

"On balance it has to be considered the most successful social system in human history. It was the model upon which a hundred other nations based their systems.

"The light of the world? A beacon for others to follow?"

"Absolutely. It provided hope to billions."

"Indeed. But what of the last forty years? After the Soviet system collapsed, what happened, David?"

Again the newsman hesitated.

"Your decline was rapid, was it not? The behavior of your financial institutions ruined your economy, persistent unemployment destroyed your middle class, poverty and crime rates increased. In the end your system could not provide for its citizen's most basic needs—food, housing, medical care, infrastructure, education. It entered a kind of death spiral."

"Our system did not fail," Simone said sharply. "People failed the system."

Chen turned to Simone and said, "It is the same thing."

"No! It is not the same. Our system rested on a social contract—individual freedom was exchanged for individual responsibility. The system produced freedom, but many citizens failed to behave responsibly."

Chen sighed. "People are fallible. Some are lazy, some are greedy, some are weak. If a system is to survive and prosper it must recognize these facts and protect itself. Yours did not. It placed too much faith in people. It asked far too much of them."

"And what of your system," Craighill asked. "It seems to me yours places too little faith in people. It treats them like cattle."

Chen nodded. "Ours failed also. While yours was producing global chaos, ours was producing economic stagnation. In the years before the war overcaution erased much of the progress we had made since the turn of the century. We avoided your disaster, but the cost to individual Chinese and to China herself was great."

The furrows in Craighill's forehead deepened. "You admit failure?"

"Of course I admit it. I cannot ask you to be realistic unless I am prepared to be equally realistic." Chen paused, waiting for the impact of this statement to be felt. Then he said, "We have forced you to endure these classes so that you would understand what we are now prepared to sacrifice. Gentlemen, it is time for both of us to discard our traditional loyalties and our preconceptions. Our systems have failed and must now be replaced. We must devise a new system, which balances opportunity and responsibility and asks only what is possible of its citizens. I am asking you to join with me in the work of creating that system."

Chen paused and hearing no immediate response from any of the Americans continued, "Gentlemen, we have collaborated in the destruction of our globe; we must now cooperate in its rebirth. The Chinese occupation of North America has reached a point of stability—order has been restored and the farming and manufacturing economies are being reestablished. But it is nevertheless a hostile occupation. Chinese rule is being imposed on the North American population. We are anxious to end this relationship. We wish to relax the security restrictions currently being imposed in the camps and begin normalizing the continent.

"Our goal is the creation of a new North American state, an autonomous, self governing population in which Americans and Canadians and Hispanics and Chinese are integrated into a single society. Ultimately, we intend to create six continental states joined in a global federation. Consider what this can mean. Humanity united. An end to nationalism and war. An opportunity at last to address global problems on a global basis. A chance to allocate global resources equitably. All this is possible."

The Commandant paused again, clearly expecting some reaction. This time he was not disappointed.

"A grand dream," Sandiman said. "But hardly original. China uber alles, is that what this is all about? You plan to make Beijing the new capital of the world?"

Chen smiled. "As a matter of fact, Mr. Sandiman, current plans place the Global Capital at Athens." His eyes scanned the room. "Anyone else?"

Craighill said, "I'm willing to hear more, I suppose. But I can't offer much enthusiasm. You now hold territory by force of arms. I know my countrymen; they won't be easily persuaded to accept you as fellow citizens of some new continental state, regardless how much sense you think that makes. The moment you relax your security, you'll have a revolution on your hands."

"I believe you are wrong," Chen said. "But I agree with you to this extent—the new state must be created first. The machinery must be established and functioning before the security is relaxed. That is precisely why we have recruited this group."

Chen nodded to Ho-ting and the senior guard moved an easel, which had been standing nearby, into position beside the lectern. The easel held a large tablet of paper, in sheets about a yard square. The top sheet, the only one visible, was blank. Chen glanced at the easel, then back to his audience.

"At our first meeting two weeks ago I told you that we hoped to enlist your cooperation in the North American reconstruction. A few minutes ago I told you that we must both be prepared to discard old philosophies in order to make that cooperation possible. What we are proposing is the creation of an entirely new social order. It will be neither Chinese nor American, socialistic nor democratic. Instead it will combine elements of both pre-war systems, elements which *the test of history*—he looked directly at Craighill as he spoke these words—has proved worthy of inclusion.

"Please understand, none of what I am about to show you is etched in stone. I said this is to be a cooperative undertaking and I meant exactly that. We want your input. Where you feel these plans are flawed, criticize. If you have changes to suggest, suggest them. Keep in mind that we are designing our common future. We must all live in the world we create."

He stepped from the lectern to the easel, lifted the blank cover sheet and folded it back, revealing what appeared to be an organizational chart and said, "We will begin with the structure of the continental government."

For the next half hour the prisoners listened attentively. But none responded to Chen's appeal for participation. Then Wiedemier asked for a minor clarification. A while later, Sandiman objected to what he called "social engineering," concluding, "We're supposed to be organizing the activities of human beings here, not programming machinery."

When Chen had responded to this, Simone asked, "What about religion? Are we all expected to become Buddhists?"

Other questions followed and the meeting quickly began to assume the form Chen had intended. No longer a lecture, it became a spirited round-table discussion. Everyone contributed, and on several occasions heated arguments erupted. The coffee and tea breaks, which had become a familiar part of the school routine, were dispensed with. Instead the guards kept the pots full and steaming and delivered refreshments to the participants on request.

In the third hour, Chen abandoned his station at the lectern and seated himself with the others. The Americans hardly seemed to notice and no one apparently recognized the significance of the gesture—the commandant had won. For the moment at least he was enjoying a complete and unqualified victory.

The forum continued into the late afternoon and would have gone much longer except that Chen finally rose and announced that it was time for dinner.

"We will meet again in several days," he said. "In the meantime I will interview each of you individually. This meeting was the easiest way to provide all of you with an overview of our thinking, but it is no substitute for quiet and reasoned contemplation. You will now be given an opportunity to reflect. I want each of you to review what you heard here and consider your reaction. We value your opinions and want your contributions."

Several of the Americans expressed disappointment and a desire to continue the discussion, but Chen would not be swayed. "I appreciate your enthusiasm," he assured them. "But I must ask that you defer to an old man's wishes on this point. It is late and I am tired. You will each be given an opportunity to express your views." He bowed and left the room.

As they left the barracks, Ho-ting looked at Chen and smiled broadly. "I believe it went well, Commandant. Did it not?"

"It went even better than I had hoped," Chen replied. But he was not smiling.

"Yet you do not seem pleased. Have I misunderstood something?"

Chen shook his head wearily; the long day had left him exhausted. "No," he said. "You have misunderstood nothing, Captain. What you see is merely the unreasonable caution of an old man. I fear it went too well; that concerns me."

Ho-ting considered this as they walked, decided it made no

sense to him and dismissed it. A few yards further on he said, "You told them about many things today, but I noticed you did not tell them about the ships. When will they be told about that?"

Chen abruptly slowed his pace and looked angrily at Ho-ting. "They will not be told about the ships, Captain, not until it becomes impossible to keep them from knowing. If news of the ships reaches them prematurely, I will hold you personally responsible. Do you understand?"

Ho-ting was so surprised by his commandant's anger that he did not answer. But his expression left no doubt that he had understood.

FIFTEEN

Devin was sleeping. Katie looked down at him and smiled. It was amazing, she thought, that he was able to shut everything out like this and abandon himself to his contentment. She could never do it.

She could share his passion; she could shut everything out then. When they made love the world receded further and further until there was nothing but the two of them merging into one, combining to form something completely new and different from anything in her previous experience, something wonderful. But afterward, the world always intruded and she returned to herself. She envied his ability to remain where they had been. She wished that she too could remain and forget. And yet she loved these moments. She loved looking at him and knowing that she was capable of giving him such peace.

She drew her blanket close around her and sat gazing up at the sky. They were in a small hollow in the lava field, near the top of a low hill fifty yards from rest of the north McKenzie camp. She and Devin had been working for three days to create their home, with Cox's help. Tomorrow they would begin building the roof. In a week it would be finished. Just in time, she thought. The snow would come soon.

There was still a little light in the west but no color now, only a narrow band of pale grey above the irregular skyline of mountain peaks. Overhead, the grey shaded quickly to deep indigo, and stars were beginning to appear; in a half hour the heavens would be ablaze. The recent brilliance of the night sky testified to the fact that the earth was finally purging itself of the war's nuclear refuse. Everyone at McKenzie saw this as a hopeful sign.

"Cold?"

Startled, she looked down at Devin. "I thought you were asleep."

"Almost," he said. "I was watching you. What were you thinking?"

125

"Just looking at the sky." She raised a hand and pointed. "That's Polaris, the pole star, the tip of the handle on the little dipper, Ursa Minor. There's the big dipper, Ursa Major. And straight up is Cygnus, the swan."

He rolled onto his back and looked up as she pointed. "Where'd you learn all that? I thought you were a history teacher."

"I was. I only know a little about astronomy. But it interests me. The sky just overwhelms me; it makes me feel small. Don't you feel it?"

"You like feeling small?"

She could barely see him in the fading light but she knew that he was smiling at her.

"Not always. But there are times when it's useful. When I have problems or if I feel scared, I look at the sky and nothing down here seems important. The stars are always the same. No matter what happens here, they endure. Knowing that makes me feel safe. It makes me feel like a little girl again." She hesitated for a second and when she continued, her voice sounded husky, strained. "When I was a kid I used to go out into my yard at night and lie on my back for hours looking at the sky. And fifty feet away, I knew that my father was watching TV and my mother was reading romance novels and my brother . . ."

Her words trailed off and Devin could tell that she was fighting back tears. He wrapped an arm around her and pulled her to him.

"God, I miss them so much." She put a hand to her face and dabbed at a tear. "I'm not cut out for this fighting, Ben. I'm no good at it; I don't belong here. Deep down, I just want to go home."

"None of us belong here," he said soothingly. "We're just doing what we have to do. I know how hard it is, Katie. I lost my family too. My wife, my boys."

She drew back in embarrassment. "I know," she said. "I'm sorry. I didn't mean to sound so selfish. Forgive me?"

"Forgive you? Hey, I bawled like a baby at first. We all did." He leaned forward and kissed her cheek. "You're incredible, Katie. I don't know why it took me so long to realize that."

She pulled her blanket from one shoulder and wrapped it around him. "C'mon in here," she said. "I'm cold."

They huddled together for several minutes in silence. Then Devin said, "It won't be like this forever. There are positive signs. That sky, for instance; it didn't look like that last year. And

Anderson's docimeters have been clean for six months now. There's no more radiation, at least not here. Someday, the war will be just a memory. Our grandchildren—"

Katie shuddered involuntarily, and Devin wished immediately that he could take back what he had just said. For two years, long term radiation effects had been a subject of constant speculation in the McKenzie camp. Anderson's instruments told them that they had all received a cumulative dosage of between fifty and one hundred REMS before the radiation cooled, but none of them were sure about the implications of that level of exposure. Even David Cox, who had been a medical technician before the war and was now acting as the clan's doctor, couldn't tell them what to expect. They knew the danger of primary radiation sickness was past—if they weren't sick yet, they weren't going to get sick—but what of secondary effects? Would cancers be induced? If so, how soon? Had they suffered genetic damage that would produce mutations in the next generation? Most of the clan members had made their peace with these questions by now, but Katie was still troubled by them. She was twenty-five years old, one of only five women in the camp in the midst of their childbearing years, and the possibility of genetic damage frightened her. She had tried to hide that fear from the others, to keep her own counsel on the subject, but Devin had suspected. He wasn't sure exactly how he had known but he had known. And then, in a careless moment, he had forgotten.

"Katie," he said gently, "I'm sorry. I didn't mean to . . ."

"It's all right. Really. It's just that talk of children and grandchildren scares me. We don't know what could happen. And there's also that business about John's new rules."

At the mention of John's name, Devin sighed. During the long meeting the night John visited the McKenzie camp, Devin had supported every one of the stranger's proposals except the one to which Katie now referred.

"Pregnancies," the Californian had insisted, "cannot be tolerated in our camps. Infants are a liability and pregnant women must therefore surrender themselves to the Chinese." Devin had argued against the rule, in part because of the new relationship he and Katie had formed on the trip back from the microwave tower, and in part because he couldn't accept the prospect of voluntarily condemning any clan member to the Chinese camps. But he had been outvoted. John's arguments had persuaded the others.

"I always thought I wanted children," Katie said. "But not

under these circumstances. Ben, I don't know what I'd do if it happened to us. I couldn't turn myself in to the Chinese. I couldn't leave you."

"You wouldn't have to. In the first place, it isn't going to happen to us." Devin paused suddenly and Katie could feel his eyes on her. "Unless you're saying . . . You don't think that . . ."

"No," she said quickly. "No, Ben!"

"You're sure?"

"I'm sure." She placed a hand on the back of his neck, pulled him toward her and kissed him. "I'm absolutely sure. Okay?"

"I wouldn't let you leave," he said. "The hell with John. If it came to that, we'd go off on our own, find another group to join. I'm in love with you, Katie."

She smiled, "I know. Ain't life grand!"

They lay back for several minutes, looking up at the stars. Finally, she said, "Zachary's in California by now, isn't he?"

"According to John they should have arrived three days ago. Zack should be starting back about now."

"Then we'll know soon, won't we?"

"Know what?"

"Whether John was telling the truth. Whether Zack will come back alone or John will march in leading a division of Chinese troops."

Devin laughed. "That sounds like something Anderson would say, Katie. When did you get so cynical?"

She smiled sheepishly. "That was mean, wasn't it?" She wrapped her arm around him and pulled herself close. "I guess . . . Hello, what's this, Sergeant? Private Devin is full of himself again!"

Ben grinned. "He's operating without orders; Should I have him stand down?"

"Hell no!" She kissed him. "I have a better idea. That sort of initiative should be rewarded, don't you think?"

Devin enthusiastically agreed.

SIXTEEN

Across the face of the North American continent preparations had now begun, according to orders handed down from continental administrator Lin Chiao-tu. In a hundred separate cities damaged electrical equipment was repaired, long idle switches were thrown and dormant machinery hummed back to life. In the countryside old transmission towers were refurbished and new towers erected. Everywhere, the dish antennas were adjusted and aimed at a new satellite launched only a week earlier. Soon the entire system would be operational.

Lin scanned the reports with satisfaction. Construction of the final link in the chain, the new facility at Sacramento, was actually ahead of schedule. It was all going very well.

Other reports on Lin's desk brought more encouraging news. The agricultural production tallies revealed a harvest 10 percent better than predictions, primarily as a result of late rains in the parched midwest. Perhaps global weather patterns were at last returning to normal. On the western Snake River plain there was news of an irrigation project restored to full operation; next spring it would bring one hundred thousand acres of crop land back into production. A truck manufacturing plant near Nashville was scheduled to reopen in two weeks, an oil refinery near Tulsa had resumed operations only yesterday, and numerous smaller factories were going on-line daily.

To Lin it appeared that a significant corner had been turned. It was still far too early to declare success, but at least the reconstruction of North America was finally proceeding.

Only a single source of irritation remained to cast a shadow over an otherwise promising record of recent accomplishment, and that problem would soon be remedied. Within a week the annoying rebel bands around Omaha, south of Wheeling, in the mountains east of Salt Lake City and in twenty other locations would be eradicated, swept away like so much dust before the wind.

His only regret was that he would not able to witness these final victories in person.

SEVENTEEN

Thursday, October 28

I was served breakfast in my room this morning and have been confined to quarters all day. It is now early afternoon.

I have spent the time reviewing the notes I made last night and considering the proposals which were presented to us yesterday. My impressions at the moment are as follows:

The enthusiasm we all shared yesterday has now diminished. (At least mine has.) The old suspicion and skepticism have returned and today I find myself preoccupied with the subject of Chinese motives.

Chen claims that his people have learned from the past and are now prepared to abandon much of their Communist dogma (the party line described to us in our classes) in order to create an enlightened and enduring global state. "We have been given a blank sheet of paper," he said. "We have the whole of human history to guide us and no one opposing us so there can be no excuse for failure. We must produce nothing less than a new genesis for mankind."

These are fine sentiments, and I accept them from Chen. But I find it difficult to believe that he speaks for the Chinese leadership in this. I sincerely doubt that they are prepared to surrender all that he has offered.

Yet Chen speaks from a position of authority here, a position granted him by that same leadership. What then is the truth? Is Chen deceiving us? Is he himself being manipulated? I have no way to answer these questions.

The system he described to us is an amalgam containing elements drawn from many pre-war systems. The basic structure—six autonomous continental states joined in a global federation—is much like the structure of pre-war China. Aside from this point, however, the entire system seems more western than eastern in character.

The continental states are to be democracies, with the leadership chosen in free elections. Vast, capitalistic private sectors are to be created because, in Chen's words: "Private capitalism clearly produces goods and services more efficiently than does government." (Is this really the new view of the Chinese leadership?)

There are, of course, socialistic elements included as well. Health care is to be state administered, as is all scientific research and development. Education is to be entirely public. This is necessary, Chen explained, because education is the key to the most fundamental of his proposals—wage regulation.

In order to direct society's efforts along desirable productive paths, all wages are to be strictly regulated. All work in both public and private sectors will be compensated at rates which reflect two fundamental standards: first, the social benefit produced by the work and, second, the level of education required to perform the work. The highest wages will be paid to highly educated men and women whose work directly benefits society— medical professionals, scientists, engineers, educators and so on. Admission to the schools and universities which prepare students for these opportunities will be awarded strictly on the basis of merit.

On the surface, this part of Chen's program seems unremarkable. In China (and in the Soviet Union a half century ago) similar inducements were offered to gifted students for the same reasons. And government always determined wage rates. What is different here, however, is that a capitalistic private sector is proposed and the predetermined wage rates have been extended to include private sector jobs. An employment market is thus created in which government and private sector employers will compete for employees. Neither is permitted to offer higher wages, so both are obliged instead to offer more attractive working conditions and other non-monetary incentives in order to attract the best workers.

Chen seemed very pleased with himself as he explained all this. I can summarize his presentation as follows:

"You can see what it accomplishes. Every worker is encouraged to excel, while every employer—including government—is compelled to respect the workers. The system will succeed because it is based on economic reality rather than ideology."

Chen contends that our pre-war systems failed because

131

they were too theoretical, too unrealistic. Communism destroyed individual incentives and produced economic inertia. Capitalism made a god of self-interest and failed to protect itself against the destructive implications of that theology.

There may be merit in all of this, but again, I cannot believe the Chinese hierarchy is prepared to conduct such quasi-democratic social experimentation. I have asked myself, How would the American leadership behave if our positions were reversed? Would we be so magnanimous? I don't believe so.

There are other interesting aspects of the program outlined yesterday. Income taxes, for instance, are to be completely eliminated. This is necessary, Chen explained, for two reasons: First, income taxation would distort the regulated wage structure and this cannot be permitted; wages at all levels must remain absolute, accurately reflecting the standards applied in determining them. Second, no income tax is equitable; flat rate taxes are regressive, and graduated taxes destroy incentives.

Only three taxes are therefore to be employed: (1) a sales tax, with necessary commodities bearing the smallest burden (basic foods will be exempt) and luxury products and services (automobiles, restaurant meals, etc.) paying the highest rates; (2) use taxes to be levied on automobiles, television, etc.; (3) investment income taxes levied on a graduated scale.

I don't pretend to be a sociologist or an economist, but on the whole these proposals (along with the additional details contained in my notes of last night) seem doomed to failure. They are much further removed from the pre-war Chinese system than I would have anticipated, but they are also far removed from pre-war western systems. I fear they will satisfy no one. They do appear to represent a legitimate attempt to provide humanity with the new genesis of which Chen speaks and that is seductive. But appearances can be deceiving.

It is clear that a lengthy transition period would be required before very much of this could be put into practice. During that transition, some form of cooperation will be required of me and my fellow inmates. So the old questions must now be asked again. Should we cooperate in whatever they are planning to ask of us? Do they really intend to implement Chen's new genesis, or is Chen's program merely a carrot he is dangling before us to invite our collaboration?

My newsman's instincts are useless to me on this. I have no information, no hard evidence to support any conclusion.

Finally, there is the subject of the language. The last thing Chen told us yesterday was that English is to be adopted as the new global language. Why? Are we supposed to accept this as a grand concession which confirms their sincerity, a proof that they don't intend to impose their will (or their language) on the world. Chen claims there is logic in the choice. English has long been the global language of commerce and is understood by more people than any other single tongue. Perhaps this is true, but it seems suspiciously convenient.

I have a great many questions to put to Chen when I am granted an interview.

Friday, October 29

I met with Chen this morning. It was in the great hall and we were alone except for Ho-ting, who kept his distance and displayed little interest in our conversation.

Chen seemed very tired, which prompted me to approach him somewhat more gently than I had intended. But I nevertheless conducted what could properly be characterized as an interrogation. He received my attacks with a kind of weary good humor. (I suppose the six who preceded me must have asked many of the same questions and displayed similar skepticism.)

On the fundamental question of whether the program he had presented to us was legitimate, I received no satisfaction.

"I am what I appear to be, David," he said. "No more, no less. If you aren't yet convinced of my sincerity, there is nothing I can say now to persuade you."

"It's not your sincerity that concerns me," I said. "It's the sincerity of your superiors. I respect you, Chen, but I find it hard to believe that you speak for China."

He frowned at this and said, "You speak of respect, then accuse me of being a puppet. I find that curious. In my culture we do not respect puppets."

When I raised the language question, he responded, "I suppose I could show you photographs taken at various sites around the globe which you would undoubtedly recognize. You could see then that the street markers and the billboards and the signs on the busses are now in English. But would you believe the photos have not been altered? Really, David, what proof can I

133

possibly offer you?"

After several more futile attempts to resolve my basic doubts I finally asked what he wanted to talk about. He said he wished to discuss his program.

He produced a printed summary of the presentation he had delivered to us and handed it to me, saying, "It cannot be perfect, nothing is. So I am anxious for your comments."

We proceeded down the list, reviewing each point in turn. As we did the fatigue seemed to melt away from him. He sat up straighter, his voice grew stronger, his eyes brightened. The energy he displayed was remarkable; his enthusiasm was unquestionably genuine.

It was during this discussion that I realized how little real attention I had devoted to the study of Chen's plan. I had been preoccupied with my suspicions and had hardly considered the possibility that these proposals might be worthy of realistic evaluation. As a result, I had little criticism to offer. The few superficial comments I did manage were rebutted easily and on the whole I'm certain he was disappointed with my contributions. There were, however, two occasions when my questions evoked impassioned responses.

The first question related to the subject of private sector capitalism. Chen's plan attempts to channel society's ablest individuals into science, medicine and education. The reason for this is self-evident. But the plan also recognizes the fact that the needs of commerce must be served. In Chen's own words, "Capitalism invigorates society." So the plan attempts to encourage innovation and risk taking by providing an alternate track to those "who fail to qualify academically for the most desirable positions, or who prefer the risks of business to the rewards of public service." It accomplishes this by permitting successful capitalists to accumulate profits. The wages they will be permitted to pay themselves, even in businesses they control, will be strictly regulated, and they will be lower than the wages paid to highly educated public servants. But the accumulation of profits will enable them to amass net incomes which may exceed even those of the highest paid public sector professionals.

As we reviewed this element of Chen's plan, an obvious objection suggested itself to me. "Your purpose here is clear," I said. "But you can't rescind the laws of human nature. Even if these capitalists are prevented from flaunting their wealth, they will still possess it. Wealth is power and ultimately that power *will overwhelm all your good intentions. It will destroy your system as it destroyed ours."*

Chen nodded appreciatively at this and said, "You express the typical views of an occidental, David. You speak as your western experience instructs. But men are not always as venal as you suggest. Your fear was warranted in your pre-war environment, but in other environments human beings are capable of far more enlightened behavior. The pre-war West was philosophically barren and cynical. It lacked a clearly defined cultural imperative. When you say that 'wealth is power' you confirm this fact. And you ignore the existence of more humane philosophies. In the world we intend to build, power will not spring from wealth. It will spring instead from the fertile soil of the culture. It will not be expressed in economic terms, but in terms of honor and accomplishment and the respect of other men. No individual will be able to purchase it but every individual will be granted the opportunity to earn it."

I think he honestly believes this. Despite his education and experience, I'm afraid he is at heart a hopeless romantic.

The second objection to which Chen reacted strongly was not really an objection at all. It was merely an aside, an offhand comment. We were near the end of our review of his plans when I told him I was uncomfortable with the whole idea of utopian dreams. "They seem always doomed to failure," I said. "You aren't the first and you won't be the last to make this attempt, but I'm afraid perfect human social systems are quite simply impossible."

Chen responded, "None of us is really comfortable with the idea of utopia, David. We are only comfortable with things we understand, and by definition utopia—perfection—is beyond our understanding. We can comprehend the process by which we hope to move toward perfection, but the ultimate goal, perfection itself, is inconceivable. You see this expressed in our religious beliefs, especially in our concepts of the next life. Has it occurred to you that none of the world's religions are ever specific in their descriptions of heaven? They are often specific with regard to the other extreme, they describe hell in horrifying detail. But the idea of heaven is incomprehensible, so we make no real attempt to describe it. Instead, we content ourselves with statements such as, 'It is more beautiful than anything we can imagine.' Earthly utopias are equally difficult to conceive. We cannot imagine them because their existence would be too terrible. Think of it! A perfect society. A world where nothing remained to be discovered or accomplished. All questions answered, all needs satisfied, all knowledge obtained."

He paused, apparently expecting some reaction.

"It would be the end of everything," I said. "There would be no place for man in such a world."

"Exactly! And yet we must pursue the quest. It is our primary reason for being."

In practical terms I must consider this meeting with Chen, which lasted perhaps an hour, a failure. He answered none of my questions directly and resolved none of my doubts. And I provided him with little of what he had hoped to gain from me. Yet I am encouraged. I am left with an impression, however vague, of increasing comfort (no other word accurately describes my feelings). Slowly, steadily, I am growing comfortable—with him and with the idea of his new world. Should I resist these feelings? Are they the first step toward collaboration with the enemy?

Tonight I intend to study Chen's plans until I understand them as well as he does.

Wednesday, November 3

It has now been five days since Chen first presented his plans to us and our routine continues unchanged. First, we meet together in the great hall for a group discussion. Then we are confined to quarters for two days while Chen conducts his individual interviews, after which we meet together again and the cycle repeats. Today was our third group meeting. It was shorter this time and definitely less enthusiastic than the first two. The reason for this is obvious. We are tired of the repetition and anxious to know what they intend to ask of us.

Virtually everything that was discussed today has appeared in my earlier notes so I have little to record. There is, however, one item of interest.

At one point this morning Billy Dupree, our young musician, asked Chen what status the Arts would enjoy under the new federation. The question was greeted with sarcastic laughter, and Grant said loudly, "I'm afraid rock music isn't art, Billy."

Chen himself laughed at this, then looked at Grant and said, "I quite agree, Mr. Grant, most rock music is not art. But then, neither are your films." More laughter, louder this time. Grant's face reddened.

"But Mr. Dupree's question did not concern rock music," Chen said, looking at Billy. "Did it Mr. Dupree? Shall I tell them or would you prefer the honor?"

At this, Billy's face reddened and he mumbled something incoherent. Recognizing his discomfort, Chen spoke for him.

It seems our Billy wasn't always a rocker. Before he took up smashing guitars for profit he was an accomplished classical pianist/composer/conductor. Billy Dupree is a Juilliard graduate!

"In answer to your question," Chen assured Billy, "Art and science are the only enduring monuments produced by any society; all the rest is mere social mechanics. So they will be afforded the highest possible status and it will never again be necessary for you to abandon the music you love in order to earn a living."

Friday, November 5

We have finally been told why we are here and what they want from us.

As we guessed weeks ago, celebrity is our common bond. The Chinese have selected us because we were all well-known before the war and, more to the point, well-liked and/or respected by the public. For this reason, Chen explained, we are ideal spokesmen for the new federation.

We have each been offered a position in the North American Continental Administration. We were given few details today but the basic assignments are as follows:

Eugene Palitz is to participate in the organization of the North American Health Agency. His background is in research and he was assured that eventually he would be allowed to return to that work, but his pre-war prominence makes him more valuable now in a more public capacity.

Dr. Summerland will be assigned to the Research and Development Agency. Chen did not describe his public duties.

Wiedemier is to function as a kind of general spokesman

for science and to promote science as a career choice.

Jack Fogarty, the former editor of "Whistleblower" magazine, will put together a new magazine to be called "North America."

All the rest have been assigned to a new continental media center under construction at Sacramento.

Roger Simone will write television scripts.

Grant and Sutton will act in the plays Simone writes.

Billy Dupree will compose music for television.

The remaining four will form the nucleus of a new North American News Agency.

I am to anchor a nightly newscast, with Sandiman and our attorney, Pete Bell, doing field reports. Kowalski will report on sports. (This has us all baffled. What sports? As far as we know, there won't be anything for Kowalski to report!)

Chen and his guards left us alone in the great hall most of the day to decide on our response. There was little disagreement. None of us is willing to commit yet—there are still a number of question which must be answered—but we are all tending toward the same conclusion. We have been invited inside the Chinese hierarchy and if they are willing to provide us the freedom they are promising in the conduct of these jobs, we feel we must accept them. With regard to this decision, Chen has stressed the distinction between cooperation and collaboration. We accept neither of these characterizations. In our discussions today we substituted the word "infiltration."

EIGHTEEN

It was finally beginning. After two days of planning, two hours in the trucks and an hour-long march, the young captain's effort would soon be rewarded. He was about to fight his first battle.

He smiled as he bent over the folding table upon which were arrayed the maps and reconnaissance photos of the target area. He had been cautious as he prepared the assault. His troops had dismounted the trucks miles beyond the perimeter they had now established and marched here in silence so their approach would not be detected. Some might say such caution was unnecessary—this was a simple operation. But these bandits were clever and the first rule of warfare was "never underestimate the enemy." In his first engagement, the young captain was determined to make no mistakes, certainly none as foolish as that. He would win victory today and it would be the first of many victories, the beginning of a brilliant career.

A lieutenant appeared at his side and saluted stiffly. "All is ready, Captain."

"Is Hua's squad in position?" The captain pointed to a ridge line on the map, running north and south along the eastern boundary of the target area.

"Yes, sir. Everyone is in position."

"Then let us proceed, Lieutenant. Radio the helicopters."

The lieutenant hurried off and the captain looked out across the strange, alien landscape that confronted him. He had never before seen anything quite like the McKenzie lava fields. Except for the few stunted trees scattered across its barren surface, it resembled the ruined city of San Francisco; it did not look natural. Overhead, slate grey clouds drifted slowly and the pines swayed in a frigid breeze. Soon, he thought, it would begin snowing.

He could hardly imagine a more desolate, forbidding place. He shivered and pulled his collar up around his neck. Then he checked the map one final time and looked left and right along the line of his troops. Everything was ready. In moments the

139

helicopters would arrive and the assault would begin.

"Strange place to hide, isn't it, Sir?" The lieutenant had returned.

Without looking at him, the captain said solemnly, "A stranger place to live. They've been here for two years, do you realize that? It seems impossible."

The lieutenant nodded. "It's almost as though they wanted to deny that they really were alive. Nothing really lives here. Look at the trees. They're like old men, grey and bent. They seem more dead than alive."

"Make no mistake," the captain said. "These bandits are very much alive. And they are dangerous."

The lieutenant started to say something further, but the captain held up a hand for silence. Then he cocked his head to the side, listening. In the distance he heard the faint whine of engines, accompanied by the dull thump-thump of rotor blades.

"Collect the maps," the captain barked. "I want to move as soon as the helicopters report the target in sight. And I want the radio here with me."

A minute later, three helicopters passed overhead at an altitude of two hundred feet and moved out over the lava field, tracking directly toward the north McKenzie camp.

A half mile from the target they descended to a hundred and fifty feet, then a hundred. On the ridges a mile to the east and north, and from behind a low hill to the south, three hundred Chinese troops began to advance, picking their way slowly over the volcanic rubble.

The helicopters bore in, strafing the target with machine guns. Then, directly over the camp they released their bombs. Black canisters tumbled through the air and exploded on striking the ground. A grey-brown fog enveloped the tiny village.

It was more than a half hour before the first of the soldiers reached the McKenzie camp. Their gas masks and camouflage uniforms gave them an otherworldly appearance, like grotesque, two-legged insects. Most of the chemical fog had dissipated by then, although some lingered in the low places, swirling around the soldier's feet as they passed through it.

"They must have died in their shelters," the lieutenant said to the captain. "They didn't fire a shot!"

The captain shook his head. "This was too easy. Much too easy. Check the shelters. That one there, Private! Corporal, you take that one!"

One by one the soldiers entered the shelters. One by one they returned, each reporting the same thing—the shelters were empty.

"Lieutenant, come here!" The captain was standing by the entrance to Anderson's house. "This looks like the headquarters." He pointed at the door and waited impatiently as the lieutenant pulled it open and disappeared inside.

On a hilltop nearly two miles distant, three figures crouched on a rocky bluff, observing through high-power field glasses.

Anderson turned to Devin and said, "I hate admit it but the arrogant bastard was dead right."

Devin lowered his glasses and nodded. "He knows his business. There's no more doubt about his loyalty, that's for sure."

"We'd all be down there if he hadn't warned us," Zachary agreed.

Anderson raised his glasses and continued his observations. The last of the soldiers had now reached the camp and the three helicopters, which had flown off to the west after their initial attack, were back, circling at low altitude a few hundred yards from the camp.

Devin placed a hand on Anderson's arm. "We'd better get moving. Those choppers are going to start looking for us any minute."

Anderson shook him off. "Just a second," he said. "I want to see this."

"See what?" Devin raised his glasses just in time to learn what Anderson had meant.

Most of the Chinese troops were gathered around the perimeter of the camp. Only a few were in the central courtyard. Of these, two stood at the entrance to Anderson's shelter. As Devin watched, one threw open the door and went in. A moment later, a brilliant flash of orange flame erupted from the doorway throwing the second soldier backward like a rag doll. The stone roof of the shelter heaved upward and collapsed in on itself. Black smoke burst from the door and billowed skyward from the crater where the roof had been. Several seconds later the three observers heard the sound of the explosion.

Devin lowered his glasses slowly and glared at Anderson.

The clan leader smiled back at him. "I had to leave them

something to remember us by."

Zachary, in obvious disgust, said, "But John told us . . ."

"The hell with John," Anderson snarled. "Dammit, this is war! And regardless of what John says, I'm going to fight."

NINETEEN

Sacramento. For David Craighill, the prospect of seeing the California capital again brought back a flood of memories. Before the war his job had taken him to Sacramento frequently and he had known it well. He was there in the final days before the Chinese victory and heard the surrender announcement in Sacramento. He saw the Chinese soldiers march into the city.

He recalled sitting for a long while that final afternoon, waiting and watching from a second-floor window of the hotel where the American Disaster Authority had billeted him. At first there had been only Americans in the streets, walking very quickly and nervously or very slowly with their heads bowed. Then the Chinese column had rumbled into view—foot soldiers, trucks, tanks, APCs, mobile rocket launchers. At its head was a single Chinese officer, standing in the front of a large open truck, straight-armed with his hands resting on the top of the windshield frame. He was lean and hard-looking, and even though he remained stiff and motionless as the truck rolled by, he somehow managed to convey an impression of strutting egotism. The soldiers who followed immediately behind seemed to reflect the character of their leader. They too were grim and humorless, precise and intense. They all had rifles slung over their shoulders at exactly the same angle and they marched stiffly.

Further back in the column however, a more relaxed attitude prevailed. The soldiers riding the tanks seemed to be enjoying themselves. Almost without exception they were smiling and talking and pointing to sights along the way. Craighill recognized immediately what this signified. The casual, cocky assurance displayed by the tank crews was a reflection of their status—it was the arrogance of armor. Because they rode the tanks, these soldiers felt superior, impregnable. There was a lesson in this fact which the newsman had filed away for future reference then and remembered now: The Chinese worker's paradise these soldiers represented had not yet begun to purge itself of class distinctions.

But the thing Craighill remembered most about that day was neither the strutting leader, nor the grim foot soldiers, nor the arrogant tank crews. It was a young Chinese private who passed by in the back of an open truck near the end of the column. It was a large truck, but the soldier was its only cargo. He was standing with his elbows hooked over the truck's wooden sideboard. As he approached, his eyes met Craighill's and the newsman found himself unable to look away. Something in the young conqueror's expression was familiar. Craighill struggled to identify it and finally succeeded. The soldier's eyes conveyed the same lonely desperation he had seen recently in the eyes of many Americans. The soldier was frightened. He was only a boy, thousands of miles from home and caught up in something he didn't understand.

They watched each other as the truck approached and as it moved past. Directly in front of the hotel, the soldier waved to him. There was no taint of ideology in the gesture, no identification of oppressor or oppressed. It was merely one victim, sharing a moment of common pain with a fellow victim. They were both trapped by events and standing on the threshold of changes too enormous for either of them to fully comprehend.

Craighill smiled and waved back.

Those were some of his memories of Sacramento. There were others.

In the last days before the Chinese conquest, the American military had decided not to make the city a battleground. It was awash in civilian refugees and the outcome was by that time inevitable. Further fighting, they concluded, could only produce unnecessary destruction and bloodshed. So Sacramento was delivered to the Chinese intact, and they had quickly transformed it into a gigantic refugee processing center. Craighill's most vivid memories were of the city as it had been then.

The crowds were unimaginable, the lines interminable. The city had been divided into nine geographical units, each a completely separate self-contained camp. The key factor determining the unit to which each American applicant was assigned had been "former occupation."

The largest of the nine units housed all those whose former occupations had been in some form of skilled or unskilled manual labor. These included factory workers, carpenters, bricklayers, mechanics, electricians and so on. The Americans referred to this as the blue collar camp and it was apparent that the Chinese had assigned it and the agricultural camp their highest priority. The

144

other units included engineering and technical, pure sciences, education, medical, administrative and sub-administrative (clerical). These were Craighill's characterizations. Exactly what the Chinese called them, and exactly how each applicant's assignment was determined, only the Chinese knew.

There was a final, ninth camp, to which Craighill himself had been assigned. These were the "Others," the misfits, those whose former skills were unnecessary in the new Chinese world. They were attorneys, accountants, salesmen, clergymen, entertainers, athletes, politicians and anyone whose occupation had been unique to a decadent, capitalistic society. Morale in this camp was extremely low. Craighill distinctly recalled the fear and uncertainty that haunted its occupants. They were, it seemed to them, dangerous to the Chinese, or at least potentially dangerous. Almost without exception the Others had been successful in the old world. Most had tasted relative wealth and influence. A large number had enjoyed a degree of celebrity. In general, they had lost more than the average American and were better equipped to become the leaders of any resistance that might develop. For these reasons, they half expected to be lined up against a wall and shot.

Apparently, however, the Chinese did not share these concerns. For the most part the Others were treated with unexpected kindness and consideration. They were among the last to be processed out of Sacramento, but one by one their assignments finally did arrive. Most, including Craighill, were sent to agricultural "stoop labor" camps.

Craighill recalled one thing in particular about this period—his persistent and futile attempts to gain some information about his family. Before the Chinese victory he had pursued this search tirelessly with the American authorities, without success. During the long, tedious months in Chinese Sacramento he renewed these efforts. At first his requests were met with excuses and indifference, but later he had found cause for encouragement. Family reunification was being pursued diligently, he was told. Toward the end, however, he had become convinced that these assurances were illusory. "Further inquiries are pointless," a sympathetic clerk had finally admitted. "We are doing our best, but there are nearly eighty million requests exactly like yours. The probability of success is not high."

In the two years since that time, he had never completely given up hope. But he had gradually resigned himself to the reality of the situation. In all probability Anne and the boys were lost to

145

him forever, and in his mind he would always associate that loss with Sacramento.

His last memory of the city was of the bus ride from the processing barracks to his first farm camp. The route toward I-5 for the trip north had taken them through the center of the downtown area, and the city he saw then bore little resemblance to the city he had known before. The buildings were unchanged, but the streets were nearly deserted. There were a few pedestrians, a few bicyclists and a few vehicles, mostly trucks and busses, but the bustling vitality of pre-war Sacramento and the huge crowds and confusion of the months just before and after the Chinese occupation had vanished completely. The storefront signs, once so bright and vibrant with flashing color, were now dark. Many of the stores stood empty and others, which the signs mutely identified as restaurants or women's wear shops or gift boutiques, now served as warehouses or offices. Even the traffic lights had been turned off. An eerie quiet had settled over the town. Despite the fact that he was seeing it on a warm spring day, a cold and forbidding midwinter mood gripped the city, a dormant feeling, as though it was suspended halfway between life and death.

He had been glad to escape. If this was what the new Chinese urban world promised, he wanted no part of it. Better to pass his remaining days surrounded by sunshine and fresh air, even if that meant accepting a lifetime of labor in the camps.

He never wanted to see Sacramento again.

And now he was returning.

"It is a beautiful city," Chen had assured him at their last interview. "You will be pleased, David. I am certain of that."

He hoped that the old man was right.

The trip provided him with a number of conflicting signs. The aircraft, a Boeing 767, had been an immaculate example of pre-war western luxury. He had expected a military transport or one of the cramped and uncomfortable Chinese domestic airliners. The Boeing was an unexpected surprise. There were no refreshments served and no flight attendants, but on a flight that lasted less than an hour that hardly mattered. On the whole he was greatly encouraged.

The Sacramento air terminal had also presented a surprisingly western look. It was not busy but it was clean. And all the signs were working! The coffee shop was even open for business.

146

When they boarded their ground transportation, however, things began to deteriorate rapidly. It was a school bus, still painted orange. A cursory attempt had been made to mask its pre-war identity but the words "Yolo County Schools" were still faintly visible on its flanks. Its engine clattered ominously and it trailed a plume of blue smoke as it bounced and rattled its way southward toward the city. Some of the bouncing was due to the condition of the bus, the rest to the condition of the road. Craighill wondered how this main route could have fallen into such disrepair in just two years.

"During the war," Chen explained, "Travis Air Base was destroyed and the U.S. military moved their operations to the civilian field. There was much fighting in the area, and tanks and heavy equipment used this road. It will be repaired eventually, but not until more urgent needs have been met. For now, it is still . . ." At that moment, the bus hit a large pothole and both men were launched to an altitude of three or four inches above their seats, each landing with a thump. "Serviceable!" Chen concluded, laughing. "Priorities, David. It is all a matter of priorities."

There were sixteen aboard the bus, not counting the driver—Craighill and the other seven members of the new media team, along with Chen and seven guards. To Craighill, this level of security was troubling. His group had made it clear that their work could not proceed if they were to be kept under constant scrutiny, and they had been promised substantial freedom in the conduct of their new jobs. Had Chen already withdrawn this promise? Or was he merely observing some standing order regarding the transport of prisoners? There was no need to ask these questions now; he would know the answers soon enough.

The condition of the road improved as they approached the city. The bus ceased its pitching and bucking and they were able to relax and observe the roadside scenery. The northern suburbs seemed deserted, but after they crossed the American River, Craighill noted with surprise that there was a fair amount of street traffic and the traffic lights were working. Pedestrians, mostly Americans, were everywhere, not in the numbers he would have seen pre-war, but in far greater numbers than he had seen the last time he passed this way. There were many trucks and busses and a few cars. And there were hundreds of bicycles. The people looked reasonably content, well fed and well dressed. Their attire was probably the thing that most surprised him. It seemed typically western. Casual clothing predominated, and much of it was quite

147

colorful.

Chen offered no comment on any of this. He seemed content to allow his charges to form their own opinions.

When they left I-5 and entered the city center, Craighill received a somewhat less positive impression. Here again, the traffic lights were working. So were the shop signs. And there was even more traffic, of every kind; the city bustled with activity. But at many of the downtown intersections large banners were displayed. Some were stretched across the faces of buildings; others spanned the streets: ONE PEOPLE, ONE WORLD, one announced. Another, WHAT EACH OF US DOES ENRICHES US ALL. Still another, FREEDOM THROUGH EQUALITY. One said simply, "NEVER AGAIN."

To Craighill, these banners conveyed a very distasteful message and a totalitarian mentality. They represented everything he had hated in the pre-war Communist world, and he was certain that these old, discredited techniques, hauled out of mothballs, dusted off and translated into English, could not possibly succeed here. They hadn't really succeeded in China in 1949, where the population was illiterate and poverty-stricken; they were even less appropriate in the twenty-first century United States. It was inconceivable that American citizens, accustomed to affluence, freedom of choice and freedom of expression could find satisfaction in a bicycle, a new sport shirt and a slogan.

He confronted Chen with this opinion.

"You are overlooking a great many things," Chen said patiently. "First, the America you recall had ceased to exist long before we Chinese arrived. It had been replaced by anarchy and disorder. You were a nation of refugees, confused and hungry. We brought order. I admit that slogans are not a permanent substitute for all that you have lost, but they are part of the ultimate solution. They are a beginning. Look around you, David. The people are no longer confused. They are busy and they are beginning to feel that they have purpose. They are even learning to smile again."

The bus stopped at an intersection as Chen concluded this statement and Craighill saw a young woman standing at the street corner beside them. A small boy was at her side, holding her hand. The child looked up at her and giggled about something and she smiled back.

Could Chen be right? Except for the banners, the scene Craighill was witnessing could be taking place ten years ago on this same corner. But he quickly rejected the notion. It meant nothing, he realized. The feeling between a mother and child was beyond ideology. Their apparent happiness at this moment had nothing to do with the mother's feelings about the Chinese presence.

"Are you claiming that success is already at hand?" Craighill asked. "Do you really believe that these people have already discarded their former identity?"

Chen replied, "I am saying that as time passes there will be fewer and fewer problems. They will realize that it is their society they are building. Theirs, David, not mine. That process is already beginning. You see?" He waved a hand, indicating the streets around them. "How few police?"

Craighill had to admit that there were few police in sight. And no military. In all, this new Sacramento had an appearance of settled normalcy about it. And yet he was not convinced. He imagined a street corner in Paris might have looked much the same on a typical afternoon during the German occupation of World War II.

"Have all the restrictions been lifted?" Craighill asked. "At the relocation camps and on the prison farms we were all confined to barracks in the evening."

Chen did not answer. He was busily consulting a list he was carrying. The bus was rolling to a stop in front of a building that had formerly been a large midtown hotel.

Chen rose. "Mr. Grant and Mr. Sutton," he announced. "Please take your belongings. These are your new quarters."

Grant and Sutton left the bus in the company of two guards.

At subsequent stops, each within four blocks of the first hotel, this process was repeated. Each time, two more graduates of Chen's academy were led away by two guards. At the forth stop, however, only Simone was dismissed. He left with a single guard. Chen and Craighill were left alone on the bus.

The newsman, who had started to get up with Simone, sat back down at Chen's instruction and eyed the old man curiously. "Have I been singled out for special consideration?"

"I have arranged a surprise for you," Chen replied. "And I wish to present it in person."

Several blocks farther on, they arrived at their destination. Craighill recognized the building. Not far from the Capitol, it had once been a lavish, luxury condominium. It looked neglected now; the paint on the front door was peeling and the shrubbery was ragged and overgrown. But it was nevertheless a palace compared to the barracks he had called home for the past two years.

He nodded appreciatively. "You're trying to bribe me, Chen," he said smiling.

Chen led the way through the lobby to the elevators. Craighill noted without comment that the building entrance was unguarded. They boarded an elevator and a minute later stepped out on the twelfth floor. A short distance down the corridor, Chen paused and produced a key, which he handed to Craighill.

"Your new home," he said, pointing to a door.

The apartment was modestly but attractively furnished. Directly opposite the door was a glass wall with a balcony beyond, overlooking a grassy park.

Craighill walked to the glass and gazed out at the view. Without turning, he said, "It's lovely, Chen. I'd almost forgotten that places like this existed."

"Then you are pleased?"

Craighill turned and faced him. "Yes, of course. Pleased and very surprised. Thank you."

Chen smiled. "But this is not the surprise, David. This is merely your apartment."

"No? Well—what then?"

From behind him, Craighill heard the sound of soft footsteps on the carpet. Chen nodded in their direction and Craighill turned.

"Hello, Pug."

For a moment David Craighill was stunned into total immobility. He felt the strength drain from his body. His eyes filled with tears and he reached out and placed his hand on a chair to steady himself.

"Annie?" His voice was barely audible, a whisper. "Oh God, Annie, is it really you?"

He moved toward her clumsily; his whole body trembling. She stepped toward him. Then, for an instant, both of them stopped, inches apart, afraid to touch each other, afraid that what they were seeing wasn't real, was only a mirage. Then he threw his arms around her and the tears flowed in great shuddering bursts.

"I thought you were dead. I thought . . ."

"I know, Pug," she said, pressing herself against him. "I know."

"I looked for you. I drove the authorities crazy."

"I looked for you too. For so long"

150

Neither of them noticed Chen's departure. Neither heard the door as he closed it softly behind him.

TWENTY

About an hour after Anderson, Zachary and Devin fled the lookout from which they had observed the Chinese attack, they heard the first of the jets.

All three men stopped and looked toward the sound. Devin cursed under his breath.

"There!" Zachary pointed. His pilot's eyes were the first to find the target, moving almost directly toward them. "Six or eight miles, at about two thousand feet."

Devin raised his binoculars while his companions waited.

"Well?" Anderson asked anxiously.

"Shit!" Devin spat, letting the glasses drop to his chest. "We have to find cover. Fast!"

"The trees!" Anderson yelled, and started down the rocky slope toward a stand of pines fifty yards away.

But Devin shouted after him, "Not the trees, Tom! We have to get under something solid." He pointed. "That overhang. Over there!"

Devin and Zachary scrambled across the steep hillside to the spot Devin had indicated, under a large rock shelf. A moment later, Anderson joined them.

They waited, listening to the whine of the approaching engines. Anderson fidgeted impatiently. Zachary asked Devin, "What the hell is it, Ben?" He had rarely seen the ex-Marine so concerned and Devin's concern worried him.

"A Bat," Devin replied. "I didn't know they were any stationed near here. I haven't seen one since the war. Not one, damn it! DAMN IT!"

The sound was growing louder, the aircraft was closing. Anderson leaned out and peered up, hoping to catch sight of it. Devin grabbed his collar and pulled him back roughly.

"Damn it!" the clan leader snarled, glaring angrily at Devin.

"Sorry, Tom, but that was necessary. If your boot was exposed or even a gloved hand, he might not see it. But he'd sure as hell see your face. Any exposed skin—you might as well send up a flare!"

"You're serious?" Anderson looked suddenly contrite. "I didn't know."

"Its sensors detect heat. If it knows where to look it can find a single spent rifle cartridge at a range of ten miles. It can't see near as well scanning a wide area, but it's still damned effective."

The Bat was very close now. The whine of the jets peaked, then dropped in pitch. The sound began to diminish as the aircraft moved away. Devin clambered from the hiding place, stood up slowly and watched as it continued on its southward course.

"It sees infrared," he said, turning to face Zachary and Anderson. "But it can be evaded."

Anderson asked. "Did we evade it just now? Do you think it saw us?"

Devin looked at the aircraft. "It isn't turning," he said hopefully. "But I don't know. There's no way to know."

Zachary looked over Devin's shoulder at the retreating plane. "It's going south, Ben. It's heading straight toward Sparks Lake."

Devin's eyes met Zachary's. "I know. But Cox and the rest should have reached the shelter by now. If they stay inside, they'll be all right."

"Do you really think so?"

"Yes," Devin said. "I really think so." But he could see that he had not convinced Zachary.

When Zachary first delivered John's warning of the impending Chinese anti-guerrilla campaign, the north and south McKenzie clans quickly met to plan their strategy. There were fifty-five men, women and children in the two camps, but only thirty-seven adults; so they were going to be vastly outnumbered. In any event, the children had to be protected, and this made defense impossible. Escape was the only reasonable option. But escape to where?

They couldn't go north. John's intelligence suggested that the Chinese would be there too, searching for the rebel groups near Mt. Hood. They couldn't go west. To the west was the Willamette Valley with its closely guarded prison farms and ten thousand Chinese soldiers. To the east there was only barren, open desert, stretching for hundreds of miles. And if they went to the southern Cascades, they would run the risk of leading their pursuers to the many groups already hiding there.

Only one sanctuary was available—California! John was convinced that the clans there were unknown to the Chinese. The journey would be difficult, requiring a march of over three hundred miles. Zachary had just made the trip, but he had been very lucky with the weather. It was now mid-November; nighttime temperatures in the high country could dip well below zero and the heavy snows that came every year were already overdue. It would be hard for all of them, especially hard for the children, but they had no choice.

There were too many of them to travel as a single unit. A party of fifty-five would be slow, easy to track and easy for the Chinese to spot from the air. So they decided to split into five squads, three from the northern clan and two from the smaller southern clan. They planned their escape with great care.

They reasoned that the Chinese would approach by road rather than by air because it would be too difficult for helicopters to land troops on the lava field. The garrison at Redmond was small, so they wouldn't come from there; they would come instead from the west, up Route 20 from Corvallis or Route 126 from Eugene, or both. They would attack both camps from the north, coming at the northern camp from Route 20, the southern camp from Route 242. No other approaches were possible.

The escape routes were self-evident. The two southern squads would head south and west toward the Diamond Peak Wilderness, maintaining a minimum five-mile separation until they had traveled at least seventy-five miles. Only then would they join up and travel the rest of the way together. The northern squads would begin their journey to the east, turning south along the eastern slopes of the Three Sisters Mountains to the shelter at Sparks Lake. Then, on the morning of the second day, they would separate and fan out to the south and east. They would rendezvous far to the south, near Sugarpine Mountain, before continuing on to California.

With these plans established, they had abandoned their homes at daybreak, just seven hours before the Chinese attack.

The northern clan cleared the lava field at 9:00 a.m. and headed south. Zachary, Anderson and Devin remained behind—to confirm the predicted attack, to see if the Chinese were pursuing them and, if necessary, to lead any pursuit away from the rest of the clan. They saw the attack and saw also that following the attack

154

the Chinese mounted no immediate pursuit. The three observers had been puzzled by this at first, but finally guessed correctly that Anderson's booby trap must have killed or badly injured the strike force commander. An incredible stroke of luck! It provided them exactly what they needed most—time. Time to move south. Time to get away clean. They were hurrying to tell the others when they saw the Bat.

The sighting of the Bat was completely unexpected and changed everything. It cancelled the advantage they thought they'd gained and cast a shroud of doubt over all their subsequent planning. It instantly skewed the odds in favor of the Chinese.

Had the observation team been detected? They didn't know. And not knowing made it difficult to decide what they should do next. Continue on to Sparks Lake to warn the others? Strike out in another direction in an attempt to lead the Chinese away?

After some discussion, Anderson said firmly, "We have no choice! No one at the lake even knows these Bats exist. We have to warn them. Without that information, they're completely helpless."

There was no argument. They headed for the lake but followed a roundabout course, backtracking twice. They heard jet engines several times but saw no aircraft. It was well past dark when they reached the shelter.

Cox and the others also heard the jets, but they were sure none had passed directly over the narrow canyon in which the shelter was located. That meant that the Bats could not have had line-of-sight, so they could not have seen the shelter. The clan members who had stood sentry duty since the group's arrival at the shelter confirmed this.

"They seemed to be concentrating their search west of here," Jack Norris offered. "West and south, on the far side of the Sisters, over toward . . ." His voice suddenly caught in his throat.

"Over toward the South Clan's escape route," Anderson said, completing his thought.

Norris looked shaken. "Yes," he said numbly. "That's exactly where they were."

Anderson glanced at Devin, who was standing on the far side of the room next to Katie. The ex-Marine nodded. This afternoon, he and Anderson had noticed that the jets seemed to be patrolling the area southwest of the lava fields and they discussed the implications of this development.

155

"We're going to have to change our plans," Anderson said to everyone gathered around him. He dropped to one knee, spread a large map on the dirt floor of the shelter and pointed to their present location. "Here is Sparks Lake. Down through here are the routes we planned to follow tomorrow."

The clan members drew themselves into a tight circle around the map, some kneeling, some standing. All were paying close attention to what Anderson was saying.

"Unfortunately, the members of the South Clan know we planned to follow these routes, and there is now a strong possibility that some of them may have been captured. So those routes must be abandoned." He directed their attention to a different area on the map. "Our new routes will be further east. The country there is more open and there are more roads. Ben and Zack and I discussed these problems and we still believe we will be safer there. Are there any objections? The floor is open for discussion."

There were no objections but there was much discussion. Details of the new routes were decided upon. They would travel well east of the old routes, then south to a rendezvous near Thompson Valley reservoir. When that was settled Devin conducted a brief class in techniques for avoiding Bat detection.

"Caves or rock ledges provide the best protection," he explained. "But there won't be much cover like that where we're going so the next best thing is trees. If a tree is large enough it will screen you from the sensors as long as you keep it between you and the Bat. Get right up against the trunk and when the Bat comes close to you, press your face against the bark. Kiss that tree . . ." Several of the children giggled at this. "And cover the sides of your face with your gloves.

"Now, if you find yourself in the open with no cover, you still have a chance. Find the lowest spot you can—a shallow ditch, a stream bed, anything. Lie in it, face down, and cover yourself with the camouflage blankets you all carry. Make sure to cover your head and stay there until you're absolutely certain the aircraft is gone.

"One final warning: never look at these planes. If you look at them, they will see you. I guarantee it."

One of the children, an eight-year-old boy named Jimmy, said, "It's just like the bombs then, isn't it, Mr. Devin?"

Devin looked at him uncomprehendingly. The boy seemed proud of his observation but Ben had no idea what he meant.

156

"They told us not to look at the bombs when they explode," the boy explained. "This is just like that, isn't it?"

There was no distress or fear in the boy's voice, merely childish curiosity. Two separate facts had come to his attention, and they seemed to be related. He was trying to arrange them in his mind, to see how they fit together. So it was a reasonable question. Yet somehow its matter-of-fact tone chilled Devin to the bone. A child should fear these things! This boy should be terrified by what he had just been told, not merely curious.

"A bomb and a Bat aren't the same," Devin explained. "But they're both very dangerous. They can both kill, so we need to treat them the same. Do you understand, Jimmy?" He wanted to say more. He wanted to say something that would shock the boy back to reality and convince him that nuclear bombs and heat-seeking Bats and soldiers who chased people from their homes were not elements of a normal life and should not be discussed so casually. But there was nothing he could say. Jimmy was a child of the war; he remembered almost nothing before the war. There was no longer any such thing as a normal life for him, for any of them, not anywhere in the world if John was right. "Normal" was yesterday; it was gone forever.

"Sure," the boy said brightly. "Sure, I understand."

Devin hardly slept that night. Huddled in the small shelter with the others, not even Katie's warmth pressing against him provided any comfort. He thought about the boy, Jimmy, and about his own sons and his wife. Perhaps his wife and his boys were the lucky ones. He thought about the dangers of the journey that would begin tomorrow and about the thirty people who were depending on him, trusting him to protect them. And he thought about the twenty-four members of the south McKenzie clan, people who had also trusted him, people he had failed. Had they been captured or killed? He was almost certain they had been. And he alone was responsible. Of all the members of the McKenzie clans, he alone had known of the existence of the Bats. He alone had seen them before and understood what they could do and how to evade them. But he had failed to warn the others. Among all the myriad details discussed at the planning meeting, why had that single, most critical item slipped his mind? He knew the answer, of course; he could explain how it had happened—for two years there had been no Bats so he had not expected them now—but he could not excuse it. It haunted him.

He stood sentry from 2:00 a.m. to 4:00 a.m. and when his

157

relief came he remained outside. He couldn't sleep anyway and two sentries were better than one. The sky was overcast and the night was coal black; he could see nothing. He heard nothing either—no soldiers, no gunfire, no aircraft.

A half hour before dawn it began to snow.

The snow was falling lightly as the three squads left the lake shelter and headed out along their separate routes. It was reducing visibility and making it harder for the soldiers to find them, but it was also causing them to leave tracks and filling those tracks very slowly. And it was not falling hard enough to ground the Chinese helicopters and Bats.

By noon they had heard no aircraft. But they were worried. Had the Sparks Lake shelter or their tracks been discovered? Were soldiers already pursuing them? What they needed was a real storm. Heavy snowfall would ground the aircraft and cover the clan's tracks. It would also make navigation more difficult but they could deal with that. The three squad leaders—Anderson, Devin and Cox—knew this country better than anyone else and Zachary knew it almost as well. They could find their way in any condition short of a blizzard.

By mid-afternoon, however, the sky had lightened perceptibly and the snow had almost stopped. This was very bad, the worst possible situation. The three squad leaders responded according to their prearranged procedures. They changed direction frequently and left the valleys for the heavily forested ridges whenever possible.

Just after 3:00 p.m. Anderson's squad, the one traveling farthest west, heard aircraft, both helicopters and Bats, a few miles west of their position. An hour later they saw a single helicopter. The squad was traversing a ridge at the time and they watched it fly south down the center of a valley immediately to the east of them.

"It's between us and Cox," Jack Norris said to Anderson. "They've found something, Tom. Oh, Jesus, they know we're here!"

"Not necessarily," Anderson argued. "They're sweep searching, that's all. Hoping to stumble across something obvious. I don't think they've found anything yet. If they had, they wouldn't be moving so fast."

Fifteen minutes later the same helicopter flew rapidly up the valley just west of them, moving north. So it looked like Anderson had been right.

158

There were no more aircraft that afternoon. But the next day, Bats overflew all three squads several times. The squad members used all of Devin's tricks. They kissed the trees and wrapped themselves in blankets and ducked into culverts. Then they moved on, hoping it had worked. They watched the sky and prayed for snow.

They were nearly twenty miles southeast of Sparks Lake now, and they knew the odds should be tilting in their favor. Except for the tracks. Behind them stretched thirty miles of fresh tracks in fresh snow. The tracks were in the trees so they couldn't be seen by the helicopters, and of course, they couldn't be detected by the Bats. But once the ground troops located them and saw which way they were heading it would be just a matter of time. The aircraft would come then and the troops would surround them and they would die.

They needed a storm.

They got it on the morning of the third day. It swept in from the central Pacific and it was huge. It came in waves, like surf rolling onto a beach, blanketing the west coast from northern California to Vancouver Island. In twelve hours the first wave dropped two and a half inches of rain on northern California, three and a half on the Willamette Valley. Then it drove east into the Sierra Nevada and the Cascades.

It was snowing heavily at first light and there was already two inches of new snow on the ground. In the camps of all three squads the clan members cheered. This was the opportunity they had hoped for. With the Chinese aircraft grounded and their tracks disappearing behind them they could race to the south. The soldiers would never find them now. They would plunge into the belly of the storm and vanish.

By noon the snow was a foot deep. Walking was becoming difficult, especially for the children, but no one was complaining. By three o'clock, nearly two feet blanketed the ground, and the clan members strapped on their snowshoes. By 4:30, with the snow falling even more heavily, Anderson led his squad to a log cabin nestled in a low hollow beside a small creek and called his lieutenants into conference.

"I've lived in this area all my life," he told them. "I've seen a lot of storms, but very few like this. There's already two and a half feet on the ground and no sign that it's about to quit." He paused and looked at each of them in turn. "For the present I think we can

159

forget about the Chinese. They aren't the problem now. We can't allow ourselves to be trapped here. But we may not be able to move much further; we may not be able to reach Thompson Valley."

"Where then?" Bill Kileen asked gravely. He and the others were well aware how serious their situation could become.

"I'm not sure," Anderson admitted. "Zachary is the key. He's the only one who knows John's route to the south and the locations of the shelters John showed him. In this weather we're definitely going to need those shelters."

"But Zachary is with Cox."

Anderson nodded. "So we're going to have to find Cox if the storm continues. Tomorrow morning, if it's still snowing, I'll leave you here and look for him."

Kileen and Norris both frowned. Norris started to say something but Anderson cut him off.

"It's not as bad as it sounds. I anticipated this, so this afternoon I cheated our route a mile east of where we were supposed to go. I know where Cox is supposed to be; it's only about two miles from here and I'm pretty sure I can find him."

They talked for another half hour, laying out contingency plans in case Anderson didn't return. Then they ate dinner and turned in for the night in front of a warming fire they had allowed themselves because the storm would prevent its detection. If it stopped snowing, whoever was standing watch was instructed to douse it immediately.

The fire was still burning when they awoke, and the snow depth had reached three feet. Anderson ate a light breakfast and set out in search of Cox at first light.

Zack Zachary was the most accomplished mountain man in the McKenzie clan. When the storm stuck he read the signs quickly and concluded that it was going to be a monster; he could feel it in his bones. He was certain it would defeat their Chinese pursuers, but it was also going to badly disrupt their own escape plans. By noon of the first day, with a foot of snow on the ground, he was convinced that the rendezvous at Thompson Valley could not take place.

"We have to pull the squads together now," he told Cox. "We have to close up or we'll never see each other again. At least, not till we reach California."

Cox had learned long ago to respect Zachary's opinions on

such matters, even when they seemed to be based on nothing more than instinct and intuition. But this time he was sure the baby-faced woodsman was overreacting. Did he really expect them to abandon all their careful planning because of a mere foot of snow? Cox asked Zachary to explain exactly what he was proposing.

"You stick to this route and maintain a normal pace," Zachary instructed him. "That will keep you even with Anderson. I'm going east to find Devin. I'll bring his squad back to our camp tonight. Tomorrow we'll go after Anderson."

But Cox wasn't convinced. "I don't know," he objected. "If it stops snowing we could all be caught together."

"It isn't going to stop snowing," Zachary insisted. "Not today and probably not tomorrow."

He finally left without Cox's blessing. He didn't need it anyway, and, whether Cox agreed or not, he knew he was right.

Devin was a good soldier—his squad was exactly where it was supposed to be and Zachary found them at mid-afternoon. The snow was nearly two feet deep by then and Devin could read weather signs too; he accepted Zachary's assessment without hesitation.

They found Cox's trail just before dark and tracked him to an old, half-collapsed farmhouse. His squad was holed up in the garage. He greeted them with a sheepish shrug.

"What can I say," he admitted to Zachary. "You were right."

The next morning the two squads remained at the garage while Zachary, Devin and Cox fanned out to the west looking for Anderson. They didn't find him or the cabin where he'd left his squad, but Anderson found their farmhouse. He was waiting for them when they returned late that afternoon.

They discussed their options over a dinner of freeze-dried tuna casserole and coffee, cooked over a camp stove. The snow had stopped a half hour earlier, so the fire had been put out. It was bitter cold in the garage.

Devin and Cox were in favor of picking up the route to Thompson Valley; it was further east and they didn't think the Chinese would look for them there. Zachary and Anderson disagreed. John's route was only twelve miles west of their present location and offered five secure shelters—two caves and three cabins—that Zachary was certain were going to be very important to them. "This storm isn't over," he asserted stubbornly. "There's

161

more snow coming, a lot more."

Zachary and Anderson prevailed.

The next morning they left the farmhouse and trekked to the cabin where Anderson's squad was still waiting. Then the entire clan marched west, toward the first of Zachary's shelters. Four feet of new snow crunched underfoot as they headed out under a featureless, steel-grey sky. The air was calm and no snow was falling. But that was soon to change.

The second wave of the great storm was already climbing the western slopes of the Cascades. It carried less moisture than the first but far more force. Where the first wave had been benign, even beautiful, this one was malignant.

Light snow began falling shortly after noon. By two o'clock it was coming down as heavily as it had the day before. Still, they saw no cause for concern. They had already traveled nearly ten miles and were making steady progress. Only two miles remained to their destination.

An hour later, however, they were laboring to maintain their pace. Strong, gusty winds, blowing in from the west, stirred the tops of the heavily laden trees and brought snow cascading down from the swaying branches in mini avalanches, forcing them to repeatedly divert around the resulting drifts and follow a zigzag course. In the open areas, clear of the trees, it was even worse. There, the swirling wind drove falling snow before it like frozen shrapnel. The wind swept up clouds of icy powder from the ground and the nearby woodlands and sent it churning in the air like glistening, crystal fog. It stung exposed flesh and reduced visibility to forty yards, then twenty.

They were well clothed against the cold. All had donned ski masks and goggles, so they could endure that part of the storm's fury. But they knew there was no possible protection against the ultimate danger a mountain blizzard could impose—whiteout! If this storm got much worse it would rob them of all visual reference and imprison them where they stood.

About four o'clock, Anderson fell in step beside Zachary at the head of the column and asked anxiously, "How much further?"

"A mile," Zachary replied dully. "Maybe less." His voice was muffled by the ice that caked the mask in front of his mouth and Anderson could read no expression in it. But the words themselves confirmed his worst fear; it was not like Zachary to be so imprecise.

"Are you sure where we are?" he asked.

162

Zachary didn't look at him; his gaze remained fixed on the terrain in front of them. "I've only seen a storm like this once before," he said to the clan leader. "In Montana, about fifteen years ago. A friend of mine died in that storm. Left his house to check on the animals in his barn and got lost on the way back. Wandered around in circles in his front yard until he froze to death because he couldn't find his own house! This storm's not as bad as that one yet. But this isn't my front yard either."

"I understand," Anderson said. "How much longer will you keep looking?"

"If I don't see something I recognize in the next half hour, we'll have to start digging snow caves."

Anderson nodded, then dropped back and fell in behind Zachary.

About twenty minutes later, Zachary found what he had been looking for—a recognizable landmark. It was a dead tree, split in half by lightning along its entire length to within eight feet of the ground, just three feet above the present snow line.

Zachary stopped in front of the tree and stood, head bowed and hands folded in an attitude of prayer for at least a minute while the snow swirled and the clan gathered around him. Then he turned to Anderson, pointed to the south, and said, "That way."

He had led them to a spot only three hundred yards from his target, a large cave complete with a natural rock chimney that permitted them to build a roaring fire inside. Under the circumstances it was an incredible feat of backwoods navigation, roughly comparable to Lindbergh's crossing the Atlantic by dead reckoning. Zachary had known John's route and he had known exactly where the farmhouse from which they had started the day's trek had been located. But he had never seen the country in between. Yet he had brought them through it in a howling blizzard. He admitted later that there had been moments when he thought he was hopelessly lost and feared that his failure had killed them all. But he had pushed on, driven more by blind faith than any flagging belief in his own ability. "I didn't deliver us here," he said humbly. "The Lord did." It was the first time any of them had ever heard him mention his faith.

They remained at the cave for four days while the second wave of the storm raged and then abated and was followed by a third and finally a fourth wave. And when at last they set out to continue their journey, a total of seven feet of new snow blanketed the mountain landscape.

The snow slowed their progress and forced them to plan each leg of the trip with meticulous care. The tedious pace stretched their food supplies to a bare subsistence ration, and the numbing cold took its toll on their strength. But they pressed on, moving steadily southward, resting and warming themselves for several days at each of John's secure shelters and supplementing their rations when they could. They caught five fish in the Lost River and called the resulting feast Thanksgiving despite the fact that it was celebrated on December fifth. Once, Devin shot a wild dog—thousands of wild dogs had roamed these mountains since the war. Twice they bagged rabbits and Anderson got a deer.

It snowed frequently, but there was no repetition of the terrible storms of the early days. This snow was welcome, they felt it protected them. They saw no aircraft on the entire trek and encountered no Chinese troops.

They entered California on December seventh. Eight days later, cold, hungry and weak, they made contact with the most northerly of the Shasta clans. Six of their number, including three children, had suffered frostbite and would lose fingers or toes. But they had survived. Not a single clan member had been lost.

They were welcomed as heroes. The day after their arrival a celebration was held in their honor complete with venison and beer and music. There was singing and much laughter, and Zachary's extraordinary skill was toasted over and over again. Only Devin seemed subdued, and only Katie understood the reason for his mood.

There had been no news of the south McKenzie clan.

TWENTY-ONE

David Craighill had always hated Christmas in California. Despite the fact that he lived in Los Angeles for twenty years before the war his heart remained in the east. Each year he longed for the crisp, clean winter air of his youth, the smell of wood smoke and bare trees silhouetted against a cold December sky.

But now all that had changed. He knew that in future his most cherished Christmas memories would be of this year in Sacramento. Chen's gift had made this holiday season the most joyous of his life. It had redefined Christmas for him.

Until the moment he had seen Annie again, he had not realized how much he had needed her or how empty his world had been without her. The years had fallen away then and he felt young again, reborn. He had remembered then. Throughout their life together Annie had nourished him. She had provided support when he needed it, comfort when he was discouraged, wisdom when he was uncertain. She had been his rock and his anchor and he had withered in her absence. He thought his black moods were because of the war and the prison camps, because the Chinese had beaten him down. But that had only been a small part of it. Mostly, it had been because he needed Anne.

And now she was back and he was whole again.

Was it possible that Chen had understood all this? Had the old man somehow known Craighill even better than Craighill knew himself and arranged the reunion simply because he needed the newsman whole? Craighill would never know the answer to that question, and he finally decided that it really didn't matter. All that mattered was that he and Anne were together again.

It had now been a month and a half since their arrival in Sacramento and life had settled into a comfortable pattern for the Craighills. David was very pleased with the progress at the television station. The facilities and the new equipment were first rate, the Chinese technicians were first rate and preparation for the premiere broadcast was proceeding on schedule.

Anne was equally satisfied with her job. She had been a

hospital administrator before the war and was now working in a neighborhood medical clinic. Daily supply shortages were a source of constant irritation, but she nevertheless took pride in the fact that the clinic's doctors and nurses still managed to deliver quality care.

"And the Chinese speak English so well," she had remarked once, after her first few weeks there. "It's really quite amazing, Pug; I often find myself forgetting that they are . . ." She paused, searching for the right word.

"The enemy?" he suggested. It was a reference to their single continuing disagreement—he was generally sympathetic to the Chinese; she openly distrusted them.

"That isn't what I was going to say," she objected. "I was going to say foreigners."

"Were you?" He raised an eyebrow in exaggerated surprise. "Does this mean that . . ."

"It means nothing," she said sharply. "Except that doctors are doctors, not soldiers or utopian social planners like your Mr. Chen. They have a job to do and they do it. They are above politics."

"I see. Then you haven't changed your mind generally."

"No, I haven't. And I don't care to talk about it now. You know my feelings so there's no point in starting another argument about it."

"Chinese doctors are above politics, but all other Chinese are suspect. Is that right?"

She sighed, but said nothing.

"What about the waitress at the restaurant last night? Was she . . ."

"David!"

That stopped him. Whenever she called him "David" he knew he was skating on thin ice. In the years before the war he had fallen through that ice often enough to know just how frigid the water beneath could be. So he let it drop.

For the next month he had carefully avoided any reference to the subject. He mentioned Chen on occasion—it was impossible not to—but aside from that he honored her wish absolutely. Not being able to talk to her about such a basic element of their new life frustrated him, but there was no help for it.

It was she who brought it up the next time. On New Year's Eve.

They were attending a hastily contrived New Year's dinner

166

at a small restaurant a few blocks from their apartment. Paul Sandiman was there, along with Derek Kowalski and Roger Simone and Pete Bell. They had just enjoyed a delightful meal and were about to toast this most memorable New Year with a rare, pre-war California Riesling. December thirty-first was a date of no particular significance to the Chinese, so the six of them were almost alone in the restaurant.

As the waiter stood by, Craighill took a sip of the wine, rolled it around on his tongue and swallowed with undisguised relish. "Wonderful," he said. "It reminds me of . . ."

"London," Anne said quickly. "That little pub in Chelsea."

He regarded her with surprise. "How did you know what I was going to say?"

"It wasn't difficult. An empty restaurant, the fog outside. I was thinking the same thing myself. And I hadn't even tasted the wine yet."

"This will be fine," Craighill said to the waiter. "And bring us another bottle, would you?" He filled Anne's glass and handed the bottle to Sandiman. Then he looked out the window at the street lights glowing dimly in the mist. She was right, it had been the fog that triggered his recollection. He hadn't realized it himself.

"Am I so predictable?" he asked her. "That must be boring for you, Annie."

"Not predictable, Pug, just familiar." She laid her hand on his and laughed. "And never boring. Not for a second."

He took another sip of wine and looked around the restaurant. It was getting late and he wondered if he should have ordered the second bottle; perhaps they should be leaving. But there were two Chinese couples in the far corner of the room and both were still eating. So they could stay a while longer.

"Did I tell you what Chen said to me today," he asked her.

Anne set her wine glass down, rested her elbows on the table and laced her fingers together. "No, dear," she replied, "What did the great man say today?"

His antennae rose instantly. In his wife's address code, "dear" ranked below "David" in order of belligerence but still well above "Pug." Why had she used it now, in response to such an innocuous comment? And why the sarcasm regarding Chen? The great man! He had no idea what was troubling her, but he could feel the ice forming beneath his feet.

He took a long swallow of wine and retrieved the bottle to

refill his glass, stalling for time while he mentally strapped on his skates. "The great man!" he said finally. "I had no idea you thought of him that way, Annie."

"I don't. I only said it because you think of him that way." She was smiling but there was a curious gravity in her voice. He wasn't sure how to read the conflicting signs.

"I guess we all think of him that way," Kowalski said. He was sitting across the table from Anne, cradling a coffee cup in one large hand. Since their arrival in Sacramento, Craighill had seen a lot of Kowalski. The halfback had taken to his new duties with unexpected enthusiasm and David had grown to like him. "Chen's quite an impressive fellow," Kowalski concluded.

Craighill nodded in Kowalski's direction. "You see? I'm not alone, Annie; we all respect him. Do you think that respect is misplaced?"

Anne rested her chin on her fingers and drew a deep breath. "Frankly," she said, "I believe it is."

Kowalski looked on with innocent interest; he had no knowledge of Anne's opinion of the Chinese. But Craighill frowned.

"Annie," he said, "It's New Year's Eve. Why don't we talk about this some other time." He picked up the bottle and offered to fill her glass. "More wine?"

"No," she said. And the sharpness of her tone told him his caution had come too late.

"I thought you didn't want to talk about this," he said.

"I've changed my mind. We've danced around this subject for six weeks, Pug. I think it's time we discuss it."

"Now?"

"Now. Most days we barely see each other. If not now, when?"

"All right," he agreed, after all he too had been wanting to talk it out. And she was back to "Pug", so apparently the danger wasn't as acute as he had feared. "Fire away, if you must."

She began carefully, as though reciting a memorized text. "I'm concerned about your participation in this television project," she said. "And about your relationship with Chen. You were always cautious, Pug, fanatical about confirming information sources. Yet you seem willing to accept whatever Chen tells you on blind faith."

Now that it had begun he was anxious to clear the air. He responded without hesitation, "I believe in his sincerity, if that's what you mean. And his intelligence. Those are qualities I respect."

She tilted her head to one side considering his response. "Sincerity and intelligence—I'd agree with those characterizations. But I suppose the same could have been said of Adolph Hitler."

Kowalski stared at her, wide eyed. For an instant, David was too stunned to react. "Hitler!" he said finally. "My God, Annie, you don't mean that you think of Chen as . . ."

"Of course not!" Anne said curtly. "I only mean that, by themselves, sincerity and intelligence aren't enough. To earn the kind of trust you've granted Chen, he must also be right."

Simone and Sandiman and Bell, who had been talking among themselves, stopped abruptly and looked over at them.

"And you think he's wrong? About what?"

She had everyone's attention now.

"I believe he is different, that he comes from a different background, a different culture. His attitudes and opinions may make perfect sense within the context of that culture—but to suppose that they are right for the entire world . . ." She shook her head. "I simply can't accept that. He represents a foreign power, Pug. His interests and ours are not the same."

He had known she distrusted the Chinese, but the depth of conviction he now heard in her voice and saw in her expression surprised him. It frightened him too. He and Anne apparently stood on opposite sides of a question so fundamental that it could, if left unresolved, threaten the foundation of their future life together.

"I believe you're wrong, Annie," he said carefully. "I believe his interests and ours are the same. You weren't in Chen's camp with us and you don't know him as we do. I was skeptical myself at first."

"But he convinced you. Yes, I know, Pug." Her tone was sympathetic, but insistent. "I admit I wasn't there, but I've read your camp journals. You're right, I don't know Chen as you do. But I've heard you talk about him almost daily since we arrived here. And I'm not convinced. He's a charming man, in some ways an impressive man. But he's only one individual. Chen is not China, Pug. And even if he isn't the enemy, China is."

She was throwing his own doubts back at him, doubts that he and the others had wrestled with for months and resolved. He was certain he was right about this, but how could he convince her?

"No," he said. "China is not the enemy, Annie. The past is

169

the enemy. The paranoia we all accepted as normal is the enemy. That past is dead now and we have to put it behind us. We have to learn to trust each other."

Pete Bell said suddenly, "Perhaps you've forgotten how it was, Anne, before the Chinese came. We brought this on ourselves, they didn't create it. Our cities were armed camps; our homes were like foxholes where we hid from each other. It was horrific."

She nodded. "I remember, Pete."

"The national debt was making us a third world country. Globalism was forcing millions of Americans into poverty. And we couldn't muster the political courage do anything about it. Right to the end, the people who could have done something about it did nothing. They buried their heads in the sand."

Simone said, "We all remember, Pete. We all agree."

"We were all scared," Sandiman said. "Politicians were afraid of offending powerful lobbies. Businessmen were afraid of how the security markets or the stockholders would judge them. We were afraid of losing our jobs or crossing the wrong people or just looking foolish, so nobody took the initiative. Nobody knew what to do so they did nothing. That might have been the worst fear of all. Nothing produces paralysis quicker than uncertainty."

"You know what it reminded me of?" Kowalski said, looking at Bell. "You said our homes were like foxholes, Pete; it reminded me of that. My grandfather fought in World War II. He was caught in the Bulge; his whole company was pinned down somewhere in Belgium for five days, under constant artillery attack. And you know what he told me? This was incredible—he said that two men in his company went to sleep in their foxholes, in broad daylight in the middle of the worst shelling. They weren't tired, just terrified. It was too much for them. They felt completely powerless and trapped; so their minds just shut down. It was the only way they could escape.

"I think we acted like those soldiers. I think we felt powerless so we curled up in our foxholes and went to sleep, hoping it would all be over when we woke up."

"Exactly," Bell said. "That's exactly what we did! The crisis lasted for years, and we simply slept through it." He turned to Anne. "But now Chen is trying to do something. Can't you see that, Anne?"

But she was still unconvinced. "No," she answered. "What I see is that you've been seduced, Pete, you, Derek, Roger, all of you."

"We were not seduced," Craighill said angrily. "We were skeptical, we asked questions. We demanded assurances and they were given. Chen made promises to us and those promises have been kept. We've been allowed to pursue any news we felt was important. Roger has written scripts that accurately portray life in the camps, warts and all, and those scripts are being filmed. We've been granted permits to travel freely. In two days . . ."

"David!"

He saw the expression on her face and realized he had been arguing a little too enthusiastically. In a far corner of the room one Chinese couple was preparing to leave; the other was still seated. All four patrons and the waiter were looking at him.

Anne pushed her cup toward him and said, "Coffee, please."

The Chinese went on about their business.

He filled her cup and replaced the coffee pot on the table. Then he lowered his voice and continued, "In two days, Paul is leaving to film stories on three continents. He's going to Asia, Europe and Africa. Those destinations were our choices. Ours, not theirs. Good God, Annie, what more could they do to prove their sincerity? They've given us a free hand. They're allowing us to create a free media."

Sandiman said, "That's all true, Anne."

"Not entirely!"

Craighill settled back in his chair. "Not entirely?"

"You told me yourself, there are restrictions. You aren't allowed to talk about the war or anything that happened before the war."

Craighill pursed his lips in an expression of frustration. "Even without restrictions, we wouldn't be talking about the war. The war is history, not news. We're newsmen; our purpose is to report what's going on now, to bring people up to date. There's no point in opening old wounds; that would only reinforce the hatred that's already out there. Too many people are living in the past, they need to be shown the present."

"Do you really believe that, Pug?"

"Yes, I really believe that."

"But don't you see what you're saying? You're admitting that the purpose of your broadcasts is propaganda, that they are intended to convince people to cooperate with the Chinese."

Craighill sighed. He had known it would come down to this. It had taken months of agonizing appraisal and reappraisal

171

before he was convinced—she was no different. Her beliefs ran deep and would not be easily shaken. If only he could expose her to all the proofs that had persuaded him: Chen's school, Chen himself, all the things he had seen as the stories for the coming newscasts were being put together. But that was impossible.

"Propaganda is an ugly word, Annie," he said. "And it simply doesn't apply here. We aren't going to try to convince anyone of anything. We're going to report the news exactly as it happens, just like we did in Los Angeles. That's going to open some eyes, I admit, but I think that's good. Too many people have been wearing blinders for too long."

She held her coffee cup between her hands, rolling it back and forth and staring at it with a faraway expression as he spoke. When he finished, she said, "You think I'm wearing blinders, Pug? I don't think so."

"I think that, like many people you've been forced to form your opinions in a vacuum. You don't have the facts. Until six weeks ago you were locked in a camp. The Chinese were your only source of information and you didn't believe anything they told you. We've seen the world beyond the camps and we have the facts. If you had them too, I think you'd feel differently." He paused and leaned toward her. "I could show it all to you, Annie. Tomorrow you could come down to the station and . . ."

The waiter suddenly appeared beside their table. Sandiman acknowledged him and the waiter asked, "Will there be anything else, Sir?"

"Just the bill," Sandiman said.

They sipped their wine and waited until he had retreated out of earshot, then Anne said, "You talk about facts, Pug. But what about the facts you've chosen to ignore?"

"Such as?"

"In your journal you mentioned that three prisoners in Chen's camp disappeared. Why? Where were they taken? And there was also that business about the drugs. Why were you all drugged?"

She waited for a response but he said nothing. Neither did the others, so she continued.

"You can't answer those questions, can you? Oh Pug, I don't want to sound unreasonable. Maybe you're right, maybe Chen is exactly what you think he is and the Chinese are honestly trying to help us. But I want you to be sure. I want to know positively that what you're doing—what I'm doing too, for that matter—is right."

The waiter presented the bill and they paid him with crisp new five credit notes. No one spoke while they waited for their change. In the pre-war world they would have told the waiter to keep it, but tipping was prohibited in the new North American State.

The waiter made change from a small pouch hung from his belt. Sandiman thanked him, complimented him on the meal and wished him a Happy New Year.

The waiter smiled broadly. "And a Happy New Year to you," he said with genuine warmth.

"Well," David addressed the others at the table. "It's late and we old folks need our rest."

New Year's wishes were exchanged all around and Anne offered a brief apology to the group. "I hope I haven't ruined your evening," she said. They assured her she hadn't. David and Anne left them to their wine and coffee.

The temperature outside was in the mid fifties, but the fog made it seem much colder. Anne fastened the top button on her coat and pulled her collar up around her neck. She wrapped her arm around her husband's waist and he circled his around her shoulder. They walked for some distance without speaking.

"Your thoughts?" she asked finally.

Her cheerful tone startled him. "I was just thinking," he replied, "how much you mean to me and hoping that this disagreement won't come between us."

"Come between us? What do you expect me to do, lock you out of our bedroom?"

He laughed. "Something like that, I suppose. You sounded very serious back there."

"I am serious. And opinionated. And stubborn. But I made my point and I know you'll consider it."

"I will. I always consider your opinions, you know that."

"Do you really?"

"Always."

"Good. Then I won't make you sleep on the couch tonight."

"Oh? And what about tomorrow night?"

She smiled and tightened her grip on his waist. "We'll see about that tomorrow."

TWENTY-TWO

The announcement was made everywhere at once, in the rural camps and in the cities. There was no advance notice, no publicity; the Chinese wanted it that way. They did not wish to have the impact of the premiere diluted by premature speculation. At the end of the evening meal everyone was simply ordered back to their barracks. "The evening free period is canceled," the authorities announced. "Something special has been prepared. Attendance is mandatory."

In rural camp 454, at the northeastern corner of the Sacramento valley near Shingletown, reaction to the order was typical. The workers grumbled and complained, but they obeyed. They filed from the mess hall and made their way slowly back toward their barracks.

"What is it this time?" Jason Becker muttered. "Another boring lecture, I suppose."

The man walking beside him shrugged indifferently.

"You don't know?" Becker eyed his companion with sudden concern. Cal Triplett's information sources were famous; he and his associates in the camp were constantly rooting out intelligence and exchanging it with the resistance groups on the outside. They were the camp's early warning system, an invaluable resource. "But you know everything, Cal," Becker said anxiously. "If you haven't heard about this, it could be bad."

"It's nothing like that," Triplett said curtly. Becker was a perpetual worrier and Triplett had no patience with his recurring paranoia. "I heard something but it was only a rumor. There was no reason to pass it on."

This was not completely true. Triplett was quite certain of his information but had kept it quiet to protect his source.

"What is it then? What did you hear?"

"I'm not sure. I told you, it was only a rumor. Anyway, we'll all know soon enough."

When Triplett and Becker arrived at their barracks, the small dayroom was already buzzing with conversation. A ten-year-

174

old Sony television set had been installed in one corner and the furniture was drawn up in front of it. Most of the chairs and sofas were already occupied and the set was on. But the screen was blank so the prisoners were talking among themselves. Becker joined friends on the far side of the room; Triplett remained near the door, observing.

"This show is boring," someone shouted. "Somebody change the station; maybe there's a football game on."

Scattered laughter.

"The hell with football," said another, "I want to see some sex. Flip to the movie channel, will you, Fong."

The lone Chinese guard, who was standing next to the television, grinned and said, "No football. No movies. Just one channel." He held up his index finger and waved it. "Only one!"

This announcement was met with a chorus of groans.

"So what are you going to show us?"

Fong said nothing.

"A lecture," a voice offered. "That's it, isn't it?"

More groans, louder this time.

Fong laughed and said, "No lectures."

"What then? Are you going to . . ."

A stylish logo suddenly appeared on the screen, a circle with block letters—G T N—at the center and the words Global Television Network inscribed around the perimeter.

All conversation ceased; all eyes turned to the television set. Music began to play, softly at first, then louder. The insistent, staccato rhythm was reminiscent of pre-war newscast themes. It was very "American" music.

Fong keyed the remote to adjust the volume. As the theme continued, the GTN logo dissolved and was replaced by the image of a distinguished-looking gray-haired man seated at a desk. Behind him was a greenscreen projection of the logo above script letters announcing "January 15." The music faded slowly and the man said, "Good evening, I'm David Craighill and this is the news."

Someone in the day room said, "It is! That's David Craighill!" Several others confirmed the identification.

The newscast that followed was slick and totally professional. Craighill made no inaugural announcement, no statement of goals or purpose. He simply reported the news as though this was one more in a continuing series of routine broadcasts. He reported stories from Sacramento to Baltimore,

Calgary to Mobile, with film from each location. He reported positive stories (a factory opening near Wichita) and negative stories (a fire at a hotel barracks in Des Moines). He did two stories on Houston, referring to the city matter-of-factly as "the Continental Capital." Then he introduced a European remote.

Paul Sandiman appeared. He did a tongue-in-cheek piece about the transition to the English language in Europe. He showed film taken in Marseilles, Venice and Munich, and needled the French mercilessly about their "linguistic arrogance." It struck exactly the right tone and twice evoked hearty laughter from the barracks audience.

Next, Derek Kowalski amazed everyone with film of a recent intercontinental (Asia vs. Europe) soccer tournament contested at Ankara. North America was not represented, he explained, because soccer leagues had not yet been organized here. He assured his audience, however, that they would be organized soon, as would basketball leagues, with football and baseball to follow later.

The newscast lasted a half hour. Craighill returned frequently to introduce stories by correspondents from around the world, and closed with a capsule summary of the continental weather. His final sign off was a simple, "Until tomorrow, this is David Craighill. Good night."

The GTN logo reappeared and the theme music began playing.

A man in the front row said, "Tomorrow? Fong, are there going to be regular broadcasts?"

"There will be broadcasts six days a week," the guard replied.

There was a moment of stunned silence. Then everyone in the room began talking at once.

Fong pounded the floor with the butt of his rifle. "Silence!" he commanded. "Silence!" When he had regained their attention, he said, "Beginning tomorrow, you may ignore these broadcasts if you wish. Today your attention is required."

Before Fong had finished this announcement, the news theme ended and a voice-over announcer began outlining the balance of the evening's programming. First up was a program titled "Our World," which was described as a video magazine. This would be followed by a documentary on the rapidly improving condition of worldwide coastal fisheries. The final offering of the evening was to be a program called "Barracks 25," which was

176

touted as "a delightful comedy."

"And now," the announcer concluded, "Our World."

The video magazine was fascinating, a collection of interviews with ordinary people—a farmer from southern Africa, a factory worker from Shanghai, and a clerk from Seattle—who described their lives and the work they were doing. The American and the south African spoke fluent English; the Chinese worker required the assistance of an interpreter. Only the Chinese seemed totally satisfied with the circumstances of his life; the others expressed hope for the future but little present enthusiasm. On the whole the barracks audience was surprised by the program's apparent balance and honesty.

The documentary was less well received. Its subject matter was important, but by comparison with the newscast and "Our World" it was dreadfully dull. If Fong had not been present, very few members of the audience would have watched it.

The final program, however, "Barracks 25," proved to be the highlight of the evening. It's portrayal of life in a typical North American agricultural camp was almost painfully realistic. And it was funny. Especially loud laughter greeted the consistently foolish lines delivered by one Chinese character, a dim-witted guard, and the pompous pronouncements of one of the Americans, a self-declared barracks aristocrat played by John Grant, who the other characters ridiculed behind his back. The audience enjoyed the show enormously and applauded when it was over.

Fong, however, did not seem amused. He frowned darkly at many of the lines delivered by the foolish guard. And when the final "Barracks 25" credits had rolled he switched the set off and announced stiffly, "Lights out in fifteen minutes."

As he left the barracks, the prisoners fell into small groups of two or three and the room hummed with the sounds of excited conversation. Everyone was anxious to express an opinion about what they had just seen.

There were only two exceptions to this rule, two individuals who stood apart, seemingly lost in their own thoughts.

Since the beginning of the evening, Cal Triplett had not left his station near the door. All night he had been observing his barracks-mates. He had studied the broadcast, of course, but he had paid even closer attention to his fellow prisoner's reactions to the broadcast. He was frowning now; their reactions clearly troubled him.

The second individual, a tall, muscular black man, was

standing at the far side of the room. Like Triplett, he was ignoring the conversations going on around him. Like Triplett, he looked troubled. He had recognized something on the telecast that no one else in this barracks could have recognized and it alarmed him.

Like the others he had seen Craighill and Paul Sandiman and Derek Kowalski on the newscast. He also recognized John Grant and James Sutton among the actors on "Barracks 25," and saw Roger Simone's name on the writing credit. But unlike the others he was aware of the common tie that bound the newsmen and the actors and the writer together. He alone understood what their appearance on this television premiere signified. It all made sense to him now: The strange prison in the desert, the old Chinese Commandant, the lectures, the drugs. This broadcast had not been what it appeared to be. The newsmen and the actors and the writer were pawns, carefully trained collaborators. And he was the only one who knew it.

He realized what he must do. Others must be made aware of these facts, others who might be able to take action.

Carefully, he picked his way through the crowd toward the door where Cal Triplett was standing.

"Cal Triplett?" he said, extending his hand.

"Yes?" Triplett was over six feet tall but when he turned to answer he found himself looking up at the speaker. "Murphy, isn't it?"

"That's right. Lonnie Murphy."

"Used to play for the Lakers."

"In another life," Murphy said.

Triplett looked past him to the crowd and nodded toward the television set."Well, what did you think?"

"It worried me. I think it's dangerous. I need to talk to you about it."

Triplett grew suddenly cautious. "Me? Why me? We've never even met."

Murphy lowered his voice. "I have information about tonight's broadcast, information your people should have."

"My people?"

"Your people on the outside."

Triplett shrugged. "I don't know what you're talking about."

Murphy's eyes narrowed. This denial seemed pointless to him; he had no time for it. He wrapped a long arm around Triplett's shoulder and guided him several steps further away from the others. "Let's not play games," he said. "You're in touch with the resistance. Everyone knows that."

Triplett pulled away. "Mr. Murphy, I don't know anything about any 'resistance'. But if you want to talk, I'll be glad to talk to you. Fair enough?"

Murphy glared down at him, then nodded. If Triplett was determined to play it this way Murphy had no choice but to play along. After all, he was new to the camp and Triplett didn't know him.

"Let's go back to the bunk room," he said.

"No!" Triplett's tone was firm.

Murphy started to object but realized he was in no position to argue the point. Triplett obviously wanted time to check him out and, from Triplett's perspective that was reasonable.

"When then?"

"Maybe tomorrow. Maybe the next day. I'll look you up."

Murphy sighed, clearly displaying his irritation. He hated feeling that he was suspect and he wanted Triplett to know it. Triplett's people on the outside needed his information and this delay was infuriating, more so because it was unnecessary. But of course, Triplett didn't know that.

"Fair enough?" Triplett asked.

Murphy nodded his reluctant agreement. "I can't tell you how to run your business," he said. "But I believe time is important here. So make it tomorrow, not the next day. All right?"

Again Triplett shrugged. "I'll try," he said. "I'll do what I can. Fair enough?"

Murphy didn't answer. There was nothing left to say.

TWENTY-THREE

As always, the lunch wagon was right on time. Fong and the other guards blew their whistles as it approached. The workers put down their tools, plodded through the mud to the rutted dirt road that ran along the south boundary of the field and queued up for lunch. It was a bright, sunny day, unseasonably warm for mid-January and everyone was in high spirits. Most of the conversation in the line was about the previous evening's television programs, as it had been every one of the six days since the first broadcast.

Cal Triplett was standing at the head of the line when the lunch wagon arrived. He was always granted that position when he needed it, even if others had arrived before him, and he needed it today. The guards never seemed to notice this deferential treatment; they ignored the workers during lunch breaks, preferring their own company and their own food, which they ate at a table some distance away.

The driver flashed a broad grin as the wagon rolled to a stop, and called out a greeting to Triplett. She was about his age, thirty-five, and nothing ever seemed to dampen her mood. Triplett liked her and she returned the feeling. Twice, on those rare occasions when the Chinese had distributed birth control devices and permitted fraternization, they had spent the night together.

"'Lo, Meggie," he called, as she climbed from the cab and disappeared into the back of the ancient Ford van.

The wide awning on the van's side panel swung upward and she fitted the supporting prop into its socket. "Morning, Cal," she grinned. "Gorgeous day, ain't it?"

"You got that right. If I wasn't so damned busy I'd be tempted to play hooky and go fishing."

She laughed. "So what'll it be? Coffee, tea, or . . ." She left the sentence hanging and winked at him.

"Sorry," he said, "You can't tempt me today. Gotta save my strength. Coffee, I guess."

She poured a cup, handed him the coffee and a small bowl and said, "Bon appetit.

180

"Careful," he cautioned. "They don't even let Frenchies talk like that anymore."

He left the truck and walked to the east, away from the field where he had been working. About ten yards from the road was a large oak tree nestled up against a fence that marked the farm perimeter. Beyond was a dense thicket of brush, its tangled branches extending through the fence.

Triplett settled down and leaned back against the oak's trunk. He sipped the coffee and set it on the ground beside him. Then he looked at the guards' table. It was at least fifty yards distant and none of the guards were looking his way.

"You there, John?"

A voice answered from the thicket behind him, "I'm here. What's going on, Cal? Anything important?"

"Yeah. Something very important." Triplett examined his bowl and sampled the contents. It was some kind of meatless stew. He couldn't identify all of the contents but it didn't look half bad, better than usual anyway. "I told you a week ago that they were planning a television program. We expected a lecture or some national announcement, you remember? Well, it wasn't anything like that. They've set up a whole damn network, just like pre-war. They're broadcasting every evening. And here's the kicker—it's run by Americans!"

"Americans?" John's usually calm voice jumped in pitch slightly. It was the first time Triplett could ever recall hearing any expression of alarm from him. "Go on. Let's have all of it."

For the next ten minutes Triplett described the broadcasts between bites of his lunch. He concluded, "This stuff is dangerous, John. Very slick, very effective. I can feel the impact in the camp already. The anchorman, Craighill, is an old pro. The others are believable too."

"I remember Craighill," John agreed. "Used to watch him in L.A. I liked him; he had a fatherly quality."

Triplett took another sip of coffee and checked the guards. They were still eating, still paying no attention to him. "That's why he's so dangerous. Everybody likes him. They like Sandiman too. So they're starting to think, 'If Craighill and Sandiman and Kowalski believe in this new world, maybe there's something to it.' They watch the stories and the documentaries and they see some positive things and some negative things. That tends to make them think it's all honest. And because most of it is good news they're beginning to believe that maybe the Chinese should be given a chance, that maybe we should be helping them instead of doing only what we're forced to do. We have to change that, John, and fast, or the game could be over."

"What do you suggest?"

Triplett scraped the last of the stew from his bowl and savored it for a moment. "That's your department," he said. "I'm just a field worker, remember? You're the warrior strategist."

A wry laugh from the bushes. "I wish I were. Anything else?"

"One thing. It's related. There's a guy named Lonnie Murphy who claims to have some information about the broadcasts. He wants to meet with you about it."

"With me? Why? What does he have?"

"He won't tell me. Says he won't talk to anyone but you."

"Bullshit! Tell him we have procedures. Tell him he has to talk to you."

"I told him already. He says it's too important. Says he can't trust anyone on the inside with it, not even me."

"Do you trust him?"

"I'm not sure. He seems okay, but he's new to the camp. Arrived just three months ago."

"So he could be a Chinese plant."

"The thought had crossed my mind. He's a brother, if that makes any difference."

John laughed. "You mean a bruthuh?"

Triplett downed the last of his coffee. The guards were rising from their table; lunch was about over. "He was a basketball star before the war. Played for the Lakers."

"I see," John said. "We're talkin' 'bout *that* Lonnie Murphy."

"The guards are up," Triplett said, getting to his feet. "What do I tell him?"

John hesitated, thinking. Then he said, "Tell him I'll meet him tonight. Bring him to the usual place."

"Fair enough." Triplett started to leave.

"And Cal . . ."

Triplett paused.

"If we still aren't sure about him after he says what he wants to say, he won't be going back with you. Understand?"

Triplett nodded and continued on his way back to the fields.

That same morning, Lin Chiao-tu had scheduled his first inspection tour of the new Sacramento television facilities. Chen himself showed the Administrator the studios and the newsroom and introduced him to the staff. On their return to Chen's office, Lin was in an expansive mood and lavish in his praise of Chen's accomplishment.

"My reports indicate that the impact of your broadcasts is far greater than we predicted. It is difficult to quantify such data, but the camp populations seem to be responding with much enthusiasm. Already, they are expressing a new spirit of cooperation and new interest in their work."

"We have only exposed them to the truth," Chen said modestly. "We have shown them that there is light at the end of the tunnel. That prospect is new to them."

"I suppose so," Lin agreed. "Whatever the reason, you are to be congratulated."

"Much of what they have seen in the past week had been presented to them before in lecture programs," Chen continued. "But television is a powerful medium, especially here. We have presented images to them which they can neither ignore nor deny. We have shown them that conditions in other parts of the world are better than here and they have apparently concluded that, if they cooperate, things can improve here as well."

"Perhaps." Lin said, pouring himself a cup of tea. "But my reports indicate that they are responding primarily to the personalities you have placed on the air. It is the people you trained, Comrade Chen, who are the real key to your success."

Chen nodded; it was almost a bow. "My people have done excellent work, I agree."

Lin sipped his tea, then said, "That brings me to my next subject—your camp. How is it progressing? How soon may we expect more graduates?"

"I have prepared a report." Chen retrieved a copy from a briefcase which was standing beside the tea table. "As you will see, it is progressing quite well." He handed the report to the Administrator.

For the next several minutes, Chen summarized the report's contents while Lin followed along on his printed copy. A second small class had graduated three weeks earlier—Lin was already aware of this—and three of these graduates were already in Sacramento working at the television studios. More would arrive shortly, mostly writers and actors who would be assigned to the

183

production of new dramatic and comedy series. The camp was now operating at near capacity, and within a month graduates would be emerging on regular five-day cycles. Most would be administrators, scientists and teachers.

"We have little immediate need for additional public personalities," Chen explained. "This is due in part to the remarkable acceptance rate of the first class which, you will recall, was 80 percent. Our initial estimates projected a probable rate of 60 percent and we still believe this is a more realistic goal. The second class did run 60 percent and the classes now processing, the ones which have reached the point where rejections are considered, are maintaining that same level. So I am prepared to stand by our original estimates. Within four weeks we should begin delivering about fifty new graduates each month."

Lin seemed well satisfied with this. Again, he offered his congratulations. Then he set down his teacup, slipped Chen's report into his briefcase, and stood up. Chen stood also and the two men exchanged bows.

"Continue your good work," Lin said with a broad smile. He hefted his briefcase and started toward the door. Then he paused abruptly.

"One last thing," he said. "I fear your security here is inadequate. There should be more guards posted."

Chen was surprised by the comment and dismayed by it. It ran counter to everything he was trying to accomplish here.

"But Sacramento is an open city," he objected. "A model city. Surely you don't mean to turn the information center for the new continental state into an armed garrison. We've been working here since November without such precautions and I see no need for them now."

Lin listened politely, then said, "You misunderstood me. I was not talking about the entire city, only this building. I agree, it would not do to make a general show of force. But I would like the guard here doubled. Please see to it."

"As you wish," Chen replied coolly.

When Lin had left, Chen stood for some time at his window, looking out at the city.

The man is a fool, he thought angrily. He understands nothing! We are finally succeeding, and our continental administrator has absolutely no idea why.

They crept out under cover of darkness. It was easily

accomplished; a child could have escaped from this camp. Murphy was surprised by the lack of security; Triplett, of course, had known what to expect. For over a year the prisoners here had given their jailers no reason to distrust them. There were no escape attempts, no riots, no trouble. From the Chinese perspective, 454 was a model camp.

It was all part of John's plan. Patience was the cornerstone of his strategy. "We will lull them to sleep," he said. "And someday their sleeping will work to our advantage. Someday, the right opportunity will present itself and we will be ready."

There had been dissenters. Both inside and outside the camp a few had viewed John's patience as cowardice. But each time the strategy had been put to a vote, John had won. Because what he said made sense. And because no one had ever suggested a convincing argument for any other course of action. In over a year, no opportunity worth surrendering their advantage had presented itself, so they still waited. And each month the Chinese grew more careless.

Lonnie Murphy knew nothing of this history. He had never even heard John's name. He knew only that nothing ever seemed to happen at 454 and the inmates cultivated an unusually cordial relationship with their guards. Long before the first television broadcast these things had made him suspicious. That suspicion was the reason he had refused to tell Triplett what he knew. It was the reason he was now following Triplett into the night.

They moved quickly but carefully, hiding behind barns and outbuildings, crawling on hands and knees along a barrow pit beside a dirt road, crouching low as they crossed the corner of an open field. Finally they skirted a fence line bordering a woodland on the eastern perimeter of the farm. Triplett directed Murphy to climb through the fence and led him down an embankment to a spot beside a small stream. They were perhaps four hundred yards from the nearest barracks.

"Now it's a clear night," Triplett warned. "And there's no wind. Sound carries a long way in these conditions, so keep your voice down." Then he turned and began climbing back up the embankment.

"Wait!" Murphy called out in a hoarse whisper. He reached out and grabbed Triplett's pantleg.

"What?"

"Where are you going? And where's your friend?"

"I'll be up by the fence. You said you wouldn't talk to me

185

anyway."

"And I'm right here," a voice said. It came from the shadows a few feet off to Murphy's right.

Murphy turned and looked in the direction of the voice. He could make out the faint silhouette of a man sitting on the embankment. The man was slightly built and appeared to be alone.

Murphy released Triplett's pantleg and heard him climb up the slope to the fence.

The man said, "It's your move, Mr. Murphy; you called this meeting. Now what is it you want to tell me?"

The athlete strained to see the speaker. He was slowly growing accustomed to the darkness of the meeting place and he could now see the man's clothing. He could discern its color, even its texture—military fatigues in a camouflage pattern. But the face was still indistinguishable. Then, suddenly, he understood the reason. The man was black! He hadn't expected that. He had pictured the rebels as a band of militant rednecks who had stockpiled arms in the mountains before the war. Triplett had told him this man was their leader and he had assumed the leader would be white.

"Who are you?" Murphy asked.

"Cal told you who I am," the man replied, then added impatiently. "Now let's get on with it."

The impatience irritated Murphy. After all, he was offering valuable information. In exchange, this man should at least be willing to identify himself.

"I want a name," he insisted. "What do I call you?"

The shadowy figure leaned toward him. "My name would mean nothing to you and your knowledge of it would place me at risk. That should be obvious. Call me anything. Call me John, if you like."

Murphy felt suddenly foolish. The rebel was right, he saw that immediately.

"Unless you'd prefer some other name."

Ignoring the sarcasm, Murphy said, "John is fine."

He told the rebel leader all he knew about the strange indoctrination camp where he and the others had been held. He described the location in a remote corner of the southwestern desert, the secrecy and the extreme security, the inmates with whom he had shared the experience, the games they played, the old Chinese professor who had acted as Commandant, and finally,

186

the drugs, which even the eminent Dr. Palitz had been unable to identify.

"It was a confusing experience," he said in conclusion. "I was never able to make sense of it until I saw the first broadcast four days ago. Then I knew instantly. There they were—Craighill, Sandiman, Kowalski, and Bell on the news; Sutton and Grant on 'Barracks 25,' Simone writing the script—all of them together on television! It made perfect sense then."

John shook his head doubtfully. "You actually believe all these men are being controlled somehow?"

"I'm absolutely certain of it. I got to know them fairly well in the time I had there. By the way, I just remembered, there was another I didn't mention before; didn't notice his name myself until yesterday. Billy Dupree. He's writing music for most of the shows. He was in the camp too. That makes eight in all, and none of them were sympathetic to the Chinese when I knew them. Sandiman in particular was a rabid patriot, almost irrational about it. He would never have collaborated willingly. Grant might have, he didn't seem to believe in much. And I'm not sure about Kowalski. But the rest of them were all level-headed. They never would have done this." "You think they're being forced to participate?"

"Forced, manipulated, drugged, what's the difference? The point is that they're being used. The Chinese are propping them up like puppets, trying to convince the rest of us to cooperate—that's the obvious purpose of these broadcasts. And it's working! So it has to be stopped. If it isn't stopped, they win; it's as simple as that."

John glanced up to where Triplett was standing watch. "I believe that much," he said. "Cal told me the same thing. He's worried too. He sees the same danger you see."

"So what can we do about it?"

"I don't know yet."

Murphy said, "Whatever you do, I want to be part of it."

"You will be part of it," John assured him. "You're already part of it. Your special knowledge will be extremely valuable. I need you to monitor future broadcasts and tell Cal . . ."

"No," Murphy said firmly. "That's not what I mean." He pushed himself to his feet and stepped closer to John. "I mean I really want to be part of it. Whatever you do, I want to be on the team. On the outside. I'm not going back to camp with Triplett; I'm going with you."

"Like hell you are!" It was Triplett. He came skidding down the embankment to where Murphy was standing and added threateningly, "You'll go where you're told to go. Or you'll go nowhere at all."

Murphy met his gaze with a sneer. He had disliked Triplett the moment they met at the first broadcast and nothing had happened since to change his opinion. The man was a strutting peacock; he knew the type well. Triplett thought he was tough, but Murphy knew better. He was tempted to prove it now. He had seen the flash of a knife blade in Triplett's hand as he scrambled down the embankment. He could see the foolish arrogance in his eyes now, the total absence of fear. It would be easy.

"Exactly what do you mean by that," Murphy asked.

Triplett's confidence was unwavering; he was absolutely sure of his ground and his ability. He said, "I mean just what I said. You'll take orders like everyone else, Lonnie, or . . ."

Murphy cut him off. "Or what?"

"Or . . ." Triplett began.

But John interrupted. "What Cal means," he said, "is that discipline is necessary in any organization, and ours is no different. You have to understand this, Lonnie. We simply can't tolerate . . ."

When Murphy saw his opening he moved so quickly that neither Triplett nor John realized what was happening, more quickly than it seemed possible a man his size could move. There was incredible ease in the movement and a fluidity born of twenty years of concentrated training and conditioning. He moved like a cat, with grace and power and precision. It was over in an instant. Triplett was left prostrate on the ground with Murphy standing over him, holding the knife.

Murphy looked at John. "You were going to say insubordination, weren't you? You were going to say you can't tolerate insubordination. Well I can't tolerate this!" He threw the knife far back into the brush beyond the stream. "You lead and I might follow, John. But not if he's standing behind me with a knife." He pointed at Triplett.

Triplett's eyes were wide with astonishment. He lay motionless at Murphy's feet. John glanced down at him, then looked back to Murphy and shook his head.

"You didn't learn that in the NBA. You've done time on the streets. Where was it?"

"Kansas City," Murphy replied. Then he reached down and

offered a hand to Triplett. The barracks captain took it and allowed himself to be lifted upright. "It was a long time ago, but that kind of thing stays with you."

"Obviously." John looked at Triplett. "You okay, Cal?"

"I'm fine." Triplett seemed to have overcome his initial shock, but embarrassment still prevented him from looking at John.

"All right. Then I guess we're about done. Cal, you head back now. I'm taking Lonnie with me."

Triplett and Murphy were both surprised by this sudden announcement, Triplett especially. He blurted, "What?"

"You have a problem with that?" John asked. "What is it? You expect recriminations in the camp?"

Triplett's face was contorted with rage. "I don't know," he snapped. "I haven't thought about it."

"Well, think about it. I need to know."

The barracks captain looked away. When he turned back, the anger was gone, or at least under control. He said, "It's an escape of course. That's never happened before, but it's only one man. No, I don't think there'll be much trouble. Especially because it's Murphy. He's new and a loner so I don't think they'll tie him in with the rest of us."

"Good," John said. "I'll see you in a week then to let you know what we're planning."

"But, John!"

The rebel leader placed a hand on Triplett's shoulder and led him several paces away from Murphy. "Look, Cal. I know you don't agree with this but I think it's going to work."

"You're sure?"

"There's no way to be sure. But I think I can use this guy. I think his skills will be more valuable on the outside than on the inside."

"His skills? You mean that sucker punch? Shit, John, it's dark and I was looking the other way. I don't think . . ."

"Cal! We've never argued; let's not start now."

Triplett nodded reluctantly. "Okay. If that's the way you want it."

"I'll see you in a week."

Several minutes later, Murphy and his new clan leader were headed east toward the mountains. They moved briskly, with John leading and Murphy following.

John called back over his shoulder, "You don't like Triplett. Why?"

"Because he thinks he's better than he is," Murphy replied. "He's pretty good, I'm not denying that. But he thinks he's even better and that's dangerous. In a ballgame or a fight, that's always dangerous."

"He doesn't like you either, you know. He says you sucker punched him."

"That's just another part of the same thing. People who think they're better than they are always call it skill when they win, but when they lose it's because the other guy broke the rules."

"Did you sucker punch him?"

"Of course I did. But I didn't break any rules. There are no rules in that kind of fighting. He had the knife; all I had on my side was speed and surprise."

John slowed and allowed Murphy to pull up next to him. "You did have those," he grinned. "It was a beautiful thing to watch."

Murphy eyed him curiously. "You don't like Triplett either?"

"Oh, I like him well enough. Before the war he was an attorney and I was an engineer. So we have a lot in common. Back then I probably would have liked him better than I would have liked you. But now?" He speeded up and resumed his course along the stream bed.

Murphy fell in behind him. "I don't understand. What's different now?"

"I thought that was obvious. You're a born guerrilla fighter, Lonnie. Right now, that's exactly what I need."

"You do have a plan, don't you! You're going to do something about the broadcasts."

"Not exactly. I have an idea, but it's not a plan yet. As soon as it is, I'll let you know."

"Is that a promise?"

"That's a promise."

The night grew rapidly colder as they climbed into the hills, but Murphy hardly noticed. For the first time in a year and a half he was free and doing something important. At last he was fighting back. The game was finally on.

TWENTY-FOUR

Chen Lo-yung could not remember the last time he had felt so good. He had slept long and well, he was experiencing no fatigue or pain and it was a beautiful morning. He knew there could not be many mornings like this left to him and he luxuriated in it. He lingered longer than usual in his bath, shaved with meticulous care and laid out his best suit. Then he called the transport desk at his hotel and dismissed his driver.

"I will not be needing him," he announced. "This morning I prefer to walk."

He arrived at the studio building fifteen minutes later than usual. The sight of the doubled security guard idling in the lobby caused him to frown briefly as he passed them, but he had dismissed this irritation even before reaching the elevators. There was nothing he could do about Lin's foolishness and he was determined not to let it ruin his good mood.

He could not, however, dismiss the surprise which greeted him when he reached his office. David Craighill was sitting in the reception area sipping a cup of coffee. The newsman was clean shaven and well dressed, but, beyond that, looked barely presentable. His eyes were bloodshot and he wore the haggard expression of a man badly in need of sleep.

"David!" Chen exclaimed with genuine concern, "You look as though you've been up all night."

"I have." Craighill rose. "May we talk?"

"Of course." Chen motioned toward his office. As Craighill preceded him toward the door, Chen looked questioningly at his secretary.

The secretary, an attractive middle-aged Chinese, shrugged. "He was waiting in the hall when I arrived. He's been here . . ." She glanced at the wall clock. "about a half hour. And your first appointment is in fifteen minutes."

Chen nodded. "I may have you cancel that. Bring me some tea, please, and coffee for Mr. Craighill. Make a fresh pot; he looks as though he needs it."

"Yes, sir."

As he entered the office, Chen saw that Craighill had already settled into a chair. He closed the door behind him, walked to the far side of the desk and seated himself. Craighill looked nervous.

Chen said, "You seem troubled, David. What is it? How can I help?"

"To be perfectly honest I doubt that you can help," Craighill said. "But I feel obligated to let you try. I believe I owe you that much."

The gravity of the newsman's tone alarmed Chen, but he nevertheless managed to force a smile. "Go on. Exactly what don't you think I can help with? I may surprise you."

Craighill did not answer immediately; he seemed to be gathering his courage. Finally he said, "This is difficult for me, Chen. Because it is going to sound as though my comments are directed at you personally. They are not and I want to avoid giving that impression. I have the highest regard for you. Nevertheless—there's simply no easy way to say this—I'm afraid I can no longer continue at the station. I've come to submit my resignation."

"I see," Chen said, although he did not see at all. Craighill had always been the one he was most certain of. The tests had shown him to be the least dogmatic of his group and therefore the most receptive to the idea of the new order. Only last evening he had appeared before the cameras as usual and given no indication of the dissatisfaction he was now expressing. What could have happened between then and now?

"Can you explain your reasons?" Chen made no attempt to hide his surprise and disappointment. Craighill's loss, he feared, would be more damaging than the loss of any of the others; it could be disastrous. "Have I failed to keep my promises to you?"

"No, you've kept your promises; I admit that. But as I said, this isn't really about you. In fact, it isn't about anything specific. It's about the aggregate, the sum total of a number of small things. May I be completely candid?"

"Of course."

"All right, I'll begin at the beginning then. Months ago, before we came to Sacramento, you made a proposal to us. We accepted, but not because we were convinced that we should—in fact, none of us was fully persuaded by your arguments. We accepted because we were not convinced that we shouldn't. That may seem a fine distinction, but it was critical to us. It meant that we arrived here uncommitted."

"We understood that," Chen said. "That's why we've been so careful to keep our part of our bargain. We knew we had to prove to you . . ."

"Please!" Craighill held up a cautioning hand. "Let me finish."

Chen made a gesture of deferral.

"There was information we wanted, tests we needed to apply. We needed to see the world beyond these television studios, beyond Sacramento. That's why we insisted on so much freedom. You granted that freedom and, for me at least, that concession lulled me into a kind of complacent daydream. There was so much work to do preparing for the first broadcast that I literally forgot why we had come here and behaved as though I was completely committed. Looking back on it now, I'm not proud of the way I behaved during those months. I think my relationship with you had something to do with it—I really did grow very fond of you, Chen. And I know that Anne's presence was a factor; I can't thank you enough for that. Still, my behavior then troubles me now. It wasn't normal.

"A few weeks ago, I finally began to recognize these symptoms. During the week before the premiere, I noticed that we had collected quite a number of negative stories. A soldier had raped a girl in one of the camps; in another camp a guard had beaten a male prisoner senseless over nothing, that sort of thing. In the cities there were several stories about Chinese officials taking advantage of Americans. One had systematically shorted the rations in all the barracks mess halls he controlled and then created a black market to sell the food back to the very people he'd stolen it from. We discussed these stories at editorial meetings and decided to run only a few because we felt they weren't typical and emphasizing them would portray an incorrect impression of the camps.

"But they were there. They did happen. And as our reporters covered more ground, they found more of them. Finally, I began to wonder if they represented a pattern. And if they did, why hadn't I noticed it earlier? Had I been wearing blinders, seeing only what I wanted to see? What you wanted me to see? Why had I been so uncritical?"

There was a knock on the office door and Chen's secretary entered the room. Craighill settled back and waited as the tea and coffee were delivered. When she had finished Chen instructed her to cancel his appointments for the next hour.

When she had gone and they were alone again, Chen sighed thoughtfully. "David," he began. But again, Craighill insisted on continuing.

"After the premiere, the workload stabilized. It seems ironic, but once the broadcasts actually began, there were fewer demands on my time. Things settled into a routine. That allowed me time to think, to reflect. And I didn't like what I saw. Out there," He waved a hand, vaguely indicating the world outside the office window. "this brave new world we're supposed to be creating isn't working. Your people aren't running it the way you told us they would.

"Now, I'm not naive or stupid; I know what you'll say to that. You'll say Rome wasn't built in a day and the transition will take time and errors are inevitable. I agree with all of that. But I have a problem with it just the same. The problem is this: Progress toward the implementation of your program could be stopped at any time, but the impact of the work I'm doing is irreversible. I think you know what I mean by that; I think you've always known. I didn't anticipate what's happened, but I recognize it now. Our broadcasts are pacifying the camp populations at an amazing rate. They are encouraging people to believe in the new federation, encouraging them to cooperate."

Craighill paused, and Chen said quickly, "David, you're very tired. You are in no condition to discuss this now. You should go home and rest. Perhaps tomorrow . . ."

"No!" Craighill picked up his coffee. "I am tired; I can't deny that. It took me all night to come to this decision." His hand was surprisingly steady as he lifted the cup to his lips and drank. "But I am perfectly capable of discussing this now. I have finally realized how much effect my work is having and that changes everything. I realize that I must decide now whether I believe your program will really be implemented. If I do believe it, then cooperation in the camps would be a good thing; it would speed the implementation. But if I'm not sure, if I'm afraid your superiors may pull the props from under the transition once my work has reduced the population to a herd of braying sheep, then I must resign."

He studied Chen's reaction to this and finally concluded, "I want to believe you, Chen, but I no longer trust my own judgment. My track record lately is so dismal it frightens me. So if you want me to continue, perhaps it's time for you to administer another injection."

"Injection?" Sudden recognition flashed across Chen's face. "Is that what this is about? The drugs?"

"The drugs were part of it, yes, an important part. But there were other things as well. The three prisoners who disappeared—Murphy, Hammil and Moore—why were they dismissed while the rest of us were kept? Was it because you discovered that we were susceptible and they were not? And what happened to them? Were they killed?"

For a long moment, Chen did not respond. Instead he waited, expecting more. Then he shook himself, finally realizing that Craighill was finished. He sighed and ran a hand slowly through his thinning hair.

"David," he said carefully, "I see a certain logic in what you are asking, but I honestly didn't anticipate it. I suppose I should have. As to your basic concern—I assure you, there has been no manipulation. The drugs were given for an entirely different purpose. With regard to the rest, I'll take your questions one at a time if you will allow me."

Craighill nodded his assent. "Please understand," he said. "I want to believe in you. But I don't know you well enough to be certain of your motives. You have not taken me into your confidence. You must see how that appears."

"I do," Chen agreed. Craighill's attack had finally made him angry, but he sympathized with the newsman's anguish. These doubts were reasonable. "But you must understand something as well—it was not possible to tell you everything until I was certain you were committed. Clearly, you are still not committed and so I still cannot tell you everything. But I can tell you what matters.

"You are concerned about the drugs. The drugs were necessary but they were not primary. They served only to prepare your mind, to render it accessible to certain tests. They were merely the preliminary step in a process. You see, we have developed a remarkable device. The drugs prepared your mind for the testing, and the device allowed us to analyze your thought processes. That analysis was the key. It enabled us to chart your most fundamental reactions to the lessons we were presenting in the school. Were you open to the possibilities of the new world we hoped to create? Were you sufficiently free of ideological bias and dogmatic adherence to pre-war loyalties? Did you possess the intelligence and independence to make real contributions to our

195

program? We had to know these things. Murphy and Hammil and Moore failed these tests; the rest passed. But I assure you, David, there was no manipulation. We merely analyzed your thoughts; we did not influence them in any way. We could not even if we had wanted to; the device does not have that capability."

For a moment Craighill seemed too stunned to respond. Finally, he said, "This is your explanation? You defend yourself with a fairy tale? It's preposterous, Chen! No such device exists. You can't possibly expect me to . . . My God, I'm surprised you can keep a straight face as you tell it!"

"Oh, it exists. I'm surprised you don't remember."

The newsman started to laugh but checked himself. Chen's gaze was unwavering; he seemed completely sincere. It was impossible, wasn't it?

"I remember being wired to a machine. A lie detector, I think. That proves absolutely nothing."

"You see, you do remember. We were frankly amazed by the results. I have always held the American people in high regard, and your group was made up of exceptional individuals; still, none of us expected a success rate of 80 percent. Twelve of fifteen satisfied the testing criteria, a remarkable performance. It demonstrated to us that, deep down, most of you truly believed in the core philosophy upon which your democracy was founded. How could a nation of such enlightened citizens produce such a corrupt culture? Can you explain that to me?"

This time Craighill allowed himself to laugh. "I can't tell whether you're trying to flatter me or insult me," he said. "Either way, it isn't persuasive. I ask for an explanation, for proof of your sincerity, and you offer this absurdity."

"It is true, David."

"Then produce my records. Let me see the thoughts your machine drew from my mind."

"I don't have your records. Even if I did, they would mean nothing to you, just as they meant nothing to me. Only a trained interpreter can read them; to anyone else they appear as gibberish."

"How convenient," Craighill hissed. But there was no force in the exclamation. The anger he had intended to convey was swallowed up in an overwhelming disappointment. He had come here hoping to be convinced, hoping that Chen could somehow reassure him. He hadn't completely realized that until this moment, hadn't realized how much he wanted to believe in Chen.

Because if Chen's promises were false, there was nothing left for him, for the entire world, no hope for the future. And Chen had offered only excuses and evasion. So Anne was right! He felt suddenly empty and very tired.

"David."

Craighill returned the old man's gaze but wasn't really seeing him. A vast weariness had settled over him, leaving him drained and numb.

"Everything I've told you is true," Chen said. "But I have no way to prove it. What proof can I offer? What would convince you?"

"I honestly don't know," Craighill muttered. "This is your game, Chen. I'm only a pawn."

Chen scowled thoughtfully. "My game," he said, so softly that Craighill barely heard him. Then his eyes widened and he smiled. "Of course! My game! That may work. I think I can prove it to you."

He turned his chair around, withdrew something from the low cabinet behind him, and turned back to Craighill. He set the object down on the desktop. It was a maze game, exactly like the ones the prisoners had played at the desert camp.

"The drugs we gave you have two functions," Chen said as he began arranging discs on his side of the board. "Here, David. Set your pieces." He pushed a plastic box containing the second set of discs across the board.

Craighill had no idea what purpose this might serve, but he was encouraged by Chen's sudden enthusiasm. Without comment, he began arranging his discs.

"I have already explained the testing machine's first function—to evaluate mental profiles. But it can also be used to enhance mental capability. It can't specifically teach, not in terms of imparting knowledge or information, but it can help to stimulate and organize human thought processes, increasing the mind's power by refining its ability to concentrate on a problem." Chen placed his last disc and looked up at Craighill. "The drugs you are so worried about are necessary for this procedure also, so I have taken them myself."

Craighill placed his last disc and looked up with surprise. "You?"

"Yes. That should prove something to you." Chen pressed the button on the side of the game board and the red barrier fences rose into position. "You begin. Make the first move."

197

"I've only played once before," Craighill objected. "I'm no good at this. Beating me will prove nothing."

"I have no intention of beating you. A few moves will prove my point. Please!"

The newsman moved a disc, then glanced curiously at his opponent.

Chen stared at the board, his brows knitted in an expression of intense concentration. He remained like that for perhaps ten seconds. Then, suddenly, he relaxed. "There. Your move."

"My move? But you didn't . . ."

Chen nodded toward the board. Craighill looked down and saw that one of Chen's discs had moved.

"It has been some time since I last attempted this," Chen said. "I am out of practice. It should not have taken so long." Then, recognizing Craighill's skeptical expression, he added, "Go ahead, examine it."

Craighill reached out and touched the displaced disc. It moved normally.

"Pick it up, David."

Craighill complied, examining it closely. It looked exactly like all the other discs.

"It is aluminum." Chen said. "Non-magnetic."

The disc did appear to be made of aluminum. Craighill frowned. "I don't know how it was done but I'm certain there's a simple explanation. Can you do it again?"

"Certainly."

"But this time, I'll select the disc to be moved."

"I should be insulted," Chen said. But he was clearly not insulted. To the contrary, he seemed to be enjoying himself.

"That one," Craighill instructed him, indicating a disc near the left side of the board.

Again, Chen concentrated. And this time, the newsman saw the disc move. It quivered momentarily, then slid smoothly forward into the next space.

Again, Craighill picked up the disc and examined it. "A neat trick," he said. Then he pointed to a disc in the center of the array in front of Chen and commanded, "Now that one."

"That one?" Chen looked suddenly deflated. "I cannot move that one."

Craighill sighed. "I thought not."

"To move that one I would have to lift it over the discs

around it. I am not that good."

"Or perhaps this board is not that good. Chen, this is a parlor trick. It's extremely well done, I admit, but . . ."

"It is no trick," Chen snapped, suddenly and finally angry. "David, I sympathize with you; I understand your doubts. But have you considered what you are accusing me of? Do you really believe that I have prepared an elaborate ruse here merely to deceive you? I didn't even know you were coming."

Craighill glared back across the desk, returning the anger he saw in Chen's eyes. His first impulse was to argue, to point out that the trick could have been prepared long ago, as insurance against the chance that some member of the team might someday raise the very objections he was now raising. But he could see that Chen was genuinely offended. There seemed no doubt the old man's anger was sincere. Quickly, his own anger abated and he sighed.

"I don't want to accuse you. But try to see this from my perspective. I came here hoping for proof that I have not been induced to betray my country. And you respond with this?" He waved a hand over the game board. "I need something more substantial. You must see that."

Chen shrugged helplessly. "I do. I do see that. But I have no other proof. Listen to what I'm telling you, David. The drugs were not what you feared; they were merely a step in a process. They enabled me to do this." He pointed to one of the discs he had moved. "I admit, by itself it is nothing. I am a weak old man. But there may be no limit to what younger, stronger minds can accomplish. Others have already . . ." He stopped abruptly. "The demonstration! I have a disc!"

He rose from his chair and walked around the desk to a tall cabinet on the far side of the room. "Bring two chairs over here!" As Craighill complied, Chen opened the cabinet. Inside were a TV and a video cube player. From a drawer, Chen produced a disc which he inserted into the player. Then he turned on the television.

"Take a seat, David. Now, a brief explanation before I start. I told you that the machine can enhance concentration. You've seen that it can enable even an old man to move maze discs. But it can do much more. We have been conducting experiments to determine how much enhancement is possible. We use the maze game because the results are so easy to quantify and so dramatic. This cube demonstrates how much progress has already been made."

Chen activated the player and settled into the chair next to Craighill. The television came to life, revealing a small room with a high ceiling. On the far wall was an analog clock with a large sweep second hand. There was a square table in the foreground with plain, upright chairs on opposite sides. On the table was a maze game board. It was very large, perhaps four times the size of the board on Chen's desk, with four times as many squares and discs. Above the table, a pendulum was suspended from the ceiling. It was at least eight feet in length and hung to within three feet of the board surface.

Three Chinese entered the room, a woman and two men. All appeared to be in their mid-twenties. The woman and one of the men seated themselves in the chairs while the second man walked to the far side of the table and faced the camera. He reached out and lifted the weight at the end of the pendulum. It was apparent from the effort required that the pendulum was quite heavy. It was also apparent that the line on which the weight was suspended was flexible rather than rigid, it was a rope or cord of some kind.

"A time reference," Chen explained. "A proof. Once the pendulum is set swinging, it cannot be manipulated as the second hand on the clock could be."

Craighill nodded his understanding, although he had no idea why this fact was significant.

The man allowed the pendulum to hang to its full extent, steadied it, then gently pushed it to his right. It swung through an arc perhaps two feet in each direction, four feet in all. As it swung through its first cycle, Craighill noticed that a light, mounted in the ceiling next to the pendulum mount, caused the pendulum to cast a shadow on the game board. The shadow moved back and forth with the pendulum, first toward one of the seated players, then toward the other.

"Now watch closely," Chen cautioned.

The referee pressed the familiar button on the side of the game board and the maze barriers rose from the enormous playing surface. The camera zoomed in closer so that the board and the players now filled the frame, with the wall clock visible beyond them. The pendulum weight and the lowest foot of the cord on which it was suspended could still be seen at the top of the frame.

The players studied the board for perhaps fifteen seconds. Then, abruptly, the silver and gold discs began to move.

Craighill stared in disbelief. The players were sitting with their hands folded in their laps. Only their heads moved as they strained to follow the rapidly accelerating action.

At first, the discs appeared to move individually; one would move at one end of the board, then, a second later, another at the opposite end would move. But as squads formed and entered the maze, individual movements became much more rapid and more difficult to discern. A minute into the contest, the squads seemed to have merged into coherent units which flowed through the corridors like liquid. The pace was astonishing. In five different places at once they approached one another. In two locations, stalemates were established; in three others, squads advanced, met, and then retreated, winding and twisting through the maze. Repeatedly they approached, retreated, and approached again. Several times, squads on both sides merged with other squads to form small armies which flowed toward one another, touched, diverged and touched again in another location. Several times these split, reformed and spilt again. Back and forth, the discs flowed like molten metal, approaching and retreating over and over with dizzying speed.

Craighill was completely unable to comprehend what he was witnessing. The pace of the play was far too rapid for him to follow, the maze too huge and complex to grasp, the players' strategies unimaginable. It all seemed to be happening on an entirely different plain of mental capability. Normal minds could not understand this, let alone initiate it. He was even more astounded when he considered that the players were not only managing the play, but mentally moving the pieces as well.

It was impossible, he decided. It had to be a trick. The time frame must somehow have been manipulated.

He studied the movement of the pendulum, its shadow on the game board, its relationship to the steady progress of the second hand on the wall clock. He focused his attention on the players, first one and then the other. He watched the motion of their heads, the way the girl's long black hair shifted on her shoulders as her head swayed from side to side. He saw a bead of perspiration trickle down the male player's cheek and down his neck until it vanished beneath his collar. He examined the referee's movements, the way he paced slowly back and forth in a random pattern, occasionally nudging the pendulum when it slowed. Craighill tried to convince himself that some part of it seemed false, out of place with the rest. He failed. It was all utterly consistent. The evidence was beyond questioning; he saw no way the video could have been rigged.

The contest lasted fourteen minutes and ten seconds. The female player won.

"Now do you believe," Chen asked as he switched off the television.

Craighill was speechless.

"What I find most interesting is that the players you just saw, while they are easily the most proficient game players we tested, are otherwise unremarkable. Their general intelligence is no higher than average. Initially, their profiles were charted, just as yours were at the school, and their subconscious interests and abilities were determined. Based on this, we were able to assign them to this experiment because game playing suited them. The machine was then used to refine their powers of concentration and, of course, they spent thousands of hours practicing. The results speak for themselves."

"They certainly do," Craighill said absently. He was still feeling somewhat overwhelmed and struggling to fit this new information into the context of his present discussion with Chen. Even if what he had just seen was true—and he saw no way to refute it—did it prove Chen's claims? Craighill had seen no evidence that linked the game playing experiment with the drugs he had been given. Were they actually related? There had been a machine at the school, but did that machine have anything to do with these game players? He had only Chen's word on that.

"Think of the implications," Chen continued. "The impact this can have on future generations. Someday, it may be possible to test everyone to determine the work they are best suited for, the work they would be happiest doing. And when we then enhance their ability to do that work, can you imagine what that would mean? Of course . . ."

Was Chen's word enough? That was what this finally came down to. Craighill studied the old man sitting beside him. Who was he? A utopian dreamer? Perhaps. A political operative sent to deceive him? No, that was absurd. Chen was a teacher, a diplomat, a scholar. *I trust him*, Craighill thought. Regardless of what Anne believed, he knew in his heart that Chen could be trusted. He had doubted it an hour ago, but no longer. *I do trust him.* Despite the fact that he had no proof because no proof was possible, he knew that it was true. Chen could be trusted. *I trust him completely!*

So he had finally resolved his doubts and it was over. With

this decision came a feeling of profound relief.

Chen was saying, "It will make the greatest difference in technical disciplines, engineering and science, for example. Some work will be relatively unaffected, but in the fields of . . ."

"Chen!"

The old man stopped in mid-sentence.

"I believe you've proved your point. Please accept my apology. If I have offended you, I am sorry."

"No offense was taken, David. No apology is necessary."

Wearily, Craighill pushed himself to his feet. He felt completely exhausted. "I am tired," he said.

Chen rose also and together they walked toward the door. Then Chen took Craighill's hand and said, "I must ask that you tell no one what I have shown you this morning. Very few people know of these experiments."

"But then, why did you tell me?" Craighill's surprise was genuine.

"You required proof. This was the only proof I had to offer." Chen shook Craighill's hand. "Now go. Get some rest. Great things are possible, David, but there is much work to be done before they can become probable."

When Craighill had gone, Chen stood for a while, looking out his window at the skyline of Sacramento. The exuberance he had felt earlier this morning had now vanished, drained away by the strain of his unexpected confrontation.

A small price to pay, he thought, for such an important victory. It had not been absolute, of course; it would be a long time before Craighill and the others learned to trust him completely. But victories were never absolute. Still, there was no harm in savoring them a little.

He keyed the intercom on his desk and said, "Shu-lin, cancel the rest of my morning appointments. I am too tired to see anyone right now."

Then he lay down on his office sofa, closed his eyes and went to sleep.

TWENTY-FIVE

By the time John and Lonnie Murphy reached the rebel camp John had decided on a course of action. The twelve-hour trek up from the valley had given him ample opportunity to consider his options, and the details of his plan were now laid out like a blueprint in his meticulous engineer's mind.

He did not keep his promise to Murphy—he did not tell Murphy what he had decided to do. If the Chinese decided to launch a search for Murphy in these mountains it was possible that some of the Lassen camps might be found and clan members captured. That was a risk John had been forced to accept. But he would accept no further risks; he would take no one into his confidence unnecessarily. Others would be told of his plans only on a need-to-know basis and, at this moment, Murphy did not need to know.

Upon arrival at the camp, he promptly handed Murphy off to one of his lieutenants and retired to his room to begin making preparations.

His first task was the selection of personnel. There were six separate clans in the Lassen area, with a total population of one hundred ninety-three individuals (one hundred ninety-four with the addition of Murphy). Eliminating the women and children left eighty-six able-bodied men. Of these, he was able to quickly discard about sixty. Those that remained were an impressive group—the leaders of the various clans and a number of others with special qualifications, whose names he had mentally filed away for consideration on occasions such as this. He listed them down the left side of a lined legal pad and began making notes beside each name. Most of the notes were positive, a few were negative.

Beside Ben Devin's name he wrote: Combat experience. Smart. Tough. He drew a star in the left margin.

Beside Murphy's name: Street fighter. Knows all the broadcasters. Again, he drew a star.

Zachary: Combat experience. Guide. Led McK. clan to

Calif.

Anderson: Combat experience. Tough. Self-centered.

He reached the bottom of the page without drawing a third star. Four names had been scratched from the list, two had been chosen for the team; nineteen candidates remained to fill four vacancies. He needed a total of six good men.

Returning to the top of the page he started down the list a second time, carefully considering each man's qualifications and adding additional comments. Expert marksman. Good mechanic. Too reckless.

He drew a third star and eliminated two more names on this second pass.

Selection of the last three was more difficult; it took him a half hour to complete his work. Four were newcomers: Murphy, Devin, Anderson and Cox (chosen primarily because of his medical knowledge). Only two were long-term members of the Lassen clans. This ratio would be unpopular, he knew, but that couldn't be helped. Combat experience had weighed heavily in his considerations, and even the best of the long-term Lassen clan members had done very little fighting. Besides, the locals would be far more valuable here in northern California when the balloon went up. He would just have to convince them of that fact.

The next step was to gather the team together here at the Hot Springs camp. Devin was already quartered at Hot Springs, as were Murphy and Jacob Yang, the local who had been selected largely because he was the only Chinese-American in the six clans. But the rest were in other camps, scattered across three thousand square miles of mountain wilderness. Anderson was quartered in one of the most remote camps, nearly fifty miles away.

They could be contacted quickly. The Lassen clans communicated with one another by means of signal guns which John had fabricated in the first year after the war. These consisted of small, high-intensity flashlights fitted into rifle-like stocks, with long barrels made of plastic tubing an inch and a half in diameter. The flashlights were sealed in the stocks so that light escaped only through the barrels. They were actuated by external triggers, could be aimed like rifles and were visible at a range of up to fifty miles. Because of the barrel arrangement, however, they were visible only to an observer located at or very near the aiming point. Just one degree off line the light was invisible. This made it virtually impossible for the Chinese to intercept their messages. Established signaling sites near each camp were manned at six hour intervals, so the four absent team members could be called in on short notice.

But there was no way to shorten their travel times. Anderson could not reach the Hot Springs camp in less than two days. It was regrettable but it was a fact of life. The Chinese had spy satellites, aircraft and a massive array of ordinance at their disposal. The resistance fighters had only their legs to carry them and a few small arms.

John composed the necessary messages for his signalman to transmit, then prepared to get some sleep. There was nothing more he could do until tomorrow. He had been going steadily for two and a half days without stopping. In that time he had hiked thirty miles down to the valley, visited three different camps, met with Triplett and then with Murphy, led Murphy back to Hot Springs and begun making plans for the long-awaited revolt. It had been a grind and weariness now descended upon him. Exhausted, he stretched out on his bed and fell into a deep and satisfying sleep.

Hot Springs camp was a remarkable facility. The members of the McKenzie clan had been amazed when they first saw it. Compared to the shelters they occupied on the lava field, the accommodations at Hot Springs were palatial.

The camp consisted of five structures—four barracks and a central meeting hall—huddled on a wooded hillside beside a small creek. They were crude and rough-looking on the outside, half buried in the hill, with dirt roofs and few windows. Inside, however, the cabins were fitted out like modern pre-war houses. Double airlock entrances opened to cozy interiors with wood plank floors and log walls. The furnishings were all pre-war manufactured goods of excellent quality.

"This is no guerrilla headquarters," Anderson huffed when he first stepped into the central hall. "It looks like one of those weekend retreats where corporate executives go to unwind."

It was comfortable. The residents at Hot Springs had not been fighting the Chinese, so they had had ample time to improve the camp. Under John's direction they had built: A dam that diverted water from the creek into a covered cistern for distribution to the camp buildings (so they had running tap water), a second dam that powered a small turbine generator (so they had electricity), and a second cistern where steaming hot water from a thermal spring was collected for use in heating the camp buildings.

The buildings themselves were of double-wall construction and heavily insulated. This made it unnecessary to augment the hot water heating system. Even in the coldest weather the buildings stayed warm despite the total absence of fireplaces or stoves. All the cooking was done in microwave ovens.

To Anderson and several others from McKenzie, all this luxury seemed unnecessary and frivolous. The Californians, they concluded, were soft and clearly more interested in maintaining their cozy mountain empire than in fighting the Chinese.

On the day before the McKenzie clan was disbanded and its members sent out in small groups to live in the various Lassen camps, Anderson had argued with John on this point. He had called John a hypocrite, saying, "Your high sounding guerrilla theory is all bullshit, isn't it? All you really care about is your comfort!"

John had defended himself calmly and logically. "This all serves an important purpose," he said. "These projects have kept us busy, taught us to work as a team and instilled pride. And the comfort we enjoy as a result discourages defections. We live better here than the prisoners in the Chinese camps, so no one is anxious to leave. The electricity is necessary to recharge the batteries for the signal guns and to allow us to cook without burning wood. The hot water heat is important for the same reason; we never have to build fires, so we are invisible to the spy satellites. What would you have us do, give up our comfort and our security along with it? Huddle in crude shelters like you did in Oregon? Why? What would we gain as a result?"

When the confrontation was over, neither man had succeeded in persuading the other. But they had defined their positions to one another and to the rest of the camp population. Afterward it was clear that a seed of doubt, however tiny, had been planted in the minds of some clan members. John's arguments were far more sensible than Anderson's, but still, two years without fighting was a long time.

On the day Lonnie Murphy was led into camp, therefore, John's position was already marginally less secure than it had once been.

Murphy's first impression of the Hot Springs was nearly identical to Anderson's. He was spoiling for a fight, anxious to take action to counteract the Chinese television broadcasts and hoping to enlist the aid of an avenging army. He found instead a settled and complacent-looking band of pretenders, the exact opposite of what he had expected. They reminded him more of vacationers than guerrillas. So he took it upon himself to light a fire under them.

Capturing their attention was easy. While John planned and later slept, Murphy addressed the clan. Its members gathered around him in the meeting hall, anxious for news of the camps and to hear about his escape. He told them everything, about the new television network, the broadcasts to the camps, the reactions of the prisoners and, finally, his experience at Chen's school.

When he was finished, one female clan member asked, "Then you think Chen let you go because the drugs didn't affect you?"

"That's my best guess. He couldn't control me so I was useless to him."

"And you believe the others are being controlled?"

"I never saw the others again until the broadcasts started. But what they're doing now speaks for itself. I know these people; they wouldn't have sold out like this. There's only one possible explanation."

The woman who had been asking the questions looked worried, almost frightened. She said, "And you really think this is dangerous?"

"It's worse than dangerous, it's brilliant. For eighty years, television ruled American culture. For a lot of people it was the most important thing in their lives. Now the Chinese have given it back to them. It looks and sounds exactly like pre-war U.S. TV. That's why it's working. In the barracks, people are acting as though the dead past has been resurrected. The pictures show a completely different world, of course, not the old world resurrected. But they see what they want to see. The newscasters and the music and the sets and the actors all seem familiar, so they accept them without thinking. I might have been fooled myself if I hadn't recognized Craighill and Sandiman and the others.

"I don't know who thought it all up—recruiting Americans and staging it like American TV—but it's been incredibly effective. It's doing exactly what the Chinese want, breaking down resistance in the camps. In six months it'll all be over. The people will have accepted the New Order."

Murphy looked from the woman to the rest of his audience, wondering if he had convinced them. Had he shaken them from their lethargy? Would they be willing to fight now? Even if they were willing, after two years of inactivity, would they be any good at it? He remembered how rusty he used to be after the off-season, and how badly his Kansas teams had played each year after the layoff for semester exams. After a one-week layoff! And they had been finely conditioned, highly focused athletes, almost professionals. These rebels weren't soldiers to begin with. Most of them had never been in a real fight in their entire lives. So how good could they be?

"Lonnie!" It was not the woman this time; it was a man's voice. Murphy turned toward the speaker.

"Are you saying it's too late, that we've already lost?"

"Hell no! But I am saying we don't have much time left."

The man's concern was obvious. "Time to do what?"

Murphy glanced around the room. The clansmen were hanging on every word now, it was going even better than he had hoped.

"Can anyone tell me," he asked, "just how many guerrillas there are in these mountains?"

The camp was quiet when John awoke. It was four o'clock in the morning. During college he had always done his most productive studying in the hours just before sunrise and it was still his favorite time of the day. He climbed out of bed, flipped on his desk lamp, and dressed hurriedly. Then he sat down at the desk, turned to a clean sheet of paper on his legal pad, wrote "Local Teams" at the top of the page and began making notes.

He worked for several hours. Then he placed all his notes from this morning and yesterday afternoon in a desk drawer, turned off the light and walked from his barracks to the meeting hall. It was there he learned about Murphy's polemics.

The hall was empty when he arrived. Usually there would have been four or five clan members up by this time, but he dismissed their absence as unimportant and set about brewing a pot of coffee. Five minutes later, Dave Adrian appeared through the main doorway. In the informal command structure of the Hot Springs clan, Adrian was John's second in command.

"Morning, John," Adrian said.

John waved a steaming cup at him. "Join me, Dave?"

Adrian nodded. He poured himself a cup of coffee and joined John at one of the mess tables.

"We've got a problem," Adrian said.

John sipped his coffee and waited.

"It's the new guy, Murphy."

"What about him?" John had spent twelve hours with Murphy yesterday. His instincts told him Murphy had been telling the truth and was not a turncoat. So this shouldn't be too serious.

"Well, you know how tense everyone's been lately. It's been a long hard winter and we've all got cabin fever. Then there's the stories the crowd from Oregon has been telling about all the fighting they did up north. Together, these things have created a situation, John. The clan is anxious for some action."

Adrian seemed to be dancing all around his subject and choosing his words very carefully. His caution was beginning to worry the clan leader. John said, "Get to it, Dave, what did Murphy do?"

"He stirred things up," Adrian said finally. "He held court in here all yesterday evening and pretty well convinced everyone who would listen that it was time to start the revolution. He told them things were changing fast in the camps because of some new television programs the Chinese were broadcasting. He said we needed to act now. He claimed—"

"How bad is it?" John asked. "How many did he convince?"

"I didn't come in until very late," Adrian said carefully. "That's why I didn't get you up last night—everyone went to bed a few minutes after I got there. But a lot of people seemed ready to fight. At least half of them, I'd say. The rest wanted to know what you were planning. Ben and Katie were in that group and, of course, I sided with them. But Murphy is a persuasive bastard. He wanted to organize an immediate invasion of the northern California camps. Once the revolt got started, he said, it would be like a snowball rolling downhill. It would spread all over the country, he said, and we could drive the Chinese back to China. A lot of people agreed with him."

John's mouth was drawn into a tight, thin line. He said icily, "Exactly how many, Dave?"

Adrian hesitated, then replied quickly, as though finally resigned to get it over with. "Most of the camp was there, John. Twenty-five or thirty people. Twelve or fifteen seemed very enthusiastic about Murphy's plan."

The clan leader's expression remained fixed.

"I tried to reason with them," Adrian said. "So did Devin. But Murphy had facts on his side, things I didn't know anything about."

John sank back in his chair, shaking his head. "This wasn't

your fault, Dave; it was mine. I wanted to keep this particular genie in its bottle for a while, but I ignored Murphy's ego. I recognized it, but I still ignored it. That was stupid." He drummed his fingers on the table. "So what's needed now is some damage control. I have to put a muzzle on Mr. Murphy and remind everyone who's in charge around here before this goes any further. I hate to play dictator, but sometimes it's necessary." He downed the last of his coffee. "Okay, here's what we're going to do."

A meeting was called for 10:00 a.m. Every adult resident of the Hot Springs was required to attend, with the exception of the six sentries. (John had doubled the normal number, on the chance that the Chinese might be searching for Murphy.) These sentries had been hand-picked for this shift by Dave Adrian; they had all been in the hall with Murphy the night before, and had sided with Adrian and Devin. John had instructed Adrian to make these assignments because he wanted to be sure that all Murphy's followers heard what he planned to say at the meeting.

He entered the hall and walked to the head of the room at precisely ten o'clock. There was no podium and he carried no notes. Thirty-one anxious faces greeted him.

"I'll make this short and sweet," he began. "I've been told about the informal meeting that was held in this room last night and I know what was discussed. I don't agree with Mr. Murphy's actions, but I agree with several of his conclusions. First, I agree that the recent Chinese television broadcasts are dangerous. As a consequence, I also agree that immediate action is required to counter the effect of the broadcasts. I cannot, however, agree with his proposal for a northern California revolution. Such a plan would be ill advised and futile. Even if it succeeded in accomplishing its short-term goals, its ultimate failure would be inevitable because northern California can easily be isolated from the rest of the country. To the west is the Pacific, to the north, in Oregon, are a large number of heavily garrisoned camps. To the east, hundreds of miles of uninhabited desert and to the south, the population centers of Los Angeles and San Diego. It is therefore evident that any action begun here would also end here. The Chinese would bring in reinforcements and cut off the few escape routes available to us. Mr. Murphy's revolution would not spread and blossom, it would wither and die." He looked at Murphy and said, "Lonnie, if a successful revolution could begin in the northern California camps we would have started it long ago."

211

Many in the audience appeared embarrassed by what John had just said; Murphy did not. He rose to his feet and faced the clan leader. "Does this mean," he asked sharply, "that you plan to do nothing? What will it take before you stand up and fight?"

"Sit down, Lonnie!"

Murphy seemed startled by the authority in John's voice. He hesitated momentarily, then said, "First I want an answer. We all want an answer."

John's face was an ebony mask, stern and hard. He and Murphy were standing only a few feet apart, and although the newcomer towered above him, somehow John seemed the more imposing figure. He said, "You have no standing in this clan. You are here as a guest. And if you continue to disrupt this meeting you will be removed." Then he looked back to his audience. "In a sense, the revolt has already begun. Preliminary planning is complete, the other clans have been contacted, and their representatives will begin arriving here this afternoon. In the meantime, there is a great deal of work to do."

Murphy sat down.

"Mr. Murphy's arrival yesterday has exposed us to special risks; the Chinese may already be searching these mountains for him. For that reason, and because what we're about to attempt is of such critical importance, the strictest possible security will be maintained from now on. We're going to do everything we can to reduce our risks. That means that each one of you will be told only what you absolutely need to know about our plans in order to do your jobs. And you will not know even that much until the last possible moment. You all understand the reason for this. There is going to be fighting and some of us may be captured. We can't allow captured individuals to compromise our operations.

"For now, you should have no questions. You don't have enough information yet to ask questions." John forced a smile and nervous laughter rippled through the audience. "So this meeting is adjourned. I need to see the following individuals in my quarters immediately: Lonnie (he nodded to Murphy), Ben Devin, Jacob Yang, and Dave Adrian."

Five minutes later, John and the four men he had named were gathered in his room.

"First things first," John began. "Lonnie, I want you on this team but only on my terms. I'm in charge; that has to be understood. If you can't accept that condition, you can leave now. I won't hold it against you; you'll be assigned to another team."

Murphy shook his head. "I'll stay," he said. "I want to be part of this."

John fought back a wry smile. "Apology accepted," he said. "Now let's get started." He pulled his notes from a desk drawer and thumbed through them briefly before saying, "Gentlemen, our patience has finally been rewarded. The Chinese have given us everything we need. They've handed us the keys to the revolution. Let me explain what I mean.

"When Ben's group came down from Oregon, we found out that the Chinese used chemical weapons against them. That was the first key; it demonstrated their inhumanity and gave us something we could use against them. Now Lonnie has told us that all the Americans on the broadcast crew were drugged into collaborating. That's the second key. Next there is Sacramento. Because there's been no guerrilla activity in California, Sacramento has been made an open city. Security is lax; the city is accessible. Finally, there's the new television network. It broadcasts nationwide and its studios are in Sacramento. Those studios are the fourth key."

Adrian whistled softly. "We're going to Sacramento, aren't we?"

John nodded. "We're going to capture that brand new television studio and tell everyone in North America what vicious, hateful bastards the Chinese really are. We're going to tell them about the chemical weapons and the drugs, and then we're going to tell them to take control of their camps. We're going to explain to them that if they all act at once the Chinese will be powerless to stop them."

"You really think we can do that?" Murphy asked. "You think we can go in there and get back out alive?"

John said, 'I do. Two minutes after our broadcast begins, Sacramento will be a war zone; the streets will be impassable. The Chinese will shut us down eventually by cutting the power, but by then it'll be too late. I've already rough-drafted our announcement. I figure it'll take no more than four or five minutes."

"Five minutes sounds like a lot," Devin said doubtfully. "You can't be sure how people will react, in Sacramento or anywhere else. The streets might not be impassable, at least not right away."

John smiled knowingly. "We have friends in Sacramento," he said. "Take my word for it, we'll have our five minutes."

For a moment, the room fell silent as each man privately

213

pondered the enormity of what John was proposing. Finally, Yang broke the tension. "We have to try," he said simply. "This is the chance we've been waiting for."

"Agreed," Murphy put in.

Devin and Adrian nodded their approval.

"Good," John said. "Very good. Then the first thing we need to discuss is team assignments."

John's plan for the revolt was the product of years of preparation and included many elements. Only John knew them all. The Sacramento team had no knowledge of what the teams in northern California were planning and the northern California teams did not even know of the Sacramento team's existence. They knew that the revolt was about to begin and what they must each do to prepare, that was all.

Every able-bodied man in the Lassen clans had been assigned to a team. Most were to be stationed near the farm camps in the northern Sacramento Valley. They would be armed with side arms, assault rifles, mortars, and even a few portable rocket launchers, retrieved from hidden bunkers before they marched to their stations. Their mission was to move in and support the camp populations when the rioting started.

Smaller teams were to leave the Hot Springs immediately, days before the Sacramento team departed. These consisted of only two or three men each, bound for Oregon and Washington and the mountains of the Coast Range on the far side of the Sacramento Valley and the Owyhee Mountains in southern Idaho. Their mission was to contact the rebel clans known to be hiding in those locations and prepare them to support the camp populations in their areas.

The critical element in all of this was advance notice. John was certain that many camps could be taken from the inside. But he was equally certain that, without outside support, many could not. His greatest fear, which he revealed to no one, was that the success they all anticipated on the west coast would not be duplicated east of the Sierra Nevada mountains. The clans to the east must be contacted. The mission would be extremely dangerous. There was only one way it could be accomplished and only one man who could do it. When the meeting with the Sacramento team was over, John summoned that man to his quarters and explained exactly what would be required of him.

Zachary volunteered without hesitation. "I haven't done

that kind of flying for a long time," he said with a grin. "Not since I left Alaska. I've missed it. You bet I'll go."

"Good man," John said gratefully.

He wanted to say more; he wanted to offer a personal warning, because he was sure the boyish daredevil hadn't fully understood the difficulty of what he was being asked to do. But he was afraid Zachary might change his mind if he did understand, so John kept his warnings to himself.

The day before the Sacramento team was scheduled to depart, Zachary and a mechanic who knew where the aircraft was hidden trudged off through the snow toward the east. No one but John knew where they were going.

The plane, a fifty-year-old Cessna 180 fitted with skis and long range fuel tanks, was hangared in an old barn near Susanville. It was ideal for Zachary's mission. The fuel tanks were full, and a cabinet in the barn held a complete library of VFR charts covering the western U.S., all carefully cataloged and indexed.

"The old boy who owned this bird was a meticulous son-of-a-bitch," Zachary observed when he saw the charts.

The mechanic shrugged. "I didn't know him," he said disinterestedly, then set about his work, draining the oil from the engine and heating it over a portable gas stove.

They installed the battery they had brought from Hot Springs and were amazed when, despite the fact that it was only 22 degrees in the barn, the engine caught after just three revolutions of the prop and ran perfectly.

"A very meticulous old boy," Zachary repeated with genuine admiration. He listened to the engine for only a minute, then shut it down. The mechanic wanted to let it run a while longer and check a few things, but Zachary refused; he was satisfied and didn't want to burn any more fuel.

It was near dusk. Zachary stepped outside the barn and gazed down the length of the field that would serve as his runway the next morning. The snow was about eight inches deep and crusty. There was a low line of hills running along the north side of the field and a single hill about three hundred feet high directly in line with the runway, a mile to the east. Piece of cake, he thought; unless the wind was strong from the west, forcing him to take off in that direction.

He would leave just before first light. Maintaining his runway heading, he should clear the lone hill by several hundred feet, then pass over the small population center at Susanville while everyone was still asleep. By sunrise he would be flying low and slow over central Nevada, carefully choosing a route that would avoid the few towns and ranches where the aircraft might attract attention. From there his route would take him across southern Utah and into Colorado where there were supposed to be large rebel clans headquartered between Aspen and Gunnison. His fuel would be just about exhausted when he reached the area and the rebels would be invisible from the air anyway, so he would simply have to take his chances about where to go down. If he could establish contact quickly, and if the Colorado clans had good communications, the whole vast Rocky Mountain region could participate in the revolt. It might mean the difference between ultimate success or failure.

John had told him to abandon the aircraft. "There are no secure landing fields anyway and no fuel, so there's no advantage in staying with it. Once it hits the ground, that aircraft will provide the Chinese their only clue to your location. So I want you to jump. Let the aircraft go down by itself. Let it lead them away from you."

This was the only part of the mission that troubled Zachary. He didn't mind jumping—he'd made seven jumps one summer, just for the experience—but the thought of ditching this lovely old bird caused him real pain. Airplanes were living things to Zachary. In Alaska he had counted several among his best friends and seeing this one reminded him of those days. Maybe it was the skis. Or maybe it was just because he was about to fly again for the first time since before the war. Whatever the reason, he wished the ditching was not necessary. But he knew that John was right. Abandoning the aircraft made sense; it would have to be done.

He took one last look down the runway, fixing the location of the obstacle, the lone hill, in his mind. He would not be able to see it in the morning, but it would be there, lurking in the darkness. So he would need to visualize its position.

Satisfied with this part of his preparations, he turned and walked back to the barn. There was still much to do. From the old farmer's files he pulled the charts he would need, as well as charts covering areas to the north and south of his intended course. He studied these for an hour, selecting his route and noting landmarks he should be able to identify from an altitude of only one or two hundred feet. Next, he retrieved the pilot's handbook from the aircraft and refreshed his memory of the 180's performance—rate of climb, stall speed, cruising speed. A little quick math confirmed what he suspected. The long range tanks held seventy-five gallons of fuel; the airplane would burn just under twelve gallons per hour at a speed of 130 mph, and it was nearly eight hundred miles to Aspen. So he could make it, just barely.

His last item of business was the parachutes. Why had the old farmer kept parachutes anyway, when most pilots had never even seen one? Was he that cautious? Zachary doubted it. More likely, the parachutes were another example of John's remarkable foresight; he had probably acquired them elsewhere and stored them here with the airplane just in case they might someday be needed. But could they be trusted? There was only one way to be certain. He picked one, unpacked and examined it, and found it to be in perfect condition. He carefully repacked it and placed it in the aircraft.

His preparations were complete. He and the mechanic ate a dinner of Spam and canned potatoes, then climbed into their sleeping bags. He slept soundly and awoke, without benefit of an alarm clock, at exactly 5:00 a.m.

A half hour later the Cessna was out of the barn and standing in the snow at the west end of the field. It was a clear, calm morning and the sky was full of stars. But there was no moon, the lone hill at the end of the runway was lost in shadow. The mechanic wished him luck. Zachary waved, eased the throttle forward and felt the airplane shudder. The snow yielded reluctantly to the skis at first, clinging to them as the plane struggled to gain momentum. The first hundred yards went by very slowly. Then, finally, the airspeed indicator quivered and rotated off its peg. He eased the yoke forward. The tail lifted and the airspeed began to build. Snow hissed beneath the skis. At seventy miles per hour the airplane lifted free.

Zachary maintained forward pressure, allowing his speed to build before starting his climb and straining to catch sight of the hill. He never saw it but he knew where it was and as he eased the yoke back and watched his altimeter's steady upward progress he knew he would clear it easily. Finally he could relax. The steady drone of the engine was like music and the star-strewn sky above seemed suddenly familiar, so did the featureless void below. He had almost forgotten how beautiful it could be. It was a fantastic sensation, the freest feeling in human experience, he thought, to be alone in an airplane at night.

About a thousand feet above the ground he saw the sky to the east beginning to lighten and his first landmark, Hot Springs Peak, silhouetted against the pale horizon. He had timed it perfectly. He flew directly toward the peak for several minutes, then, once he was past Susanville, swung to the southeast and followed the valley toward Nevada.

As the sky lightened further, permitting him to see, he descended. By the time he reached the northern end of Pyramid Lake he was flying just a hundred feet above the desert. Had his presence been detected yet? By someone in Susanville? By radar? By satellite? There was no way to know and no point in speculating. *Follow the mission plan*, he told himself, *that's the only thing you can control.*

He crossed the barren wastes of Nevada without incident and entered Utah.

His fuel consumption was running lower than expected because he had realized several hours earlier that he should screw the mixture down as lean as possible. He wouldn't do that to an airplane he was going to need again tomorrow, but he could do it to this airplane because it was going to be scrap tomorrow. So he now had a couple of unexpected gallons in his tanks and was gaining nearly a gallon every hour. He felt good about that.

Zachary reached the Colorado border at 11:15, thirty miles north of I-70 and only a hundred and thirty miles from his target. He was on time and had twenty minutes of extra fuel on board. So far he had been incredibly lucky; everything had gone perfectly. He had seen no one and he didn't believe anyone had seen him.

But his luck was about to run out.

East of Grand Junction, the western slopes of the Rockies soared upward and disappeared into clouds. A winter storm blanketed central Colorado.

Zachary had only a few minutes to consider his options. If he bailed out here, on the western fringe of the storm, he would be facing a hundred mile march before he would reach the area where the rebels were believed to be hiding. Would he reach them in time? He doubted it. But if he flew into the storm he would be accepting enormous risks. The rebel positions were in the very heart of the Rockies, south of Aspen, where many mountains rose to more than fourteen thousand feet. He would be entering that area blind, navigating by dead reckoning and flying, quite literally, into the condition pilot's laughingly called "cumulo-granite clouds"—clouds full of rocks! Under any other circumstances he would have refused. But on this day he had no choice.

North of De Beque he trimmed the Cessna to maintain a 300-foot-per-minute climb and circled while he gained altitude. To the southeast he could see Horse Mountain; beyond, everything was swallowed in grey mist.

When he reached ten thousand feet he took up a heading that would carry him directly over Crested Butte, noted the time as he passed over I-70 and proceeded southeast into the clouds. He continued climbing until he reached thirteen thousand feet. Then he trimmed the airplane for level flight and climbed into his parachute harness. He would take no foolish chances, he told himself; he had already cheated his course a few degrees to the south to ensure that he would miss Castle Peak. He would bail out long before there was any chance of hitting the sentinel peaks along the Continental Divide, thirty miles east of Crested Butte. But despite these precautions, his heart was pounding as the minute hand on his watch slowly approached his calculated jump time. Four minutes remained, then three. His mind raced. "Jump now! Play it safe!" it screamed at him. But he knew that every minute he waited was carrying him over two miles closer to his target. Two miles of rugged, snow covered terrain that would take hours to cross once he was on the ground. Two minutes remained, then one. Turbulent air churning around the nearby peaks buffeted the Cessna.

He cracked the door, recoiling as snow swirled into the cockpit. Then he pulled the throttle back, trimmed the airplane for ninety miles an hour, secured his jacket hood tight around his head and forced the door open.

He jumped. The airplane was now a death trap and he wanted to get away from it as quickly as possible. He saw it hanging above him for only seconds as he fell away from it. Then it was swallowed up by the featureless grey void that surrounded him, and he was alone.

He pulled his release handle immediately and felt the familiar drag of the chute feeding out behind him. There was a jolt as the canopy filled, then absolute perfect silence.

TWENTY-SIX

Tuesday, January 25

    The banners came down today. At seven this morning they were still mutely declaring their simplistic messages; by noon they had been stripped from the streets and the buildings. As a result, the city now looks more like its old self and less like occupied territory. I consider this a victory of some significance; first, because we all played a part in winning it (we have been lobbying Chen on this subject since our arrival here two and a half months ago), and second, because it is another example of the growing spirit of cooperation and flexibility being displayed by the continental administration. We are all encouraged by it.

    The business with the banners may seem a small thing, but in the long run it is the small things that matter most. The ultimate success or failure of the Chinese experiment here will depend not merely on its philosophy, but on whether everyday reality coincides with its philosophy. In my view this is exactly what destroyed our American experiment—for most of us, everyday reality did not coincide with the philosophy expressed in our founding documents and engraved on our monuments. The removal of the banners is a step in the right direction. There have been many such steps lately and we pray that the trend will continue.

Thursday, January 27

    During my life as a newsman I have witnessed firsthand much of the human misery of the last forty years. I have seen populations ravaged by war and famine, cities destroyed by floods and earthquakes, nations held hostage by terrorism. Two and a half years ago, I saw the horribly disfigured victims of our final madness as they hobbled or crawled or were carried into refugee camps. I thought these experiences had taught me the meaning of the word "disaster" but I was wrong. I was completely unprepared for what I observed today.

220

It was Sunday. Global Television currently broadcasts only six days a week; as more staff is added this will change and we will broadcast every day, but for now we are all given Sundays off. The forecast was for beautiful weather and Anne and I wanted to do something special. Last night I asked Chen if he could suggest something. He looked thoughtful and said, "You've never seen a dead zone, have you, David?"

Under different circumstances this suggestion would have been intriguing, but it did not appeal to me on this occasion. A tour of a dead zone would undoubtedly be conducted by some military PR type who would spend the entire day declaiming the evils of pre-war nationalism. I was in no mood for such an ordeal; I wanted to enjoy the day unencumbered. I declined.

"Until you've seen one," Chen insisted, "You'll never really understand what happened to our world."

Again, I refused. "I've often considered asking to see San Francisco, Chen," I said. "But not tomorrow.

"I can't say you'd enjoy it exactly. But you would both find the experience valuable. You can drive yourself. I'll arrange for a car and you can have it for the whole day. Go anywhere you wish."

I couldn't believe I'd heard him right. We could drive ourselves? With no guide, no military escort? Not even our news crews are afforded such freedom, they are always accompanied by military escorts when they leave Sacramento. Sandiman has a lieutenant with him on his current trip around the world.

"I could arrange for someone to drive you if you prefer," Chen said. "But I assume you'd rather be alone."

The offer was too good to pass up. I accepted without even asking Anne.

The car was delivered to our apartment at 7:00 a.m., complete with travel permits, maps and passes to the San Francisco Restricted Area. We were on the road by 7:10.

The six-year-old Nissan Mentor was tiny, cramped and underpowered. It bounced along pothole-strewn I-80 like a basketball being dribbled, and its engine sounded like a swarm of angry hornets. But the computer on the dash told us it was getting seventy-four miles per gallon and that meant that our five gallon fuel supply would take us over three hundred and fifty miles. The car was rough and uncomfortable and we loved it. It reminded us of the Mini Cooper we owned the year we were married, while we were both still in college. The sensation was absolutely delicious, we felt freer than we had felt in years. There was almost no traffic on the roads and that added a subtle note of danger and adventure. It made the familiar countryside seem strange and full of menace, but at the same time inviting, as though it existed only for us. Exactly the way the world had looked to us forty years earlier, we recalled.

We laughed a lot as we drove west, remembering the Mini Cooper and friends we knew and things we did long ago. I made a mental note to thank Chen when we returned, and Anne, reading my thoughts as she often does, said at that precise moment, "Pug, we must do something for Chen when we get home. Invite him for dinner one day next week, will you?" I will never understand how she does that.

The first checkpoint was at Fairfield. There were chain link fences along both sides of the road for several hundred yards as we approached, with radiation warning placards hung every fifty feet or so, directing us to a narrow barricaded checkpoint with vehicle gates on either side of a small, wood-frame structure. Off on the north shoulder of the road was a metal trailer, set on blocks, with electric and telephone wires connected to it.

A uniformed guard emerged from the booth as we pulled to a stop at the barricade. He walked to the car and asked for my papers. He recognized me and called me by name even before looking at the papers, but his manner was very officious and he seemed quite surprised to see two Americans alone in the car. He muttered something about verifications, left us and walked to the trailer, presumably to make a phone call. It was a full five minutes before he returned and handed us a packet of maps and literature. He also gave us two docimeter badges and instructed us to wear them at all times.

"The roads are color-coded," he explained and warned us not to leave the green routes. Then he checked his watch, told us we must return no later than 2:30 and abruptly returned to his booth. A moment later the barricade opened and we drove through.

Anne read aloud from the literature as we climbed into the hills west of Fairfield. There was a great deal of information about estimated radiation levels immediately after the bomb and comparisons with current levels. Color-coded zones were drawn on the maps to indicate approximate current radiation levels. It was pointed out that the hilly terrain of the bay area played an important role in determining which areas suffered the greatest blast damage, but that residual radiation outside the downtown core was primarily the product of wind-driven fallout. "Someareas which appear to be COOL may in fact be quite HOT!" the brochure said. "DO NOT BE MISLED BY THE ABSENCE OF BLAST DAMAGE. PAY ATTENTION TO POSTED SIGNS AND MONITOR YOUR DOCIMETER BADGE!"

There was also information about EMP (Electromagnetic Pulse) effects. "Tens of thousands of abandoned vehicles litter the area," the text stated. "These were rendered inoperable by EMP. So were some aircraft, radio and television broadcasting and receiving equipment, computers, and anything else electrical. Derelict vehicles have been removed from posted routes, but many secondary roads remain impassible, even in outlying areas. DO NOT LEAVE POSTED ROUTES."

"What vehicles?" Anne asked after reading this. "We've seen no abandoned vehicles."

"That's true," I agreed. "But this is a posted primary route and we're still thirty-five miles from San Francisco. I imagine we'll see what they mean once we clear these hills and drop down into Vallejo."

I remember feeling rather smug as I spoke those words. I'd never seen a dead zone but I knew what to expect. Or so I told myself.

We saw hundreds of abandoned cars in Vallejo. Only a few stood on the shoulders of I-80 and Route 37 (the green route we had chosen to follow around the north shore of San Pablo Bay), but they were everywhere on the side roads. There were other unnatural signs as well. The trees and shrubs in Vallejo seemed sick and stunted. Grass grew on the lawns and in the parks, but it was weak and ragged looking stuff.

"It's winter," Anne argued when I pointed these things out. "The plants are all dormant."

"Maybe," I said, "but no one's cut this grass for two summers. So it should be waist high even if it is dormant now." I was frankly surprised to see radiation damage this far northeast of the city; everything I'd heard indicated that the fallout from the San Francisco bomb had been carried off to the south and west. Anne's maps confirmed that this area was supposed to be cool; the zone around Vallejo was shown as green or nearly normal now.

Further on, the marsh grasses skirting the bay looked

healthy. But I'd only driven this route once before in my life. Was the grass really healthy or should it be taller, denser? I couldn't be certain. West of the bay, however, as we reached Route 101 and turned south, the signs became unmistakable. At first there were sick trees and stunted grass, a little worse than in Vallejo. Several miles further on it became worse still, and dead trees began to appear. By the time we reached San Rafael, even the conifers looked dead, the grass was brown and the shrubs were withered. Abandoned vehicles stood along the shoulders of the main highway here. Most of the buildings we passed had broken windows and many had been burned. Blast effects? Surely not at this range, not the fires at least. We were still more than fifteen miles from ground zero and sheltered by the rugged hills of the Marin Peninsula. More probably this damage had been the result of rioting and looting. I tried to imagine the scene—the roads jammed with useless vehicles, the southern sky ablaze, the air heavy with smoke and panic-stricken people screaming in the streets. All telephone service, television and radio destroyed by EMP, the entire population here cut off from any information and feeling abandoned. It was easy to imagine that some of them would have lashed out in blind rage.

But where were they now? They could not have all simply walked away. So some of these buildings, possibly many of them, must be tombs. Quiet now. Eerily quiet. We had not seen another car since Vallejo.

We drove on past the Richmond Bridge (which appeared intact), past Tiburon and Mill Valley. The damage was growing visibly worse with each mile now. Nothing was alive in the area we were driving through. The trees were blackened and charred as though from a firestorm. Firestorms were a phenomenon I associated with ground zero, or very near ground zero. Could there have been a firestorm here, beyond Sausalito, almost ten miles from ground zero according to the radiation maps? It certainly appeared that there had been. Structures were still recognizable but almost none were intact. Few had roofs and most retained only one or two standing walls. Rubble was everywhere. The neighborhoods we could see from the highway looked like photos of Berlin or Dresden after World War II. It was difficult to tell where the streets had been.

The highway itself was now in terrible condition, so much so that I began to wonder if the bomb had triggered an earthquake. (I had heard no such report at the time.) The road surface was cracked and irregular, heaving upward in places and sunken in others. The shoulders and the center strip were a jumbled litter of discarded cars and trucks and buses, which had been unceremoniously bulldozed from the road to clear a passable route.

Finally, there was a massive barricade with a large placard directing us to exit.

At the base of the exit ramp was another checkpoint. Our papers were examined again and we were given a new packet of literature and maps. These maps were a much larger scale and very detailed, showing only the southern tip of the Marin Peninsula. We noticed that our route on this map was no longer green, but red. It wound its way westward into the hills, then south to the old World War II fortifications overlooking the Golden Gate. A checkpoint guard demanded our docimeter badges and examined them. Apparently satisfied, he returned them and withdrew a small area map from our packet. It showed the observation points at the extreme southern tip of the peninsula.

"You will park here," he said gruffly. "But you may remain no longer than a half hour. You will see a footpath leading around this hill." He pointed with his finger as he spoke. "You may walk to this point but no further; it is clearly marked. The view is like no other on earth so you may want to remain for some time, but you must return to the parking lot within five minutes. To stay longer would be very dangerous. Do you understand?"

"How hot is it?" I asked him.

He ignored my question. "Five minutes," he repeated. "No more." Then he backed away from the car and returned to his shelter, which was not like the guard's shelter at Fairfield; this one was made of heavy metal and its windows were narrow slits fitted with thick grey glass. I had no doubt that the guard was telling the truth—this was not a place where we should linger unnecessarily.

We followed the red route into the hills and found the parking lot without difficulty. It was on a windy bluff facing the Pacific, high up on the headlands just north of the entrance to the bay. It was completely barren now, stripped of all vegetation. Even the trees that had once grown there were gone, only charred stumps remained. I didn't really recognize the place, but I did remember it. Anne and I had come here shortly after

225

moving to California. We toured the Bay Area like typical vacationers on that trip. Alcatraz, Ghiradelli Square, Fisherman's Wharf, Coit Tower, we saw them all. And this spot— or rather the spot we were about to see overlooking the Golden Gate and the city—had provided my most vivid memory of that trip. It was, I thought then, one of the most spectacular views in all the world.

What would it be now?

I stepped from the car into a chill, January gale. And that too seemed strangely familiar. Had it been January when we last came here? Or was it always this cold on these bluffs?

I buttoned my coat and walked around to help Anne from the car and was surprised to find her fighting back tears. "I can't do it, Pug," she said, her chin quivering. "You liked L.A. but I never did. San Francisco was my city and I don't think I want to see it the way it is now. I thought I could do this, but I can't. You go. I'm staying here."

I don't know why, but at that moment it seemed important to me that she should see it. "You have to see it," I said. "It's history, Annie. We've come all this way and it's so close now."

She shook her head and said solemnly, "It was the most beautiful city in the world, Pug. I loved it and I want to remember it whole."

I walked to the lookout alone. There was a large photograph in a glass case showing the city as it once was, and three short rows of benches facing its charred corpse. I sat on a bench for three minutes looking at it, then left. I could endure no more.

The city is simply gone and the place it once occupied is now vacant, as though nothing ever stood there. According to the maps, ground zero was the Embarcadero, but there remains no evidence that such a place ever existed. Not even rubble marks the spot. Instead, there is a slight indentation in the earth, perhaps a half mile square, which glistens dully in the sunlight like black glass. The landscape on all sides has been swept clean. In the downtown core of the city, between the crater and the place that was once the Presidio, shattered remains of only twenty or thirty buildings stand tall enough above the general level of rubble to be identifiable. They look like stumps in some long dead forest. They are dark grey and everything around them is dark grey. To the east the Oakland Bridge has vanished, leaving only stumps where its towers once stood. In the entire area only two recognizable landmarks remain: Alcatraz Island and the towers of the Golden Gate Bridge. The bridge span that carried the highway is gone, the south tower is twisted and leaning, and from the north tower huge cables, which once arched gracefully across the narrows, hang limp. Alcatraz fared better. The foliage that once softened the island is gone, of course but its stone buildings are still recognizable.

A prison and a bridge; there are no other memorials. All the rest is black and charred and looks like the surface of the moon. And over it all hangs an immense, suffocating stillness. Nothing moves. No bird soars on the sea breeze, no boat plies the waters of the bay. There is no sound but the shrill whistling of the wind.

I said nothing when I returned to the car. Neither did Anne. We followed the red route back to the last checkpoint, regained the highway and headed north. Just past San Rafael we saw a bus going south, full of children, smiling and laughing, apparently enjoying a day's outing. They were bound for the overlook we had just visited, this road went nowhere else. I wondered what they were expected to gain from the experience. What could it possibly mean to them?

"Do you still think I was wrong?" Anne asked. She too had been watching the bus.

"Wrong?" I said.

"Do you still think I should have gone with you back there?"

"No," I said. "You weren't wrong. There was nothing there for you."

"And for you, Pug?"

I am still considering the answer to that question.

Saturday, January 29

Two days ago, I looked upon the charred corpse of what was once the most beautiful city on this planet. It sickened me to think that human beings had wished such hideous destruction on other human beings. It made me angry. Now, however, with the benefit of a little quiet contemplation and 20/20 hindsight I find myself less certain of my right to criticize the perpetrators, at least not until I have faced up to my own responsibility. I believe many people contributed to the destruction of the San Francisco

227

Anne loved so much, me more than most.

It began four or five decades ago. Like other American cities, San Francisco's traditional neighborhoods were sold to the highest bidders. A small coterie of investors, developers and affluent newcomers made the place over in their image. They called the process "renewal" and claimed that they were revitalizing neighborhoods, reducing crime, making the city safe for their children. But the effect was elitist and exclusionary. San Francisco's traditional populations were driven out, and its vitality eroded away.

Who was to blame? The easy answer is the perpetrators themselves, the smug, self-satisfied clique who saw the city as nothing more than valuable real estate in need of improvement. (The mobs certainly blamed them in that last terrible year before the bomb.) But these few were not really at fault; they were merely acting as their culture instructed. They were successful and seeking to enjoy the rewards of that success.

The real villains were the system that spawned them and the material ethic that appointed them trustees over all the system's business simply by virtue of their bloated bank balances.

I myself was a trustee. My bank balance was substantial before the war and I admit to occasional smugness and self-satisfaction regarding my status. I felt I had earned my affluence and the benefits it afforded me were right and proper. I didn't support what was happening in San Francisco or Los Angeles or a thousand other places, but neither did I object to it. I was neutral. When I observed American culture disintegrating (it was my job to observe it) I reported what I saw but took no action to stop it.

I came to my senses very late. Not until the population's frustration became rage, spilled out onto the streets and erupted into open warfare did I begin to understand that the America I loved no longer existed. We were no longer a great culture, but a hundred separate and distinct subcultures, each divorced from the others; one living in splendor and all the rest consigned to the surrounding ghettos.

San Francisco brought all this back to me; it is a fitting monument to our failure. Chen is right—every American should see it. We cannot allow the lesson of its final decades to be buried with it.

TWENTY-SEVEN

Katie awoke at first light. The sky was growing pale beyond the eastern ridges and one by one the stars were winking out. Today would be their last day in the mountains. Tonight they would sleep in Sacramento, in the basement of a safe house.

She pushed herself to a sitting position and looked down at Devin. As usual, she was the first one awake; as always, he was snoring softly. She would never understand how he did it—he could sleep like a cat when it was necessary, with one eye always open, but when it was not necessary he could slumber right through breakfast. Her habits were more consistent; she always rose with the sun.

Something else had been consistent lately, she thought ruefully. Every day for the last two weeks her stomach had churned like a cement mixer and she had been sick. She'd missed her last period and suspected the worst; this was confirmation. She wondered if Devin knew yet. He always seemed to sense what was going on with her and what she was thinking, but she didn't think he'd guessed this. If he had known, he wouldn't have allowed her on this trip, wouldn't have forced John to include her in the assault team.

Usually the nausea didn't bother her until she was up and moving around, but today it was starting early. She hurriedly unzipped her sleeping bag, pulled on a shirt, pants and boots, and stood up. Several yards away Anderson was already making coffee over a small camp stove. He nodded to her. "Morning, Katie."

"Tom," she replied curtly, hoping he hadn't recognized her discomfort. Then she headed off into the trees, affecting a careless, easy stride until she was out of his sight. When she was sure he could no longer see her she broke into a run. A hundred yards from the camp she dug a small pit in the half frozen ground with the toe of her boot, threw up into it and covered it over with dirt. The whole process had become routine now and no longer bothered her. She was getting good at it and she was proud of the fact that she had managed to fool everyone for so long.

She sat down for a minute, thinking and chewing on her

tongue to raise some saliva to rinse her mouth with.

A week ago she had been terrified by her suspected pregnancy. She hadn't been sure what it would mean for her or for Ben. Would John really banish her from the clans? Would Ben come with her? Even if they were allowed to stay, she didn't think she wanted to bring a child into this world. But the thought of abortion was against everything she believed in. She had felt lost and very much alone.

But now everything had changed; Ben was the first to see that fact. When John explained his plan to the six hand-picked men he chose for the assault team, Ben objected immediately. Dave Adrian told Katie later what he said. Devin delivered an ultimatum to John; he told John he wouldn't go to Sacramento unless Katie was included on the team. "Whether we succeed or fail," he insisted, "all hell is going to break loose and none of us is ever going to see the Hot Springs again or any of the people we leave behind. So Katie is going where I go. You can take us both or leave us both, but we won't be separated."

John objected strenuously, but Anderson and Cox supported Devin. "She won't be a liability," Cox assured John. "She's a better soldier than most men, and because the Chinese are so chauvinistic, they'll ignore her; that could prove useful to us." John finally relented.

These expressions of confidence had imposed an additional burden on Katie of course but there were compensations. Leaving the Hot Springs camp relieved many of her previous concerns. The question of banishment, for example, was now moot. They would reach Sacramento today and, as Ben had pointed out, would probably never return to the mountains. So the world of the clans was behind them now, they were about to create an entirely new world.

Would the new world welcome her child? She could not answer that question until the new world began to take shape. Should she tell Ben about the child now that it no longer posed a threat to their standing in the clans? She had asked herself this question many times in the last few days, and the answer was always the same—Ben must not know until the mission was completed. There were only eight members on the team; each was important, but Ben's leadership was critical. If she told him, his attention would be diverted and the mission compromised. So the child would have to remain her secret, at least for a few more days.

She could hear activity in the camp now and knew the team

would be moving soon. She rubbed her teeth with her tongue, rolled saliva around in her mouth and spat it out, then stood up and blew into her hand to test her breath. It wasn't kissing fresh, but it would have to do.

As she started back, she saw that the sky was already turning a deep, rich blue and the valley fog had begun to burn off. It was going to be a beautiful morning.

The assault team had been thoroughly briefed about the situation in Sacramento before leaving the Hot Springs. John had told them it was an "open city" and that getting in would be easy. Still, they were amazed at just how easy it proved to be.

"There is no curfew," John had explained, "But movement after dark is still more likely to attract attention than movement during the day. So we are going to walk in at the busiest time of day, late afternoon."

They came in from the east, down the American River from Folsom Lake. It was mid-afternoon when they reached the point where they were to split up and blend with the crowds. It was too early; the streets were almost deserted. So they waited for several hours, hiding in some shrubbery below one of the bridges crossing the river. Their destination was a small house in Arden, two miles distant. While they waited, John grilled them on the separate routes each was going to follow.

About 4:30 the streets began to fill with traffic, mostly pedestrians and bicyclists. One by one, the members of the assault team climbed up from the bushes to the bridge and disappeared into the crowds. An hour later, they had all arrived at the safe house. None had experienced any difficulty, only two had seen policemen.

"You did very well," John said when they were assembled in the basement of the safe house. The residents of the house and several other urban guerrillas were there with them. "And so I am now free to tell you something I did not tell you before because I didn't want to worry you. We have already survived the most dangerous part of the mission—the two miles between here and the river." He paused, allowing this to sink in, then continued, "Look at yourselves! We've been living in the mountains. We're dirty and conspicuous here in the city, although I admit I did see several locals even dirtier that we are. More important, we had no credentials, no papers. If any of us had been stopped for any reason, they would surely have been arrested and the mission would have been placed in jeopardy. You will not be exposed to these risks again. Tonight we'll get cleaned up and, thanks to Mark and Jenny, we will all get new clothes." He nodded in the direction of the couple whose house this was. The seven team members applauded. "Then Roger there . . ." John motioned toward the three men standing next to Mark and Jenny, the one in the middle waved his hand. ". . . will take pictures for your IDs. We want to minimize his risks as well as ours and one way to do that is to let him leave here as soon as possible. It won't do for him to travel late and attract the attention of some policeman while carrying all our photo data. So the first thing we have to do is get cleaned up. Don't shower yet, just scrub your faces, trim your hair and beards and put on clean shirts. Roger needs to leave here within an hour. Then I believe Jenny has some dinner for us. I think that's all for now, so let's do it!"

Roger and his two companions left at ten minutes to seven. Dinner was buffet style; Mark and Jenny's dining table would not accommodate six, so the small band of conspirators filled their plates and took seats in the living room. Then Mark disappeared into a bedroom and returned with a small portable television set. Everyone but John stared at it in amazement.

"How the hell did you manage that," Murphy asked. "I thought the Chinese confiscated all electronic equipment last year."

"Black market," Mark replied, grinning with undisguised pride. "Whole televisions are impossible to get but components can be had. I built this one just for this occasion. You people need to see a broadcast so you'll understand what we're fighting, and so you'll recognize Craighill and the rest of them when you get inside the station."

Katie watched him as he plugged the set in and adjusted the antenna. He was probably older than she was by several years, she thought, but he had a boyish quality and an enthusiasm she found appealing. He reminded her of Zack Zachary.

She asked him: "Do you mean that the people here in Sacramento haven't seen the broadcasts? I don't understand. Are they intended only for the rural camps?"

"Oh no," Mark said. "There are thousands of sets in Sacramento. The apartment dormitories all have day rooms with televisions and in neighborhoods like this one there's a house

232

every few blocks that's been designated as a community center. But we can't risk going to the local center. Any stranger would be noticed there and the appearance of eight strangers would be like sounding an alarm."

Anderson scowled darkly at this. "You're saying there are Americans at the center who would turn us in?"

"There are some, yes. The police pay rewards for that kind of information and there are plenty of takers. And there are Chinese at the center too; not many but a few. They live in the neighborhood and they work alongside the Americans. It's all part of the long-range plan the continental administration is always talking about. Eventually, they claim, we're all going to be one big happy society."

The television set was already on and its blank screen flickered to life as Mark was speaking. The Global Television logo appeared and the music started to play. Everyone but Murphy stared intently at it. Murphy was glancing around the room, studying the reactions of his colleagues. He didn't even look at the set when he heard the familiar voice announce, "Good evening. I'm David Craighill and this is the news."

Someone whispered, "Jesus! I wouldn't have believed this if I hadn't seen it myself. It's just like before the war."

"Believe it," Murphy said. "And remember that face. David Craighill is the key to this whole operation."

Tape of the first story rolled at that moment, so no one reacted to Murphy's pronouncement. But John had heard it and it infuriated him. Murphy was still trying to run things! He was a prima donna and that was trouble; it would have to be dealt with tomorrow. Tomorrow, he thought, was going to be one hell of a busy day.

TWENTY-EIGHT

Paul Sandiman's plane touched down at 11:05 a.m. His trip had been a grind, an endless succession of airports, interviews, taxi rides, uncomfortable beds and bad food. He had been sick twice and separated from his luggage three times. He was glad it was finally over. The last leg, a direct flight from Honolulu, had been so rough that that his old fear of flying had been rekindled. He felt shaky and looked tired as he emerged from the gate into the Sacramento air terminal with his Chinese cameraman and the Chinese army lieutenant who had accompanied him on the journey.

He scanned the few faces gathered near the gate and, seeing no one he recognized, said testily to the lieutenant, "Well, damn! It looks like no one's come to meet us."

As he spoke, a scrubbed and anxious looking young man stepped toward them and addressed Sandiman by name.

Sandiman regarded him questioningly. "Yes?"

"Mr. Craighill sent me. I have your car."

"Do I know you?" Sandiman was pleased that Craighill hadn't forgotten him, but irritated at being met by a total stranger. Was he that unimportant?

"Jason Keeler," the young man said, extending his hand. "No, you don't know me. There are lots of people at the station you don't know now. You've been gone almost a month; it's grown a lot in that time."

As they collected the baggage and drove into the city, Keeler brought Sandiman up to date. Chen's desert academy was spitting out new graduates every week and the station staff was growing rapidly. Soon the program schedule would extend to seven days a week. A second comedy and a half hour drama were about to be added to the schedule, and there was talk that the news might be expanded to a full hour. Sandiman could see that he had a great deal of catching up to do.

At the station, he was received with considerable fanfare.

234

Welcoming banners hung from the ceiling and from the furniture; there was a chocolate cake with his route around the world depicted in white icing, and there were congratulations from everyone. Craighill was the first to greet him.

"I apologize for not being at the airport," he said, "But I wanted to put tonight's newscast to bed early so we could have the afternoon to ourselves. That is, if you feel up to it. You must be exhausted."

Sandiman smiled crookedly. "I look like hell, I know. And I am tired, probably as tired as I look. But I do want to talk. I have a lot to tell you."

He was dragged off by Derek Kowalski before he could say more and it was nearly an hour before he and Craighill were able to escape to the privacy of Craighill's office.

"Can I get you something," David asked as they sat down on opposite sides of his desk. "A drink?"

Sandiman waved a hand in a gesture of mock surrender. "Please, no. I'm already sloshing." He patted his stomach. "I didn't expect anything like this party. I'm a little overwhelmed."

"We're glad to have you back."

"I don't know half of the people out there."

"They all know you. You've done a hell of a job, Paul."

Sandiman nodded. He felt somehow that the occasion called for a memorable summary statement, like Neil Armstrong's "One small step for man . . ." But he was too tired for eloquence. He settled for a simple, "Thank's, David."

"So," Craighill said. "Tell me all about it. What does our new world really look like?"

"It looks like the tapes I've been sending you each day," Sandiman said. "You've seen the cities and the countrysides and the faces of the people. But that's all superficial. What I couldn't put into those three-minute stories and interviews was what it feels like. We're going to have to put together longer features and documentaries to capture that. I have it all on tape but I'm going to need help with the editing. I can tell you this—it doesn't feel like I expected it to. From what we were told before I left, I could not have anticipated what I found out there."

Craighill looked concerned. "You're not implying anything sinister, I hope."

"No. Everything Chen told us was true. But he omitted certain facts. He might have been unaware of them, or maybe it was simply a matter of interpretation. I'm a pragmatist, David;

235

when I look at the present, I see the present. But I believe when Chen looks at the present, he sees the future. We both know he's a dreamer; I believe he sometimes sees what he wants to see."

"Stop talking in riddles," Craighill said impatiently. "Exactly what did you find?"

Sandiman leaned forward over the desk. Despite his fatigue he was clearly excited and anxious to share what he had learned. "Let me take it in order; it's easier for me to remember it that way. In Europe things are very much as they were described to us. Only two cities were bombed so the initial impact was primarily economic. The blasts and the EMP destroyed most computer records in Brussels and London and that wrecked the whole European financial complex. The entire continent quickly reverted to barter. Longer term, however, disease played the most significant role because the Europeans weren't as fortunate with the weather as we were.

"Have you ever stopped to consider how lucky we were? Chicago was bad, of course, but we got off very light on the west coast. In California we couldn't have fared much better, at least from the standpoint of weather."

"Yes, I had noticed that," Craighill agreed.

"The Europeans had it much worse. The winds carried fallout east into Germany, Switzerland, Austria, and so on. They had a horrible time with radiation casualties, and all across northern and central Europe, even the survivors were weakened by exposure to it. Last year that weakness led to an epidemic. It was a virus, some form of influenza. It would have been nothing for a healthy population, but it killed over 35 percent near the fallout zones. Large portions of southeast England and northern Europe are now uninhabitable. The total population of Europe is barely 70 percent of what it was before the war. The bombs took some, radiation took some, the epidemic took a large number and the rest starved during the first winter. It makes you realize how lucky we really were.

"Anyway, the Europeans who remain are doing fairly well. That's what I meant when I said the situation is about as Chen described it to us. They have less food than we have here, but they have enough. Spain and Italy and southern France have become the breadbaskets of the continent. The language transition is proceeding, the economy is beginning to regenerate, and the people seem reasonably optimistic."

Sandiman paused momentarily and Craighill interrupted.

"You say they have less food that we have? I thought food distribution was being balanced worldwide."

"That's the goal. And officials everywhere were constantly reminding me of it. But it's not the reality, at least not yet. It's worst in Africa.

"Africa is starving, David. The Chinese presence is limited to the coastal areas and a few inland cities, so I wasn't able to visit the remote interior. But I did interview people who had been there. Radiation is not a significant problem anywhere in the Southern Hemisphere, but the climatic changes in the first year after the war reduced agricultural yields everywhere. And of course, all the aid Africa used to receive ended before the war. Considering all of that, the Chinese, even with the whole world to draw from now, don't have the resources to feed Africa and rebuild the developed world at the same time. So they are doing almost nothing in Africa.

"I was appalled when I saw that. I was angry with them. But later, after I had seen the problems they face in India and heard about South America, I began to understand. They've been forced to establish priorities. They've developed a kind of triage system and assigned each area of the globe to one of three categories: The first category is those who need aid to become self-sufficient; the second is those who are already self-sufficient and need only administrative guidance; the third is those for whom no available amount of aid or guidance will ever produce self-sufficiency.

"Unfortunately, much of interior Africa falls into the third category. The land is poor and the population is too large to ever sustain itself without importing food. In a case like that, the Chinese believe that aid which served to perpetuate a pattern of dependency would benefit no one. So they withhold the aid.

"That sounds callous and harsh, I know, but let me tell you what one Chinese official I met in Africa said to me. I asked him what he thought would happen to all the people he was refusing to help. He said, 'They will do one of two things: they will leave their homes and come to the coast or they will die. If they come to the coast we will help them; we will educate them and find places for them; we have already made this offer. But we will not force them to come to the coast. If we did, they would resent us. Eventually they would strike back at us. So it must be their choice. They must come to us voluntarily.'"

"Are they coming?"

"A few are, but only a few. They don't seem to understand the magnitude of the changes brought by the war. The governments of most of the interior nations are still resisting. They constantly warn the Chinese against interfering in their affairs while lobbying for aid. The people receive information from their governments, not the Chinese, so at present there is little progress. It's very bad. The Chinese believe millions are dying, but they claim there is little they can do about it. They're willing to help those who accept help on their terms, the rest they are ignoring."

Craighill's expression had grown pensive as he listened to this. When Sandiman finished he said, "Paul, do you think there's any chance that racial bias could be playing a part in all of this?"

Sandiman didn't seem surprised by the suggestion, but he was quick to discount it. "That thought crossed my mind when I was there," he said. "But the situation in Africa is not unique; I realized that later. In South America and Australia too, the Chinese have taken control of the coasts and left the interior to the native populations. On all three Southern Hemisphere continents the reason is the same—the land masses are so huge that the Chinese have decided military campaigns into the interiors can't be justified. At least, that's what they told me. But I suspect there was another reason.

"The Southern Hemisphere, remember, suffered very little from the bombs. The Australians and the nations of Africa and South America still had intact military organizations and their economies were still functioning. In Africa and South America they also had a new source of pride—they were no longer third world; they were now among the most powerful nations on earth! So as the invasions proceeded, I'm sure the Chinese met stiff resistance. They did manage to lay claim to the coastal areas and establish defensive perimeters. But in all probability, many of the armies they defeated are still there, just beyond those perimeters.

"No one would confirm any of this for me, but I suspect that the Chinese are up against well organized resistance throughout the whole Southern Hemisphere. I'm not sure they could move inland from the coasts even if they wanted to."

Craighill looked doubtful. "That's a very different picture than Chen painted. Are you sure about this?"

"Reasonably sure, yes. But I'm describing the present situation; I think Chen is projecting the present situation to its logical conclusion. He's anticipating the future."

"You think the resistance is doomed? Is ultimate Chinese

victory the only logical outcome?"

Sandiman shrugged. "If you pressed me on it, I'd have to say that ultimate Chinese victory is more or less inevitable. They are rebuilding the areas they control and growing stronger while the populations in the interiors are growing weaker. Eventually, more and more will defect and the resistance will collapse."

"So it's a war of attrition. In effect they've thrown up a blockade around their remaining enemies and are starving them into submission. They've placed whole continents under siege!"

Sandiman smiled. "You make it sound barbaric."

"It is barbaric. My God, Paul, are you defending it? You said yourself, millions are starving to death. Women and children are dying, not just soldiers."

"No, I'm not defending it." Sandiman sighed. "It's just that I've seen so much in the last month. In a sense, we caused all of this, David. So frankly, I don't feel I'm entitled to criticize Chinese methods."

Craighill saw Sandiman's sadness and understood completely. "I know," he said. "I saw San Francisco last weekend."

It was some time before either man spoke again. "Look," Craighill said finally, "You've had a long trip. Maybe we should take this up tomorrow."

Sandiman, who had seemed lost in his own thoughts, looked up at him and said, "I am tired. But there's one more thing I wanted to tell you. I think it's important. You know that on this trip we changed our schedule frequently. Chen told me we could if we felt the need, and that we would be free to go anywhere we wanted to go. I took advantage of that and caused problems for the transport authorities many times. Everywhere I went, despite the trouble I was causing, the Chinese were extremely cooperative; they made every effort to accommodate us. Except on two occasions. Twice they denied my applications for travel permits. I was intrigued by those denials and I did some digging. David, something is going on in China, specifically in Guangzhou and Shanghai, something they don't want anyone to know about."

Craighill, too, was intrigued by this. "Go on," he said.

"I was in Hong Kong when I was turned down for Guangzhou. I met a man at a travel office there, a Chinese who spoke fluent English. He told me he'd been trying to get a permit to Guangzhou for nearly a year, to see his family. He warned me that I was wasting my time. You won't get to Guangzhou, he said, unless you have special credentials. I asked him where I could apply for special credentials and he said no one knew. He had talked to every authority he could ask; no one would tell him anything.

"Guangzhou is only about eighty miles from Hong Kong and there are four ways to get there: bus, train, plane, and boat. I tried them all. There were plenty of people coming and going, but—this was very strange—the passengers were all Chinese. I mean ALL Chinese! No westerners, no Africans, and no other Asians."

Craighill frowned thoughtfully. "Some sort of health problem?" he suggested. "An epidemic of some kind?"

Sandiman shook his head. "If that was it, they wouldn't be letting so many in and out."

"Civil unrest then. Riots or a local revolution."

"No. Most of the passengers I saw were civilians. Many were women and children. There was no tension on any of their faces. They looked like typical travelers."

"What then? You must have some idea."

Again, Sandiman shook his head, frustration and fatigue were both evident in the gesture. "I heard some rumors but nothing solid. Guangzhou and Shanghai are both ports with large shipyards. Apparently, there's strict security around those shipyards and a lot of activity. The rumor is they're building ships, a lot of ships."

Craighill said, "Ships? Why would they be building ships? And why all the secrecy?"

"I don't know. But I imagine Chen could find out. I think we should ask him to look into it."

"Chen's not here today; he's at the school. But he'll be back tomorrow. I think we should meet with him together."

"Then you agree? You think this might be important?"

"I don't know. But it's sure as hell worth looking into."

"Good." Sandiman pushed himself to his feet. "I think I'll go home and unpack."

Craighill walked him to the door and, just before opening it, asked him a final question: "Paul, you said the Chinese cooperated with you completely on this trip. Because of that cooperation you discovered some unpleasant things in Africa and you also stumbled onto this business about Guangzhou. Why do you think they ran the risk? Why did they invite us to send you around the world?"

Sandiman said, "I can't be certain. But I think they did it

because they're convinced they're behaving responsibly. They believe they're doing everything that can be done and they think we'll agree once we have the facts."

Craighill nodded. "Do you agree?"

"I'm not sure. Do you?"

"I want to. But I'm a skeptic by nature."

"So am I," Sandiman said. "So am I."

TWENTY-NINE

At the house in Arden the television came to life at 7:00 p.m. Again, the Lassen clansmen and their Sacramento counterparts gathered around. Again, all conversation ceased when Craighill's face appeared on the screen. This time, however, the atmosphere in the room had subtly changed. It was a change Lonnie Murphy found familiar.

Last night, the clan's mood had reminded Murphy of the first time a team sees game films of its next opponent. Everyone was loose and there was a fair amount of banter as they watched the news, even more when the documentaries and series programs ran. Tonight was different. Tonight was like the second time a team sees those same films. Now there was no joking, everyone was concentrating and the tension was heavy in the room. Murphy had seen this many times before and it felt good to him. He thought the level of intensity was just where it should be. He thought this team was ready and would do all right.

John was less certain. Throughout this long day he had drilled his clansmen on every aspect of the assault plan. They had studied maps of Sacramento, bus routes and schedules, photos of numerous downtown landmarks and architectural schematics of the Global Television building, obtained from a local clansman who worked for North American Telephone. Over and over they had reviewed their individual routes to the rendezvous point, their plans for gaining access to the television building and their assignments during the assault. They had covered everything, left no detail unattended. Yet John was still uneasy. He couldn't explain why, but a vague doubt gnawed at him. He felt he had forgotten something. But what? Had there actually been an oversight, or was it simple nervousness? Was he merely imagining it? After all, the pressures on him were enormous. He had waited so long for this and the stakes were so high.

At least he had no worries about the IDs. Roger and his team had performed their task with consummate skill; the small red and gold laminated cards were flawless. Visually, they could not be told from the real card Mark had shown them for comparison. The fake cards would not pass scrutiny by police electronic card readers, of course, but only squad cars and a few motorcycles were equipped with card readers, and the police rarely used them unless an individual was already under considerable suspicion. "Act natural," Roger instructed them. "Hold your card up when asked and they'll wave you on just like everyone else."

But despite the fact that he was pleased with the cards and the drills, John's mind kept returning to his doubts. What had he forgotten? Something about Murphy perhaps? He recalled his concern of last evening regarding Murphy; the athlete had angered him. But today Murphy had done everything that was asked of him and behaved like a responsible member of the team, so John had decided not to confront him. Had that been a mistake? Perhaps. But even if it was, he didn't think it was the thing that troubling him now. There was something else, something he was missing, some detail that was escaping his attention.

Or perhaps there was nothing at all.

It was maddening, but there was no help for it. All he could do was hope that his mistake, whatever it was, would occur to him during the next few hours. He had two chances left. He would drill the team once more after tonight's broadcast ended and again tomorrow morning. Then, in the early afternoon, they would begin leaving Arden by their separate routes for the journey downtown. Whatever was left undone then would remain undone forever.

Sacramento was now an experimental city, the first place in North America where the theories of the new global society were being put into practice.

Equality was a major long-term Chinese goal. They envisioned a world in which all racial, ethnic and cultural subsets would eventually mingle in perfect homogeneity. To this end, they had already begun integrating Sacramento. Everywhere, former Americans were being elevated to positions of responsibility. Everywhere, the Chinese were stepping aside, becoming less and less visible. Except on the police force. The police force was the last stronghold of overt Chinese dominance in Sacramento. It had not yet been integrated on even the lowest level. Every street patrolman, every officer, every file clerk was still Chinese.

It was 7:15 a.m. when Sgt. Yu Feng strode to the small podium at the head of the shift briefing room. Arrayed before him

243

were the faces of forty-two street patrolmen. A few were yawning, but most looked bright-eyed and attentive.

"I have just one piece of business this morning," Sgt. Yu said, in his customary clipped monotone. As he spoke he held up a sheaf of papers on which were photographs of a black man. "This is an escapee. Name: Lonnie Murphy. You saw these sheets four days ago, so you should remember this individual. He escaped from a rural camp one hundred miles north of Sacramento ten days ago. Ten days ago, gentlemen, and he is still at large! The continental administrator has expressed personal interest in the recapture of this individual. Status has therefore been raised to priority two. I want spot checks of cyclists, pedestrians, bus passengers and so on. You know the routine."

In the front row a patrolman raised his hand. The sergeant pointed at him and barked, "Chou?"

The patrolman did not stand; such ceremony was not required here. Unlike other shift commanders, Sgt. Yu liked to keep his briefings informal. It was one of the things his men liked about him.

"Do we know that Murphy is in Sacramento?" the patrolman asked.

Yu eyed the young man indulgently for a moment before answering. "If you mean 'has he been sighted?' the answer is no. But this individual's roots are urban, so he's not likely to stay long in the countryside, living on berries and tree bark. He will hide in some city and Sacramento is his most likely choice. Does that answer your question?"

The sarcasm in Sgt. Yu's tone was not lost on the young patrolman. He nodded sheepishly and said, "Yes, Sergeant."

Yu then directed his attention to the others in his audience. "Gentlemen, we believe this man is in Sacramento. The continental administrator wants him and I want him. So we are going to find him. Put the word out to all your informants and keep your eyes open. That is all for this morning. Dismissed!"

The water truck arrived promptly at 10:00 a.m. Two young women and a fifteen year old boy jumped down from the truck and moved into the fields, each carrying a pair of water cans. The cans were heavy, but each pair was connected by a broad yoke which the water carriers slung over their necks, spreading the weight. It was an archaic system—it looked like something from an early Hollywood biblical epic—but it had the advantage of delivering the water directly to the workers so they never had to move from their stations. The Chinese camp managers considered this significant.

Cal Triplett saw the water carriers approaching and slowed the pace of his digging. Like all the other workers at camp 454, Triplett understood the importance of occasional respites from the back-breaking stoop labor they were required to perform and had learned how to appear busy while doing very little. "Resting in place" it was called. Cal always rested in place when the water carriers were making their rounds.

As he rested on this day his eyes nervously scanned the nearby woodlands. He was looking for a sign, some indication that the armed rebel forces Dave Adrian had promised him were now in position around the camp perimeter.

"The new war is about to begin," Adrian said at their last meeting. "We will be ready and you must be ready too."

Triplett had asked for more information. Exactly when would it begin? How would it begin? But he was told only that he would receive instructions at the proper time and that he must be prepared to act immediately. "You will know when it is beginning," Adrian had assured him. "It could happen in four days or five or six, but it will be soon. And we will be here to support you when it begins."

That conversation had taken place four days ago and Triplett was now growing anxious. Preparations inside the camp were complete. He had taken into his confidence everyone he was certain could be absolutely trusted and told them to prepare. But prepare for what? They had all asked him that question and he had been unable to answer. Would the rebels attack from the perimeter? He doubted that. Adrian had said that the rebels would provide support—that seemed to indicate that the fighting would begin inside the camp. But how could that be? How would the prisoners inside the camp know when to start the fighting?

It was all very frustrating. Triplett had been the rebels' primary source of intelligence for nearly two years. He had proved his trustworthiness many times, and being told so little now would have made him angry if he did not have such complete faith in John. He knew that everything Adrian had told him was part of John's plan. That knowledge soothed his frustration. John knew what he was doing. If John felt that this maddening secrecy was necessary, then it must be necessary.

"Water, Mister?"

Triplett turned and found one of the water carriers

245

standing beside him. He had been so deep in thought that he hadn't noticed the boy's approach.

"Yes," he said. "Thank you."

The boy filled a small metal cup from one of his cans and handed it to him. As Triplett drank, the boy asked, "Is it today?"

"I don't know." Triplett sighed. "I wish I did, Kevin." He wiped his mouth with the back of his hand and handed the cup back.

"Could it be today?"

"It could be."

Kevin nodded. "I hope it is. Everyone is ready."

As the boy headed off toward the next worker, Triplett scanned the nearby woodlands one last time before returning to work.

Just before noon, a van turned off Capital Avenue and drove past the entrance to the Global Television building in Sacramento. When it reached the driveway leading to the building's garage it turned in and stopped short of the guard booth that stood halfway between the street and the garage door.

There were two uniformed policemen in the booth, both were young. Guard duty was the dullest, most tedious assignment policemen were required to endure, so it was reserved for new officers and those who had incurred the displeasure of their superiors. These two were new to the force and to Sacramento. One of them walked from the booth to the van as the driver stepped out.

"What do you have for us today," the guard asked smiling.

"The usual," the driver replied, "Just the usual."

Together they walked to the rear of the van, where the guard waited while the driver opened the double doors. Inside were the familiar racks of bread and baked goods to be delivered to the restaurant on the first floor of the building. This same guard had inspected these same racks of baked goods every day for the last two weeks and the driver was now well acquainted with his routine.

"What are those," the guard asked, pointing.

"They're called cream puffs," the driver answered. "They have cream filling on the inside." On any other day he would have been pleased with this question—the young Chinese usually selected something expensive; today he had chosen modestly—but on this particular day, the driver had other things on his mind.

246

"Do you like chocolate," he added, anxious to complete the transaction.

The guard grinned. "Yes, I like chocolate very much."

"Then take one, please. And one for your friend, of course."

The guard reached out to collect his prize, then hesitated. His eyes narrowed and he drew back his hand. The driver realized immediately that he had allowed his impatience to show. That had been an error, a violation of the subtle protocol that had evolved around these daily negotiations; it had made the guard suspicious. But how suspicious? Would he now insist on carefully inspecting the entire van? The thought brought a sudden flush of color to the driver's cheeks.

"You seem to be in a hurry today," the guard said. "Is there something you don't want me to notice?"

"Of course not," the driver objected, forcing a casual smile. "Take your time. Look again. Take anything you want."

The guard's eyes roamed over the array of cakes and pastries on the racks. He stroked his chin with his thumb and forefinger and made an exaggerated display of careful consideration. Finally, he collected two of the cream puffs and announced, "No, you are right; I do like chocolate." He waved one of the pastries at the driver, indicating that he could now close the doors.

Half a minute later the electric door was raised and the van rolled down the ramp into the garage. Neither guard seemed to notice the thin-lipped tension on the driver's face as he passed, or the perspiration beading his forehead. They were too busy eating.

Inside the garage, the van backed up to a loading dock and the driver wheeled a large dolly cart filled with baked goods across the platform and into an interior corridor. Halfway to the elevators he stopped beside a door marked "maintenance" and stood for several seconds listening. Satisfied that he was alone, he opened the door. Inside was a small room full of mops, brooms, vacuums and other cleaning equipment. He removed two pastry trays from the dolly cart, and set them on top of the cart. Then, from the space behind the trays, he hurriedly withdrew four small Uzi machine guns, a number of extra ammunition clips, three pistols, four hand grenades and two small packages of plastique explosive. These he carefully placed in the bottom of a hamper in one corner of the maintenance room and covered them with the dirty rags that half filled the hamper. Then he closed the door to the room, replaced the pastry racks in the dolly, and proceeded to the

247

elevators.

He had not been seen and one more element of John's plan was now in place.

Eight hundred miles to the east, the rebels' luck was running even better. What Zachary had found in Colorado far exceeded anything John had anticipated or even hoped for.

Seven days earlier Zachary had emerged from storm clouds two thousand feet above mountainous terrain and guided his parachute to a landing in an open meadow. His descent was observed and the local rebels found him and escorted him to their camp less than six hours later. The rebels were all in uniform and their camp looked very military. They claimed not to be rebels at all, but a still active Special Forces unit of the United States Army.

They subjected Zachary to thirty-six hours of continuous interrogation, after which he was permitted to sleep for nearly a full day. On awakening, he was told that the wreckage of his aircraft had been located.

"We are not pleased with the hasty decisions taken by your leaders," the commander of the camp had told him. "Their action is premature and has preempted our own plans. Under the circumstances, however, we seem to have no choice but to support you."

Zachary was elated. The memory of his interrogation was still painful, and he immediately recognized the magnitude of this concession. The residents of this small camp clearly believed that they were among the last U.S. military units still operating, and that their commander, a full Colonel, was probably the highest ranking U.S. military officer still in the field. That made him, in effect, the Commander-in-Chief of the entire U.S. military and, arguably, the acting President of the United States, a responsibility he seemed quite willing to accept. He was arrogant and pompous and jealous of his authority. His offer of help was completely unexpected.

"What will you do," Zachary anxiously asked the Colonel. "Can you communicate with other rebel groups?"

"We can and already have," the Colonel replied, flashing a self-satisfied smile. "Come, I'll show you."

When Zachary saw the communications center, he realized immediately just how valuable the Colonel's help could be. The Colorado unit was operating an elaborate and sophisticated radio.

"But how can you use radio," Zachary asked. "Won't the

248

Chinese . . ."

"Monitor and triangulate our signal?"

"Exactly."

Again the Colonel smiled. "You've never heard of L-RAD, have you?"

Zachary admitted that he hadn't.

"Laser Radio," the Colonel explained. "You see, we have a small transmitter here that fires a discrete beam to a relay satellite. The satellite then transmits a similar beam to a receiver somewhere else. The signal that reaches that receiver is only a few hundred yards wide when it strikes the ground, and it can be picked up only by receivers located within that small area. That makes enemy monitoring and triangulation virtually impossible."

"Just like our signal guns," Zachary observed.

"Excuse me?"

Feeling suddenly foolish, Zachary quickly said, "Nothing. It wasn't important." Comparing a flashlight and a plastic tube to this sophisticated technology was absurd, he realized.

The Colonel explained further that there were fourteen similar radios still in operation, scattered over a vast area from Colorado to Virginia and from the Gulf Coast to the Great Lakes. "At any time, we can instruct the satellite to broadcast a wide-area alert signal," he said. "Each radio operator then signals the satellite, which records his position so the next transmission can be relayed to his exact coordinates. This allows us to quickly establish contact, even if all the radios have recently been moved."

Zachary asked why there were no radios west of the Rockies.

"Simple bad luck," the Colonel replied. "At the time of the Chinese invasion we had hundreds of L-RADs in the field. Now we've lost all but fourteen, including every one west of here. There's no reason for it, it just worked out that way. It's been a problem because it's prevented us from telling anyone west of here what we were planning. We thought we'd eventually have to start the war without you. Now it turns out you decided to start without us." He sighed. "Damn it, Zachary, do you realize what this could mean?"

Zachary nodded. "For want of a nail the shoe was lost."

"Precisely! Only this time, the line might read: For want of a radio, the whole damn continent was lost."

In the days that followed, Zachary learned to like the colonel. The old soldier was clearly frustrated with what was about to happen but nevertheless totally committed himself and his troops to the support of John's plan. On one occasion he actually thanked Zachary for what he had done, saying, "I don't like any of this, son; I don't like it one bit. But I'm sure as hell glad you risked your neck to tell us about it. It would have been a disaster if you hadn't come. Hell, it may still be a disaster, but at least now we've got a fighting chance."

Of course, John had no way of knowing that Zachary's mission had been such an unqualified success. It had seemed almost an afterthought at the time, a shot in the dark. But it might now prove to be the most important single element in his entire plan. The unexpected bonus of the L-RAD had served to place vast new populations on notice of what was about to happen and spread the impending revolt across the entire face of the North American continent. As far east as Virginia, camp prisoners and rebel clansmen were now watching and waiting for John's signal, ready to take action.

It was a cool, sunny afternoon in Sacramento. The first members of the assault team had departed the Arden house at 1:30; it was now nearly three o'clock.

Katie Hogan sat on a bench at one end of the public transport kiosk on Fair Oaks Boulevard. It was a large facility, one of the thousands built with Federal mass transit money during the fuel crisis of the late teens. During rush hour it would be jammed with people, but it was not crowded at this time of day so Katie had a clear view of the street and of the black man standing at the far end of the kiosk. A bus approached down the boulevard and she glanced at the man, waiting for his signal. He looked disinterestedly at the bus and returned to the copy of *North America* magazine he was reading.

Five minutes later, another bus approached and Katie watched the man again. This time he folded the magazine under his arm and stepped toward the loading ramp. She rose and moved toward the ramp also. The bus hissed to a stop. Katie and John and three other passengers boarded.

The bus was only half full. Katie saw John take a seat in the third row and selected a place several rows farther back for herself. A moment later the engine roared and they pulled away from the kiosk onto Fair Oaks Boulevard. The bus pulled to a stop almost immediately at a red light and she saw Devin walking down a side street toward the kiosk. She also saw a police car, moving very slowly toward her along the same street. It was moving only a little faster than a man could walk and seemed to be following Devin.

Her stomach knotted itself into a fist as she watched the car move closer to him. With an effort, she resisted an irrational impulse to cry out or bang her fists on the bus window and forced herself to remain calm. The car pulled even with him. One of the Chinese officers inside was looking directly at him, studying him! Nausea stabbed at her and for an instant she thought she was actually going to be sick.

Then the car was past him. It turned onto Fair Oaks and moved away. Devin reached the corner and stopped at the curb, waiting for the light, which had just changed. The bus accelerated and Katie finally released the breath she had been holding for the past twenty seconds.

At that same moment, a mile closer to the center of the city, a three wheeled bicycle cart was moving slowly west on "H" Street. The front of the cart consisted of a large metal box painted bright white with pictures of hot dogs stenciled on its front and sides. A thin metal sign standing in a slot on the top of the box announced, SOLD OUT.

The driver braked to a stop at a red light, looked quickly around him to ensure that he was alone and, without taking his eyes off the road ahead of him, said softly, "Lonnie!"

From inside the hot dog box, a muffled voice replied, "What is it? Trouble?"

"No," the driver said. "I just thought you should know there were police at a bus stop we passed a couple of blocks back. They boarded a bus. I think we were right; I think they were looking for you."

"I hope they were," Murphy said irritably. "I'd hate to think I was going through all this for nothing. My right leg's been asleep for a half hour and I'm sweating like a pig."

The driver grinned as he pushed off to continue his journey toward downtown Sacramento.

THIRTY

Craighill recognized the change the moment he and Sandiman were ushered into Chen's office. From across the room he could see that the old man seemed to have difficulty rising to greet them. As they drew nearer, the signs became even more evident. But it was not until he took Chen's hand that full realization struck him.

Chen was in his late eighties; he had always "looked his age," but seemed robust for that age. Now, suddenly, he appeared weak and frail and his hand quivered in Craighill's grasp. How could this have happened so suddenly? Craighill had seen him less than a week earlier and noticed nothing. How should he react? What did Chinese custom dictate? Should he offer sympathy or pretend he was not seeing what he was seeing? Chen quickly released him from his dilemma.

"As you see," he said, "I have been ill."

Craighill felt immediate relief; the voice, at least, sounded as strong and firm as ever.

"Unfortunately, old age and illness are frequent companions, as you shall both learn one day." Chen offered his hand to Sandiman, and Craighill saw surprise and compassion in Sandiman's expression too. "But I am better now, and it is a subject I don't wish to dwell upon. So I suggest we proceed to our business. Please be seated, gentlemen."

There was an awkward pause after they took their seats. The two Americans had come to lodge an official complaint. Their recognition of Chen's condition now left them feeling uncomfortable about that. It was Chen who finally spoke. "I suppose you've come to report on Paul's trip."

"We have," Sandiman replied.

"Was it successful?"

"Long and tiring but very successful. I brought back forty-five hours of recorded material."

"Excellent. How many stories will it produce?"

"I'm not sure. It depends on what we decide to make from it. It could produce as many as a hundred five-minute spots, I think, but perhaps only three or four hour-long documentaries."

"I see," Chen nodded. "Then you have not yet begun your editing?"

Sandiman shook his head. "We begin tomorrow."

Chen looked questioningly at Craighill, then back to Sandiman. "I'm pleased the trip went well, gentlemen. But you requested an urgent meeting. How can I help you?"

Sandiman started to answer but Craighill put a hand on his arm to stop him. He knew Chen better than Sandiman did and it was clear to him that the old man's condition was more serious than he was admitting. Craighill did not think this was the time to confront him about Africa or the withheld travel permits.

"When we asked for this meeting," Craighill said, "we did not know you had been ill. There were several things we wished to discuss, but they can certainly wait until you are feeling better."

Sandiman looked at Craighill, then back to Chen and nodded his agreement. "Yes, of course. They can wait."

"Nonsense!" Chen huffed. "One more thing you will learn one day—when you are old you do things immediately." He smiled wryly at them. "Because you may not be able to do them tomorrow. It's true, I do not feel as well today as I did a week ago. But I feel well enough. So get on with it; ask me what you came to ask."

Craighill was encouraged by the spirit and humor displayed in this statement, but he was also disturbed by the literal meaning of the words. Was Chen really so ill that his recovery was in doubt? The idea struck like a hammer blow. He had grown very fond of the old man. He saw that Chen was looking at him and waiting, but this entire meeting seemed suddenly unimportant. "If you insist," he said reluctantly. "Then Paul will explain."

Sandiman launched into his subject with enthusiasm, displaying none of Craighill's hesitancy. He described his African discoveries in some detail and concluded, "What I need to know now is whether I will be allowed to broadcast these facts. They do not portray the federation favorably, and if they are going to be suppressed I would rather know it before we waste weeks editing stories we cannot use."

Chen seemed more surprised than angered by Sandiman's accusation. "Suppressed?" he snapped. "When has anything been suppressed? You may broadcast what you wish—I told you that when you came here and it is still true."

"Yes, you did tell us that. And I believed you. But you also

253

told us the entire globe had been pacified and that unified world government was an accomplished fact. We now know that isn't true. What I saw in Africa contradicts you, Chen, and that contradiction forces me to doubt other things we've been told. You must see that."

Chen eyed Sandiman narrowly. "I see no such thing," he said. "I told you that we control the entire world and that is true. The contradictions you speak of are of no consequence. You say we must subdue the scattered populations of the continental interiors before we can claim control? You are arguing semantics, nothing more. As for the business of the 'triage' as you call it, that is a complex subject; we could discuss it for hours but I fear I am too tired. In this instance, therefore, I will accept David's offer of deferral; we will talk about that another day. Now, is there anything else?"

Craighill could see that Sandiman was not pleased to have been so bluntly dismissed. But Chen had, in fact, answered his primary question—he had told him he could pursue his editing without fear of censorship. He had also admitted his fatigue, so the interview was clearly at an end.

Just as Craighill was about to thank Chen for his courtesy in seeing them, however, Sandiman preempted him, saying, "There is one more thing, Chen. When I left for this trip I was promised complete freedom of movement. That promise was usually kept, but there were exceptions. I was twice denied travel permits."

He paused, awaiting a response, and Chen asked, "Under what circumstances were these permits denied?"

"I really have no idea. Both times, when I applied for Guangzhou and later for Shanghai, I asked for explanations but no one would tell me anything. You must recognize how intolerable this situation is. We believe a formal protest is in order and we are therefore requesting your assistance. Frankly, we aren't sure how to proceed."

Craighill didn't know whether Sandiman saw Chen's uncharacteristic reaction to this statement, but he saw it. A shadow passed briefly over the usually impassive landscape of Chen's face. Then the old man quickly composed himself. What did it mean? Was Sandiman right? Were these places, Guangzhou and Shanghai, important? Or had Chen's apparent reaction to their mention somehow been a product of his illness?

"I have no knowledge of this," Chen said, nodding

affirmatively. "But I will certainly make inquiries."

"I would appreciate that," Sandiman said.

With this exchange complete, Craighill pushed himself to his feet. He thanked Chen for his trouble and wished him a swift recovery. Sandiman echoed these sentiments. Chen remained seated as they made their way from the office, which served to renew Craighill's fear for the old man's health. At the door, Craighill turned and bowed, making no attempt to hide the concern he was feeling.

When they were gone, Chen immediately picked up his phone and placed a call to Lin Chiao-tu. Lin was in conference and it was a half hour before he returned the call. Their conversation was brief.

"The permits should have been granted," Chen said angrily. "The reporter, Sandiman, would not have known what he was seeing. Ships are being built—it would have meant nothing to him. But now he is certain that important information is being withheld."

Lin, however, was adamant. "I will not argue the point," he said. "The policy has been in effect for a year. If we had made an exception for this reporter we would have to let them all in. Eventually one would ask the wrong questions."

"He is already asking the wrong questions," Chen countered. "He wishes to file a formal protest over the incident. Don't you understand the implications of this situation? We promised these people freedom of movement in order to enlist their cooperation. We have now won their confidence and they have become our most valuable asset. But that confidence can still be lost. And if it is lost, they can become dangerous enemies."

"Comrade Chen," Lin growled, "These are your people. They are your responsibility. If you cannot control them, I will find someone who can."

There was a click as Lin switched off, leaving Chen cursing under his breath.

THIRTY-ONE

The last member of the assault team to reach the rendezvous point was Jacob Yang. It was just after 6:00 p.m. when he emerged from the rush hour crowds and turned down the narrow alley separating the Global Television building from the building next door. He glanced at the Global building as he entered the alley, then quickly averted his eyes, determined to do nothing that might appear suspicious. Then he began counting his paces. Twenty-six paces down the alley, at the rear of the building opposite the television studios, there would be a door where he was to knock.

He found it easily, tapped lightly, and the door opened. A moment later he was led down a flight of concrete steps to a basement mechanical room where the team was waiting. The place smelled musty. The only sound was the faint humming of the building's furnaces. His guide, a young man he had never seen before, pointed to a door then turned and started back the way they had come. Yang pushed the door open and stepped through.

He realized immediately that something was wrong. No one greeted him; at first, no one even looked at him. They were all wearing long faces. He stood in the doorway for a moment, anxiously waiting, then demanded, "What is it? What's happened?"

Several of the team members turned to him. Katie Hogan said, "The police have John."

"He's been captured?" Yang winced as the words tumbled involuntarily from his mouth—foolish words, like bad dialogue from a low budget movie. "How?" he added solemnly. "When?"

Devin appeared soundlessly from the shadows to Yang's left and pushed the door closed behind him.

"They took him off our bus," Katie said. "Two policemen came down the aisle checking IDs. Not everyone's, just the black men. They took all the IDs and ran them through the reader in their car. Then they came back and took John."

"They were looking for Murphy," Dave Cox said angrily."We expected that and protected Murphy. We should have

256

guessed that John would be checked too. It was stupid, unbelievably stupid."

Tom Anderson spat on the floor and said, "Bullshit! There's no way we could have seen this coming." He pointed at Murphy. "Look at him! Clean shaven where John wears a full beard. He's also eight inches taller and outweighs John by sixty or seventy pounds. Stand 'em side by side, they look like David and Goliath. I still can't believe the police checked John. But I know this—we can't waste any more time worrying about it. We've got to be inside the building next door in . . ." He checked his watch. ". . . thirty-five minutes. And we can't do it the way John planned it. We have to design a new plan."

"A new plan?" Cox shook his head doubtfully. "Everything depended on John deactivating the security system. There's nobody else here who can do that. Can you do it?"

Anderson said, "No, but . . ."

"I think I might be able to do it." It was Mark, the man whose house had been their headquarters in Arden. Everyone turned and looked at him.

"You really think you can?" Anderson asked.

"I know a fair amount about electronics."

"But do you know enough? Are you sure?"

"I'm willing to try. What other choice do we have?"

Anderson shook his head. "We can't take that kind of chance."

"No we can't. It's way too risky!" Murphy stepped to the center of the room. "We aren't talking about a portable television set here; we're talking about a sophisticated security system. If it goes off, that building will be locked down and crawling with police in two minutes! No offense, Mark, but we need to be certain."

Anderson regarded Murphy coldly. He had disliked the basketball player from the moment he had met him, because he was black, because he had been a celebrity before the war and because he possessed the kind of effortless charm that Anderson always distrusted. He suspected that everything had always come easily to Murphy. Such people, he had observed, rarely appreciated the rewards society lavished on them. "What do you suggest, Lonnie," he asked, with a touch of sarcasm in his voice. "Do you have a plan?" To his disappointment, Murphy was better prepared to answer than he had expected.

"As I see it we have two advantages," Murphy said. "The

257

first is surprise, the second is our man on the inside, who was going to meet John in the lobby and get him past the guards. We could still use his help to get one or two of us in. But without John to deactivate the alarms we can't open the rear door and the rest of us would be left on the outside. So I propose that we rely on surprise. We all go in through the front door, take out the guards, and seal the building. That way we never have to touch the security system."

Murphy paused and everyone stared mutely at him for a moment. Then Mark said, "That's it? You want us to storm the building?"

Murphy smiled confidently. "I'm not talking about a cavalry charge. Two of us go in alone, walk to the guard desk, and take out the guards. Then the rest come in and lock the doors. It's clean, it's direct, and it'll work."

"No it won't," Mark said. "To begin with, both guards aren't always at the desk. They make rounds on an irregular schedule, they go to the can . . ."

"If there's only one guard, it'll be that much easier," Murphy interrupted.

"And the other guard?"

"We take him out when we find him."

"You mean *if* we find him. What happens if he doesn't show up for five minutes? Or ten? The second guard is a wild card, Lonnie, a loose end we can't afford. And there's an even bigger problem. This is a television studio. The employees don't work nine to five. There are going to be people in the lobby, maybe a few, maybe a lot. You plan to take them out too?"

"The Chinese we take out. The Americans . . ."

"Oh Jesus!" Mark laughed aloud. "You think the Americans are going to cooperate with us? You think they'll be glad to see us? Not a chance! I live here; I know. Half the people in this city already believe in the new Chinese world; most of the rest think of us as crazies with no chance. They'll turn us in for the reward money. So to be safe, you're going to have to take out everyone who happens to be in the lobby. That could get messy. And noisy! Unless you plan to run around knifing them all. You see my point? In order for this to work we need fifteen minutes upstairs, undetected! During that time, everything downstairs has to look normal. If we go in through the lobby, we won't have that."

Murphy glared at Mark, but seemed to be considering what he had just said. Anderson looked on, displaying a small, satisfied smile. It was Katie who spoke.

"Exactly what do you think we should do then," she asked Mark. "Take the chance that you can deactivate the alarm, or give up completely for tonight?"

"Well, we can't give up," Mark said. "Tonight is our only chance, that's obvious. The Chinese will eventually make John talk and John knows everything. He might hold out until tomorrow or even the next day, but not forever. And when they break him they'll come after all of us. So we have to act before that happens. We have to act tonight because of the weapons in the basement storage room. Those weapons will be discovered tomorrow morning at the latest. When they are, the Chinese will turn that building into an armed fortress."

Katie chewed thoughtfully on her lip as she listened to this. When Mark had finished she turned to Devin and said, "He's right, isn't he, Ben? We have to go tonight."

Devin had been standing with his arms folded across his chest. At Katie's question he leaned toward her and nodded. "He's dead right. But so are Tom and Lonnie; they're each right about part of it. The problem is none of them is right about all of it."

Despite the fact that it had been intended only for Katie, his comment attracted everyone's attention. Mark, who had grown to respect Devin's opinions in the last two days, said quickly, "If you have a solution, Ben, let's have it. We're running out of time."

"Hell yes," Anderson put in. He too had great respect for Devin. "Don't keep it to yourself."

Devin asked, "Are you all through arguing then?"

Mark and Anderson nodded. Murphy seemed less certain. "I can't make any promises," he said cautiously. "Until I hear what you have to say."

Devin wasn't sure whether Murphy's reluctance was the product of honest concern for the mission or a simple desire to see Devin's plan rejected as his own had been, but he didn't think it mattered. Murphy would come around once he learned how Devin planned to use him.

The ex-Marine faced the group. "Tom and Lonnie believe there's too much risk in letting Mark try to neutralize the alarms. I agree. But I also agree that Lonnie's frontal assault won't work. Mark's right about that; we can't get around the problem of the lobby guards. That leaves us only one option—we go in through the garage."

"The garage?" Anderson's disappointment was obvious.

"But the garage guards are outside in a free standing booth! An attack there could be seen from hundreds of yards away."

"No, it couldn't," Devin said. "Visualize the building schematics, Tom. The garage ramp is thirty yards from the main entrance; it's poorly lighted and there's shrubbery on both sides of it, heavy shrubbery on the side toward the entrance and toward Capital Avenue. The guard booth can be seen clearly from only one spot, the area directly in front of the ramp. And at 6:45 there'll be very little traffic on the street." He looked at Mark. "Isn't that right?"

"Almost no one," Mark agreed. A few seconds earlier he had been eyeing Devin skeptically; now he seemed more receptive.

Anderson, however, was still unconvinced. "I don't know," he said, "It still seems awful chancy."

"It is," Devin admitted. "But not half as chancy as our other choices. We have to face facts, Tom. Nothing we do now will be as safe as what we originally planned to do. John's loss hurt us. But if you'll all listen to me, we can still get this job done. All right?" He didn't wait for an answer, instead, he turned to Murphy and said, "Lonnie, I understand you're good with a knife." Murphy stared back at him, expressionless. Devin could never read Murphy; that bothered him a little now, but he didn't have time to worry about it, so he proceeded as though Murphy had told him what he wanted to hear. "You and I are going to be the first team. We'll take out the guards. Then I'll trip the garage door while you and Yang pull the bodies into the bushes and get Yang into a uniform. That'll make you the last one into the building. You have a problem with that?"

"No problem," Murphy said, and it sounded to Devin like he meant it.

Next, Devin turned to Jacob Yang. "You heard what I just told Murphy?"

Yang said yes.

"I'm sorry we have to leave you down there alone but . . ." Devin shrugged.

"Don't apologize. I've known since John picked me for this team that it might be for something like this. I'm the only one who can do it."

"The uniform will be messed up. We'll try to damage only the back but I can't promise anything. Anyway, you get into a uniform, then get into the guard booth. I don't think anyone will come in at that time of night, but if anyone leaves just stay in the booth and wave them past. Whatever you do, try not to leave the booth; they can't see you very clearly in there so they won't notice that you're not the regular guard."

"I'll be fine," Yang said.

Devin proceeded around the room, delivering assignments to each team member. Cox and Anderson were to collect the weapons from the basement storage room and take them to the elevators. Mark was to secure the elevators. Katie and Devin and the one team member who was not in the room, the one now guarding the alley door, would search the garage to make sure no one had seen the break-in and hidden there. Then they would join the others at the elevators. As each new detail of the plan was revealed, the team seemed more convinced that it could work. Confidence flowed out from Devin and drew them together.

"When we get to the sixth floor," Devin said in conclusion, "we go back to the original plan, John's plan. Any questions? All right; now I want to go through it all once more. Only this time, each of you is going to tell me what you're going to do." He pointed at Murphy.

As Lonnie began repeating his orders, Anderson glanced at his wrist watch. It was fifteen minutes past six.

THIRTY-TWO

He was in a large room with a big table in the center. He couldn't remember how he got there or how long he'd been there but he didn't care about that. He was sitting at the end of the table and there was a man sitting beside him and looking at him. At the far end of the table—a long way off—there were two more men. They were not looking at him. They were looking at each other and jabbing the air with their fingers, like they were angry with each other. He didn't know why they were angry. In fact, he couldn't imagine why anyone was ever angry; he was feeling good and as far as he could remember he had always felt good. So their anger fascinated him and he watched them for a little while. Then he got tired of watching them and turned to the man sitting beside him.

He must have turned his head too quickly, because the turning made him feel dizzy and he had a little trouble focusing on the man's face. For a few seconds, the face seemed to drift and circle and he had to concentrate very hard to steady it so he could see it clearly. When he did finally steady it, he saw that it was a pleasant face, but also a strange kind of face, broad and flat, with eyes that turned up at the corners and skin much lighter than his own, but not as light as the skin of white people. He found the face even more interesting than the anger of the men at the far end of the table.

"Oriental," he heard himself say. "You're o-ri-en-tal, aren't you?" Then he heard himself giggle like a small child.

"You've asked that five times," the man said to him. "Don't you remember? The answer is still yes. Yes, I am oriental. But let's talk about you some more. You said your name is John. John what? What is your last name?"

The man looked at him and he looked back. It all seemed familiar to him. The man had asked this question before, he remembered that. *What is my last name?* He remembered trying to recall his name before, and he remembered that he hadn't been able to think of it. He realized that he still couldn't think of it and that made him feel suddenly embarrassed.

"You go first," his child's voice said. "You tell me your name, then I'll tell you mine."

"That's fair," the man said. "I am Yu Feng. Now, who are you?"

"Yu Feng," John repeated. And he frowned thoughtfully. Then he said it again, very slowly, "Yuu Feenng," as though he was carefully considering the strange syllables. Actually he was only stalling for time. He wasn't really interested in the man's name, he was trying to remember his own. And still, it wouldn't come. *I must know my own name!* But he did not. His mind would not cooperate. "I can't remember," he heard himself whimper. "I want to, but I can't." He felt a tear trickle down his cheek.

Yu Feng looked at him with an expression that was at once sympathetic and impatient and said, "That's all right, John. Let's try something else. You were on a bus when we found you. Do you remember the bus?"

He did remember the bus! And remembering surprised him and made him feel better. He nodded enthusiastically and said, "Yes, I remember the bus."

"All right. Now, do you remember where you were going on the bus?"

Again, he remembered. "I was going to meet my friends," he said. He was so pleased with himself and so intent on pleasing Yu Feng that he didn't notice that the two men at the far end of the table had ceased arguing and were now watching him with great interest.

"Go on," Yu Feng prompted. "Tell me about your friends. Who are they?"

"Just friends," John said.

"Good friends?"

"Best friends. We live together."

"Who are your friends, John?"

He thought about that for a moment. "Well, there's Ben and Mark and Lonnie and Katie and . . ." His voice drifted off; he had lost interest in what he was saying. Talk suddenly bored him. He wished Yu Feng would let him do something else.

Sgt. Yu glanced briefly at the men at the far end of the table and one of them returned an anxious expression. Then he looked back at John, who seemed to be intently studying the grain pattern in the top of the wooden table at which he was seated. He was tracing the curving grain design with his finger.

Yu said, "John, where do you and your friends live?"

263

John sighed. He liked Yu Feng very much, but he was beginning to feel tired and a little dizzy. All this thinking was hard.

"You aren't from here, are you?" Yu asked.

"Oh no," John said. And he smiled as he thought about his home. "We live in the mountains."

"You came to Sacramento from the mountains?"

John nodded.

"Why John? Why did you come here?"

John looked up at Sgt. Yu. "We came to start the revolution," he said.

Yu Feng's eyes widened and he blurted out, "When?" But John didn't answer and Yu said, more calmly this time, "When is the revolution going to start, John?"

John wanted to answer, but Yu Feng's face had begun drifting and circling again. He looked up the table toward the two other men. They were drifting and circling too. John's head felt heavy then, and he let it drop back and found himself staring at the light fixture on the ceiling. It was then that he saw the fragments of color, swirling and tumbling in the air. "Oh, look," he said wonderingly, "fireflies!"

"John," Yu Feng said, "John, you must tell me when the revolution is going to begin. What were you and your friends going to do?"

But it was too late. Head back and eyes closed, Yu Feng's prisoner had fallen into a deep sleep.

The two men at the far end of the table rushed forward. One, the medical doctor who had administered the drugs to John, began examining his patient. The other, a police captain named Quon Duo, fell into conversation with Sgt. Yu.

"I heard the last of it," Captain Quon said. "But what was there before? Did he tell you anything more?"

"You heard him say they were planning a revolution?"

"Yes, I heard that."

"And you heard him mention the name Lonnie?"

"That too."

Sgt. Yu shrugged. "Then you heard everything that was important."

Lt. Quon cursed under his breath. He looked at John, then at the doctor. "Well, doctor," he snapped. The doctor looked up from his patient. "Can you revive him?"

The doctor shook his head. "Not for some time. Eight

hours, perhaps ten."

"That will not do."

"I'm afraid it will have to do. As I was explaining to you a minute ago—"

"I will accept no more excuses," Captain Quon hissed. "This is a prisoner, not an experimental subject. He and his fellow conspirators are planning to overthrow the government. If you cannot revive him, then it is time for you to demonstrate your remarkable machine. We must know what this man knows."

The doctor sighed. "I would help if I could," he said. "But what you ask is impossible. You see, the effect of this drug is progressive; the first dose merely initiates the process. Attaching him to the machine before he has been given the second injection would produce nothing. You would learn nothing."

"Then give him the second dose now," Quon demanded.

The doctor shrugged helplessly. "Again, that is impossible. Administering a second dose prematurely could induce irreversible catalepsy. It could even kill him. We must wait until—"

"If you inject him now, would I get my answers?"

"You might, but—"

"Then do it!"

"I will not!" The doctor took a step back. "You're asking me to—"

"You misunderstand me," Quon said icily. "I am not asking you, doctor, I'm ordering you. Do it! Do it now."

THIRTY-THREE

It was now over an hour past sunset. The sky was clear and the temperature was dropping rapidly; it was going to be a cold night in Sacramento. The two guards were in their shelter beside the driveway ramp, trying to keep warm. The last car had left the garage fifteen minutes earlier and there was no longer any traffic on the streets. They were talking idly about local girls and home when a drunk staggered into view.

"Look," one said to the other, pointing. The drunk weaved unsteadily along the sidewalk near the ramp entrance, tripped over the curbing where the ramp met the sidewalk, and stumbled into the bushes. Both guards laughed.

Devin picked himself up and started toward them.

One guard pushed open the door to the booth and called out, "Hey, you're going the wrong way!"

Devin paused and stood swaying. "Says who?" he demanded. Then he lowered his head, leaned forward purposefully, and continued up the ramp.

The guard who had called out to him left the booth and walked toward him. They met halfway between the sidewalk and the booth. The guard pointed. "The sidewalk is back there."

"Back there?" Devin turned his head in the direction the guard had indicated, and appeared to lose his balance. The guard reached out and grabbed his shoulder to steady him. Devin turned back, suddenly clear eyed, and placed the point of a knife against the guard's throat. The guard gasped and stiffened.

Devin wrapped his free arm around the guard's shoulder and held him fast. "Call your friend," he commanded. "Tell him you need help."

The guard obeyed. He was no more than twenty years old, Devin guessed, and looked terrified.

The second guard stood in the booth door and called back, "What's the trouble, you can't handle a damn drunk?"

"Act like you're struggling with me," Devin whispered, as he dropped to one knee, pulling the guard down with him.

266

The second guard muttered a curse in Chinese and started toward them. He had taken only a few steps when he heard a sound off to his right and turned to see Lonnie Murphy rushing toward him from the bushes. For an instant, he froze. Then he saw the knife in Murphy's hand, realized what was happening, and reached for his pistol. His hand closed on the grip and he almost had it clear of its holster when Murphy drove into him. The pistol flew from his grasp and clattered across the concrete as Murphy thrust with the knife.

It was over in a second. Murphy had won, but the guard had nearly twisted free at the last instant and his twisting had ruined Murphy's aim; the knife was embedded in the guard's chest as he slumped to the pavement.

Devin saw all this and realized immediately that Murphy's failure had left him no options. He looked at the terrified boy in his arms and, in one motion, drew back the knife, flipped his hand around, and brought the butt of the knife down hard. The blow struck the boy on the temple; he uttered a small grunt and slumped unconscious. Devin lifted him to his shoulder and quickly carried him to where Murphy and the others were waiting.

"Here's your clean uniform," he said to Jacob Yang, as he lowered the boy into the bushes beside the guard booth. "Tie his hands and feet together behind his back and gag him." Yang nodded.

Murphy dropped the second guard beside the first, extracted his knife, and wiped it clean on the guard's jacket. Then he turned to Devin. "I screwed up," he said sheepishly. "Sorry."

"You did fine," Devin said.

Katie glanced sympathetically at the boy. "Do we really need to gag him," she asked. "He looks like he'll be out for hours."

"Bind and gag him," Devin repeated to Yang. "Take no chances." He didn't look at Katie. "All right everybody, you all know your jobs. Now move!" He disappeared into the booth and tripped the switch for the garage door as the others headed down the ramp.

Two minutes later they were gathered in the garage-level elevator lobby, armed with the weapons from the maintenance storeroom.

"What comes first?" Devin asked as they boarded the elevator. "What's most important?"

"The control room," Anderson answered. "Cox and I have to secure the control room and make sure nothing gets shut down."

"The east coast tapes are already running," Cox added. "In the east they run the taped schedule first and the news last. We can't allow that broadcast to be interrupted."

"Right," Devin said. "Okay. Next?" He pointed at Mark.

One by one the team members repeated their assignments. They had been over John's plan twenty times before, but no one objected; they all understood the reason for Devin's concern. It had been only a drill before, now it was real. They were inside, their hearts were pounding and the adrenalin was flowing. They all knew they would only get one chance at this; they couldn't afford a single mistake.

The elevator doors closed at 6:48. They were exactly on schedule.

Craighill was just completing his rehearsal for the evening newscast, reading the copy aloud just as he had done in Los Angeles before the war. He even repeated his daily sign off. Then he looked at his wall clock and noted the time. Ten seconds early. Years of experience had taught him exactly how much to adjust his normal pace to add or subtract time; it was as though he had a silent metronome ticking inside his head. Tonight he would dial the rate back ten seconds.

"You finished?"

He looked up and found Paul Sandiman standing in his office doorway. "Hello, Paul. Yeah, I'm done. Come in."

Sandiman stepped into the small office and sank into a chair.

"Did you get far with your editing?" Craighill asked.

"I started, but my heart wasn't really in it. I think you know what I mean."

"You're still upset about the travel permits."

Sandiman nodded. "You've had a couple of hours to think about it now. I was wondering what you decided."

Craighill leaned back and laced his fingers behind his neck. "I decided to wait until tomorrow. I want to hear what Chen finds out."

"What Chen finds out? He already knows, David; he was only stalling for time. My God, you didn't believe him, did you?"

"I'm not sure. This business about the ships might be important or it might be nothing. Let's give him the benefit of the doubt. Let's wait until tomorrow, okay?"

Sandiman said nothing.

"Okay?" Craighill repeated.

Sandiman said, "Okay."

Craighill glanced up at the wall clock. "Eleven minutes to air. Let's talk later, over dinner. You deserve a home-cooked meal. How about it?"

Sandiman was about to answer when they both became aware of a commotion in the hall. They heard loud voices and scuffling footsteps. Then a man appeared in the doorway. He was dressed casually, in typical Sacramento fashion, but something about him alarmed Craighill.

He seemed extremely nervous, almost frightened.

Sandiman bolted to his feet and blurted out, "What the hell!"

It was then that Craighill saw the weapon which Sandiman's body had blocked from his view until Sandiman moved. It was an Uzi assault rifle. The intruder was pointing it at them.

"CRAIGHILL, SANDIMAN," he barked. "IN THE HALL!"

The two newsmen exchanged an anxious glance.

"MOVE DAMMIT! NOW!"

The gunman's nervousness seemed to be increasing and that frightened Craighill. He pushed himself to his feet, held his hands up at shoulder level, palms out, and said, "All right, all right, we're coming."

At that moment, someone flashed by the door behind their captor. Craighill wasn't sure, but he thought it had been a young woman. She had been armed with a large automatic pistol, which she held in both hands beside her ear, pointed at the ceiling. He had seen this posture at a police training academy he had visited once for a story. He had also seen it in thousands of pre-war cop dramas. He wondered if it meant the woman had received training, or if she was merely imitating what she had seen on television.

"OUT," the gunman commanded. He stepped back into the hall and waved the Uzi. "THAT WAY!"

The newsmen obeyed.

As they started down the corridor they could see other members of the evening broadcast staff, which numbered about fifteen in all, being herded into the reception area. They also saw three more armed men. Craighill was now guessing that they must be resistance fighters, the last remnant of some die-hard guerrilla

269

band. (If the one with the Uzi was typical, they were certainly not professional soldiers.) Their presence here must mean they planned to broadcast some message to the population. But what could that accomplish? With the exception of a few places like Sacramento where restrictions had been relaxed, the entire population was under constant guard. A broadcast directed at them would be an exercise in futility—it could win the guerrillas nothing. It was madness, a desperate act by desperate people!

Craighill felt a sudden chill as he repeated this last thought, because it seemed to lead to only one possible conclusion—these guerrillas were not seeking victory, they were seeking martyrdom! They had to be; nothing else made sense. They could not expect to escape from Sacramento and they certainly had not come to invite capture. They were hoping to become symbols, perhaps even expecting to die on camera!

He had just begun to consider what such fanatics might do to him and the rest of the station staff when Sandiman's voice interrupted his thoughts.

"Good God!"

Sandiman had stopped abruptly at the entrance to the reception area. He was staring at something. Craighill's eyes followed his gaze.

Several staff members were standing just in front of them; others were beyond, sitting on the floor in front of the elevators. Two guerrillas were shouting commands, instructing the new arrivals to take places beside the ones on the floor. One of the guerrillas was a tall, muscular black man. "Isn't that . . ." Sandiman started to say. But he was cut off by the guerrilla behind him jabbing the Uzi into the small of his back.

"Murphy!" Craighill said, completing Sandiman's sentence. "Lonnie Murphy!"

As Craighill spoke the name, Murphy turned and faced them. "Craighill, Sandiman." His voice was as hard as his expression, conveying no hint of pleasure at the reunion. He pushed roughly past one of the newly arrived captives and pointed a pistol at Craighill. "Into the studio, David. You too, Paul."

"Lonnie," Sandiman objected. "What the hell is going on here?"

"The studio," Murphy repeated, pointing the way with the pistol. They started down the hall toward the newsroom. Murphy fell in behind them. "There's no time for explanations," he said. "We're on the air in ten minutes."

270

The statement confirmed Craighill's suspicions. Seeing Murphy had momentarily led him to hope he had been wrong about these rebels—Murphy was no fanatic. But he now realized that he had not been wrong; they were planning exactly what he had guessed they must be planning. But then, how did Murphy figure in the scheme? Where had he been all these months? And how had he become involved with these guerrillas?

There were four people in the newsroom when they arrived, two cameramen, the boom mike operator, and another guerrilla, armed with a pistol which he pointed at the technicians. Through the glass windows separating the control booth from the studio they could see another rebel guarding the engineers sitting at the panel. The atmosphere here was calm, Craighill noted. The guerrillas in the studio were more businesslike; they seemed to know exactly what they were doing. The one in the control booth looked at Murphy as he followed the two newsmen in and announced, "Everything's ready. The east coast tapes are still rolling."

Murphy nodded and directed Craighill to take his place behind the anchor desk. "You stand there," he said to Sandiman, indicating a spot beside Craighill's chair. Then he reached into his back pocket and withdrew several folded sheets of paper, which he spread out on the desk and creased against the fold so they would lay flat. "We've brought you a new script for tonight's broadcast," he said, handing Craighill the sheets.

Craighill had not anticipated this. He had assumed the guerrillas wanted television exposure for themselves. "You want me to read this? On air?"

"The people trust you," Murphy replied simply.

"But . . ."

"Time is short, David. Read it. Then we'll talk."

"That's right," Captain Quon Duo spat into the phone, "The Global Television studio! We need every man you can mobilize, Lieutenant. Silent alarm, no sirens!" He paused to listen as the lieutenant made some reply. "Six minutes?" Quon seemed pleased. "Good! And, Lieutenant, no one enters the building except on my order. Is that understood?" He slammed the receiver down and turned to Sgt. Yu. "There is a team on the way to the helipad already. You know as much about this as I do, and there is no time for briefings so I want you to command the helicopter team. Secure the roof of the building and wait for my orders. Now go!"

Yu Feng was out the door almost before the captain had finished speaking. His mind raced as he rushed toward the helipad. A few minutes earlier he had been feeling sympathy for the American prisoner they had been interrogating; he had thought Captain Quon was overreacting when he ordered the doctor to administer the fatal drug. But Quon's instincts had proved accurate; the prisoner's death had been justified. It was incredible, unbelievable! A small band of Americans was actually planning to overthrow the continental government! And now, good fortune had granted Sgt. Yu the opportunity to stop them. It was the chance of a lifetime!

He could not disobey his orders, of course, but he had already decided what he could do. Quon had not thought of it, but he had. It was so simple! If it worked it would forever mark him as a hero of the new federation.

At the helipad, he found the chopper waiting, its turbine engines whining and its rotors already spinning in preparation for takeoff. His team—seven men—were already aboard. Yu leapt into the vacant copilot's seat. "Go!" he shouted to the pilot. "That way!" He pointed toward the west, toward the tall buildings that clustered around the Capitol dome at the heart of downtown Sacramento.

It was 6:53 when Craighill finished reading the script Murphy had written out in the basement of the building across the alley. John was supposed to have written it but in his absence the task had fallen to Murphy. The athlete knew his text was less than eloquent—he didn't have John's facility with words—but the facts were all there. And the facts were what mattered.

"Well?" he asked, when he saw that Craighill had reached the bottom of the third and last page. Devin and Katie had now joined him in front of the anchor desk. Anderson stood several steps away, guarding the cameramen and the sound technician. Cox was in the control booth, holding a pistol on the engineers there.

Craighill looked up, disbelief written in his expression. The script had been exactly what he expected it to be—a venomous piece of propaganda full of half-truths and outright lies. It distorted everything the Chinese had accomplished or were trying to accomplish. Yet the anxiety he had just noted in Murphy's voice seemed completely genuine. Was it possible he actually believed this fiction? Murphy was too clever too be fooled easily. Craighill wondered how the rebels had enlisted him and convinced him to join them. Then a disturbing thought flashed across his consciousness: Was it possible that any of this was true? He demanded, "Can you prove any of these claims?"

Murphy replied gravely, "It's all true, David."

"Tens of thousands of armed rebels still hiding in the hills?" Craighill shook his head incredulously.

"Maybe a hundred thousand; we aren't sure of the exact number. But certainly enough to start a massive revolt. All they need is the order to begin. You're going to give them that order."

"Where? Where have a hundred thousand people been hiding?"

"Everywhere. From California to the Carolinas. They're there, David." This was a lie. Murphy had no knowledge of Zachary's success in Colorado and no specific knowledge of rebel activity east of the Sierra Nevada; he was only sure of the rebels in California and Oregon. But his bluff was so convincing that Craighill did not recognize the deceit.

From the control booth Cox announced: "SIX MINUTES" over the studio speakers.

"For two years," Murphy continued, "the only things preventing a revolt have been the prisoners' lack of weapons and their fear that beyond the boundaries of their camps there was no one to help them. Once they know that there are armed guerrillas beyond the boundaries, and that everyone is going to begin fighting at once, they will respond. And once the first spark catches fire . . ." He left the thought hanging.

Craighill returned his gaze without speaking. If there really were a hundred thousand armed rebels out there, he realized, this scheme might not be madness. Was that possible? There were probably no more than twelve or fifteen million Chinese in North America, only a fraction of which were military and police. There were nearly two hundred million prisoners in the camps and the cities. If a real revolt started, could the Chinese contain it? Maybe not. But there weren't a hundred thousand armed rebels out there. There couldn't be! Murphy was lying about this and about the rest of it too. The things he was claiming were absurd.

Craighill scanned back through the script and pointed to an item on page two. "Here," he said to Murphy, "You claim the Chinese have been torturing prisoners in the camps?" He knew this was untrue; in the last few months his reporters had visited a hundred camps and found no evidence of torture. There had been

273

scattered cases of abuse—a rape, several beatings—but those had been isolated incidents.

"We have very reliable intelligence," Murphy said confidently. "There has been torture."

"No," Craighill objected. "I've been to the camps myself; I've talked to the prisoners. I saw nothing to support this. You're asking me to believe things that . . ."

Murphy glared at him. "Dammit, David, don't you understand what's been happening here? They've been using you! You, Sandiman, and everyone else here. They've shown you only what they wanted you to see. They've programmed you!"

Craighill recognized unmistakable sincerity in this statement. Murphy clearly believed what he was saying! That shook him for an instant. After all, he had recently entertained these same doubts himself; only a week ago, he had confronted Chen about them. And Chen had resolved his doubts.

Chen! The image of the old man's face flashed before him now. Craighill respected Murphy's sincerity, but he could not believe Murphy without disbelieving Chen. Had Chen lied to him, manipulated him? He couldn't accept that. The facts, as he knew them, supported Chen.

"I don't believe that," he said flatly. "Neither do you."

Murphy shook his head in frustration. "Afraid to admit you've been wrong, is that it? But you have been wrong, David. We're giving you a chance now to correct that wrong."

Sandiman, who was still standing next to Craighill, leaned close and said, "He may be right, David. Remember Guangzhou."

"FIVE MINUTES," the studio speakers announced.

Craighill's head snapped around and he glared up at Sandiman. "Are you willing to read it, Paul? Are you that sure he's right?"

Sandiman drew back. "No," he admitted. "I'm not sure he's right. But I'm not sure he's wrong either. Neither are you."

"We don't have time for this," someone shouted angrily. It was not Murphy. Craighill turned and looked at the speaker.

Anderson took a step toward the three guerrillas clustered in front of the anchor desk and continued, "He isn't going to cooperate, Lonnie, so give it up. Let Sandiman read the damn script."

"No," Murphy said firmly. He did not look at Anderson as he spoke; his eyes remained on Craighill. "David is one of us. He's an American and he's going to read it. Aren't you, David?"

Craighill looked from Anderson back to Murphy. His first impulse was to say "No!" and thereby relieve himself of responsibility for the rebel broadcast. But he hesitated. The very fact that he feared that responsibility prevented him from refusing. Why was he afraid? If the rebel claims were untrue, then the broadcast would accomplish nothing and his participation could do no harm. Only if the script was accurate would he be forced to accept responsibility for his action, because only in that case would it produce consequences. Revolution! Was it possible? Was Murphy right? Had Chen deceived them? Used him? These guerrillas believed it. Sandiman believed it. If it were true, then he should read the script; he should play his part. But he couldn't believe it. He still trusted Chen. The old man had not lied to him. *He took me into his confidence and showed me things none of these others have seen. I know more than they know; I know I am right.*

And yet the doubt still gnawed at him. Somehow his trust in Chen was not enough. He had to be sure it was the rebels, not the Chinese, who were lying.

"You haven't convinced me yet," he said to Murphy. "You still haven't proved any of these claims." He looked quickly down the page in front of him and his eye settled on another item. "Here, for example, you claim the Chinese have used chemical weapons."

Murphy nodded and began to say something, but Devin preempted him. "I'm positive of that," he said. "I saw the gas canisters myself."

Craighill had noticed Devin earlier and wondered why he had been so quiet; he had the look of a man accustomed to command. He had guessed, correctly, that Devin's responsibilities were probably military, and that Murphy was acting as spokesman here in the studio because of his previous relationship with Sandiman and himself.

"That's a serious accusation," Craighill said to Devin. "You may have seen canisters, but how can you be sure what was in them. Were they labeled in English?" It was a facetious question, almost sarcastic.

"They were used against my group," Devin replied evenly. "I'd seen them before and I knew what was in them. It was a nerve gas called Sarin, one of the oldest chemical weapons in the Chinese arsenal. Cheap but effective."

Murphy added quickly, "Ben was a Marine before the war. He knows weapons. There's no doubt about this, David, nerve gas was used. Ben's group was lucky; they were warned and they escaped. But others were massacred."

"I have personal knowledge of that too," Devin said.

Craighill was almost certain that Devin had told the truth about the nerve gas. He had less faith in Murphy's claim of a massacre. But Devin had confirmed that too. David wanted to know exactly what they were talking about. "Who was massacred," he demanded. "And when?"

"It was in early November," Devin answered. "There were two groups. Mine and—"

Anderson shouted, "Damn it, we're wasting time. Don't you see what he's doing? He's stringing us along. And we're down to . . ." He turned to look at the studio clock just as Cox announced: "FOUR MINUTES."

"It's okay," Murphy said. "We have time. Go on, Ben."

Anderson turned away, muttering angrily as Devin continued. "As I was saying, both of our groups got out before the gas was deployed. We followed separate escape routes and the Chinese never found my group; we got away clean. But they found the others, twenty-four people, five children—not a single one survived."

Craighill saw genuine pain in Devin's expression as he said this. He clearly believed what he was saying. But there was something in his eyes besides mere pain. There was a look of guilt that Craighill didn't understand. This man felt somehow responsible for what had happened, personally responsible. Was the burden of that responsibility coloring his perception of the incident? He hated to ask his next question, but he had to know the answer.

"Are you certain they were killed? Did you see . . ."

"Did we see bodies?" Devin's eyes narrowed. "You still want proof, is that it? You want absolute assurances of who's right and who's wrong? Well, I can't give that to you."

Katie moved closer to Devin as he said this. She placed a hand on his arm and squeezed gently, reassuringly. Craighill watched her with sudden fascination. She was beautiful. He hadn't noticed it until this moment, but he was suddenly struck with the impression that she seemed completely out of place here.

"No one can make this easy for you," Devin was saying. "There are no assurances anyone can give you, no absolutes. But I know this—the Chinese attacked us with lethal gas. So it's clear they had no intention of taking prisoners." He paused and

276

Craighill looked away from Katie back to him. "What they did can't be defended," Devin concluded.

Murphy stepped closer and placed his hand on the script. "So, David, will you read it?" He seemed to believe Devin's arguments had been persuasive and that this was the moment to press that advantage.

But Craighill was still not convinced. All the evidence had been inconclusive. He believed Devin about the nerve gas, but the rest was mud. Had there been a massacre? Even if there had, did it represent a pattern or was it an isolated incident? Did it prove deceit on the part of Chen and the Chinese hierarchy, or were these guerrillas merely seeing what they wanted to see? "I'm not sure," he said to Murphy. "Give me a moment more."

"No more time!" Anderson shouted. And this time Murphy agreed. "You have to decide now," he demanded, his tone finally angry. "If you won't do it, Sandiman needs time to get ready."

Why is this so important to me, Craighill asked himself. Why don't I simply allow them to remove me, wash my hands of it? He felt vaguely aware that there was something he wasn't seeing, some consideration that hadn't occurred to him yet. But what? Perhaps he should simply agree, tell them he would read it just to buy himself a few more minutes to think. "I . . ."

He was cut off by one of the guerrillas bursting through the door into the studio. "Ben!" the man said breathlessly, "We've got problems. A helicopter! I think it landed on the roof!"

"Shit!" Murphy hissed. "They know we're here!"

Devin bolted for the door and Katie followed him. Anderson started after them, then pulled up abruptly, wheeled, and trained his weapon on the technicians in the studio.

Devin faced the guerrilla who had just come in and asked in a voice so calm that it surprised Craighill, "Are the elevators locked down?"

The newcomer said yes.

"Is the stairwell secure?"

Again, the answer was yes. "We've got charges set on both landings, above and below," the guerrilla said.

"Then we should be able to hold them. All right, get back to your post." He turned to Katie and said firmly, "You stay here."

"Here? No, Ben! I'm not needed here!"

"No arguments! I say you stay and you're going to stay." He leaned forward and kissed her. Then he reached out, placed a hand on her stomach, and smiled. Craighill was certain he saw her blush.

A moment later, Devin was gone and Katie was left standing by the door, looking worried and anxious. Only two guerrillas remained in the studio, Murphy and Anderson.

Murphy looked toward the studio clock as Cox's voice sounded over the speakers. "Two minutes, fifty seconds, Lonnie. I forgot to call three minutes. Sorry."

Murphy waved to him. The oversight was certainly understandable. Murphy was feeling suddenly shaken; Cox probably was too. They were both beginning to recognize the full implications of what had just happened.

It wasn't supposed to be this way. No one was supposed to know they were here until the broadcast aired. The streets were supposed to fill with rioters then to cover their escape. What had gone wrong? The Chinese must have gotten the information out of John. So now the rebels were trapped and they would never know if they succeeded or failed. They would all probably die. Even if they didn't die, they would be subjected to unimaginable torture. Given those prospects, Murphy was amazed at how calmly he was accepting it all. Perhaps he was simply numb. He turned to Craighill, no longer angry, now merely determined to do what must be done. "Well, David," he said. "What's it going to be?"

"I'll do it," Craighill said. "I'll read your script."

At the garage entrance, Jacob Yang had seen the helicopter. It had come in from the northeast, and he had heard it long before he caught sight of it. He had paid little attention at first. Then, as it drew nearer, he looked up and watched it emerge from the blackness of the night sky, dimly illuminated by the lights of the city. Was its appearance just coincidence, he wondered—the street was still quiet. Then he noticed that the helicopter was showing no lights and that the word POLICE was emblazoned on its underside. He saw also that it was descending, moving toward a landing on the roof of the studio building. So it was no coincidence. The Chinese knew they were here!

He was gripped with sudden panic. What was his duty in this situation? He had been posted here so the assault would not be detected, so the authorities would not be alerted before the broadcast aired. Now that the authorities knew, was his presence still necessary? Should he abandon his post and join the others in the building? No, he decided. No, he should do whatever he could to delay the police! He should try to buy the team more time! But how? What could he do? He looked frantically around the small guard booth and his eye fell upon the switch that operated the garage door. That was it—he would immobilize the door.

He examined the switch mechanism. It was a simple toggle mounted on a steel plate. Behind that plate, he knew, there would be wires leading to the switch. But the plate was held in place with screws and he had no screwdriver. He did, however, have a knife. He tried the knife but its sharp, pointed tip was useless on the philips head screws.

Suddenly, he heard the sound of engines and squealing tires. He looked up and saw two police vans, then a third, turning off Capital Avenue and racing toward him. He had no more time! The wires leading to the plate—where would they come from? From below! They would be laid in conduit from the garage to the booth. He picked a spot directly below the switch plate and began stabbing the inner surface of the wall with the knife. In seconds he had opened a fist-sized hole in the gypsum board and could see the wires. He hooked a finger around one, pulled it out through the hole and, cut it with the knife. Then he stuffed both ends back into the hole, pushing one up and the other down. He guessed it would take the Chinese at least two minutes to find the wires and repair the damage. Two minutes wasn't much, but it was something.

When he looked back to the street there were a total of five police vans in sight along with several patrol cars. Most had stopped in front of the building's main entrance; two vans were pulled up on the sidewalk, and uniformed police armed with machine guns were running toward the doors. A single van was just rolling to a stop on the garage ramp. Its doors flew open and six policemen jumped out and rushed toward him. The nearest one was carrying a radio and wearing the insignia of an officer.

Yang paused a moment to collect himself and brush a spot of gypsum dust from his uniform sleeve. Then he stepped out of the booth. "What's going on?" he demanded. Act authoritative, he thought, you're supposed to be a security guard.

The officer stopped a few feet in front of him. "Open the garage door," he commanded.

"Why?" Yang countered. "What's happening?"

The officer pointed at the building and said something in Chinese.

Yang stiffened. He was fourth generation Chinese-American and didn't understand a word of his ancestral native tongue. His mind raced—there was only one thing he could do.

"Speak English," he shouted angrily. "You know the law!"

The officer glared back at him, his eyes wild with sudden rage. Such insolence was intolerable! He pushed Yang aside and stepped into the guard booth. He flipped the garage door switch, then exited the booth and barked orders, again in Chinese, to the other policemen. They started down the ramp toward the garage.

The officer then turned on Yang and began cursing at him. He was interrupted almost immediately by a shout from one of the men on the ramp. He looked at the garage door. His expression revealed surprise, then sudden recognition. "So!" he said, with obvious pleasure. His hand closed on the grip of the AK-47 he had slung over his shoulder and he leveled it at Yang as he stepped back into the booth and looked at the switch plate.

He jabbed a finger into the hole below the plate. Yang raised his hands in a gesture of surrender. The officer looked at Yang and smiled briefly. Then he fired a short burst. All four rounds found their target; Yang was dead before his body struck the pavement.

"You," the officer shouted to one of his men, while pointing at Yang, "move this garbage off the road." Then he addressed another of his men, the one who had been driving the van. "Xia! The van! We must break the door!"

The garage door was constructed of lightweight aluminum. Xia had no difficulty driving the van through it.

It was all growing clear to Craighill now. In the brief time since he had agreed to cooperate, Murphy had left him alone to prepare himself and he had used that opportunity to order his thoughts. He now understood what he had failed to recognize earlier. All the things they had been discussing—the chemical warfare and torture accusations, the question of how many guerrillas were hiding in the hills, the probability that an insurrection could succeed—were secondary issues. They were important, but not central.

He had allowed his attention to be diverted by all these details and focused his deliberations on a single question: Who should I trust? It had seemed reasonable at the time, but he now saw that it was not. Trust was an elusive commodity in postwar North America. All information was suspect and nothing could be proved! It was easier to disbelieve both Chen and these rebels than to believe either one of them. The rebel Marine had been right; there could be no assurances, there were no absolutes. How then could he decide who to support?

He realized finally that what mattered was the future. Who held the key to the future? That was the question he must ask himself. And the answer must supersede all other considerations, even his natural loyalties. He was an American, so he felt sympathy for the guerrilla cause and was naturally inclined to support them. But even if these rebels were telling the truth, could their revolution yield positive results? If it ultimately succeeded in driving the Chinese from North America, what sort of society would emerge in its wake? Would it be better than the society the Chinese would build? And could it hope to survive, cut off from the rest of the world? On the other side, would the Chinese keep their promises? Could he really believe they would discard their oppressive, totalitarian tradition? Was Chen's voice the voice of a new China or merely a carefully crafted illusion? And what was happening in Guangzhou?

He weighed all these unknowns on the scales of his experience and decided what he must do.

"THIRTY SECONDS," Cox announced. Since the one minute mark, he had been calling the time every ten seconds.

For nearly two minutes now, they had been hearing the sound of small-arms fire echoing hollowly from the stairwell, and tension had grown rapidly in the studio; it was written on nearly every face. Only Murphy seemed immune. Shortly after the shooting had begun, Anderson had suggested that they kill the tapes and start the broadcast early. But Murphy had refused. "A lot of television sets won't be turned on until seven o'clock," he had argued. "We have to wait!" Craighill had felt grudging admiration then for Murphy's cool behavior under fire, and nothing had happened since to erode his new respect for the former basketball player.

Suddenly, an explosion rocked the building. The glass panels separating the studio from the hallway rattled and flexed. Anderson winced and looked anxiously toward the studio door. Katie, who was standing near the door, jumped sideways, retreated and took up a new position nearer to Anderson and Murphy. Craighill felt a rush of sympathy for her. He wasn't sure whether the fear he saw in her eyes was for herself or for the rebel who had kissed her earlier, but he imagined it was the latter. Her attention seemed to be directed toward the hallway more often than toward the activity in the studio.

"That was one of the stairwell charges," Murphy observed.

"I know," Anderson said. "They're getting close."

"TWENTY SECONDS."

More small-arms fire echoed, nearer this time. Murphy looked at Craighill. "Are you ready, David?"

Craighill nodded. Perspiration beaded on his forehead and he dabbed at it with a handkerchief. The last time that had happened was at least thirty years ago, he recalled; it was going to look bad on camera. Strange, the things a person thought about at a moment of crisis.

There was another explosion. Again, the glass wall rattled.

"The second stairwell charge," Anderson said. "They must be coming from below and above."

"TEN SECONDS! The logo is coming up."

Unaccountably, there was a sudden lull; the shooting stopped. Anderson looked curiously at Murphy, who responded with a frown. Five seconds passed. Then the shooting started again.

"The music is up! CUE CRAIGHILL," a voice commanded. It was not Cox this time, it was the chief engineer. "AND GET SANDIMAN OUT OF THE SHOT!"

Sandiman was still standing beside Craighill. No one had told him to move and he had not moved. Murphy waved angrily at him and he stepped aside. Craighill glanced at the control booth and smiled to himself. The chief engineer was Chinese; he should be trying to sabotage this broadcast. Instead, he was simply doing his normal, thorough job. A professional to the end, Craighill thought.

"Go!" Murphy said, pointing at the anchorman.

"Good evening," he began. "I'm David Craighill and this is the news."

From somewhere down the hallway a shout was heard, then more shooting. It was much closer this time and there was no echo. It seemed to be coming from the hallway itself. Craighill hesitated and Murphy leveled his pistol at him.

"This evening," Craighill said, looking straight into the camera, "the studios of Global Television have been captured by a small band of terrorists."

Anderson, who had been facing the studio door, whirled, his eyes wide with surprise. "That's not in the script!" he bellowed. "What's he doing?"

"They are demanding that I read a statement they have prepared."

"Shoot him!" Anderson screamed. "Damn it, Lonnie, shoot him!"

But Murphy did not shoot. His expression conveyed not anger, but a profound sadness. "Don't do this, David," he said, shaking his head slowly. "You can't."

There was another explosion, in the hallway this time. The glass studio wall shattered and fell inward, spilling glass shards across the studio floor. Smoke and dust billowed in through the opening. Katie stumbled into Anderson, knocking him off balance. He went down on one knee. There were more shots from the hallway, very loud now. It sounded like the battle was taking place inside the studio.

Murphy lowered his pistol and stared disconsolately at Craighill. He started to speak but seemed unable to find the words.

Anderson leapt back to his feet and snarled, "Well if you won't do it, I will!" He raised his pistol and aimed it at Craighill. David stared at him numbly. There was no cover, nowhere to hide. The desk behind which he was sitting was made of plywood and, he knew, would provide him no protection.

Katie saved his life. As Anderson's gun hand came up, she screamed, "NO!" and grabbed his arm. The two came together; there was a shot, and her eyes opened wide in an expression of disbelief. Then she went limp and slumped to the floor.

"Bastard!" someone shouted. "Maniac!"

Craighill looked toward the sound and saw Devin standing just inside the studio, his feet in the pile of broken glass. His face was half obscured by blood flowing from a head wound he had suffered in the battle. As Craighill watched, horrified, the Uzi in Devin's hands chattered.

Anderson's chest erupted. He was at least eight feet from the anchor desk at that moment, but blood still splattered on Craighill. Anderson staggered backward against a television camera and fell sideways to the floor.

In the control room, Cox placed his pistol against the temple of the chief engineer and said dully, "Kill it."

Craighill dropped the script he was holding and sat shaking. After a moment he took his handkerchief and began numbly dabbing the blood from his face. Devin dropped his weapon and rushed to Katie; he would do no more fighting. One of the cameramen bolted from his post and rushed toward the door. At the sound of more gunfire from the hallway he threw himself on the floor, face down. Then there was silence. Sandiman, who had dived beneath the desk when Devin started shooting, looked up at Craighill and asked, "Is it over?"

At that moment, three uniformed policemen appeared in the hallway by the shattered glass wall. Two pointed rifles at the survivors and the third commanded, "EVERYBODY DOWN! ON THE FLOOR! NOW!"

THIRTY-FOUR

In front of the Global Television building three ambulances had joined the police vans and patrol cars crowding the street. Their emergency lights illuminated the faces in the small crowd that had gathered, pulsing blue and white, like the strobes in some ancient disco club. The ambulance crews moved in and out of the building, carefully attending to the wounded and removing the dead. In the building lobby and on the plaza outside the main doors, a number of policemen stood with notepads or small recorders interviewing various members of the news staff. Remarkably, not a single staff member had been seriously injured.

It was reminiscent of scenes Craighill had witnessed hundreds of times before. This time, however, it felt very different. This time he was a participant, not merely an observer.

The policeman interviewing Craighill was a lieutenant, the only officer burdened with such menial duty. A captain named Quon Duo had assigned him personally, saying that Craighill was their most important witness and the lieutenant had attacked his task with enthusiasm. He was being very thorough.

"The man named Murphy," he asked. "Was it your impression that he was the leader of the terrorist band?"

"The leader?" Craighill considered his response carefully. At the critical moment Murphy had spared him and he wanted to say nothing now that might in any way injure the basketball player. But what answer should he give? Would Murphy receive better treatment if the Chinese believed he led the attack or if they thought he was merely a soldier? Craighill could only guess and hope.

"I don't believe there was a leader," he replied. "I saw no one giving orders. In any case, Murphy was in the studio during the entire battle; he took no part in the fighting."

The lieutenant busied himself with recording this information on his notepad and Craighill took the opportunity to look around. He saw Chen's car turn off Capital Ave. and pull to a stop behind the cluster of police vans at the curb.

"Lieutenant," he said to his interrogator, "I have to excuse myself for a moment. I'll be back."

The lieutenant muttered something David couldn't understand and returned to his writing.

Chen was just emerging through the police barricades when Craighill reached him. "David," he said anxiously. A flash from the ambulance lights played across them, revealing Craighill's blood spattered clothing. Chen gasped. "Are you hurt?"

"Not a scratch," Craighill assured him. "But I could have been. I need to talk to you."

Chen did something that surprised him then. When Craighill offered him his hand the old man took it, pulled Craighill to him and embraced him.

"Thank God," Chen said. Then he stepped back. "I came as soon as I heard. But I know very little. Exactly what happened?"

"I'll tell you everything, but first I need your help. Two different people prevented me from being killed tonight. I want you to do whatever you can to help them."

"Of course," Chen said.

Craighill led him away from the police lines to a spot on the plaza where they could talk in relative privacy.

"One of the guerrillas was Lonnie Murphy," Craighill said.

Chen's eyes widened in amazement. "Murphy? The one who played basketball?"

"Yes. He could have shot me; I think many others in his group would have shot me given the same circumstances. But he didn't. He's been arrested now and . . . is there any way you can help him?"

For a moment Chen seemed unable to speak. Finally he shook his head sadly and said, "You don't know what you are asking. I don't even know what my own position will be tomorrow. I'm going to be held responsible for what happened here."

"He wasn't really one of them, Chen. He was in your camp just three months ago. He was one of us."

"I understand, but . . ." Again the old man shook his head. "I'm not sure what may be possible. I will make inquiries but I can promise nothing. Who was the second person? You said there was another."

"Yes. There was also a girl. She's badly injured. They've taken her to hospital. I asked an ambulance attendant about her condition. He thought she would live but he wasn't positive. I tried to go with her in the ambulance but the police won't let any of us leave."

"She was one of the terrorists?"

"She was with them, but like Murphy she wasn't really one of them; I'm sure of it. She was frightened, she took no part in the fighting and she saved my life. She was shot saving me." Craighill paused. Chen's expression told him he was asking too much. But it couldn't be too much; he had to help this girl. "There's another consideration," he added. "I believe she's pregnant."

That seemed to have an effect on Chen. Craighill saw sudden pain in his eyes. "How can you know that?" he demanded. You don't know this girl do you?"

"I never saw her before tonight. But I'm almost sure, with some women you can tell.

"But what can I tell my people? What reason can I give for leniency? Do you even know her name?"

"No," Craighill admitted, then said hurridly, "Tell them anything. Tell them she was an innocent bystander. Tell them . . . tell them she's my niece!"

Chen turned away for a moment. When he turned back his face was a mask; the newsman could read no emotion on it. "Is she so important to you?"

Craighill said simply, "I owe her my life."

The old man shrugged. "Again, I can make no promises. But I will make inquiries. Is that all?" He looked very tired and Craighill suddenly remembered how sick he had seemed earlier this afternoon. In the excitement he had forgotten.

"Isn't that enough?" the newsman smiled ruefully.

"MR. CRAIGHILL!" From across the plaza someone was calling his name. David looked and saw his lieutenant, walking briskly toward them.

"That policeman was asking me questions when you arrived," he said to Chen."I have to go. But I'll find you as soon as he's finished and I'll tell you everything that happened here."

"No," Chen said. "Go to your wife; she will be worried. We can talk tomorrow."

Craighill thanked him and started to leave. Chen called out to him and he turned.

"David, one last question."

"Yes?"

"If I can help only one, Murphy or the girl, who should it be?"

Craighill answered without hesitation. "In that case," he

287

said, "help the girl."

In the woods just east of camp 454, Dave Adrian and a heavily armed band of guerrillas huddled, waiting for some sign that the fighting would begin tonight. But the camp routine seemed normal. More prisoners that usual were outside the barracks, sitting on the porches and in the camp yard and Adrian wondered about that. But there was no other unusual activity. Why weren't the inmates watching television? He didn't know. But one thing was certain: today was not the day.

In the camp itself, Cal Triplett sat on his barracks steps with several members of his intelligence team. No one could understand why there had been no broadcast this evening; there had been no announcement of a cancellation.

"Could the cancellation be the signal?" someone asked.

"No," Triplett answered confidently. The signal will be crystal clear when it comes. We will be given detailed instructions."

In Colorado, Zack Zachary and the Special Forces team of which he was now a member monitored L-RAD transmissions from across the country. There had been no newscast anywhere. What did it mean? No one knew.

In hundreds of locations from California to the Carolinas guerrilla bands checked their weapons, reviewed their battle plans and waited anxiously for a signal that would never come.

THIRTY-FIVE

Thursday, February 3

It is late and I am very tired tonight, so I will add only a few notes to yesterday's entry regarding the guerrilla attack on the television studios.

We spent today assessing the damage. We have only one working camera and will be forced to rely more than usual on previously prepared tapes tomorrow, but new equipment is being shipped in and the studio should be back to normal in a few days. The building stairwell sustained heavy damage, as did the hallway and several nearby offices. There are bullet holes everywhere.

We learned this morning that none of what happened yesterday reached the air. We had thought that fifteen or twenty seconds (including my attempt to sabotage the broadcast) had gone out, but apparently a resourceful policeman, acting without orders, disconnected the satellite uplinks and the local broadcast antenna on the roof of our building several minutes before air time. His action will not be recognized publicly because there is to be no public admission that the incident ever took place, but the policeman has been promoted and awarded some sort of medal Chen told me.

Knowledge of these facts has caused me considerable distress. Had I known at the time of the broadcast that the uplink was disconnected, I would not have refused to read Murphy's script. My gesture now seems completely futile and senseless and its terrible consequences doubly tragic. If I had not done what I did that young girl would not have been shot and the expression on her face as she fell would not be haunting me now.

I repeated my request to Chen today and he assured me that he will do whatever he can for her. She is apparently out of medical danger, and he is trying to arrange permission for me to visit her in the hospital tomorrow. I must speak to her.

Murphy's case, however, has already passed beyond the scope of Chen's influence. The evidence against him cannot be *refuted. He appears on the studio tapes of the aborted broadcast and the pistol he was holding on me is clearly visible. We also learned today that even before the guerrilla raid he was being sought on a fugitive warrant, having escaped from a rural labor camp north of here. So there appears to be nothing Chen can do for him.*

Tuesday, February 8

Chen requested a meeting with Sandiman and me this morning. He received us in his office and told us that our actions during the raid on the station had earned us the right to be told about Guangzhou. (So Sandiman was correct. Chen did withhold information from us at our last meeting.)

The following is a summary of what Chen revealed:

For the past year the Chinese have been conducting massive shipbuilding operations in three locations—Guangzhou, Shanghai, and Luta—building some ships and retrofitting others. The fleet they have been creating will eventually number nearly one hundred vessels.

The goal of this enterprise is nothing less than the eventual relocation of 75 percent of the world's human population!

"I should not have to explain," Chen said, "why this is necessary. The history of mankind is a history of conflict and oppression. No opportunity for human dispute has been ignored. We have fought over goods, territory, religion and ideology. We have shunned and abused one another because we were of different races, practiced different customs, and spoke different languages. All this must now cease."

"To this end, it is the Chinese intention to eliminate the traditional sources of human conflict by literally homogenizing the human race."

In point of fact, Chen explained, most of the people to be relocated, especially in the interconnected continents of Asia, Africa and Europe will be moved by rail or bus. Only 25 percent will be moved by ship. But the ships are the operative symbol of the program, which will not begin until they are launched. Once begun, the relocations will continue uninterrupted for fifteen years. Once complete, the pre-war world, with all its traditional conflicts, will no longer exist.

The short-term Chinese goal is to defuse any lingering

pre-war nationalism that might threaten the ordered calm of the new global federation.

The long-term goal is the absolute eradication of all racial and ethnic distinctions. With language barriers struck down as everyone adopts English, people of all races forced to live and work side by side, and interracial marriage encouraged, questions of race and ethnicity are expected to become moot within the space of four or five generations. To accelerate this process, racial and cultural ghettos are to be strictly forbidden. According to Chen, the Chinese will include themselves in this prohibition. So there will be no "Chinatowns" in the new world. The Chinese are preparing to voluntarily surrender their cultural identity and dive headlong into the global, interracial gene pool with the rest of us.

My reaction to all of this is mixed. Chen's arguments were convincingly presented and the entire program is a logical extension of the Chinese grand design for global harmony. But no mention was made of the enormous personal costs this program will impose. How will individuals react to such massive dislocations? Removed from friends and community and denied everything that is familiar to them, how will they function in the new world the Chinese are proposing? What of the loss of tradition and cultural diversity? These things were not merely sources of conflict, they were also sources of identity, stability and vitality. Are they to be discarded entirely? We have lost so much already; can we survive the loss of so much more?

I feel I am out of my depth here; Sandiman feels it as well. Could anyone answer these questions? We are both anxious to discuss this "Genesis" program (that is what the Chinese are calling it) with other members of our staff, but Chen has refused to allow this. There must be no premature announcement, he says, no rumors. I am not even free to discuss it with Anne.

I visited Katie again today. Each time I see her I become more fond of her and more determined that she must be helped. Chen is working diligently, but is still uncertain if he can save her.

Thursday, February 10

I spoke to Chen today. When I asked his opinion of the monstrous Genesis project he refused to answer, saying that his opinion was unimportant. I pressed him, explaining how much I valued his opinion, and he finally responded with something like the following:

"David, it matters little what I think; I am but one man among billions and my opinion is of no more importance than the opinion of any other man. You must reach you own conclusion.

"I realize this is difficult for you. All Americans seem to believe that the machinery of society is driven by the brilliance of a few gifted individuals, while the rest merely follow their lead. It is a cultural bias. It represents a fundamental error in your thinking, and it was a factor in your decline as a world power. Each time a crisis arose, you ignored the logical course of action—collective effort to effect a cure—and instead rushed about looking for someone who could devise a painless remedy. You persistently sought saviors instead of solutions.

"We seek no saviors, David. Everything we are doing is directed toward the goal of creating a system which will allow all to contribute, which can survive human ignorance and arrogance and all our attempts to subvert it, and deliver to our descendants a future full of promise. If you don't yet understand this, then you understand nothing."

I said, "But it is the opinion of the masses that concerns me. If they rebel, your precious system may never reach maturity; it could suffocate in its cradle. I want to know your opinion on that. How do you expect them to react? How do you plan to respond if they reject Genesis?"

"The system will reach maturity," he replied. "I cannot say how the people will react, but their initial reaction will not affect our success. If they react badly, our progress may be delayed, but we will pursuade them eventually. What is time, David? Whether the system matures in ten years, or fifty, or a hundred, the final product will be the same. And the final product is all that matters."

He would say no more on the subject.

Sandiman and I have spent long hours these last two days discussing Genesis. The more we consider its implications, the more draconian it appears. Is there no moderate alternative to this horror? Were other proposals considered?

I believe Chen shares our concern. When I spoke to him today his defense of Genesis was delivered without enthusiasm. He seemed resigned rather than committed to it. In any event,

I'm certain it is far beyond the scope of his influence.

What then can we do? We cannot support the implementation of this monstrosity, but neither can we prevent it. Perhaps we can alter its course. We will need to work slowly and carefully, for we know we are being watched. But we will have opportunities. When we recognize them, we must be prepared to act.

Thursday, February 24

Chen has finally succeeded. Three weeks of patient effort on his part has produced the result we have all been hoping for—Katie was released from the hospital today and has taken up residence with Anne and me. The authorities have officially recognized her as our niece.

I have no idea how Chen managed this incredible deception. In the days immediately following the raid on the television station the staff was subjected to interminable police interviews. Many members of the staff saw Katie armed and clearly participating in the raid, and that information must have appeared repeatedly in the interview transcripts. Yet it is now being ignored. Why? Has Chen convinced all those staff members (even the Chinese!) to retract their previous statements? Or was it in his power to simply have the records expunged? I will never know. When I asked him about it today, he merely smiled and said, "I do not believe she is an enemy of the State."

Anne is even more pleased than I am. For the past two and a half weeks she has visited Katie every evening. Chen suggested this, but I'm certain she would have done it even without his prompting. She and her new "niece" have quickly become so close that I sometimes feel superfluous in their presence.

An hour ago I actually found myself experiencing a modest fit of jealousy as a result of my exclusion. Had I carried my gratitude too far? Would I ever see my wife again? But those feelings quickly passed. I've never been a particularly sensitive man, but even I can see what Anne has recognized—Katie needs the diversion that our attention is providing her, she needs it badly. Because the gratitude with which she has embraced us and her new life here is masking a profound sadness.

She has been lucky in many ways. Her wound probably saved her life. Chen would not have interceded in her behalf if she *had not tried to save me and probably could not have helped her if the police had been able to interrogate her immediately after the raid. Then too, the bullet missed her heart by only three inches, her spine by two. But she has been unlucky as well. The father of her unborn child, Sergeant Devin, is in custody and will certainly be executed. She loves him deeply—I recognized that even in the brief moments I saw them together the night of the raid—and his loss now weighs heavily upon her.*

I wish there were some remedy I could offer to soothe her pain, but there is not. I wish Chen could help Devin as he helped Katie, but he cannot. Of course, in time she will come to terms with her pain; there is some comfort in that. And in September she will have his child. There will be real comfort in that.

Yesterday, Sandiman completed the first of the half-hour programs he has been editing from the film he shot overseas. It is marvelous work, easily the best any of us has yet produced. It would have won awards even in the competitive days of pre-war television.

Tuesday, May 10

Chen is ill again. As before, he claims it is nothing serious and talks vaguely about the miseries of old age. But his denials are becoming transparent. There is no longer any doubt—he is dying. I think I have known it for some time.

I can hardly believe I have known him only seven months. I cannot imagine the world without his remarkable presence. In my lifetime I have encountered many of the individuals who guided the course of human events: the presidents and princes, the scientists and generals and ministers whose names will dominate the future histories of our era. None has impressed me as Chen has. His passing will leave a void.

My personal feelings aside, however, Chen's failing health raises practical questions for which I have no answers. Who will speak for us in his absence? Who will advocate for the freedoms he has granted our group and guarded so jealously? Will his program survive his passing?

He must have made plans for his succession but I have no knowledge of those plans. He seems to have prepared no one to assume his duties; he has no lieutenants. I have concluded therefore that I must confront him on this subject. I plan to do it as soon as he has recovered his strength.

At home, Katie is showing some improvement. She has been teaching history at a nearby school and her involvement there has been therapeutic. But I believe the simple passage of time has had the greatest effect upon her. It has been nearly a month since Devin and Murphy and the rest were executed, and she is finally regaining her appetite and her spirits. Previously, she was eating so little that she had actually lost weight and Anne was becoming concerned for the baby's health. She took Katie to the clinic with her last week and one of the doctors prescribed an anti-depressant which seems to have helped immensely. Katie has now gained two pounds and at breakfast this morning she actually laughed at one of my modest attempts at humor. It was the first time I had seen her smile in many weeks.

In the news, the process of continental "normalization" continues. Among the items we reported today was the designation of Memphis as an open community. It is the eighth North American city to be normalized and the list is now expanding so rapidly that these designations will soon pass without mention.

Sandiman received a summons today from the continental administrator. It was in the form of an invitation, but its wording left no doubt that it was an order rather than a request. Two weeks from today he is being sent to Guangzhou to witness the launching of the first Genesis ships. Finally, we will be free to discuss Genesis.

Sunday, May 22

Chen is gone. He died quietly last evening.

Outside the television studio the flags flew at half mast today. Inside there was none of the usual chatter; long faces and an atmosphere of solemnity prevailed. To the Chinese on our staff Chen was a national hero, to the Americans he was a mentor and a spokesman. Everyone held him in high regard.

During the newscast I made a brief memorial announcement. The workers in the camps would not recognize his face or his name, I realized, but it gave me satisfaction to publicly eulogize him.

After the newscast I was summoned to Chen's office and

presented with a letter he had directed his secretary to deliver to me in the event of his death. It was dated April 25 and read as follows:

Dear David,

You have work to do and a family anxious for your company so I will keep this brief.

In the short time I have known you my respect for you has steadily grown. I have found you a man of remarkable objectivity, almost entirely free of preconception or bias. This is an extremely valuable quality in these times. Very few individuals are equipped to become leaders of our new global community; you are one.

I am therefore appointing you my successor here. As of this moment you are Director of Global Television North America. You may continue broadcasting the news if you wish, or you may concentrate your efforts on administration. That decision is entirely yours to make.

A word of caution: this position is not a gift; there will be times when you will wish to be free of it. It carries cabinet rank, and your appearance in the continental administration will be widely resented. Eugene Palitz, the Director of the North American Health Agency, is currently the only occidental serving in the Cabinet and his experience thus far has been difficult. He will be pleased with your appointment. He is a man of great ability; rely upon him.

The task I have set before you will be daunting, but you too are a man of great ability. Together, I believe we have begun well, and I am confident of your ultimate success.

One final, personal note: I shall miss you. Your friendship in these last days of my life has been a source of strength and great comfort to me.

It was signed, simply, "Chen."

I am frankly surprised by my reaction to his death. I had months to prepare, yet I am still devastated. He had made so many remarkable recoveries from his previous illnesses that I suppose I had expected him to recover this time as well. In any case, his passing is a profound shock.

Anne too seems to have been affected more than I anticipated. I found her with Katie this evening; both women were weeping. I had expected this of Katie—she had come to think of Chen almost as a grandfather—but not of Anne, who was always suspicious of Chen and jealous of my relationship with him. My expression must have conveyed my surprise, because she looked at me and said defensively, "He brought us back together, Pug." Then she reached out, took Katie's hand and added tearfully, "He brought all of us together."

There is to be no funeral here. According to Chen's request, the body will be shipped to China and buried by his father's in a small graveyard beside the Tatu River, near a historic bridge where his father participated in a great decisive battle during the Long March many years ago.

This choice of a final resting place seemed strange at first, but now I believe I understand it. At the end of life, most of us experience a sense of loss and longing for the passionate dreams of our youth. The clarity of our early visions of the world is seldom sustained as we grow old. Chen's vision, however, was sustained. It grew and evolved and nourished him to his last days, so that he was finally able to look upon his life as an uninterrupted journey and a dream realized.

Most of us are not so lucky. The dreams of my youth, which for most of my life I believed were superior to Chen's, now lie shattered. That failure sickens me, as it sickens all former Americans. We sought perfection and nearly achieved it, then allowed it to disintegrate. For that failure, that benign neglect, I feel personally responsible.

And now, I have been granted an opportunity to atone, to establish for myself and my fellow humans a new point of beginning. Tomorrow, I assume Chen's Cabinet seat beside Palitz. In the coming months and years, others will join us.

Our work will be difficult. As Chen warned, progress will be slow and we will need to tread softly; success will be measured in small increments, accumulating over years, even lifetimes. But that does not matter. All that matters is that we have finally begun.

297